A CAROL FOR THE DEAD

A CAROL FOR THE DEAD

OLIVIA TATE

ISBN: 9798298694759
Imprint: Independently published

For my family

Monday 16ᵗʰ December 1940

Night fell on the estate at Gartram Manor like Hemingway going bankrupt, slowly at first and then all at once. On this night, young Mickey Lennox was, as his mum might have said, in a right state and no mistake. He was dressed in livery only marginally less ridiculous than a clown wearing oversized-shoes and a red nose. The sight presented by the estimable young Lennox would almost certainly have induced paroxysms of pride in his mother and mirth in his father; such is the uncommon nature of women and the immaturity of men.

Mickey, just turned seventeen, had recently been recruited as a doorman for an industrial magnate and peer of the realm called Lord Hardy. He was one of the few men in England able to afford a mansion in one of the least affordable locations in Devon. Tonight, young Mickey was witnessing and bowing to a parade of the flushest and most powerful individuals, not just from the county but from all around the country.

A Bentley attracted his attention as it drew up to the magnificent mansion. From the passenger seat, stepped out a woman in her mid to late twenties. Mickey's eyes widened in shock. She was easily the most beautiful girl he'd seen all evening, if not ever. And she was unaccompanied. This was probably not so shocking given the country was at war.

As she walked up the steps, the young woman glanced at Mickey. His attempts to disguise his admiration were sadly undone by a mouth that had dropped open and an inability to tear his eyes away from her face. She looked back at him; her blue eyes narrowed faintly, then she smiled. Moments later she was away and floating into the hallway of the mansion.

Dominating the hallway was an enormous malachite staircase which led from a black and white marble floor to a second-floor landing which housed an enormous Van Dyck portrait of a Dutch woman overlooking the whole scene with all the patience, bonhomie and good spiritedness of a wife awaiting her lord and master's return home from the pub.

The staircase was lined with footmen who looked like chorus girls in a musical. The young woman walked past them towards the drawing room. The room, as far as she could see, was awash with men dressed in white tie.

Caroline Sinclair surveyed the room for a few moments. She noted, without caring too much, that many of the men aware of her arrival were surveying her also. A pity Charles was not here. He would hate it.

Across the room was Lord Peter Hardy, the joint owner of Hardy McDougall. She was inside the drawing room of Hardy's mansion a couple of miles outside Exeter. The room seemed to be the size of a small county. Overhead were two crystal chandeliers which competed unsuccessfully for attention against the *Objets d'art* which included Renaissance paintings on the walls and a Rodin bust situated at the end of the room.

Hardy turned around just as the she moved towards him. He was a tall man, around sixty, tanned with hair turning from dark to silver. His blue eyes crinkled into a smile as he saw her approach.

'I'm sorry, I didn't see you arrive, Carol. We've dispensed with announcing arrivals.'

'There's a war on, I suppose' replied Carol, 'Anyway, it's a relic from the last century.'

'I agree,' nodded Hardy. A waiter was passing with drinks; he took two from the tray and handed one to Carol. 'Champagne?' he asked.

2

'Thank you, and thank you for the invitation to your...,' she searched for the right word to convey the fact that they were amongst many of the country's leaders together at a mansion a long way from London. She settled on, 'soiree.'

This made Hardy smile and he said, 'I heard that Charles had left for the airfield so I thought this might act a pick-me-up.'

Carol smiled at this. It had. When Figgs had handed her the invitation the previous morning she had been crying in the library, a copy of *Vanity Fair* lying unread on the table beside her.

'There's a man coming towards us who I think you may want to avoid,' observed Hardy.

'Carol,' boomed a voice rich enough in timbre to suggest a long and successful career on the boards. In fact, this was not so very far from the truth as the man was playing a role. The role was as fictitious as his playing of it was true.

Both turned around to be greeted by the sight of Frederick Hughes-Norton, a gossip columnist for one of the nationals. Hardy rolled his eyes and made good his escape. 'Sorry, Carol, you're on your own with this one,' he whispered before turning to the looming figure of the gossip columnist and saying, 'Freddie, I must circulate. I'm sure you won't mind looking after Carol for me.'

'I shall be delighted,' said Freddie shaking Hardy's hand and then kissing Carol on both cheeks. 'Carol, how are you? Charles is not here, I see. I do hope he is safe and well.'

Freddie, whose intuition was tuned as he was highly strung noticed a slight change in Carol's expression.

'Please forgive me. Is Charles away on ops? I shan't ask where.'

Carol nodded and felt tears sting her eyes. Freddie took her hand and squeezed it. An inveterate gossip and snob he may have been but he was also adored by most of the people he wrote about and once upon a time, Carol had been one of those people. He smiled sympathetically at her.

'I'm happy for you that you married Charles but, I must say, I do miss you. I don't see you enough now. You were always such good copy.'

'Thank you, Freddie,' said Carol, rolling her eyes. 'I on the other hand, do not miss those days.'

'Not even a little? You had half the young men of London chasing you.'

Carol laughed at this. Then a thought struck her. She asked, 'Who were the other half chasing if not me?'

'Each other, darling,' chuckled Freddie. This prompted a giggle from Carol as well. She really did enjoy being with Freddie. It was easy to forget almost everything in his company.

Almost everything.

The fun couldn't last though. Seconds later, they heard a braying laugh from a woman who might have been in another county but was, in fact, entering the room.

'Oh Lord,' said Freddie. 'Who invited them? Sorry, my dear. I won't pretend to like her.'

Carol smiled at Freddie and said, 'I forgive you.'

'Do you want me to hide you?' offered Freddie.

'Caroline,' exclaimed the woman. 'Is that you?' Carol turned and saw the woman and the man approach. Before Carol could answer, the woman spied Freddie who was making good on his plan to escape. 'Freddie where are you going?'

'My drink is at dangerously low levels Cressida,' replied Freddie, holding up his near-empty glass of champagne. 'Toodle-loo.'

Carol and Cressida eyed each other with polite loathing. She was in her forties and probably still as beautiful now as she had been when she was Carol's age. However, they had one thing in common. They had married well. Very well. For Cressida, this had always been the goal. Not for Carol. She had married for love and then found out that what you fall in love with is not necessarily same as what you remain in love with.

4

'Hello, Jason,' said Carol to the man who had accompanied Cressida into the ballroom. 'You look well.'

He did look well. He was like a larger, older version of Charles. He had the same hint of dash in his moustache and, if the rumours were true, a wandering eye. He was also Charles' brother, Viscount Jason Sinclair. He the head of the family, a fact that Cressida was never slow to point out. While Charles was content to ignore the jibes from his sister-in-law, it was difficult for Carol not to feel wounded by every encounter.

'Is Charles here?' asked Jason, looking around the room.

'No, Jason, I'm afraid he's away at the moment,' replied Carol. She did not say more. As remote a possibility as it was, she made it a policy never to reveal Charles' whereabouts to anyone. And anyone included family.

Jason shrugged and said, 'Pity.'

Cressida, however, saw her opportunity. It was too good to pass up. Carol steeled herself for the assault.

'I think we know what that means, Caroline,' began Cressida. 'You know if you had been blessed with children, perhaps Charles would not have gotten these foolish ideas into his head and stayed where he was, safe, at the airfield, training airmen.'

Carol felt her face burn. It was true. He would have stayed had there been children. Two years of trying had yielded nothing but heartache and, in the end, resentment.

'Come now, Cressida darling. That's unfair,' said Jason. 'Charles always had that streak in him. I doubt wild horses could have held him back never mind a crying baby.'

Carol smiled at Jason gratefully. What had possessed Jason to marry this awful woman was beyond Carol. Or almost beyond her. Despite her vile nature, there was no one in the room more beautiful. Save perhaps herself, but Carol did not feel this anymore. The last few years had begun to rob her of the sparkle that had once lit her eyes, the mischievous laughter that had once acted as a magnetic contagion to any room that she entered.

5

Seeing that Carol would not rise to the bait, Cressida pointed to a man talking to Lord Hardy. She said, 'Isn't he in the cabinet?'

Moments later, she was gone, dragging Jason along with her.

Around midnight, the main dignitaries had retired for the evening. Hardy suggested they withdraw to the library for a nightcap. The library, if not as large as the drawing room, was as impressive. Books lined the walls from floor to ceiling. Some wall space was occupied by paintings from the French Impressionists who were gaining in popularity and value by the year in England.

The room was lit by an enormous crystal chandelier which had, as Hardy demonstrated, several dimmer switches around the room. Carol was surrounded by several young men displaying behaviour only marginally differentiated from a Gorilla beating its chest, only less impressive. Once upon a time, this amused Carol. No longer.

Hardy, meanwhile, went to a painting above the sideboard. He moved it to one side to reveal a safe. 'I must show you all a little trinket I acquired recently for Evelyn.'

Evelyn, Hardy's wife, an attractive woman in her fifties coloured a little with the frown that she shot in the direction of her husband.

'There were too many politicians around to show you this. Probably tax me into penury if they had.'

Hardy opened the safe and removed a small black velvet pouch. From the pouch he extracted a diamond necklace. Carol gasped involuntarily. She wasn't the only one. There were over a dozen sizeable diamonds on the chain. It was beautiful and unquestionably worth a small fortune. Everyone in the room inched forward to have a better look at the necklace Hardy had placed on the table.

Just as Hardy stepped back, the lights went out leaving the room in complete darkness. A few people screamed, even one of the women. The lights came on again after several seconds of darkness. When everyone looked down at the table, the diamonds were gone.

Hardy looked at everyone in the room, and said, 'Is this some sort of joke? If I may say, it's in very poor taste.'

Accusing looks were cast around the room, a few landing on Freddie. The poor man was more amused than offended. Weighing in at around two hundred and fifty pounds and standing six feet four, he was, by quite some distance, the least likely looking cat burglar in the room,. A herd of elephants would have made less of an impression in the darkness than Devon's foremost gossip columnist.

'Does someone wish to confess?' asked Hardy.

The assembled company were, to Carol's eyes, more likely to confess to a penchant for goose-stepping naked while singing *Deutchland Uber Alles* at midnight than to be thieves.

'Perhaps we should lock the doors,' said Carol.

'Good idea,' said Hardy. He nodded to a couple of footmen in the room. . Behind her, the footmen in the room did as they were bid. The room was silent as they waited for Hardy's next words. And then a man who had spent a portion of the evening trying to impress Carol about his job in Intelligence, decided to show her and the room why the Secret Service had come calling to Cambridge.

All eyes turned to Kim Philby.

'Well, clearly, they're hidden up above. Who's going to look?'

Everyone looked up at the crystal chandelier.

'Good thinking,' said Hardy, a smile returning to his face.

Another of Carol's admirers, a young man with a Ronald Coleman moustache, volunteered, and space was cleared for him to stand on a chair and to root around the chandelier with his outstretched hand. All this time Carol kept her eyes on Hardy. If her spider senses were not deceiving her, there was almost a hint of amusement in his eyes. He saw Carol studying him and he quickly grew serious again.

'I can't find anything,' admitted the young man, clearly shattered not to have played his part in this particular war effort.

'Oh,' said Philby, disappointed that his first stab at detection had on this occasion, been a failure. He felt a comforting hand on his elbow from Carol.

'What are you thinking, Carol?' asked Hardy. The amusement had returned to his eyes. Or was it a challenge being laid down? Carol grinned at Hardy.

Challenge accepted.

'What is that line?' said Carol. 'You know, something like ' if you can eliminate the impossible then whatever remains, no matter how improbable, must be the truth'. That's it, isn't it?'

'Go on Sherlock.' said Hardy, enjoying the moment openly now.

'Well, with that in mind,' said Carol, walking forward to the safe and looking inside, 'I would suggest that the necklace is back in the safe where Lord Hardy placed it when the lights went out.'

Carol pulled the door of the safe back for all to see.

The safe was empty.

This was greeted by a ripple of laughter. None louder than Philby, who, in a rather ungentlemanly manner, was immensely relieved that he would not be remembered as the biggest fool of the evening.

Hardy's face was non-committal. Carol turned to face the room. No one had moved except to look either at Carol or the empty safe.

'As you can see the safe is empty,' said Carol. She caught Philby's eye. The glint of triumph in his eye suggested the Intelligence man was enjoying this as much as he was fascinated by what the solution to the mystery might be.

'However, if I do this,' said Carol, pressing down on the base of the safe and extracting from the compartment underneath, a diamond necklace which he held up for all to view, 'then the diamonds reappear, as if by magic'.

Everyone broke out into spontaneous applause, none more so than Lord Hardy who was laughing in delight. Shouts of 'Bravo' filled the air. As the ovation died down one voice broke the silence.

It was Kim Philby.

'You know, my dear, we could use someone like you.'

'I thought you worked in procurement, Kim,' said Hardy. He winked at Philby whose job with the Secret Services was the least secret thing about him.

'Not of diamonds, apparently,' he complained good-humouredly.

Roger Trent pressed his forehead against the cold, rattling train window, trying to see through the cloud of his breath as the Devon countryside slipped past in a patchwork of frostbitten hedgerows and whitened fields. Christmas was looming, and the first snow of winter was beginning to settle on the highest points of the rolling hills, painting the land in hesitant, wavering strokes of white. Sheep stood like pale smudges on the slopes, and the dark lines of trees silhouetted on the horizon.

His sister Susan, at twelve, a year younger than her brother, sat opposite him, her hands folded tightly in her lap over the brown evacuation label pinned to her coat. Her long brown hair was tied back with a ribbon that had once been blue but was now frayed and grey with dust. She was staring down at the shoes she'd polished that morning in the hostel, lips pressed together in a firm line.

Beside her was the youngest of the Trent children, Benjy. He was sleeping quietly, his head lolling against her shoulder each time the train jolted. Small hands clutched a battered teddy, its fur worn thin around the ears. It was the one thing he had managed to grab before the wardens had pulled them away from the rubble, the one thing he had insisted on taking with him. Roger looked at him for a moment, a dull ache spreading in his chest. Ten years old, and too young to have to know what words like 'orphan' and 'Blitz' truly meant.

The train shrieked as it rounded a bend, a shower of sparks dancing against the darkening sky outside. Susan looked up sharply, her grey eyes wide and anxious.

'It's only the brakes,' Roger said quickly, forcing a smile he did not feel. 'We'll be there soon.'

Where though?

Ravenley.

As names went, it conjured up images that Roger tried not to think about. Despite being only thirteen, he could pass for older. He was tall for his age and he had always been more grown up. He had to be. He was the father-figure in a house without a father. He had his moments though when the headstrong child took over, like the times he snuck into the local cinema to watch films like *Dracula* and *Frankenstein*. The name of the house they were going to stay sounded like it was straight from one of these films.

Susan nodded, swallowing, and turned to the window, where the snowflakes were gathering against the glass in soft clusters before melting away, leaving streaks of water that the wind pushed across the pane.

They had left London at dawn, the city still reeking of smoke, the sky a grim, heavy grey above the ruins of their street. They had walked past the remains of their house only once before they left, the shell of it standing black and silent, its windows shattered, walls caved in. Their mother and Aunt Nell had been inside when it happened, making tea, folding laundry, getting ready for another day of ration queues, blackout curtains, and distant sirens. Roger could still hear the sound sometimes, deep in the back of his mind, the echoing boom that had rolled through the air while they had been playing marbles on the corner, a sharp finality that made Susan drop her marbles, the glass spheres rolling into the gutter.

A cough came from the far side of the compartment, where a man of about thirty-five sat with a leather suitcase by his feet, a slim black case perched on top. He had a kind, thoughtful face, with spectacles that had slipped down his nose, and a coat that had seen

11

better days. He caught Roger's eye and offered a small, reassuring smile before returning to the small book he was reading, thumb holding his place while the train swayed. Roger noticed the white dog-collar peeking out from beneath his scarf.

Susan followed Roger's gaze, her brows lifting slightly. 'Is he a vicar?' she whispered.

'Looks like it,' Roger replied softly.

The man glanced up again, catching their lowered voices, and closed his book, leaning forward with an awkward, friendly inclination of his head.

'I hope you don't mind my asking, but are you headed down to Devon for Christmas?'

'Yes, sir,' Roger said, sitting up straighter. 'We're being evacuated.'

'Ah,' the man said, his eyes softening. 'I see. I'm going down to take over a parish near Exeter. Little place, Belsaw-on-the-Moor. They said it's not much more than a handful of cottages, a church, and a tumbledown vicarage, but it will do for me.' He smiled, the lines around his eyes deepening. 'The name's Michael Denham.'

'I'm Roger. This is Susan, and that's Benjy.'

The vicar nodded gravely. 'A pleasure, Roger, Susan, and Benjy. I am glad to see you have each other. I should think, in times like these, family means more than ever.'

Roger felt a lump in his throat and looked out of the window again, unwilling to let the man see the tears that threatened.

The vicar did not press further, merely resumed his seat, folding his hands over his book. Susan, emboldened, leaned across.

'Will there be snow for Christmas, do you think?'

'I rather think there will be, Miss Susan,' the vicar replied gently. 'It looks to be coming in earnest now, and Dartmoor wears snow well, they say. It can be a cold place, but also very beautiful.'

Susan smiled, just a small one, and leaned back as Benjy stirred, muttering in his sleep. She brushed a strand of hair from his face, tucking it behind his ear, and the train rocked them onwards.

The train slowed as it rolled through Dawlish, the sea a dark, restless smear beyond the grey beach, waves flecked with white as they crashed against the seawall. Seagulls wheeled above the platform as they passed, their cries shrill in the winter air. Further along, a group of Home Guard stood on the platform with rifles slung across their backs, stamping their feet against the cold.

Roger watched them, thinking of their mother's stories of their father, whom they barely remembered. He had left when Roger was a baby, leaving their mother to raise them alone. She had been a teacher once, before giving up her post to care for them, telling them stories of kings and battles, of bravery and rightness, stories that had made the nights in the Anderson shelter seem less dark.

The war had taken her, too, in the end, and now it had taken them away from the city that had been their home, sending them into the unknown.

They passed through Teignmouth, and then Newton Abbot, the snow falling more heavily now, turning the hedgerows into soft, drifting mounds. The countryside seemed hushed, the smoke from distant cottages rising straight into the still air, the fields empty and waiting.

At last, as dusk deepened into night, the train gave a final whistle and pulled into Exeter station. The platform was busy with soldiers and evacuees, the lamps casting a yellow glow onto the wet ground, shadows stretching out in long, uncertain shapes.

Benjy woke with a start, blinking and clutching his teddy to his chest as Susan took his hand.

'Are we here?' he asked, his voice small.

'We're here, Benny,' Roger said, his own voice steady, though inside he felt a tightness he could not quite swallow down.

They stepped off the train into the cold evening air, their breath misting before them. The vicar stepped down behind them, offering a small wave as he gathered his cases.

'Best of luck, children,' he said, his voice warm. 'If you are ever near Belsaw-on-the-Moor, you must come and say hello.'

13

'Thank you, sir,' Susan said, bobbing a small curtsey that made Roger's throat tighten once more.

The vicar was met by an elderly man in a tweed coat, and the last they saw of him was as he walked away, cases in hand, disappearing into the swirl of snow and steam that rose from the waiting engines.

They stood together, the three of them, close on the platform, until a voice called out to them.

'Trent children?'

They turned to see an elderly man in a long dark coat, a peaked cap pulled low over his brow. His face was lined, but his eyes were sharp beneath heavy eyebrows, and he held a lantern that flickered in the wind.

'Yes, sir,' Roger said.

'Name's Figgs,' the man said, stepping forward. 'I'm here on behalf of Mrs Sinclair. We'd best be off before the roads freeze over.'

Figgs led them through the station and out into the dark, where the rain was falling steadily now, covering the pavements in puddles. At the kerb waited a large, old Bentley, its dark paint shining dully beneath the streetlamps. Roger could not help but stare. He had seen cars like it in newsreels, rolling past cheering crowds, but to see one here, waiting for them, was almost too strange to believe.

Figgs opened the door, and they climbed in, the smell of leather and old tobacco wrapping around them like a cloak. The seats were cold, but softer than the train benches, and as the engine rumbled to life, they felt the warmth of the heaters rising around their feet.

They drove out of Exeter, the city lights quickly giving way to dark lanes lined with hedgerows, the headlights cutting tunnels of yellow light through the swirling snow. The roads twisted and turned, climbing steadily, the trees arching over them like dark sentinels. Occasionally, they passed a cottage with a single light in the window, smoke rising from chimneys into the dark sky.

Roger held Benjy close, and Susan stared silently out of the window, watching as the snow thickened, turning the world into a blur of white and grey.

Finally, after what felt like an hour, they turned off the main road onto a long, winding drive. Tall iron gates stood open, snow piling up against them, and the car rolled slowly forward, the crunch of gravel beneath the tyres loud in the silence.

Ahead, a house rose out of the darkness, vast and foreboding, spires and chimneys black against the snow-filled sky. The windows were mostly dark, save for one, high up, where a single light burned, flickering like a watchful eye.

The car came to a halt, and Figgs climbed out, opening the door for them.

Roger stepped out first, the cold air biting at his face. Susan followed, her hand tight around Benjy's, who shivered as he looked up at the looming house.

It was the sort of house, Roger thought, that one might see in an old horror film, the sort that seemed to hold secrets in its darkened corridors, with staircases that creaked and doors that might open on their own.

But it was also, he reminded himself fiercely, a house where they would be safe, away from the bombs, away from the fires and the sirens and the endless fear of the city. They were alone now, truly alone in the world, with only each other, and whatever lay behind the heavy doors of this dark house on Dartmoor.

Figgs led them up the steps, the rain falling in sheets now, as the great front door opened slowly, revealing a warm glow from within.

They stepped across the threshold, into the unknown.

Flight Lieutenant Charles Sinclair sat rigidly in the pilot's seat of the Bristol Blenheim, the engines humming through the thin metal skin like a trapped wasp's drone. Outside, the night sky lay in heavy layers of cloud and moonlight, the horizon a ghostly, wavering line as they pushed across the Channel. Forty aircraft in loose formation, though at night it was hard to see any of them beyond the two faint pinpricks of wingtip lights that bobbed in and out of cloud.

The raid on Mannheim was retaliation. London had burned under the black rain of German incendiaries, and now Bomber Command would answer. At least that's what Sinclair told himself. He hated this business. He'd wanted to be in a fighter, not bombing factories and, despite what he tried to tell himself, innocent civilians.

The maps had been studied. The targets identified. The railway yards, the lines of warehouses, and the industrial quarter would be the focus of their bombs. He had measured the angles and plotted their run with meticulous precision, as he did with everything.

Behind him, Ralph Bolton bent over the navigation table, red pencil tapping against the paper as he checked bearings. Bolton was younger, round-faced, with an eager, almost puppy-like expression that Sinclair found quietly irritating, though he never let it show. The boy was good, even if he talked too much on the ground.

In the rear turret, Danny White manned the twin Brownings, head turning to scan the darkness. White was the only one who seemed truly relaxed in the air, always whistling softly when he thought no one could hear him. Sinclair had corrected him once about discipline, and White had nodded, but the whistling had resumed quietly the next night.

They were an efficient crew. That was all Sinclair demanded.

The Bristol Blenheim's cockpit was cramped, and Sinclair's knees brushed against the sides as he adjusted the throttle to hold formation. He caught a glimpse of the aircraft to their left: another Blenheim, flying steady, its dark shape riding the moonlight. That would be Simon Dean, his best friend, though Sinclair never called him that aloud. They had trained together in the days before the war became real, before the dark columns of smoke rose from London, before the bombed-out streets and the cries in the rubble.

Dean was everything Sinclair was not: warm, quick to laugh, fond of a cigarette shared on the edge of dispersal before a mission. The men loved Dean, but they respected Sinclair. In war, respect mattered more. Luck most of all.

'Passing over the Dutch coast,' Bolton's voice came through the intercom, shaky from the vibration of the engines. 'Course steady, two-eight-zero.'

'Maintain watch,' Sinclair replied. 'Fuel check.'

They rattled off the figures, and Sinclair absorbed them as he scanned the altimeter and the instrument panel. Their formation was climbing slowly, the moonlight glancing off the leading edges of the wings, the engines holding their beat. Somewhere ahead, Mannheim waited, and they would leave a blackened scar on its rail yards in return for the burning of London.

He could feel the tension in his neck, a tight coil that never quite left him in the air. The sky had become a place of hunting and being hunted, and even with forty aircraft in the darkness, Sinclair felt alone, the responsibility of command pressing on him with every mile they flew deeper into enemy territory.

They crossed the Rhine just after midnight, clouds rolling in over the river like dirty wool. Sinclair checked the watch pinned to his flight jacket, his gloved hand tapping once against the glass. Bolton gave him the heading, and Sinclair turned the aircraft, feeling the weight shift as the Blenheim banked into the cold darkness.

'Target should be visible in four minutes,' Bolton said, leaning forward, the pale glow of the map light making him look like a ghost.

'White,' Sinclair said, 'keep watch for searchlights.'

'Already on it, skipper,' came White's easy reply.

Sinclair could see the first glow on the horizon: the fires of Mannheim, burning from previous raids or perhaps from the eternal glow of industry. The Germans worked day and night to keep the war machine fed, and now the RAF would remind them of the cost.

The flak came first, a scattering of orange bursts far below, like a fireworks display watched from a distance. Then the searchlights, stabbing up into the clouds, sweeping in slow arcs as they hunted for the bombers. Sinclair held his course, eyes on the altimeter, trusting Bolton's calls for adjustments.

'Two minutes,' Bolton said. 'Rail yard dead ahead.'

The aircraft jolted, a sudden, hard smack from a near-miss below them, the shell bursting close enough to rock the Blenheim as shrapnel rattled against the fuselage.

'Steady,' Sinclair said, gripping the yoke. 'We stay on target.'

They dropped lower, sliding under the ceiling of clouds, the glow of fires and the criss-cross of searchlights revealing the black skeleton of Mannheim's rail yards. Sinclair could see the tracks like thin veins, the boxcars lined up waiting, the dark shapes of warehouses.

'Bomb doors open!' Bolton shouted.

Sinclair felt the vibration change as the doors opened beneath them. He held the course, ignoring the flak bursts, ignoring the sudden stab of a searchlight that caught them briefly before sliding off into the darkness.

'Steady... steady...' Bolton muttered, eyes on the bombsight.

Sinclair breathed in, held it.

'Bombs away!'

The Blenheim jumped as the bombs dropped, the weight leaving the aircraft, and Sinclair pulled up gently, banking away as the first

18

flashes lit up below. Fires bloomed among the rail yards, red-orange flowers in the dark, smoke rising as the blast waves rippled outwards.

They heard them before they saw them. A wasp's whine in the distance.

'Bandits, six o'clock high!' White's voice cracked through the intercom, the sound of gunfire snapping behind them.

Sinclair pulled the Blenheim into a shallow dive, throttling forward, the engines roaring as they sought to escape the flak zone. He saw the dark, predatory shapes of the Messerschmitt Bf 109s sliding down out of the moonlight, their wings glinting, cannons flashing in the night.

White opened up with the Browning, the twin guns chattering, tracers slicing into the darkness. One of the 109s broke off, rolling away, but another held its course, coming in fast, its cannons flickering in the night.

Sinclair threw the Blenheim into a banking turn, the engines straining, the airframe groaning as they tried to shake the fighter. The sky became a swirl of moonlight, searchlights, and tracer fire, the horizon vanishing in the chaos of combat.

'They're on us!' White yelled, the guns still firing. 'He's still there!'

The Messerschmitt closed the distance, its nose lighting up with the flash of its cannons. Bullets tore through the fuselage, a hammering rip that Sinclair felt through the floor, through the stick, through the whole aircraft as the Blenheim shuddered.

'I've lost hydraulics!' Sinclair shouted, fighting the controls.

A burst of cannon fire ripped across the starboard engine, and suddenly there was smoke, black and oily, streaming past the canopy. The engine began to sputter, coughing, the propeller windmilling as flames licked along the cowling.

'We're hit!' shouted Bolton, his voice sharp with panic.

'Fire in the starboard engine,' Sinclair snapped. 'Feathering prop.'

19

The engine refused to respond. The fire began to spread, smoke filling the cockpit, the smell of burning oil mixing with the sharp, bitter tang of fear.

'Skipper, we're not going to make it!' White called out, still firing, the tracers streaking upward as another Messerschmitt swept past, guns flashing.

Sinclair's eyes flicked to the altimeter. They were losing altitude, dropping fast. The aircraft was still flyable, but the fire was spreading, and the controls were becoming sluggish. The ground was somewhere below, invisible in the darkness, but getting closer.

'We have to get out!' Bolton shouted.

Sinclair didn't respond immediately. He held the controls, coaxing the dying aircraft out of the worst of the dive, trying to level her. If they jumped too high, they would be easy prey for the fighters. Too low, and the parachutes would never open.

Another burst of fire ripped through the wing, and Bolton screamed, a short, sharp sound cut off by the roar of the engines.

'Ralph!' shouted White.

Sinclair could see the dark shape of the fighter rolling away, banking for another pass. He pulled the Blenheim down, forcing her into the darkness, throttling back to reduce the flames, to give them a chance.

'Bail out!' Sinclair shouted. 'Bail out now!'

White scrambled toward the hatch, fumbling with his harness. Sinclair looked back once, saw Ralph slumped over the guns, blood streaking down the turret's glass. The pain was there, but he pushed it down.

Bolton was gone, the hatch open, the cold wind rushing in. Sinclair held the controls a moment longer, trying to keep the aircraft steady, to give himself a chance.

Then the Messerschmitt came again, firing, bullets slamming into the cockpit, the glass shattering. A burning pain sliced across Sinclair's shoulder, and he grunted, pulling at the harness, forcing himself toward the open hatch.

20

The Blenheim was dying around him, flames licking across the wings, the engines sputtering their last breaths. The wind howled through the cabin as he stumbled, forcing himself to the hatch, the dark void waiting.

He jumped.

The wind tore at him, the cold shock of the night air stealing his breath. He pulled the ripcord, and the chute snapped open, jerking him brutally. Above, the burning remains of the Blenheim tumbled, a comet of fire and smoke, crashing into the darkness below with a distant, muffled roar.

Tuesday 17th December 1940

Carol Sinclair woke to the pale, watery light of morning struggling through the heavy curtains of Ravenley's master bedroom. Her head throbbed a dull reminder of last night's gin-and-tonic. A bitter taste lingered on her tongue. Or was it shame? She pressed a hand against her temple, pushing away the ache as she forced herself upright.

For a moment, she simply sat there, the silence of the great house pressing in around her. Ravenley had a way of reminding her of its size in the mornings, when the halls were quiet, and the cold seeped through the cracks in the old windows. It was too large for one person, too full of shadows and memories of people who had walked its corridors long before her.

People who had belonged here.

She swung her legs over the edge of the bed, the cool air biting at her bare feet, and reached for her robe. Her hand paused as it brushed against Charles's pillow, still indented from the last time he had lain there before the war had called him away again. She drew her hand back sharply and stood, knotting the belt of her robe around her waist.

Charles had been gone for almost ten days this time. It felt as if the war were pulling him further from her. With every sortie, every mission, every bomb, he withdrew into the air force or his first love, the sky. She had tried to keep busy, to manage the estate, to maintain appearances, but the long, echoing days were beginning to fray at her composure. She had told herself she would not drink so much again. She had told herself many things.

22

She was halfway to the bellpull to summon tea when she heard it, a sound that did not belong in the quiet of Ravenley.

Laughter.

Children's laughter.

She froze, her hand hovering above the cord, head tilted as the sound drifted faintly through the thick door. It was followed by the patter of small feet on wooden floors, the creak of a stair tread, and a burst of chatter, quickly hushed.

For a moment, she thought she must have imagined it. Children had no place at Ravenley. The house had been built for quiet dinners and weekends of shooting parties, for the heavy conversations of the Sinclair men and the crisp, distant laughter of Cressida.

Not for children.

And certainly not for her.

She stepped to the door, flinging it open to the chill of the corridor. She could hear them more clearly now, scuffling feet and whispers, a door closing hastily somewhere near the back stair. Carol's hands clenched around the edge of her robe.

'Mrs Parker!' Her voice cracked as it echoed down the corridor, sharp in the morning stillness.

There was a pause, then the hurried click of sensible shoes approaching. Mrs Parker appeared at the far end of the hall, her plain black dress and white apron immaculate, her greying hair pinned tightly under her cap.

'Madam,' she said, folding her hands, eyes level but cautious.

'Did I just hear children in this house?' demanded Carol, her voice tighter than the string of the violin she used to play.

'Yes, madam,' Mrs Parker replied calmly.

'Would you care to explain why there are children in my house without my permission?'

Mrs Parker's mouth tightened. 'I allowed three evacuees from London to stay, madam. They arrived last evening.'

Carol felt as if the air had been knocked from her lungs. 'You what?'

'I allowed them to stay,' Mrs Parker repeated, with that maddening, quiet authority she had always carried, even before Carol had come to Ravenley as Charles's wife. 'They have nowhere else to go. They are orphans. I told them not to come up to the first floor. I will have a word with them. It won't happen again.'

'It won't because they are leaving, Mrs Parker. Immediately.' The older woman took a deep breath. Mrs Sinclair could be so trying. Carol had not finished. 'And you did not think to consult me?' Carol's voice was rising, but she could not help it. The walls of Ravenley seemed to close in around her, every portrait on the wall watching as she struggled to keep her composure.

'It was arranged through the local committee, madam. With the raids worsening, they had to be moved quickly...' explained Mrs Parker. It would be no use, of course. This highly strung gold digger would not understand words such as duty. Her sort never would. And so it came.

'I don't care what the committee decided, Mrs Parker!' shrieked Carol. 'This is my home, and I will not have decisions made over my head!' Carol's hands were trembling now, her headache pulsing angrily behind her eyes.

Mrs Parker's eyes flickered, but her voice remained steady. 'The children are frightened and have lost their parents, madam. I did what I felt was right.'

'What you felt was right?' Carol's laugh was brittle, sharp. 'You have always done what you felt was right in this house, haven't you, Mrs Parker? Ever since I arrived, you have acted as though you know better than I do! As though I am just some girl Charles picked up.'

'That is not fair, madam.' It was entirely fair, thought Mrs Parker.

'Isn't it?' Carol's voice cracked again. 'You made it clear from the day I arrived that I was not wanted here, and now you go behind my back, bringing children into this house.'

24

She stopped, biting down on the words as tears threatened. Children. The word itself was a wound. Two years of marriage, and nothing. The silent, crushing nothingness every month, the quiet, patient disappointment in Charles's eyes he tried to hide but could never fully mask. The guilt that rotted inside her each time she saw the nursemaid in the village pushing a pram, each time she received another letter from her sister-in-law filled with stories of her children's laughter.

The emptiness that Ravenley seemed to echo back at her, day after day.

'Madam...' Mrs Parker's voice was softer now, but it only made the anger flare hotter.

'Get them out,' Carol said, her voice low, shaking. 'Get them out of my house.'

There was a long, heavy silence between them, the space filled with the ticking of the clock on the landing, the distant caw of ravens outside the windows.

Mrs Parker's lips pressed into a thin line. 'I'm afraid I cannot do that, madam.'

Carol opened her mouth, but before she could speak, there was a knock at the door. It opened with a soft creak, and Figgs, the butler, stepped in, his lined face even graver than usual.

'Madam,' he said quietly, 'a letter has arrived. Marked urgent.'

He held it out on a silver salver, and Carol took it, the thick, official envelope heavy in her hand. She stared at it for a moment, recognising the insignia on the corner, the neat, impersonal type of the address.

Her fingers fumbled with the seal, tearing it open, the paper crumpling in her shaking hands as she pulled out the letter.

She read it once.

Then again.

'No...' she whispered.

Mrs Parker stepped forward, but Carol stumbled back, clutching the letter to her chest as if it might shield her from the words.

25

'Missing after operations over Germany,' Carol read aloud, her voice thin and breaking. 'No further news at this time.'

The paper slipped from her hands, floating to the floor like a dead leaf.

She sank down onto the edge of the bed, her robe pooling around her, the world narrowing to the crackle of the fire in the grate and the sharp, unbearable silence that followed.

Mrs Parker and Figgs stood there, helpless, the weight of the moment pressing down on all of them. Outside, the wind rattled the windows, the sound cold and empty.

After a moment, Mrs Parker stepped forward, bending stiffly to pick up the letter, folding it carefully before setting it on the bedside table. She glanced at Carol, her eyes softening, but Carol turned her face away, unable to meet that look of pity.

'We will leave you now, madam,' Mrs Parker said quietly.

Carol did not respond.

Figgs opened the door, and they stepped out into the corridor, closing it softly behind them.

The corridor felt even colder now, the quiet of the house broken only by the muffled sounds of the wind and the distant, uncertain laughter that had faded to silence.

They stood there for a moment, neither of them speaking, the weight of what had just happened settling between them.

Three children, huddled at the top of the servants' stairs, half-hidden by the banister, their eyes wide, faces pale. Roger, the eldest, stood slightly in front, his hand resting protectively on Susan's shoulder, while little Benjy stood in the middle of the corridor with all the defiance an eight-year-old can bring to bear.

They had heard everything.

Mrs Parker's heart sank as she saw the look on Roger's face, a quiet, determined hardness that did not belong on a child's face, the kind of look she had seen on young men marching off to war, knowing they would not come back.

Roger looked at Mrs Parker, then at Figgs, and then back at the closed door of the master bedroom, where Carol's muffled sobs were finally breaking the silence.

He tightened his grip on Susan's shoulder.

'We shouldn't have come here,' Roger said quietly, his voice flat, too calm for a boy his age. 'We'll leave.'

Mrs Parker stepped forward quickly, shaking her head. 'No, love, you mustn't think that.'

But Roger's eyes had already turned away, looking down the stairs, as if planning the route out of Ravenley, out of the cold, beautiful house where they were not wanted.

Where children were not wanted.

Mrs Parker reached out, her hand hovering for a moment before resting lightly on Roger's shoulder.

'Please,' she said, her voice rough. 'Just give her a little time.'

Roger did not answer, but he did not pull away either, though his chin lifted stubbornly.

They stood there in the corridor, the silence pressing around them again, as the wind rattled the windows and the weight of war settled deeper into the bones of Ravenley. And inside the bedroom, Carol Sinclair sat alone on the edge of the bed, the letter lying at her feet, her shoulders shaking as she wept for the man who might never come home, for the children she had never had, and for the emptiness that Ravenley could no longer hide.

Roger pushed open the heavy door to the unused corridor, the hinges giving a soft groan as it swung open, releasing a faint breath of cold, dusty air. A slant of winter light fell across the covered furniture: ghostly shapes beneath white sheets, hulking wardrobes, armchairs, and tables that might once have gleamed with polish but were now hidden away to save on coal and effort and the quiet guilt of living too well during a war.

Susan and Benjy followed him, their footsteps muffled on the thick, faded carpet. The air stale with mothballs, and somewhere above, a loose pane rattled in the draught.

Benjy tugged at Susan's hand, his mitten fraying at the edge. 'It's cold,' he complained, as he had complained all morning. 'Can't we go back to the warm bit?'

'You're always cold,' Susan said, not unkindly, tightening her grip on his hand.

'That's because it's always cold,' Benjy shot back, his bottom lip wobbling.

Roger ignored them, moving deeper down the corridor, lifting the edge of one sheet to peek beneath. An elegant sofa, striped in blue and cream, its legs claw-footed and curved, the kind of thing he could imagine in a grand London house, before everything was broken and blackened by falling bombs.

'Do you think she even sits on these things?' Roger asked, dropping the sheet back into place.

'Who?' Susan asked, though she already knew.

28

'Her.' Roger's voice had the disdain of a boy trying to sound older than his years. 'Mrs Sinclair.'

Susan glanced back towards the main hall, as if expecting Carol Sinclair to appear, arms folded, eyes sharp and cold as they had been that morning when they had stumbled into her shouting. The memory made her shiver, though it wasn't just the cold.

'I don't like her,' Susan said, her voice low.

'She doesn't like us,' Roger replied.

Benjy sniffled. 'I don't want to stay here.'

Susan crouched to pull his scarf tighter around his neck. 'We have to, Benjy. It's the war. Mummy said we had to be safe.'

'Safe?' Benjy's voice rose, tears in his eyes. 'I want to go home!'

'There's no home to go to,' Roger said, more harshly than he intended, and Susan shot him a look.

Benjy's sobs quieted into hiccups, and he wiped his nose on the back of his mitten.

They moved through the corridor, peeking into locked rooms through keyholes, catching glimpses of covered beds, portraits shrouded in dustsheets, fireplaces cold and empty. In one room, the corner of a mirror poked out from under its cover, reflecting Roger's pale, thin face back at him, hair too long, eyes too serious. Always so serious. He looked away. The reflection had reminded him to much of the father who had abandoned them. Their mum had kept his photograph for reasons that he could never understand.

This was only their first morning, and already he felt the weight of the house pressing down on him, the quiet cold, the ticking clocks that marked the hours in long, empty beats.

'Mrs Parker's all right,' Susan said, as they paused at the end of the corridor, where a narrow staircase led down towards the kitchen. 'And Mr Figgs too.'

'They don't talk to us like we're in the way,' Roger said, remembering how Figgs had brought them a warm pot of tea with extra sugar when they arrived, how Mrs Parker had tucked Susan's hair behind her ear when she cried that first night, whispering that it was all right, they were safe now.

'But her.' Roger spat the word. 'She looks at us like we're rats she can't get rid of.'

'She's sad,' Susan said quietly.

Roger glanced at her. 'What do you mean?'

'When you were talking to Mr Figgs yesterday, ' began Susan, 'Mrs Parker told me that she's sad. Her husband is in the RAF. He's away flying on missions. She's probably afraid he won't come back. It can't be easy for her, Roger.'

'She's still horrid,' he muttered.

They turned away from the staircase, back towards the door that led to the grounds. Snow had started to fall, soft flakes drifting down to settle on the frozen lawns, the hedges dusted in white, the air sharp with the promise of more to come.

Roger pulled the heavy door open, the cold immediately biting at their faces, the air clean and sharp after the stale dust of the house. Benjy hesitated on the threshold, but Susan nudged him forward.

They stepped out into the whiteness, the snow crunching beneath their shoes, breath steaming in the cold. The sky was heavy with clouds, the light flat and grey, but to Roger, it felt like freedom after the corridors of Ravenley.

They wandered down the path, past the bare rose garden, past the empty fountain with its cracked basin and the statues dusted in snow. Roger kicked at the drifts, sending sprays of powder into the air, and for a moment, he felt almost like a boy again, before the nights in the shelter, before the screaming bombs.

'It's cold,' Benjy complained again, tugging at Susan's hand. His coat was too thin, patched at the elbows, the buttons mismatched.

'It's always cold now,' Roger said. 'Better get used to it.'

Benjy scowled, kicking at the snow. 'I don't like it here. It smells funny. I want to go home.'

'We don't have a home anymore,' Roger said, though his voice softened this time.

Susan shot him a grateful look.

'It's not fair,' Benjy whispered, rubbing his nose.

'No,' Roger said. 'It isn't.'

They reached the edge of the grounds, where the hedges grew wilder, the trees twisted and bare against the grey sky. Beyond, half-hidden by the falling snow, loomed a great shed, its wooden boards weathered, roof patched with tin.

'What's that?' Susan asked.

Roger squinted through the snow. 'Let's see.'

'No!' Benjy wailed. 'It's cold! I'm tired!'

'Oh, come on, Benjy,' Susan said, pulling him along.

They trudged across the snowy grass, the flakes falling thicker now, clinging to their hair and eyelashes. The shed was enormous, like the barns Roger had seen in the countryside, but older, leaning slightly as if tired of standing.

Roger reached the door first, pressing his gloved hands against the rough wood. He found the latch, heavy and rusted, and pushed. It took all his weight, but slowly, with a groan of protest, the door swung open, a cold, musty smell rushing out.

Inside was darkness, the only light coming from the open door, casting a pale rectangle across the dusty floor. They stepped inside, their feet echoing on the wooden boards.

It took a moment for their eyes to adjust, but as they did, Roger gasped. There, in the middle of the shed, surrounded by crates and old oil cans, was an aeroplane. A biplane, its wings stacked one above the other, canvas yellowed with age, the nose long and sleek, the propeller still, dust clinging to every surface.

'It's an aeroplane,' Benjy whispered, his eyes wide.

'It's from the last war,' Roger said, stepping closer, fingers itching to touch it. 'A real one.'

'Do you think it still flies?' Susan asked, her voice soft with wonder.

Roger shook his head. 'No petrol. And it's old.'

31

They circled it slowly, their feet crunching on the cold, dusty floor, the biplane standing silent and regal in the gloom. It smelled of old oil and cold metal, the air sharp and still.

'You said Mrs Parker say that Mr Sinclair was in the RAF,' said Roger. 'This will be his plane. I'll bet he learned to fly in this. I wonder if his father flew in the first one.'

They all stood still for a moment, picturing it. The cold skies, the roar of engines, the chase and dive, the glory of it. Roger could almost see it, the man they had never met, tall and brave in his uniform, leaping into his aeroplane to fight, to protect them, to protect England.

'He's a hero,' Roger said softly.

They were silent for a moment. The contrast of the man fighting for his country while his wife could barely bring herself to do something that many in the country had willingly done was too great. She had a duty to support the war effort. This meant using her enormous house as a place where evacuees could go or even the army.

Sensing what Roger was thinking, Susan spoke, her voice cautious. 'She's his wife. It's natural she's afraid.' Roger's jaw tightened. Susan always took the woman's side. 'Doesn't mean she has to be mean, too.' 'We should give her time,' she added, but the words sounded thin, even to her.

Roger ran a hand along the wing of the biplane, feeling the cold, brittle canvas beneath his glove. Snowflakes drifted in through the open door, melting on the wooden floor.

'Maybe Benjy's right,' Roger said, his voice low. 'Maybe we shouldn't stay where we're not wanted.'

Susan looked at him, eyes wide. 'Where would we go?'

Roger didn't answer.

Benjy began to cry, softly at first, then harder, the sound filling the shed, echoing off the wooden walls.

'Hush now, Benjy,' Susan said, pulling him close, but he buried his face in her coat, the sobs shaking his small frame.

Roger stood there, looking at the biplane, at the old war relic that once might have meant glory and courage, and now stood forgotten in a cold shed while bombs fell over London, while their mother was gone, while they were here in a house where they were not wanted.

Snow continued to fall outside, drifting in through the open door, settling softly on the wings of the old plane, on the floor, on their hair and shoulders, cold and silent as it slowly covered the world in white.

Tuesday 10th December 1940

Ravenley was quiet that afternoon, too quiet for Charles Sinclair as he stood by the window, the light falling across the frost-furred gardens, the last of the brown leaves sticking to the gravel drive. It was the sort of silence that pressed against the ears, that made the ticking clock above the mantelpiece sound like a hammer. Behind him, Carol was sitting, half turned in the chintz armchair, her hands twisting a handkerchief in her lap.

'You could have stayed here,' she said at last, breaking the quiet in a voice that was low, almost tired. 'You didn't have to go.'

Charles's jaw tightened. He kept his gaze on the sycamore outside, its black limbs stark against the pale sky.

'I've told you already,' he said, trying to keep his voice calm, though it came out clipped. 'I won't sit here playing nursemaid to boys who can barely shave while others are out there doing what needs to be done.'

'Training them is doing what needs to be done,' Carol shot back, her voice rising despite herself. 'Don't pretend it's nothing.'

Charles turned then, slowly, his eyes grey and cold, the same cold as the air outside, and Carol felt the words catch in her throat.

'You think I should be content to sit in a warm office, flying circles over the moors while the Germans bomb London? You think I should be content to be safe while men better than me are dying?'

'I think you should want to stay alive,' she snapped. 'Is that so unreasonable?'

He laughed, a harsh sound, without any humour. 'Alive? For what, Carol?'

She flinched, looking down at the handkerchief in her lap, the fine linen twisting between her fingers.

'For us,' she whispered.

There was silence again, a silence that pressed like a stone between them. Outside, a rook cawed, the sound sharp against the glass.

'Us,' Charles repeated, the word heavy on his tongue. He shook his head, turning back to the window. 'You say that as if it's something real.'

Carol's head snapped up, colour rising to her cheeks. 'What is that supposed to mean?'

He was silent, his back to her, hands clenched at his sides. She rose, the handkerchief falling to the floor, stepping forward until she was just behind him.

'Charles,' she said, reaching for his arm, but he pulled away, stepping aside.

'No,' he said, his voice flat. 'Don't.'

She let her hand fall, curling her fingers into a fist against her skirt. She could feel the tears burning behind her eyes, but she would not let them fall, would not give him that.

'Is this about...' She swallowed, the words tasting bitter. 'Has Cressida been filling your head full of poison?'

His head turned, just slightly, but he did not look at her. 'We don't have children, Carol. We don't have anything.'

She stepped back as if he had struck her, her breath catching. Yes, Cressida had been weaving her dark magic on Charles.

'You think I haven't wanted that?' she demanded, her voice trembling. 'You think I haven't wanted...'

'You wanted a Sinclair,' he snapped, turning on her now, eyes flashing. 'You wanted the house, the name, the safety. Don't pretend you wanted me.'

The words hung in the cold air, the fire in the grate crackling softly, spitting a little as a log shifted.

Carol felt as if the air had been punched from her lungs. She opened her mouth, but no sound came out. She had wanted him.

Once.

'You're cruel,' she said finally, her voice so soft it was almost a breath.

'Perhaps,' Charles said. He turned back to the window, scrubbing a hand across his jaw. He looked tired, older than his thirty-three years, the lines at the corners of his eyes deeper than they should have been.

'I didn't marry you for the house,' Carol said, lifting her chin. 'Or the name.'

He did not turn, but she saw the way his shoulders tensed.

'I loved you, Charles.'

He closed his eyes, breathing out through his nose.

'Did you?' he asked, softly.

She felt something break inside her then, something that had been holding her upright. She turned away, pressing a hand to her mouth, the tears coming despite her best efforts.

'I don't want you to die,' she whispered, her voice breaking. 'Is that so terrible? I don't want to lose you.'

'You can't lose what you never had,' Charles said, the words falling like stones between them.

She spun back to him, anger flaring through the grief. 'How dare you,' she hissed. 'How dare you say that to me.'

He looked at her then, really looked, and for a moment, there was something like regret in his eyes, something like pain.

'Carol,' he said, softer now, but she shook her head, tears slipping down her cheeks.

'Go,' she said. 'If you want to die so badly, then go.'

He flinched, and she saw it, and a part of her felt satisfaction in it.

'Don't worry about the house, or the name, or the children we never had,' she said, her voice hardening. 'I'll manage. I always do.'

36

He looked as if he might say something else, but then he closed his mouth, his jaw clenching again. He turned on his heel, striding across the room, pulling the door open so hard it rattled in its frame.

She did not watch him go. She stood there, staring at the fire, the tears running silently down her cheeks, her breath coming in sharp, shallow gasps. She heard the front door slam, the echo ringing through the house like a gunshot.

Outside, Charles stalked across the gravel, his boots crunching, the cold air biting at his face, burning in his lungs. The sky was the colour of slate, the clouds heavy with the promise of more snow. He climbed into the Lagonda, slamming the door, the engine coughing to life with a roar that shattered the quiet of Ravenley. He did not look back at the house as he drove away, the tyres spinning a little on the icy drive.

The road to RAF Exeter was quiet, the hedgerows stark and bare, the fields dusted with frost. Charles kept his eyes on the road, his hands tight on the wheel, the cold seeping through his gloves, the wind whistling through the small crack in the window.

He could still see her face, the tears, the anger, the way her voice had trembled. He clenched his jaw, pressing the accelerator harder.

What did she know about it? About the way it felt to sit here, warm and safe, while the country burned? About the way it felt to watch boys die because they didn't know how to pull out of a dive, because they froze in the gunner's seat, because they were too young, too scared, too green?

What did she know about the guilt?

He reached RAF Exeter just as the light was beginning to fade, the sky darkening to a bruised purple, the windsock snapping in the wind. The runway was quiet, a single Blenheim taxiing slowly across the tarmac, engines rumbling.

Charles parked, climbing out, slamming the door, his boots crunching on the gravel. The cold wind cut through his coat, but he welcomed it, the sting of it on his face.

37

He strode across to the Officer's Mess, pushing the door open without knocking. The warmth hit him immediately, the smell of beer and smoke, the low murmur of voices.

'Charles!' someone called, but he ignored them, moving straight to the bar.

Simon Dean was there, leaning back on a stool, a pint in his hand, his RAF uniform rumpled, hair falling into his eyes. Like Charles, he was tall, slender, clipped of moustache, even more clipped of speech. They could have been brothers. He looked up, saw Charles, and raised an eyebrow.

'You look like hell,' Simon said, taking a sip of his beer. Far from being a mean-spirited insult, this was merely the British chap, in his natural habitat, throwing out remarks that were not poisoned darts of enmity but rather the warm pats of friendship, a ballet of barbed witticisms, each jest more blistering than the last. It made a fellow feel welcome.

'Give me one,' Charles said to the barman, who nodded, pulling a pint.

'What's the matter with you?' Simon asked, shifting to make space as Charles took the stool beside him.

Charles didn't answer until the pint was in his hand. He took a long drink, the cold beer washing the taste of the argument from his mouth, leaving only the bitterness.

'It's Carol,' he said finally, wiping his mouth with the back of his hand.

Simon sighed, leaning back. 'Ah. Cherchez la femme.'

'Ah?' Charles snapped, turning on him. 'That's all you have to say?'

Simon held up a hand. 'Easy, old man. I'm on your side, remember?'

Charles snorted, taking another drink. 'There is no side.'

Simon was quiet for a moment, studying him. 'It can't be easy for her, you know.'

38

Charles slammed the glass down, beer sloshing over the side. 'Don't you start.'

'I'm just saying.'

'I don't want to hear it, Simon,' Charles snapped.

Simon sighed again, rubbing a hand over his face. 'She's your wife, Charles.'

'Is she?' Charles muttered, staring into the glass. Simon didn't answer, and for a moment, the only sound was the murmur of voices, the clink of glasses. 'I can't sit here,' Charles said finally, his voice low. 'I can't sit here, safe, while they're out there.'

Simon looked at him, his eyes tired, understanding. 'I know.'

'She wants me to stay. Wants me to play at being safe, to pretend everything's fine while London burns' Charles said, a bitter laugh escaping him. Then he cruelly mimicked a woman's voice, 'Oh, is that one of our bombers? I do hope they come home safely. Pass the teacakes darling.'

Simon looked in surprise at Charles. He knew he'd gone too far. He turned away. Simon's tone softened. He said, 'She's scared, Charles.'

'I'm scared,' Charles said, glancing back up at him. 'But I'm still going.'

Simon held his gaze, then nodded slowly. They sat in silence for a moment, the fire crackling in the hearth, the smell of smoke and beer filling the air.

'It's not her fault,' Simon said softly.

Charles closed his eyes, the image of Carol's tear-streaked face rising in his mind.

'I've had enough of this watered-down beer. Have they nothing stronger?' he said, sharply before adding more softly, 'I know. She's scared.'

But it didn't change anything.

39

The dawn was thin and grey over the fields of Germany, the frost a silver crust over the churned earth where the Bristol Blenheim had torn itself apart. Steam rose from the twisted wreckage, a thin black smoke curling from one broken wing. The air smelled of petrol and burned oil, and the frost was turning to slush where the heat still lingered.

The German patrol arrived just after dawn, boots crunching over the frozen grass, rifles slung carelessly as they moved towards the blackened heap of metal. One of them, a young Feldwebel with a pale face and tired eyes, raised a hand as he heard something.

A groan. Faint, ragged, but there.

They stopped, rifles lifting, scanning the field for movement. Another groan, this time sharper, and they moved quickly, spreading out, boots squelching in the mud near the cratered impact site. Smoke twisted lazily into the air but there was no sign of any flames.

Near the torn fuselage, a figure was sprawled half in, half out of the twisted metal, one arm dangling, fingers twitching in the cold air. His uniform was torn, the blue-grey fabric stained with mud and oil, the insignia barely visible under the grime. One of the Germans knelt, rifle still held ready, and prodded the man's shoulder with the muzzle.

'Name?' he barked.

The man winced in pain from the jabbing of the rifle. He rolled his head slightly, eyes blinking open. Pale grey eyes, bloodshot, dazed. His hair was matted with blood where a gash crossed his temple.

'Name!' the Feldwebel repeated, more sharply.

The man blinked as he stared up into at the silhouette of soldier. His eyes shifted from side to side as he caught sight of two other bodies nearby, one slumped against the instrument panel, the other lying at an unnatural angle. He drew a sharp, rattling breath. He blinked once more at the young man standing over him.

'Flight Lieutenant Sinclair,' he said, his voice low, cracked.

The Feldwebel exchanged a glance with the younger soldier, then nodded. They pulled him clear of the wreckage, boots slipping in the mud, the stink of petrol rising in the cold air. He let out a strangled cry as they lifted him, clutching at his side, but they did not pause.

Apart from cuts and bruises, he was whole. Breathing. Alive.

They dragged him to the truck, an old grey Opel, its bed already filled with spare parts and the spoils of the morning's search. They pushed him up, his boots scraping on the wood, and he fell back against the side with a grunt, clutching his ribs.

The truck started with a rattle, shuddering as they turned back to the road, the driver muttering to himself, cigarette dangling from the corner of his mouth. Every bump sent a jolt through Sinclair's battered body, each pothole a sharp lance of pain in his ribs, real or feigned, it did not matter. The engine roared, the wind cold on his face where they had left the canvas rolled back.

He stared at the passing trees, the skeletal branches blurred with frost, the fields rolling away, empty and grey. The road was endless, the sky a dull iron above them, and every mile was measured in pain. It was if the driver had decided to attack every pothole in the road. It was scant consolation that some of the German soldiers were no more impressed by the driver's behaviour. After what seemed like the tenth pothole, the cries of protest grew louder.

The driving did not seem to improve.

After nearly an hour, the truck lurched through the gates of a makeshift camp, barbed wire strung hastily between posts, the ground churned to mud by boots and wheels. A guard stepped forward, waving them in, and the driver shouted something in return, too quick for Sinclair to catch.

They pulled him down, rough hands on his arms, dragging him across the yard. He stumbled, nearly falling, catching himself against the rough edge of a post. They ignored it, pulling him forward, past a row of sullen prisoners standing under guard, their faces pale, eyes hollow.

Two dozen men, by his count, some in khaki, others in the dull blue of aircrew, their badges unfamiliar. A few looked up as he passed, quick, measuring glances, then looked away again. One man nodded slightly, the barest flicker of acknowledgment.

They brought him to a tent near the edge of the compound, a medical tent of sorts, marked with a Red Cross that was already stained brown with mud. Inside, the air was warmer, smelling of iodine and damp canvas, the light dim.

The doctor was a thin, balding man in a frayed coat, spectacles perched on the end of his nose. He looked up as they dragged Sinclair in, setting aside a tin mug of something steaming.

'Another one?' he asked in German, sighing.

'Claims to be Flight Lieutenant Sinclair,' the Feldwebel said, pushing Sinclair down onto a cot.

The doctor stepped forward, checking him over quickly, prodding his ribs, lifting his eyelids, making a noise of mild interest at the gash on his head.

Sinclair let out a gasp, clutching at his side, his eyes rolling back.

'Internal bleeding,' he croaked. 'Can't... breathe.'

The doctor frowned, looking back at the guards. 'Leave him for now. If he dies, we will deal with it then.'

They left, the tent flap dropping closed, and Sinclair let himself slump back, breathing shallowly, eyes half closed. The pain was real enough, but he let it seem worse, clutching at his side, moaning softly until he heard the footsteps fade.

The tent was quiet. Outside, the wind rattled the canvas, the cold seeping through. He lay there, counting heartbeats, letting his breath slow, letting the pain settle into a dull ache.

Twenty minutes passed. Perhaps more.

Then, carefully, he opened his eyes fully, turning his head to scan the dim interior. There was a table with bandages and tins of ointment, a small stove with a kettle steaming faintly. A single lantern hung from a hook, swaying gently.

Slowly, he swung his legs off the cot, pausing as a wave of dizziness washed over him. He breathed through it, waiting for it to pass, then slid to the ground, boots silent on the packed earth.

He moved to the edge of the tent, crouching, fingers searching for the edge of the flap. He found it, lifting it carefully, just enough to peer outside.

The yard was quieter now, the guards at the far end near the gate, talking, smoking. The other prisoners were huddled near a brazier; their faces turned towards the heat.

Sinclair slipped under the flap, the canvas brushing against his shoulders, the cold air hitting him like a slap. He crouched low, moving between the tents, careful to keep to the shadows, his breath a white mist in the cold. The mud sucked at his boots, each step a careful, deliberate movement, avoiding the puddles that would splash, the frozen patches that would crack.

A shout rang out suddenly, sharp, angry, and he froze, dropping to one knee, his breath caught in his throat.

A moment later, a laugh, and the sound of boots moving away. Not for him. Not yet.

He moved again, slipping behind a stack of crates, edging towards the line of trees that marked the edge of the compound. The forest was dark, the trees thick, a promise of cover if he could reach them. It was around ten yards from the barbed wire. The distance he needed to cover to the wire was less than twenty yards. He was five yards from the wire when a shout tore through the air, sharper this time, urgent.

43

'Halt!'

Sinclair ran.

The crack of rifles split the cold morning, bullets snapping past him, thudding into the mud. He threw himself forward, rolling, feeling the sting of a graze across his arm as a bullet tore through the fabric of his tunic.

He scrambled to his feet, lungs burning, legs driving him forward. The wire loomed ahead, and he did not slow, throwing himself at it, hands grabbing, boots kicking as he hauled himself up.

Another crack, another bullet, and the wire rattled under him, tearing at his clothes, slicing a thin line across his palm. Then he was over, falling hard into the mud on the other side, rolling, coming up in a crouch.

The trees, he thought. Get to the trees.

The breakfast table in the Williams household was a place of quiet formality. The oak sideboard, polished to a high shine the night before, reflected the pale winter light streaming through the mullioned windows. Outside, a thin veil of frost coated the garden lawn, catching the sun in silvery patches. Inside, the smell of toast, slightly overdone at the edges, mingled with the sharper tang of Seville marmalade.

Herbert Williams, bank manager of the Exeter branch of the Southern Counties Bank, sat in his usual chair at the head of the table. His back was straight; his gaze fixed firmly on the neatly folded Times propped against the teapot. In his view, reading the paper at breakfast was not merely a habit, but a civic duty, keeping abreast of the state of the world, even if one could do little to alter it.

Across from him sat his wife, Cynthia, a thin woman with a habit of keeping her shoulders slightly hunched as though bracing for some unspoken rebuke. She poured tea with a steady, deliberate hand, the teaspoon chiming gently against the china cup. At either side of the table were their children: Roderick, seventeen and already cultivating an air of detached superiority, and Mathilda, fifteen, who had inherited her mother's pale colouring but not her nervousness.

The conversation was polite but sparse, as it always was at this hour. Herbert took a bite of toast, chewed, and then announced in the same tone one might use to discuss the market prices,

'A cold start today. We've had a dry spell, though. Could hold if the wind stays in the east.'

'Might be a frost tonight,' said Roderick, who liked to give the impression of being in tune with matters meteorological.

'Frost in the air does no harm at this time of year,' said Herbert with authority, as though delivering a verdict on the matter.

'The camellias might disagree,' Mathilda offered lightly, earning the faintest twitch of a frown from her father. Herbert Williams did not approve of levity at breakfast.

Cynthia, always keen to smooth any ripple, murmured, 'At least the sky is clear this morning. It's pleasant to see the sun in December.'

They ate in small, measured bites, spreading marmalade thickly over the toast. Herbert favoured a methodical approach — corners first, moving inward, while Roderick devoured his in large bites, unconcerned with neatness. Mathilda ate absentmindedly, her eyes drifting to the frost-fringed garden where she had said a goodbye to Lance Buckley the previous day.

The tea was poured, refilled, and poured again, steam curling in the cool air of the dining room. Cutlery chimed softly against plates. The conversation, never more than polite observations about weather or household necessities, wound down into silence.

At length, Herbert folded his napkin with military precision, laid it beside his plate, and rose from the table.

'If you'll excuse me,' he said, 'I'll brush my teeth then and be off.'

This meant he would attend to his moustache, check the precise angle of his tie knot, and ensure his shoes retained their regulation shine before venturing into the public gaze.

His absence from the room brought with it a subtle loosening of the air, as though a tightly fastened belt had been let out. Roderick slouched slightly in his chair, Mathilda buttered another slice of toast without her usual care, and Cynthia allowed her shoulders to lower a fraction. Still, they did not speak much, a habit that ran too deep in this household.

Five minutes later, Herbert returned, immaculate in his dark overcoat and scarf, bowler hat in hand. His moustache was trimmed and oiled, the silver watch chain across his waistcoat gleaming faintly in the morning light.

'Well,' he said, picking up his gloves from the sideboard. 'I'll be off.'

Cynthia rose automatically. 'I'll see you out.'

It was part of the ritual. She followed him to the front door, holding it open against the faint chill that entered with the morning air. Herbert stepped out onto the tiled porch, pausing only long enough to pull on his gloves.

'Dinner at the usual time?' she asked, more to say something than because she expected a different answer.

'Of course,' Herbert replied, and then, almost as an afterthought, 'You might speak to Mrs Denton about the mutton. Last week it was a little tough.'

'Yes, dear,' Cynthia murmured. She watched him descend the three front steps to the garden path, the frost crunching faintly under his polished shoes.

Herbert walked briskly, shoulders squared, the very picture of a man whose position in life was fixed and respectable. The frost clung stubbornly to the grass either side of the gravel, and a robin darted away at his approach.

The garden path opened onto the road; a neat residential street lined with semi-detached houses much like his own. He set off a measured pace. There was no need to hurry; punctuality was a matter of steady discipline, not frantic rush. His breath hung in faint white clouds in the air before him. His view of the weather changed as he walked. There was snow in the air. The cold was dry, with that crisp clarity to the light that only comes in winter. He was well wrapped in his overcoat and scarf. The walk would warm him up. As

47

he walked, black umbrella, tapped the pavement in a slow, steady rhythm.

This daily journey to the bank was less than fifteen minutes, and Herbert valued it as a time to marshal his thoughts, review the day's expected business, and occasionally rehearse the firm but fair tone he would use with the more tiresome clients.

As he walked on, the town slowly came into view — a huddle of rooftops and chimneys, a thin plume of smoke from the bakery's ovens, and the faint, distant clang of the church bell marking the quarter-hour. The streets nearer the centre were beginning to stir: a milk cart rattling over cobbles, a shopkeeper lifting the shutters of his draper's shop, and a small boy in short trousers kicking a frozen clod of earth ahead of him until his mother's call sent him scurrying indoors.

Herbert took it all in with the detached satisfaction of a man whose world was orderly and predictable, where everything and everyone had their proper place. The cold air sharpened his senses, but his mind was already turning to the day and dealing with the problems that faced every bank manager.

People. Either the ones he managed or the ones who came through the doors as customers.

Halfway to the high street, he came upon old Mr Lincoln from the ironmongers, a stooped figure wrapped in a scarf that looked as though it had seen three decades of winters.

'Morning, Mr. Williams,' Lincoln called, tipping his cap with a hand mottled by age.

Herbert gave a curt nod. 'Morning, Mr Lincoln. Business steady?'

'Oh, about as steady as can be hoped for, what with the war,' said the old man, his voice cheerful despite the words.

Herbert allowed the smallest of smiles. 'Steady trade in uncertain times is no small thing.' He resumed his walk before Lincoln could venture into the realm of personal conversation, a sphere Herbert regarded as a private preserve.

On the final stretch toward the bank, he passed two schoolboys in caps and scarves, one of whom whispered something to the other. Herbert caught the sound of muffled laughter and the words 'Old Marble Face,' which he suspected, correctly, was a nickname for himself.

He did not break stride, but the corner of his mouth tightened. Herbert was not a man given to dwelling on trifles, yet he made a mental note that young people today were less respectful than in his youth.

Just before reaching the market square, he met Mr. Archer, a solicitor of roughly his own age and standing. Archer was a man who took great pride in his own respectability, though Herbert privately considered him a touch too fond of convivial gatherings.

'Williams,' Archer said warmly. 'Off to keep the wheels of finance turning?'

'As ever,' Herbert replied. 'And yourself? Setting the machinery of the law in motion?'

'Trying to,' Archer chuckled. 'War work keeps us all busier than we like to admit.'

They exchanged a few more pleasantries about rationing, mutual acquaintances, and the state of the railway service, before parting with the kind of deliberate courtesy reserved for men of equal social rank.

The bank came into view, a solid Georgian building with pillars that gave an impression of sober permanence. Herbert's pace quickened slightly, not from eagerness, but because he believed a man ought to arrive at his post with an air of brisk competence.

As he approached the heavy double doors, he passed Mrs. Connolly, the charwoman, already at work sweeping the pavement in front. She bobbed her head. 'Morning, Mr. Williams.'

'Good morning, Mrs. Connolly,' Herbert said, in a tone that was neither condescending nor familiar. It was, in his mind, the correct tone to take with a person of her station — acknowledgement without undue familiarity.

Reaching the door, Herbert allowed himself one last glance over the square. The shops were opening, people going about their business, and the air still crisp with frost. Everything was in its place, exactly as it should be.

He stepped inside, ready to assume the mantle of authority that awaited him behind the bank's high counters and polished brass rails.

Watching Williams leave his house had been three men in a black car. They kept watching him until he disappeared from view. Their faces were tight with nervous energy. Surreptitious glances at one another as if waiting for someone to make the fateful decision.

'Best get a move on. Those kids will be off to school soon.'

'Aye,' came the reply.

Two men stepped out of the car. One of them was carrying a cricket bat. He'd never played cricket in his life. He swung the heavy willow implement as if he was going out to the crease.

They reached the door of the bank manager's house. One of the men knocked. Moments later they both pulled balaclava over their faces. It was this sight that greeted the rather nervous Cynthia Williams as she pulled the door open.

Williams was always the first to arrive at the bank. Although he would never admit it, it was a relief to have fifteen minutes own in the building before the staff all arrived before nine. He locked the door behind him and put the key back on the chain that was on a ring at his waste. He walked to his office behind the counter. Arriving at the door he pulled another key off the chain and opened the office door.

The phone was ringing.

He felt a flash of irritation at this. It could only be Cynthia. No one else had his private line. What could she want? She knew that this was his preparation time for the day ahead. He stalked over to the phone and gripped the handle tightly.

'Cynthia is that you?' were his first words. Before he could add anything of an equally sharp tone his wife interrupted him. The last time that had happened was never.

The next words he heard he would never forget.

'Herbert, you have to do what they say,' her voice was bordering on hysteria.

Carol's head pounded as she made her way down the sweeping oak staircase of Ravenley, one hand lightly touching the banister, the other pressed to her temple as if it might calm the storm still moving behind her eyes. Her reflection in the darkened glass of the hallway mirror was pale, her eyes shadowed, but she ignored it. She would not let them see her weakness. Somewhere in the rafters, a mouse scuttled with steps that sounded like an elephant charging at hunters.

When would this day end?

Mrs Parker met her at the foot of the stairs, hands clasped, the faint scent of carbolic clinging to her apron. Her expression was carefully neutral, but there was something in her eyes that was almost...fear.

'They're in the breakfast room, madam,' Mrs Parker said quietly.

'Thank you.'

Carol hesitated outside the door, hearing the faint rustle of movement within, a childish giggle hastily smothered. She took a breath, pressing her lips together, then opened the door.

The children sat at the long table, dwarfed by the heavy oak chairs, their feet not quite reaching the floor. The table had been laid with simple fare. Slices of bread and butter, a pot of jam, a plate of boiled eggs set with military precision, filled the table. The house was too large, too cold, and the breakfast room too formal for three evacuee children, but there was nowhere else.

Roger's eyes met hers first, dark and wary, his mouth tightening. Susan, her pale hair neatly brushed, sat straight-backed, her hands folded, and Benjy, youngest of the three, was licking jam from his fingers before hurriedly dropping his hands to his lap.

They all went still as Carol entered, the silence ringing louder than any words.

She moved to the head of the table, her slippers whispering against the polished boards, and placed her hands on the back of the chair before her.

'I owe you an apology,' she said, her voice low but steady.

Benjy looked up at her, eyes wide. Susan blinked, a faint flush colouring her cheeks, but Roger only narrowed his eyes, saying nothing.

'I said things this morning that were unkind. I was...upset, and it was wrong to take it out on you,' began Carol.

Still silence. The clock on the mantel ticked steadily, the fire in the grate giving off little heat.

Carol drew in a breath, pressing her nails into the polished wood of the chair.

'I received news this morning that my husband's plane did not return from a mission last night. We do not know if he is alive or...' She paused, swallowing. 'Or what has happened.'

Susan's eyes softened, her lips parting, and even Benjy's lower lip wobbled slightly.

'I should not have spoken as I did,' Carol finished, her voice tight now. 'And I am sorry.'

She sat down slowly, smoothing her skirt, trying to keep her hands from trembling as she reached for the teapot. The children watched her, the air around them strangely heavy, as if they were all holding their breath.

Benjy looked at Susan, who gave him a small nod.

'It's all right, miss,' Benjy mumbled, scuffing the toe of his shoe against the rung of his chair.

'Ma'am,' Susan corrected gently, giving Benjy a little nudge.

Susan looked up with solemn blue eyes. 'We didn't know. We're sorry too, ma'am.'

Carol's eyes flicked to Roger, who sat rigid, his jaw clenched, his arms folded tightly across his chest.

'You must be Roger,' said Carol softly.

He held her gaze, his eyes hard, and for a moment Carol felt as if she were looking into the eyes of a man, not a boy of twelve. Then he looked away, his mouth a thin line.

'We'll try not to be any trouble, ma'am,' he said flatly. 'We're sorry about your husband. He must be very brave.'

Carol's heart twisted. Yes, he was brave. Foolish. Angry. He was a lot of things. She did not reply. Instead, she poured tea, her movements steady, setting cups before each of them, letting the scent of the weak, stewed brew fill the silence. She passed the plate of bread and jam, the eggs, watching as the children helped themselves, their movements careful, polite, Susan reminding Benjy to say 'please' and 'thank you'.

For a few minutes, there was peace. The ticking of the clock, the clink of spoons against cups, Benjy's quiet chatter as he told Susan that he had seen a rabbit outside the window, that it had white feet, and that it had looked right at him.

Carol sipped her tea, letting the warmth steady her, feeling the knot in her chest loosen, if only a fraction. There was still one more thing to be addressed. Carol steeled herself for what she had to say.

'We have all lost...' she stopped herself at that moment to collect herself. Charles was not lost. He would return. 'I'm so sorry about what happened to you. I want you to know that you are welcome here. I don't know how long you will stay but you will always be looked after. Please consider this your home. We will need to find you a school. However, as it is so near to Christmas, I imagine that you will not start until January.'

The fact that they would not need to go to school for a few weeks was the first piece of good news that they'd had in a while.

After lunch, Figgs brought the motor round to the front of the house, the car's engine coughing in the cold air, steam rising from the bonnet. A light misty rain fell as Carol pulled on her gloves, fastening the buttons with stiff fingers, the children standing in the doorway to watch her go.

Benjy gave her a small wave, which she returned with a ghost of a smile. Susan held Benjy's hand, watching Carol with that same solemn, searching look.

Roger stood slightly apart, his hands in his pockets, his shoulders hunched. His eyes met hers, dark and accusing, and for a moment she wanted to tell him that she understood, that she too was angry with the world, with the war, with everything that had stolen her husband from her, even before he had failed to return.

Aside from a nod to Figgs, she said nothing, only turning away and stepping into the cold embrace of the waiting car. She sped off down the driveway leaving Figgs at the entrance and the three children looking out of the library window. The roads were as quiet as they were narrow. There were no tractors to interrupt her progress on the thirty-minute drive to the airbase.

RAF Exeter was a grey sprawl of runways and low buildings, the air sharp with the tang of oil and the distant echo of engines. The guard at the gate checked her papers, nodding her through with a quick, sympathetic glance. She drove towards the main building, the tyres crunching over the gravel.

The station headquarters was a red-brick affair squatting resolutely in the heart of the aerodrome, like a disapproving aunt at a cocktail party. It was a building that had clearly been designed by someone who believed that if you made a structure rectangular enough, men would march smarter in its vicinity.

The front door, forever swinging like a weathervane in a gale, admitted a ceaseless stream of men in blue uniforms, each with the air of a man who had misplaced something important, like their brylcreem. Inside, the air was thick with the scent of floor polish, pipe smoke, and faint despair, mingling harmoniously with the distant hum of an engine being tested with more optimism than precision.

A young officer in a neat blue uniform took her coat, offering her a seat in a corridor lined with wooden benches.

She sat, her hands folded tightly in her lap, staring at the floor, hearing the distant rattle of typewriters, the murmur of voices behind closed doors. After what felt like an hour, the door opened, and the young officer returned.

'Group Captain Bill will see you now, Mrs Sinclair.' She rose, smoothing her skirt, lifting her chin, and followed him down the corridor.

The Station Commander's office was the beating heart of this hive of mild chaos. A large desk dominated the room, its surface an archaeological layer of paperwork, coffee stains, and a single, fossilized bun from the NAAFI that no one dared remove.

Group Captain John Worrall Bill was a large man, broad-shouldered, his uniform immaculate, his iron-grey hair clipped close to his scalp. He stood as she entered, offering his hand.

'Mrs Sinclair. Thank you for coming,' said Bill.

'Thank you for seeing me,' she managed, her voice tight.

He gestured to the chair before his desk, and she sat, perching on the edge, her gloved hands twisting in her lap.

'I'm afraid there's very little I can tell you,' Bill said, lowering himself into his chair with a sigh, folding his hands on the desk before him. 'The details of last night's raid are classified, as you'll understand.'

Carol nodded, unable to speak.

'What I can tell you,' Bill continued, his voice softer now, 'is that it was a night raid over Germany, and that a number of our aircraft did not return. Your husband's plane was among those missing.'

'Missing,' Carol echoed, the word sharp in her mouth.

'Yes. Until we have further information, we can only classify him as missing. There is always the chance that he and his crew bailed out and have been taken prisoner.'

'Or...?' Carol's voice broke.

Bill's eyes softened, but he did not flinch. 'Or worse. We will inform you as soon as we know anything further. The odd thing about this war is that both sides play fair when it comes to informing of casualties.'

Carol nodded, pressing a gloved hand to her lips, willing herself not to break, not here, not now.

There was a knock at the door, and the young officer reappeared.

'Sir, Flying Officer Dean is here.'

Carol turned sharply, her breath catching.

'Send him in,' Bill said.

Simon Dean entered, his uniform wrinkled, his hair dishevelled, eyes shadowed with exhaustion. He stopped when he saw Carol, his expression tightening, and for a moment he looked as though he might speak, but no words came.

'Dean was on the same mission,' Bill said, rising. 'He may be able to tell you what little he knows, though I've asked him to respect operational security.'

Carol stood, swaying slightly, and Simon stepped forward, steadying her with a hand on her arm. His touch was warm, solid.

'Thank you, Flying Officer Dean,' said Carol formally. Dean had once cast his eye in her direction. This was at the same time as Charles. Charles had won/

Bill nodded, giving Simon a hard look. 'You will keep it general, Dean.'

'Yes, sir.'

They left the office together, stepping into the cold corridor, the air sharp with the scent of metal and cold stone. Simon looked down at her, his mouth working, as if trying to find the right words.

'There's a pub just down the lane,' he said at last. 'You look like you could use something to warm you up.'

She almost laughed, the sound catching in her throat, but she nodded. They walked over to a car parked in near the huts.

'It's an old thing but it should get us to a quiet place in one piece,' said Simon. Then his face drained of colour as he realised just how insensitive that might have sounded. Carol seemed not to notice. She smiled and climbed into the car. They drove out of the base along a narrow country road with hedges that seemed as if they were going to close in on the car. Simon, unlike Charles, drove at a sensible speed. How many times had she angrily told off Charles for driving like a maniac on such roads. He usually laughed it off and kept his foot firmly down on the accelerator.

The pub was small, its windows fogged with the damp cold, the scent of stale beer and coal smoke heavy in the air. A fire burned low in the grate, giving off a weak, flickering light.

Simon led her to a table near the fire, pulling out a chair for her before going to the bar. She watched him, the way his shoulders hunched, the way he ran a hand through his hair as he waited for the drinks, his movements restless. He returned with two small glasses of brandy, setting one before her.

'Drink it,' he said softly. 'It'll help.'

She lifted the glass, the scent sharp, and took a small sip, feeling the heat bloom in her chest. For a moment, neither of them spoke.

'I shouldn't be here,' Simon said at last, his voice low. 'It should have been me.'

She looked up sharply. 'Don't.'

He shook his head, staring into his glass. 'We all know the risks. But he...Charles was...'

He broke off, his hand tightening around the glass.

'You were his friend,' she said softly.

'Yes.' He looked up, his eyes bright. 'And I failed him.'

'You didn't.'

'I was flying next to him, Carol. I saw the flak, the fighters...' He swallowed. 'And then he was gone.'

Carol closed her eyes, the image rising unbidden, Charles, his face set, eyes hard, the roar of the engines around him, the cold night sky, and then nothing.

58

'You did not fail him,' she whispered.

Simon reached across the table, his hand covering hers. His touch was warm, grounding, and she let herself hold it for a moment before pulling back, her hand trembling.

'He will come back,' she said, her voice firm, though it felt like glass in her mouth.

Simon looked at her, something unspoken in his eyes, something that had always been there, in the way he had looked at her when Charles's back was turned, in the quiet moments when he had lingered a second too long.

'I hope so,' he said softly.

They finished their drinks in silence, the fire crackling softly, the wind rattling the windows, the world outside cold and grey.

When they rose to leave, Simon placed a hand lightly on her back, guiding her to the door. She let him, just for a moment, allowing herself to lean into the warmth, the comfort, the unspoken promise in his touch.

Outside, the cold air hit them, sharp and clean, and she lifted her chin, drawing in a breath.

She would go back to Ravenley. Back to the children, to the house that felt too large, too empty. She would wait. Charles was out there.

Alive.

She had to believe it.

The rain had finally stopped, leaving the sky a bright, cloud-streaked blue, and the earth beneath their boots was soft, the puddles reflecting white clouds like scraps of torn cloth. Roger led the way down the rutted track, hands thrust in his pockets, his shoulders hunched forward as if bracing himself against a wind that had long since died away.

Susan and Benjy followed, Susan carefully stepping around the muddy patches, while Benjy dragged his boots through them with glee, spattering himself in brown and grinning up at the sudden warmth of the sun.

They had not told Mrs Parker where they were going. Roger had simply announced, in the crisp, determined tone that Susan recognised meant there would be no arguing, that they were going for a walk.

'I don't like it here,' Benjy said suddenly, after they had crossed the second stile, the fields opening before them in rolling green and pale gold. 'I want to go home.'

'You can't,' Roger said sharply.

Susan glanced back at Benjy, who was scuffing at the mud with his boot, his lower lip trembling. 'He doesn't mean it like that,' she said quietly to Roger.

'I do,' Roger snapped, but he fell silent, kicking at a stone until it skittered off into the grass.

They walked on for a while, the air fresh, birds calling from the hedgerows, the sunlight warm on their faces.

'Do you think,' Roger said suddenly, not looking at them, 'do you think we could just...run away?'

Susan stopped. 'Don't be stupid.'

'I'm not being stupid. We could go somewhere. Find a boat. Go to the coast. Anything's better than this place.'

Benjy's eyes widened, hopeful for a moment. 'Could we? Really?'

Susan shook her head, her plaits bouncing. 'We can't. There's a war on. London's being bombed. That's why we're here.'

Roger turned, his face flushed. 'Maybe we shouldn't have come. Maybe they don't want us here.'

Susan's face softened. 'Carol's trying, Roger.'

'You don't know her,' he muttered.

'I know she's sad. I think... I think she's lonely. Not just about her husband. She's sad.'

Roger kicked at another stone, hard, sending it skittering. Benjy's hand crept into Susan's, and she held it, squeezing gently.

'I miss Mum,' Benjy said, his voice very small.

Susan closed her eyes for a moment, pressing her lips together, before opening them and kneeling down to Benjy's level.

'I know,' she said softly. 'We all do.'

Roger turned away, wiping his nose on his sleeve.

They stood there for a moment, the breeze lifting the loose strands of Susan's hair, the scent of grass and damp earth around them.

They were crossing a large pasture, the grass cropped short by sheep, when they saw two men by a hedge, resting on their spades, mugs in their hands, steam rising from them in the cool air.

'Morning!' called one of the men, his face weathered, a wide grin breaking across it.

Roger hesitated, but Benjy, as always, ran forward, eager for company.

'Hello,' Benjy called back, breathless. 'What're you doing?'

'Digging this ditch out before it floods again,' the man said. 'Name's Eric Fisher, and this here's Toby Hewitt.'

Toby lifted a hand, his thick fingers stained with earth, and gave a nod.

Roger and Susan caught up, standing a few paces back, wary.

Eric looked at them with kind eyes. 'You lot from the big house, are you?'

'Yes, sir,' Susan said politely.

Eric chuckled. 'No need for sirs out here, miss. Just Eric'll do.'

He glanced at Roger. 'You're the eldest, I reckon?'

Roger nodded.

Eric held out the steaming tin mug he held. 'Bit of tea left, if you'd like a warm sip.'

Roger hesitated, but Benjy had already reached out, taking the mug in both hands, gulping a quick mouthful and pulling a face at its bitterness before passing it to Susan, who took a polite sip.

'We don't see many children up this way these days,' Eric said, leaning on his spade. 'Not since they closed the school down. War and all that.'

'Did you fight in the last war?' Benjy asked suddenly.

Toby glanced at Eric, who cleared his throat. 'We were there,' Eric said simply.

They did not say more, and something in their quiet made Roger look at them with new respect. Roger held the mug for a moment, staring into it, before he spoke, his voice low.

'We were in London,' he said. 'When the bombs fell.'

Eric and Toby were silent, watching him.

'There were sirens,' Roger went on, his voice tight, 'and we all ran down the stairs. We were supposed to go to the shelter, but... we didn't get there.'

Susan reached out, touching Roger's sleeve lightly.

'Mum... she didn't make it,' Roger said, blinking hard, looking down. 'We were pulled out. The house was gone. Everything was gone.'

Benjy began to cry quietly, wiping his face on his sleeve, and Susan pulled him into a hug, holding him close.

Eric took off his cap, running a hand through his thinning hair. 'I'm sorry, lad,' he said quietly. 'I truly am.'

Toby cleared his throat again. 'Your mum would want you to be safe. You remember that.'

They stood there for a while, the children sipping the last of the tea, the steam rising between them like a fragile bridge.

'What's Mrs Sinclair like, then?' Toby asked after a moment, glancing at Eric.

Susan looked up, wiping a tear from Benjy's cheek. 'She's... she's nice. I think she's just sad.'

'Aye, she's a beautiful woman,' Eric said, 'but a bit cold, maybe.'

'Her husband's a pilot, ain't he?' Toby added, lighting a cigarette and shielding it from the breeze.

Roger nodded. 'They say he's brave.'

Eric raised an eyebrow, sharing a glance with Toby. 'Aye. Brave, sure enough,' he said, but there was a tone in his voice, just a hint of something that made Roger look at him sharply.

'What?' Roger demanded.

'Nothing, lad,' Eric said quickly, forcing a smile. 'Just that sometimes these young officers... well, they don't always think before they act, that's all.'

Toby chuckled. 'He's right there.'

Roger opened his mouth to ask more, but Susan touched his arm.

'We should be going,' she said softly.

Eric and Toby nodded, shaking hands with each of them, Benjy clinging to Eric for a moment before letting go.

'You come by any time,' Eric said as they left, 'and we'll share another mug of tea with you.'

63

The sky was paling towards evening, the shadows stretching across the fields as they made their way back. But when they reached the edge of the woods, Roger stopped, looking back at the wide, open fields, then into the dark line of trees.

'Let's go through there,' he said suddenly.

Susan frowned. 'We should get back. It'll be dark soon.'

'Scared, are you?' Roger said, raising an eyebrow.

Benjy's eyes lit up. 'I want to! Please, Susan!'

Susan bit her lip, glancing at the darkening sky. 'Just for a little while.'

They entered the woods, the air cool and damp, the smell of moss and wet leaves thick around them. Twigs cracked underfoot, and the rustle of small creatures in the underbrush made Benjy jump and laugh, clinging to Susan's hand.

They found the tree hut by accident, a ramshackle platform high in the branches of a great oak, the ladder missing, the wood weathered and grey.

Roger's eyes lit up, a rare smile breaking across his face. 'Look at that!'

'Be careful!' Susan called as he scrambled up the trunk, pulling himself onto a lower branch and then climbing higher, until he reached the platform.

He stood there, triumphant, the wind tugging at his hair, his arms stretched out. 'It's wonderful! We can fix it up, make it ours! We'll bring rope tomorrow, make a ladder!'

Benjy clapped his hands, jumping up and down. 'I want to climb too!'

'Tomorrow,' Roger called down. 'We'll come back tomorrow!'

Dusk was falling as they left the woods, the sky turning violet, the first stars pricking through the darkening blue. They were laughing, even Susan, the fear and sadness of the day lifted for a moment by the promise of the tree hut, of something that was theirs.

They were crossing the lane near the edge of the estate when they heard the car. It came fast, the headlights off, its engine growling, tyres spitting gravel as it sped past them, so close that Susan shrieked and pulled Benjy to the side. Roger caught a glimpse of the man in the passenger seat—a dark moustache, clear blue eyes, a face twisted in anger or something worse.

The car skidded to a stop, gravel spraying into the hedgerow, and then began to reverse, the engine whining.

'Run,' Roger said sharply, grabbing Benjy's arm. 'Run!'

They tore off across the field, the grass whipping at their legs, the cold air burning in their lungs.

Behind them, the car door slammed, voices shouting, but Roger didn't look back.

'Run!' he shouted again, pulling Benjy along, Susan close behind, her breath coming in ragged gasps.

They reached the hedgerow, scrambling through it, thorns tearing at their clothes, scratching their arms, then they were in the next field, running, stumbling, Benjy sobbing with fear.

The lights of Ravenley House came into view, warm and golden in the dark, and they ran towards them, the gravel of the drive skidding under their feet as they burst into the kitchen door, slamming it behind them, panting, gasping, shaking.

Mrs Parker stood there, her hands on her hips, her face dark with anger.

'Where have you been?' she demanded. 'Look at you, you're filthy! You'll all take baths this instant, and there'll be no supper until you're clean!'

Susan opened her mouth to speak, but Roger stepped forward, brushing mud from his face, his hair wild, his eyes bright.

'Yes, Mrs Parker,' he said, his voice shaking.

Because in that moment, he didn't care about the bath, or the scolding, or the cold.

They were safe.

They were home.

The road from RAF Exeter blurred under the tyres, hedgerows blackening against the indigo sky, rain beads trembling on the windscreen like tiny glass marbles. Carol gripped the wheel tightly, her knuckles white, headlights catching the gleam of puddles as she navigated the winding lanes.

She should have driven home.

Should have returned to Ravenley, to the quiet, echoing halls and Mrs Parker's concerned glances. She should have gone back, prepared herself to face the children with whatever strained gentleness she could muster.

Instead, she found herself turning towards Exeter, letting the city lights pull her in as if she were drifting, her mind adrift, seeking something she could not name. The rain had stopped, leaving the air heavy and smelling of salt, the streets glistening under the streetlamps. She drove slowly, passing shuttered shops and the dark outlines of terraces, until the road widened and she glimpsed the masts bobbing gently against the ink-black water of the harbour.

She parked the car near the quay, turning off the engine, and let the silence wrap around her. The sea was restless, slapping against the stones below, and she watched the fishing boats returning, their lanterns swinging, men calling to one another in low voices, laughter sometimes floating over the water.

Carol rested her head back against the seat, closing her eyes.

Simon's face had unsettled her. The way he had looked at her with that softness in his eyes, the careful way he had spoken her name, as if it were something fragile.

It brought it all back.

Before she was Mrs Carol Sinclair, she had been simply Carol Whittaker, daughter of a country solicitor and a mother who spent her days managing the household with a firm but kind hand. She had been twenty-three, and that spring had been full of dances and garden parties, of long evenings where laughter drifted into the dark.

Both Charles and Simon had been there, orbiting around her like moths drawn to a single flame.

Charles had walked into a room as if he owned it, that crooked smile, the glint in his eyes, the way he would lift a glass and wink, making her laugh even when she was pretending to be offended by something outrageous he had said. There had been something intoxicating about the way he had leaned against doorways, hands in pockets, eyes bright, always on the verge of laughter or a sharp, clever comment that made everyone pause.

Simon, on the other hand, had been steady, kind, the sort of man who would notice if your gloves were fraying or if you looked tired, the sort who would offer to walk you home and mean it in the gentlest sense. He was calm, warm, dependable. He had not made her heartbeat wildly, but he had made her feel seen.

At the time, she had chosen excitement.

The Sinclair name had helped, too. Charles, the younger son of a noble family, moving in circles she had never imagined for herself. There were parties, dances, trips to London, promises of a life glittering with possibility. She had been so young.

She realised, sitting there in the darkness by the harbour, that she had mistaken volatility for passion, arrogance for confidence, sarcasm for wit. Charles had been funny, but also cruel in ways that had stung when the laughter faded. He had swept her off her feet, but sometimes he dropped her, and the bruises were invisible but deep.

67

She remembered their arguments. The way he would storm out, slam doors, disappear for hours, and return smelling of whisky and cigarettes, kissing her too hard and laughing when she pushed him away.

She remembered the quiet moments, too, though they were fewer: the way he had once rested his hand on her belly, hoping for a child, before turning away, disappointed when the months turned to years with nothing but emptiness.

Simon would have been different, she thought. A steady, kind life. Less thrilling, perhaps, but less lonely.

The air smelled of fish and salt, ropes creaking on wooden posts as the boats docked. Men were unloading crates, calling out to each other, the glow of lanterns shifting on the wet cobbles.

Carol opened the car door, stepping out, drawing her coat tightly around her. She needed the air, the salt, the grounding reality of the harbour to keep her from dissolving into regret.

She leaned against the cold metal of the car, watching the water. Her reflection in the dark surface was rippled, broken, no clear edges.

She had loved Charles, she supposed. Or the idea of him. Perhaps he had loved her, in his way. But something had broken between them, and neither of them had known how to fix it. She had felt the distance growing, and she had responded with silence, bitterness, with coldness she now regretted. And now he was gone. Missing. Perhaps dead. The ache in her chest was real, heavy, but it was tangled with guilt and a sense of finality that terrified her. She pressed her hands to her face, the tears hot against her palms.

The wail of sirens cut through the night, jolting her back to the present. She turned, blinking away tears, her breath misting in the cold air.

Down the street, outside a bank with darkened windows, two police cars had pulled up, their lights swirling red and blue across the wet street. A small crowd began to gather, people emerging from nearby shops and pubs, their voices a low hum of curiosity.

She saw the door of one of the cars open, and a man stepped out, his coat flapping in the wind, his face hard, eyes scanning the crowd with a practised, disinterested sweep.

Chief Inspector Clarence Hopcroft. Everyone called him 'Chops', including Carol.

His face was long and oval, with a slightly high, domed forehead that gave him an air of thoughtfulness — or mischief. He possessed heavy-lidded, expressive eyes that could switch from sleepy indifference to piercing amusement in a heartbeat. They were set beneath prominent brows that he could arch to devastatingly dry effect. He moved with the confidence of someone who was in on the joke long before the punchline had been delivered.

He spoke briefly to one of the constables, then turned and entered the bank, the heavy doors closing behind him.

Carol stood there for a moment, watching the reflected lights on the wet street, the way people peered towards the bank, hoping for a glimpse of excitement. But she had had enough of excitement in her life. It was time to go home.

The harbour lights were still flickering on the wet cobbles outside, the rain having left behind a smell of salt and oil, as Chief Inspector Hopcroft stepped lightly out of his black Wolseley and surveyed the chaos in front of the bank.

The Devon constabulary had done its best to form a perimeter, but a crowd had still gathered, eyes wide under caps and headscarves, whispers skating over the slick pavement like leaves in a breeze. A few children in short trousers stood on tiptoes, trying to peer past the line of policemen.

Chops was in his late forties but looked older, partly because he was entirely bald except for two tufts of grey hair curled apologetically around his ears, and partly because of the long, thoughtful lines around his eyes. He was tall and slender, with shoulders that seemed permanently relaxed, as though the world were simply a stage for some great farce only he fully understood.

His black fedora was perched at a reckless angle on the back of his head, and he carried his raincoat casually slung over one shoulder. His dark eyes missed nothing, flicking across the faces, the windows above the bank, the slick reflection of the red lamps on the puddles.

He gave a small, private smile, one that did not reach his eyes, as a young constable stepped forward to speak.

'Chief Inspector Hopcroft, sir. Sorry for the mess.'

'It is rather a mess, isn't it?' Chops said, his voice carrying that refined, educated crispness that had unnerved many an unwise criminal during questioning. Cambridge, law, a mind sharpened by logic and debate before he had ever stepped into a police station. 'Thank you, Constable, you can take me in now.'

The bank was heavy with the smell of cordite and blood.

Inside, the overhead lamps buzzed, casting harsh shadows on the marble floors and the counters, the air cold despite the bodies in the room. A doctor was kneeling beside the corpse of an older man in a nightwatchman's uniform, his face pale, his hands folding up his stethoscope.

'Won't ask the time of death,' said Chops, glancing at the man's face. Fred Morrison, he thought, though he had yet to be formally introduced to the body.

'Likely within the last hour,' the doctor replied with a grim humour. 'Gunshot to the chest. He didn't suffer long.' He and Chops had known one another for fifteen years. They shared a fatalistic view of the world, of which they saw only the worst. They coped because they shared an all-too-black sense of humour that few understood except them and one or two others.

'A gunshot, you say,' Chops murmured. He stepped around the body carefully, studying the blood pooled on the marble, the drag marks, the spent casings glinting like brass beetles. No sign of forced entry on the windows or the doors, the glass unbroken.

'What did he do, Doc, crawl here to die?' Chops asked quietly.

'Possibly. Or he was dragged, though I see no bruising suggesting he was moved after death.'

Chops crouched, catlike despite his height, and studied Morrison's lined face. Fifty-nine, ex-army, ex-prison guard, now dead on a cold, Christmas night in a small Devon bank that should have been closed and quiet.

He let out a soft sigh and stood.

The door that led to the vault was wide open. Chops wandered down a narrow staircase to a small room lit by a naked light bulb.

71

The walls were all brick without any plaster. Dominating the room was the vault. The heavy steel door gaping like a toothless mouth. He walked into the vault. Inside, empty shelves yawned back at them, and scattered papers and a few coins were all that remained. The robbers had made a fairly thorough job of it. One last perusal to commit the details of the scene to memory and then he meandered out of the vault and back up the stairs.

Detective Inspector Tommy Winslow, a fair-haired man in his late twenties whose shoulders were currently hunched with stress, was speaking with a pair of constables who were dusting for fingerprints. Chops drifted over, his steps silent, causing Winslow to flinch when he realised his boss was beside him.

'Tommy,' Chops said, his smile that amused curl again, 'you look like a man who needs a warm cup of tea.'

'I'd rather have a dram, sir,' Winslow muttered, running a hand through his hair.

Chops raised an eyebrow. 'Not before we finish. What have we?'

Winslow straightened, forcing professionalism into his posture. 'No sign of forced entry, sir. Morrison was found here by Constable Yates when he responded to the alarm. No witnesses so far, though we're canvassing. The vault's been emptied.'

'And how much did they take?' Chops asked, his eyes flicking again to the vault.

'We're waiting for the bank manager, sir.'

'Alarm, you say?' said Chops suddenly. 'That seems strange.'

'Yes sir,' said Winslow. 'I thought that strange too. I mean they cleared the vault.'

Chops nodded at this and looked around at the scene at the front of the bank. He said, 'So why was the alarm set off? Could it have been the dead man?'

'He was not by the alarm but that doesn't mean he didn't set if off,' suggested Winslow, with enough scepticism to suggest that this was fanciful.

Any further discussion on the subject ended when the bank manager arrived. Herbert Williams was a man in his forties, with thinning hair, spectacles fogged from the cold, and a grey overcoat that looked too big on his slight frame. His hands shook as he approached Chops, clutching his hat as if it might fly away in the cold breeze.

'Chief Inspector Hopcroft?' he asked.

Chops nodded, gesturing him inside.

They moved into the bank, Williams swallowing visibly as his eyes fell on Morrison's body.

'Fred... Morrison was a good man,' Williams whispered. He had turned pale at the sight of the dead body. Chops was convinced there and then he had not fought in the last war. He wondered why.

'So I hear,' Chops replied softly. 'Come. Let's leave him in peace for now.'

He guided the man towards a desk, pulling out a chair for him. Williams sat, eyes darting around the ruined bank.

'How much?' asked Chops casting an eye towards the door that led to the vault.

Williams swallowed again. 'I can only give you a preliminary estimate based on how much we would normally have at this time, but I would estimate... around thirty thousand pounds, sir.'

Chops let out a low whistle, tilting his head slightly. 'That's quite a sum for a branch in Devon, Mr Williams.'

Williams nodded, rubbing his temples. 'Some of it belongs to the RAF, sir. Payroll for the airmen at RAF Exeter. It was scheduled to be distributed this week.'

'Ah.' Chops closed his eyes for a moment, as if taking in the absurdity of it all. War, airmen risking their lives nightly, and here was someone stealing their wages under cover of darkness. He opened his eyes, their dark glint sharpening. 'We'll need a full list of the denominations taken, serial numbers if you have them, and any staff with knowledge of the schedules for deliveries and vault access.'

'Yes, of course,' said Williams.

73

Chops let Williams compose himself for a moment, then glanced back at Winslow, who was scribbling notes. He nodded to Winslow and said, 'Tommy, go with Mr Williams, collect the relevant ledgers, and see that he is safely returned home afterwards.'

Winslow glanced up, eyes pleading, but Chops' raised eyebrow was enough to silence any protest.

'And Tommy,' Chops added, 'find out where Fred Morrison lived and inform the next of kin. Maybe send someone to take a look at the house.'

Winslow's face fell, the colour draining a little. 'Yes, sir.'

'It's never pleasant,' Chops said, not unkindly, 'but it's better they hear it from us. The poor man is a hero. Tried to halt a robbery in progress. I'm sure you'll think of something.'

Winslow followed Williams, who was trembling as he opened the ledgers, the papers rustling like leaves in a breeze. Chops returned to the vault, staring into its dark emptiness, his mind ticking through the facts.

No forced entry.

In broad daylight, or, at least, soon after the bank had closed.

A guard shot dead.

Vault emptied.

The alarm set off after the robbery had taken place.

Inside job, or a gang with intimate knowledge of schedules.

And the war, which should have made such a robbery harder, had perhaps made it easier. Fewer police around during the day, fewer cars on the road. Chops sighed and removed his fedora, running a hand over his smooth scalp before replacing the hat.

He stepped back to the body of Fred Morrison, the doctor having covered him with a sheet now, though the dark stain beneath still spread across the marble like a shadow.

'Who let you down, old man?' Chops murmured. 'Or did you let yourself down?'

He knew the type. Men who had fought in the trenches, survived when others had not, lived with the guilt and the memories and the

74

scars that never healed. Men who sought quiet, steady jobs to finish out their lives in dignity.

Thirty thousand pounds was enough to tempt many, even a man who had once fought and bled for his country.

But Morrison had died by the door to the vault. Protecting it, or involved in the theft gone wrong? Chops stood there for a while, the distant sound of the sea and the cries of gulls coming through the broken silence of the bank.

Outside, night had fallen when Winslow returned an hour later, his face pale, the collar of his coat turned up against the chill.

'Sir,' he said, his voice low, 'Mr Morrison had no next of kin. He lived alone in a flat on the edge of town. I've sent some men to search it.'

Winslow nodded, swallowing, as Chops turned to survey the street. People had lost interest in the scene or had simply decided it was too cold or too wet. Above them, gulls were circling, crying out above the bobbing masts, the salt breeze cutting through the lingering staleness of the bank. Chops adjusted his fedora, lifted his raincoat back onto his shoulder, and gave Winslow a small, tired smile.

'Come on,' he said. 'Let's go.' Winslow moved towards the entrance of the bank. Chops shook his head. With his eyes he motioned in another direction. Winslow turned and saw that it was a pub. It was called The Bank Robber's Arms. A sign swung lazily from the wall. It showed a man dressed like Dick Turpin holding a pistol and a bag of money.

By the time they came in sight of the house, the sky had faded into a milky dusk, clouds hanging low over the Devon hills, their boots heavy with mud and wet grass. Roger was leading, eyes bright with that restless, defiant glint that sometimes-frightened Susan, whilst Benjy trailed behind, clutching the wooden stick he had found in the wood, using it as a walking staff and a sword all at once.

Mrs Parker was waiting on the front steps.

She stood there, arms folded, apron streaked with flour, her solid figure outlined against the yellow glow of the hallway. Her face, normally so calm and round, was drawn with lines of worry.

'And where,' she demanded, 'have you three been?'

Roger opened his mouth with that stubborn tilt of his chin, but Susan cut across him.

'We were just exploring, Mrs Parker,' she said quickly. 'We went to the far fields, near the edge of the estate.'

'And the wood!' Benjy piped up, hugging his stick tighter.

'The wood?' Mrs Parker's eyebrows rose. 'You know you're not meant to go so far without telling me.'

'We didn't mean to worry you,' Susan said, lowering her eyes. 'It was just... the weather was so fine.'

Mrs Parker sighed, the tension easing slightly from her shoulders, though she kept her arms folded. 'I was about ready to send the groundsman out looking for you. I've seen children wander off and break their ankles in those woods, and with roads the way they are now—'

76

'That reminds me,' Roger interrupted. 'We saw a car, Mrs Parker. It was speeding like anything along the lane by the wood, near enough to the edge. Almost took the hedge off.'

Mrs Parker's frown returned, but it was a practical one, not the sharp worry from before. 'Too many men driving like maniacs these days,' she said. 'City men who think country lanes are their racetracks. You three be careful, do you hear me? And you–' she pointed at Roger–'you are not to go darting across roads, not for anything.'

'Yes, Mrs Parker,' Susan murmured.

'All right then,' she said, looking them over, noting the scratches on Roger's knees, the mud on Susan's stockings, Benjy's hair sticking up in tufts from the wind. 'Off with your boots, all of you. Mud stays at the door.'

The children crowded into the warm hallway, peeling off coats and boots, the smell of damp earth mingling with the faint aroma of bread baking from the kitchen. Benjy's cheeks were flushed, his eyes bright.

'Will we get some tea?' he asked, hopeful.

Mrs Parker's mouth twitched into a reluctant smile. 'Yes, you will, after you've washed your hands.'

They sat around the scrubbed kitchen table, drinking tea from chipped cups, whilst Benjy devoured two thick slices of bread with honey. Roger did most of the talking, telling Mrs Parker about the two farmhands, Eric Fisher and Toby Hewitt, describing them as 'old chaps, but decent', and recounting how they had shared tea with them, how they had spoken a little about the last war.

'And we found a tree hut!' Benjy burst out. 'A real one, high up, and Roger climbed it.'

'You'll break your neck,' Mrs Parker said without much heat, though she smiled faintly at Benjy's excitement.

Susan was quieter, her mind still on the dark eyes of the man in the car, the way Roger had grabbed Benjy's arm and shouted at them to run, how the air had seemed to thicken with a fear she couldn't quite name.

She opened her mouth to mention it again, but the sound of an engine outside made her pause.

The clock on the mantel had just struck half-past six when Carol returned.

They heard the crunch of the tyres on the gravel, the closing of the car door, the quick steps up the path. The front door opened, letting in a gust of cool air, and then Carol was there, shrugging off her coat, smoothing down her hair, her face pale and tired.

She paused when she saw the children, gathered around the kitchen table, Benjy's mouth sticky with honey, Roger's eyes watching her with that wary calculation that had grown sharper since they had arrived.

'Oh,' she said, blinking, as if she had forgotten they would be there. 'I didn't realise you were still in here.'

'We were just having some tea,' Susan said quickly, smoothing her skirt over her knees.

Carol nodded, stepping further into the kitchen, her eyes distant. She glanced at Mrs Parker, who took the kettle off the boil and poured her a cup of tea without needing to be asked.

'Thank you, Mrs Parker,' Carol murmured, wrapping her hands around the cup as if for warmth.

They sat in silence for a few moments, the ticking of the clock and the crackle of the fire filling the kitchen. Carol sipped her tea, staring into the steam.

'There's been a robbery in the town,' she said suddenly, setting her cup down with a soft clink.

Susan's head shot up. Roger frowned, and Benjy's eyes went wide.

'A robbery?' Roger echoed.

'Yes,' Carol said, rubbing her temple. 'I don't know all the details, but there was a robbery at the bank in Exeter this afternoon, or perhaps early evening. It seems they got away with quite a lot of money.'

It was Benjy who blurted it out first, unable to contain the fear and excitement that had been bubbling under his skin all evening.

'We saw a car!' he exclaimed.

Carol looked up sharply. 'What?'

'In the lane,' Roger said, his voice calm but his eyes bright. 'Near the wood. It was going fast, too fast, and there was a man in it. He looked at us.'

Susan swallowed, glancing at Mrs Parker for support, but Mrs Parker simply nodded, folding her arms.

'They told me about it when they got home,' Mrs Parker said, her eyes on Carol. 'Before they heard about the robbery.'

Carol's lips parted, then closed again. She studied each of the children in turn, her eyes sharp and assessing, trying to determine if this was some childish exaggeration or a detail worth noting.

'What did the man look like?' she asked finally.

Roger shrugged, frowning in concentration. 'Dark hair, I think, but with a moustache. His eyes were very light, blue maybe. He looked... angry. I don't know why.'

Carol's fingers drummed lightly on the table.

'And the car?'

'Dark, maybe black or dark green,' Roger said. 'Big. I didn't see the number plate.'

Carol nodded, then glanced at Mrs Parker, who nodded back.

'All right,' Carol said, standing suddenly. 'I think we ought to tell the police.'

She left the kitchen, the children following her like ducklings, as she went to the small table in the hallway where the black telephone sat. The hallway was cold, the light from the overhead lamp flickering slightly.

Carol lifted the receiver, turning the dial carefully, the clicks echoing in the stillness. They heard the faint buzz, then the voice on the other end.

'This is the switchboard. How may I connect your call?'

'Exeter Police Station, please,' Carol said, her voice firm.

They waited, Benjy shifting from foot to foot, Susan holding her breath.

After a moment, another voice answered.

'Exeter Police Station.'

'This is Mrs Carol Sinclair, at Ravenley. I believe I need to leave a message for Chief Inspector Hopcroft.'

'Yes, madam.'

She paused, taking a breath.

'I may have potential witnesses to the robbers' getaway this evening,' she said. 'Some of the children here at the house saw a speeding car near the woods, with a man inside who was behaving oddly. I think it could be relevant.'

'Yes, madam. We will pass this on to Inspector Hopcroft as soon as he returns.'

'Thank you.'

She replaced the receiver gently, standing there for a moment, her fingers still resting on the cool black plastic, the ticking of the clock in the hallway suddenly loud.

When she turned, the children were still there, waiting.

'Well,' she said, exhaling, 'that's done.'

Roger's shoulders relaxed a fraction, the tension that had been coiled there all evening easing just slightly. Susan reached for Benjy's hand, squeezing it, and he squeezed back.

'You believed us,' Roger said, and there was something almost accusing in his voice, but also relief.

'I did,' Carol said softly, meeting his gaze without flinching. 'Because you told Mrs Parker first. And because I trust that you would not lie about something like this.'

Benjy let out a breath he hadn't realised he was holding, and Susan smiled, the first real smile of the evening.

Carol looked at them, really looked at them, and for a moment the exhaustion on her face lifted, replaced by a soft, uncertain warmth.

Suddenly, she let out a small, almost surprised laugh.

'I'm famished,' she said, placing a hand on her stomach. 'Are you all as hungry as I am?'

'Yes, please!' Benjy said at once, eyes bright.

Susan nodded, and even Roger's lips quirked into a small smile.

'All right then,' Carol said, glancing at Mrs Parker, who was already moving towards the kitchen to fetch plates. 'Let's have some supper.'

They moved back towards the warmth of the kitchen, the scent of baked bread and the promise of hot soup filling the air, and for a moment, the darkness outside, the fear of the man in the car, the robbery in town, all seemed far away.

He made it to the trees. Despite his pain and fatigue, he felt as surprised as he was elated. They had noticed him more quickly than he imagined they would. They had a clear sight of him but missed. Either they were poor marksmen or they had deliberately avoided shooting him in the back. It was difficult to think of the enemy as sporting but it seemed to Charles the only possible explanation. He tore through the trees and heard a mixture of cheers and shouts behind him.

The good news was that the forest offered an abundance of trees, any one of which could serve as a first-rate shield from the bullets of irate enemy marksmen. The bad news was that this arboreal obstacle course meant he could not put much distance between himself and the enemy. He was running like a thief through car traffic. Then he heard the dogs. Not the dainty, biscuit-nibbling variety that adorn the laps of duchesses, but great, baying, bone-crunching brutes.

Perhaps it was the prospect of those hounds from hell biting him but one minute he was weaving through the trees like an outside centre in a rugger match the next he came crashing to the ground courtesy of a fallen tree branch. He screamed in agony as he fell on the side where he most probably had a broken rib or three. Pain lanced every part of his body. He rolled over and tried to get up. Behind him the shouts grew louder. More worryingly, so did the sound of the dogs.

It was over a minute later.

Rough hands grabbed his arms, wrenching them behind his back, forcing him down into the pine needles. He struggled, twisting, but a rifle butt cracked hard against his ribs, knocking the breath from his lungs. The sharp scent of earth and resin filled his nose as he gasped, the weight of two soldiers pressing him to the ground.

They hauled him up, pulling his arms tight, binding his wrists with a rough cord that bit into his skin. One of the soldiers, a thin, grey-eyed fellow with a cigarette dangling from his lips, spat to the side and muttered something in German. Another, broader, wearing a cap askew, grinned, showing yellowed teeth.

Charles met their eyes, chin lifted, forcing himself to stand straight even as pain flared in his side.

They frogmarched him through the trees, the forest closing in with the sound of boots crunching pine needles, the calls of crows overhead. At the edge of a clearing, Charles saw the camp once more. A number of fellow prisoners, for he had to accept that he was now one of them, stood in groups at the perimeter of wire.

They pushed him through the gates, a sentry eyeing him with casual disinterest, before leading him across the muddy yard towards a hut larger than the rest. A sergeant opened the door, and they shoved him inside.

The room, oddly, smelt of cologne. At a rough-hewn table was a man in Wehrmacht field grey, his tunic unbuttoned at the throat, a steaming mug of coffee in one hand. He was in his late thirties, perhaps early forties, with pale hair clipped close, blue eyes sharp beneath the brim of his cap, which rested on the table.

'You may leave us,' he said to the sergeant and the two soldiers. The soldiers hesitated, glancing at Charles, then at the officer, before saluting and stepping outside, the door closing with a thud. The officer gestured to a chair opposite him. 'Sit down, Flight Lieutenant Sinclair.'

Charles hesitated, then crossed the room, lowering himself carefully onto the chair, never breaking eye contact.

'I am Oberleutnant Ralf Ackermann,' the German said, taking a sip of his coffee before setting it down with precision. 'We will treat you according to the Geneva Convention. You have my word.'

There was a pause, and Charles raised an eyebrow, noting the bitterness in the German's expression.

'Though,' Ackermann added softly, 'there are moments when I wish I were a Nazi, because it would allow me, without scruple, to deal with time-wasting children like you.'

Charles's lips twitched despite himself, a small, wry smile. 'I suppose I should be grateful you are not.'

Ackermann's eyes narrowed, but there was no true malice there. He leaned back, folding his arms. 'You are part of the RAF, yes?'

'I am.'

Ackermann snorted, shaking his head with a faint smile. 'Always the RAF. You are the worst offenders, you know. The Army men tend to wait, hope for repatriation, play cards. The RAF... always running.'

Something in Charles's chest lifted, a brief flame of pride warming the cold in his bones. 'I'm pleased to hear it.'

Ackermann studied him for a long moment, as if weighing him, then nodded towards the door. 'You will be taken to the hut with the others. Do not cause trouble, Flight Lieutenant, or I will be forced to remove your privileges.'

'I'll bear that in mind,' Charles said, standing.

Ackermann's eyes flickered once more, the ghost of a weary smile. 'Off you go.' Ackermann shouted an order in German and the door opened. One of the men who had caught him, gestured for Charles to leave.

'So long,' said Charles, giving a lazy salute. Ackermann returned this in kind.

They led Charles across the compound to a half-finished hut, the planks of wood still raw, sawdust littering the floor inside. The door creaked on its hinges, and as he stepped in, the warmth from the small iron stove struck him, carrying the tang of smoke and damp clothes drying on a line strung across the ceiling.

The hut was crowded with bunks along the walls, blankets folded with military precision, the air thick with the smell of unwashed bodies, tobacco, and the faint edge of soap.

A man rose from a bunk in the corner, straightening to his full height, which was considerable. He was in his early forties, with dark hair just beginning to grey at the temples, a square jaw, and an expression that was both sharp and kindly.

'Flight Lieutenant Charles Sinclair, I presume?' the man said, his voice low but carrying the weight of command.

'I am,' Charles replied, managing a small nod despite the pain in his ribs.

'Major Martin Fletcher,' the man said, extending a hand. 'But you'll call me Fletcher unless I am angry at you then it will be 'sir'. Everyone else calls me Fletch when I'm not listening.'

Charles grasped his hand, the grip firm, steadying.

'Welcome to the club,' Fletcher said, stepping back. 'I wish it were under better circumstances.'

Charles glanced around the hut, noting the eyes that turned towards him, sizing him up, before returning to their card games or quiet conversations.

'I'd rather be elsewhere,' Charles said dryly.

'We all would,' Fletcher replied, with a brief chuckle. 'Now, tell me, were you alone in your little jaunt through the woods, or did you have a plan?'

Charles hesitated, then shook his head. 'No real plan, I'm afraid. I saw an opportunity and took it.'

Fletcher's expression grew serious, the lines around his eyes deepening. 'I don't discourage escape attempts, Sinclair. On the contrary, I believe it is our duty as officers to attempt to escape. However...' he paused, ensuring Charles met his eyes, 'it is also our duty to remain alive. You have a responsibility not just to your country, but to yourself, and to your family. A reckless attempt could see you shot, and that would serve no one.'

Charles swallowed, anger and shame mixing in his throat. 'I understand.'

'I'm not saying you were wrong to try,' Fletcher continued. 'I'm saying that in future, you will put any plan you have before the escape committee. Understood?'

'Understood,' Charles said.

Fletcher nodded, his expression softening once more. 'Come on, I'll introduce you to the others.'

They crossed the hut, the stove crackling as someone threw on another stick of wood, the glow briefly illuminating faces and shadows alike.

'These two are Arnie Dexter and James Hegarty,' Fletcher said, stopping at a small table where two men sat playing cards with a half-hearted air.

Arnie Dexter was a lean man with sandy hair and quick eyes, who nodded with a grin. 'Welcome to paradise,' he said, flicking his cards down.

James Hegarty, by contrast, was broader, with dark hair and the easy, rolling accent of an Irishman. 'You've missed the tea,' he said, deadpan. 'It was a right delight, I promise you.'

'They're both navigators,' Fletcher explained. 'Both shot down over France last month.'

'I thought we were in Norway,' said Arnie with a grin.

'You sound like a great navigator,' said Charles, with a tired grin. 'Pleased to meet you both.'

Noting the desolation behind the new man's eyes, Arnie smiled sympathetically, 'You'll get used to it. Just don't become too used to it.'

'No fear of that,' laughed Charles mirthlessly. He received a gentle clap on the back from Hegarty.

'Aye,' Hegarty agreed, 'but we try to keep spirits up, all the same.'

86

Fletcher led Charles further down the hut, stopping by a bunk where a man in his thirties was oiling a small wooden chess set. He looked up, a keen glint in his grey eyes.

'This is Captain Richard Cowdrey,' Fletcher said. 'He's the other member of our escape committee.'

Cowdrey stood, extending a hand, which Charles shook. 'Good to have you with us, Sinclair,' he said. 'Though I'm sorry for the circumstances.'

'Thank you,' Charles replied.

Cowdrey sat down, setting the chess piece aside. 'There are around forty of us here at the moment, but we're expecting to be moved soon. This is a temporary camp while they finish building the larger one down the valley.'

Charles frowned, glancing at Fletcher. 'And you're helping them build it?'

Cowdrey chuckled, a dry, knowing sound. 'Oh, we are helping, all right. Though I must admit, it's taking us rather a long time to complete.'

Charles's eyebrows rose, understanding dawning. 'You're planning something.'

Cowdrey smiled, tapping the side of his nose. 'Let's just say it's often easier to plan an escape from a place you're helping to build. We know the layout, the guard patterns, the weak points.'

'And we have a certain... influence over the timetable,' Fletcher added, his mouth quirking.

'Shouldn't we just refuse to work?' Charles asked, his old anger flaring. 'Go on strike, like the miners back home?'

Cowdrey laughed outright this time, shaking his head. 'We are on strike, Sinclair. It's just that we're doing it quietly. Every nail bent, every beam misplaced, every trench dug in the wrong place buys us time. We're taking as long as British workers have always done—just with a bit more subtlety.'

Charles found himself smiling, despite the cold and the hunger and the ache in his side. 'I see.'

'Good,' Fletcher said, clapping him on the shoulder. 'Get some rest. We'll speak more tomorrow.'

That night, as Charles lay on the hard bunk, the thin blanket pulled around him, the cold pressing in from the gaps in the wood, he stared up at the dark beams of the ceiling, listening to the soft snores and quiet mutterings of the men around him.

His mind drifted to Carol, to the children at Ravenley, to flatness of the Dartmoor countryside that lay beyond the wire.

They hadn't broken him yet, and they wouldn't.

If there was a plan, he would find his way back to them. Whatever it took.

Wednesday 18ᵗʰ December 1940

Carol woke with a heaviness pressing down upon her chest, as if the dreams she could not quite recall had left their residue in the air around her. Her eyes opened and took a few moments to grow accustomed to the dim light in the room. For a moment, she lay still, listening to the quietness of the house, the gentle ticking of the clock on the mantelpiece, the occasional creak of old wood.

At last, she pushed back the blankets and rose, pulling on her dressing gown and crossing to the window. The gardens below were misted over, frost sparkling on the grass. It all seemed so peaceful. So English. Then she heard the drone of an aeroplane, and the quiet beauty of the morning was shattered. Tears stung her eyes. She scolded herself for this emotion. There was no news yet of Charles. Until she knew for certain he was dead, there was hope.

She washed and dressed in a practical navy skirt and a cream blouse, pinned a brooch at her collar, and tied back her hair. There was a time, not so long ago, when Charles would have made some teasing remark as she came down to breakfast, but that was before the war, before everything had changed.

Downstairs, the dining room was empty, the long table polished and silent. A place had been set for her at one end, with a single vase of sweet peas giving off their fragile scent. Mrs Parker had left a pot of tea, eggs, and toast kept warm under a silver cover.

Carol ate alone, turning the pages of the newspaper without truly seeing the words, her mind drifting between the news of the robbery in town, the children's chatter about their adventure the day before, and the ache that never truly left her.

She had just finished the last of her tea when she heard footsteps in the corridor, and the door opened to admit Figgs, looking faintly agitated, his thin frame seeming even more angular in the morning light.

'Mrs Sinclair,' he began, clearing his throat. 'Exeter police station has just telephoned. They wish to see you at once, and they have asked that you bring the children with you.'

Carol set down her cup, a small frown creasing her brow. 'Thank you, Figgs. Did they say who I was to see?'

'No, madam, only that it was most urgent.'

Carol stood, smoothing her skirt. 'Very well. Please ask Mrs Parker to get the children ready immediately.'

Within the hour, the car was turning through the gates of Ravenley, down the drive, and onto the main road towards Exeter. The children, pressed together in the back seat, were buzzing with excitement at this unexpected summons, their faces bright with the prospect of an adventure.

'Are we in trouble, Mrs Sinclair?' asked Susan, her plaits bouncing as she leant forward.

'I hardly think so,' Carol replied, managing a small smile in the mirror. 'The police simply wish to speak to you, that is all. About the car that Roger saw. And perhaps it's time we became a little less formal. You can call me Carol. I hope you can give the police a good description of what you saw, Roger.'

'No fear of that,' Roger said, his brow furrowing in concentration. 'I won't forget the man with the hat in a hurry.'

Carol's hands tightened on the wheel, but she said nothing, keeping her eyes on the road ahead as the hedgerows slipped by, the morning sun beginning to burn off the mist.

They reached Exeter just before ten, the streets already busy with delivery carts, bicycles weaving between motor cars, the air filled with the smell of coal smoke and the cries of newspaper sellers. Carol found a place to park near the station, and they made their way up the steps, the children nearly running in their eagerness.

Inside, the lobby of the police station was bustling with constables coming and going, typewriters clattering, the scent of damp uniforms and strong tea hanging in the air. A desk sergeant, a portly man with a kindly face, looked up as they approached.

'Mrs Sinclair, I presume?' he said, standing. 'If you would follow me, please, madam, and the children too.'

They were led down a corridor lined with wooden doors, the glass panels frosted, the floor worn by the passage of many boots. At last, the sergeant opened a door and gestured them inside.

The office was small but tidy, a desk stacked with papers, a black telephone, and a typewriter pushed to one side. Behind the desk sat a young man in his late twenties, in a neat suit with a plain tie, his hair carefully combed back from his forehead. He rose as they entered, his expression polite, but there was a spark of interest in his eyes as he looked at Carol.

'Detective Inspector Winslow, madam,' he said, extending a hand, which Carol took briefly.

'Mrs Sinclair,' she replied.

'And these must be your children,' Winslow said, with a smile, glancing at them in turn. 'Roger, Susan, and Benjy, is it?'

'Yes, sir,' Roger said, standing a little straighter, trying to look grown-up.

Winslow's smile deepened, and he gestured to a row of chairs against the wall. 'Please, take a seat, all of you.'

Carol settled herself, smoothing her skirt, while the children perched, swinging their legs, glancing around with wide eyes. She glanced towards the children and said, 'One correction, Detective Inspector. The children are not mine. They have been evacuated from London.' She looked at Winslow meaningfully. He nodded as if understanding something from the look of sympathy on her face.

Winslow pulled up a chair in front of them, his notebook ready. 'Now then, I understand you saw something yesterday afternoon, near Ravenley. A car, was it?'

'Yes, sir,' Roger said, eager to speak. 'It was going very fast down the lane, nearly ran us off the road.'

'Do you remember what colour it was?' Winslow asked, his tone gentle.

Roger frowned, thinking hard. 'It was dark, I think. Black, or maybe dark green. It had mud on it.'

'And the number plate?'

Roger shook his head, looking frustrated. 'I didn't see that.'

Winslow nodded, scribbling a note. 'That's quite all right. Did you see who was inside?'

'I saw a man,' Roger said. 'He had a hat on, pulled down low, and I think he had a scarf around his neck. He looked... cross.'

Winslow's pen paused, and he looked up. 'Cross?'

Roger nodded. 'Like he was angry, or in a hurry.'

'And the time?'

'It was later in the afternoon,' Susan piped up. 'We were exploring the meadows and then the forest, and it was when we were walking back.'

'So, around five o'clock, perhaps?' Winslow said.

'Yes, sir,' Roger agreed.

Winslow smiled at them both. 'You've been very helpful, all of you. We're going to have someone help us make a drawing of the man you saw, so we can find him.'

He stood and went to the door, calling for someone in the corridor. A moment later, a tall, thin man with ink-stained fingers and a faint smell of pipe smoke entered, carrying a sketchpad under one arm.

'Feeny,' Winslow said, 'these are the young witnesses I mentioned. I'd like you to work with them on a composite sketch.'

'Of course, sir,' Feeny said, nodding to the children with a kindly smile.

92

Just as Feeny was about to usher the children away, the door opened once more, and a tall, slender man stepped inside, carrying his raincoat across one shoulder, his black fedora pushed back on his bald head with the tufts of grey hair around his ears catching the light. His pale eyes, sharp and amused, scanned the room.

'Carol,' he said, in a voice both warm and dry. 'Have you come to confess?'

'Chops,' Carol replied, with a smile that surprised even herself. 'I thought I saw you yesterday at the bank.'

'You were there?'

'Yes, across the road.'

'Arrest this woman, Winslow. Throw away the key.'

Detective Inspector Winslow looked between them, a flicker of curiosity in his eyes.

'Any particular cell?' Winslow replied, standing straight.

'No, straight to the prison at Dartmoor,' said Chops.

'It's a male prison,' pointed out Winslow, keeping his face straight. Carol merely smiled at her old friend.

'There's plenty of them. They should be able to protect themselves well enough.' Then Chops stared at the children and then back to Winslow. He asked, 'Is this a serious lead, or are we wasting our morning with children's stories?'

Winslow met his gaze without flinching. 'It's a lead, sir. It was phoned in last night. They've given consistent descriptions, and the timing fits. This young man here saw them. Roger Trent.'

Chops' eyes flickered with satisfaction, and he clapped Roger lightly on the shoulder. 'Good man.' Roger, who had been growing increasingly irritated by Chops, suddenly felt ten feet tall.

Feeny, the police artist, sensing the moment, gestured to the children. 'Come along, you three, let's see if we can get a likeness.'

They followed him out, Roger glancing back at Carol before disappearing down the corridor.

Left alone, Chops turned to Carol, his expression softening.

'How are you, Carol?' he asked.

'I've been better,' she replied honestly, folding her hands in her lap. 'But I'm managing. You know Charles is missing?'

Chops nodded, understanding without pressing, then glanced at Winslow. 'We're going for a cup of tea while your artist works, Winslow. Join us when they're done.'

Winslow inclined his head, 'Yes, sir.'

Chops offered his arm to Carol, who took it lightly, and together they stepped out into the corridor, the bustle of the station swirling around them.

As they made their way through the lobby, a thin, weaselly-looking man with a notebook in hand darted forward, his eyes bright behind round spectacles.

'Chief Inspector Hopcroft!' he called, his voice nasal and insistent. 'Dick Dalton, Exeter Gazette. Is it true you've made an arrest in the bank robbery?'

Chops did not even pause, his expression one of weary disdain. 'Dalton, when I wish to read fairy tales, I'll buy your paper,' he said, guiding Carol past without a backward glance.

Dalton's mouth opened and closed, his pencil hovering uselessly over the page as they walked past.

Outside, the air was sharp but bright, the sun climbing higher, the sounds of the city a steady hum around them.

'There's a Lyons Tea House on the corner,' Chops said, indicating with a tilt of his head. 'Come along, Carol. Let's have a proper cup while the children are with Feeny.'

Carol nodded and left the office. Chops stayed on a moment and then shut the door. He looked at Feeny.

'You went to Morrison's flat?' asked Winslow.

'Indeed. I saw the floor plans, security details of the bank laid out on the table,' said Chops.

'It looks like he was one of the gang,' observed Winslow.

'One too many,' added Chops. With this, he left Winslow and joined Carol in the reception of the police station.

They walked down the steps and crossed the street. A breeze caught Carol's hair, and for a moment, along with a light misty spray of drizzle. They headed towards the chaste and respectable exterior of the Lyons Tea House, whose large windows revealed many seated patrons taking afternoon tea. It felt almost like the world beyond the glass could be forgotten.

Almost.

Inside, it was warm and bustling, filled with the scent of toasted crumpets and fresh leaf tea, a welcome contrast to the grey drizzle outside. Chops held the seat out for Carol before sitting opposite her by the window. She looked elegant as always, though the shadows beneath her eyes betrayed the strain of recent days.

They ordered tea and then both stared out of the window at people hurrying along the street to get out of the drizzle. The ever-present expression on his face, a slight, almost amused tilt of the mouth, as if the world and all its madness was a private joke, was still there, even in the midst of a murder investigation.

'How did you come to have the children?' asked Chops.

Carol sipped her tea. 'It was quite a shock; I can tell you. I had no idea Mrs Parker had arranged for evacuees to stay at Ravenley. She never said anything to me.'

'Would you have said no?' asked Chops gently.

The silence that greeted this was its own answer.

Chops nodded, his eyes steady on her face. 'Mrs Parker is a good woman. Practical. Heart's in the right place.'

'You're afraid of her,' interrupted Carol.

'Everyone is afraid of her,' grinned Chops. 'I'm surprised we didn't just send her and other women like her to face the Nazis. She'd have dealt with them in no time.' This prompted a chuckle from Carol. Chops continued, 'Truth be told, she did the right thing.'

Carol sighed. 'Perhaps. But it caught me off guard. I've just found out they're orphans. Their mother was killed in an air raid. Poor Roger, he's the oldest, barely thirteen. And Susan's trying so hard to act grown up for Benjy's sake, but she's just a little girl herself. I'm worried about them. They should be adopted by someone who can give them the stability they need. The love...'

Chops didn't respond to that directly. He simply gave her a small, sympathetic smile and glanced towards the window, watching passers-by hurry through the damp streets.

'And what about the case?' Carol asked after a pause. 'This wasn't just a robbery, was it? I saw the way you and Detective Inspector Winslow looked at one another.'

This brought a wide grin from Chops and a shake of the head. He leaned in slightly, lowering his voice. 'You haven't lost your sixth sense, I see. And yes, it's a bit more serious than I first let on. A night watchman was killed. Shot, poor chap. Fred Morrison. Ex-Army, did a bit of prison work, like many who were demobbed. He retired from the prison service and then took this job.'

Carol paled. 'Murder? Oh my God. And Roger saw them. Or at least one of them. He was seen too, he told me. What if they come looking for him?'

Chops gave a small shake of his head. 'No need to panic. We'll be discreet. No one will know where the tip came from. Roger's name won't appear anywhere official. We're not in the habit of putting children at risk, Carol.'

She gave him a grateful look. 'Thank you.'

Chops finished his tea and placed the cup back on the saucer with a soft clink. 'What about Charles?' he asked gently.

Carol looked out of the window. The drizzle had stopped, and a faint, weak light filtered through the clouds. 'The RAF said he didn't return from a mission. No word since. They won't tell me much, just that it was a night raid over Germany. I don't know what to think. There's been silence before and then...' Her voice trailed off.

Chops placed a gentle hand on hers. 'He's a tough man, Carol. Reckless, as we both know, but tough. I wouldn't count him out just yet.'

She gave a small nod, but her eyes glistened. Her fingers clutched the teacup, white-knuckled, trembling, as if it alone could anchor her to this moment, to this dim, smoke-hazed tearoom where the world outside pressed in like a gathering storm. And yet, worse than the fear was the guilt, gnawing and insidious: their last words had been sharp, their parting cold. Had he died thinking she no longer loved him?

They finished their tea, and Chops went to pay. The rain seemed to have stopped because she could see some people taking down their umbrellas. They walked back to the police station together, the tea house now behind them. Inside, the lobby was quieter than before. Dick Dalton, the weaselly reporter from the Gazette, was nowhere to be seen. Chops opened the inner door and led her through the corridors.

In an interview room, Feeny, the police artist, was at work. The children had taken to him at once, Benjy especially, who was fascinated by the pencils and charcoals laid out in neat rows. Roger had been serious and focused, describing the man he'd seen in the car: the hard eyes, the dark moustache, the shape of his jaw. Susan chipped in occasionally to help, but Roger seemed to remember every detail.

When Carol entered, Feeny handed her the sketch. The man she saw was wearing a hat; the clear eyes chilled her. It was the face of a killer. She studied it for a long moment, her brow furrowed.

'I don't recognise him,' she said at last, almost with relief.

Chops took the sketch from her and turned it over thoughtfully. 'Doesn't look like a local face to me. Something in the cut of the suit, the style of the hair. I'd say London. Perhaps one of the East End boys. I'll get this circulated, see what turns up.'

Carol nodded, her eyes drifting to the children who were chatting now to Feeny, proud of the work they'd helped create. Roger gave her a brief, almost shy smile. She smiled back.

'You're good with them,' Chops said quietly.

'I'm not sure about that,' she replied. 'But I'm trying.'

Chops gave his usual half-amused, half-kind smile. 'I know too well how 'trying' you can be, madam.' This raised a smile from Carol.

'I'm older now,' said Carol.

'You're not even thirty,' pointed out Chops.

He walked her and the children to the front doors of the station. Outside, the rain had started again, fine and misty. Carol paused before stepping into the damp air. 'Thank you, Chops. For the tea. And for listening.'

'Always a pleasure, Carol. You mind how you go. And don't worry about the boy. We'll keep him safe.'

She turned and gathered the children, who followed her out into the car park. As they climbed into the motorcar, unseen by any of them, a figure in a long brown coat leaned against the stone wall across the street. Dick Dalton, notebook in hand, watched as the vehicle pulled away.

His eyes narrowed as he jotted down a note: Carol Sinclair and three evacuee children leave police station. Connection to bank robbery? Murder? He underlined the word twice and smiled to himself.

The light from the streetlamp caught the glint of his pen.

Back inside the police station, Chops, Winslow, and Feeny studied the face that Roger had described. The only noise in the office came from the traffic outside.

'Right,' Chops said at last, straightening up. 'If no one knows him, we'll have to make him known. Put it in the papers. Someone's seen him, maybe not here, but somewhere. Make some photographs of it and send it out to stations in the area and Scotland Yard. I want this solved before they come in and take over.'

Winslow nodded slowly. 'The Gazette's our best bet. They've a wide circulation, and their editor owes me a favour after that business with the missing heiress.' He reached for the telephone, then paused. 'We'll have to word it carefully. We don't want to start a panic, but we need eyes on this.'

Chops grunted in agreement. 'Call it a 'person of interest.' Say we're seeking information in connection with an ongoing investigation. Vague enough not to scare people off, but sharp enough to make 'em look twice.'

Winslow lifted the receiver, his other hand still resting on the sketch. The face stared back at him, blank, unreadable, yet heavy with implication. Whoever this man was, he had walked through the shadows of the city unseen. Soon, though, he would be on the front page of every newspaper in London. And then, Winslow thought grimly, they would see just how well he could hide.

'Put it in tomorrow's edition,' he said into the mouthpiece. 'And mark it urgent.'

17   Carol

The crunch of gravel under tyres broke the late afternoon quiet as Carol pulled the car into the circular driveway in front of the house. The children were chattering animatedly in the backseat, still excited from their time at the police station. Her eye was arrested by the spectacle of a lone cyclist making his way up the drive like a man pedalling through molasses.

The bicycle, one of those upright, old-fashioned contraptions that look as though they were designed by a committee of Victorian enthusiasts, bore a leather satchel strapped to its rear, giving it the air of a delivery boy on a very slow mission. The rider himself was a study in sartorial defiance. His grey overcoat, belted tightly, flapped noisily about him like the flag of the 18th green of St Andrews in the teeth of a stiff nor'wester. His trousers, neatly imprisoned by bicycle clips, proclaimed to the world that here was a man who refused to let a little thing like wind resistance stand between him and a sharply creased leg.

As he wobbled nearer, one could almost hear the bicycle sighing under the strain of its own dignity. It was the sort of approach that made you want to either salute or offer a push. He dismounted somewhat clumsily when he reached the driveway and took a moment to straighten his coat and smile, his expression cheerful and vaguely apologetic. He doffed his hat.

Carol studied him. The man was in his early thirties, perhaps, though he looked older: a prematurely lined forehead, receding hairline, and short hair, cut almost clerically close to the scalp. His teeth were slightly prominent.

'Reverend Alastair Atwell,' he said, offering his hand. 'I do hope I'm not intruding. I thought I'd call by and introduce myself. I'm the new vicar. Just arrived from London, taking over from Reverend Standish at Belsaw-on-the-Moor.'

Carol accepted his hand and smiled with faint politeness. 'Not at all. I'm Caroline Sinclair. You can call me Carol. Welcome to the parish, Reverend.'

He laughed again, a dry, fluttering chuckle. 'Ah, splendid, splendid. Thank you, Mrs Sinclair. Yes, quite a change from the smoke and soot of the city. Though I daresay I miss a good tobacconist already.'

She invited him in and led him towards the drawing room. The children, who had paused on the steps to watch the arrival of the peculiar new guest, now gathered around the door.

'Reverend Atwell, may I introduce Roger, Susan, and Benjy. They're evacuees staying here for the time being.'

The reverend bobbed his head earnestly to each child. 'Yes, I believe we shared a carriage on the way up from London. How do you do? Marvellous to have young voices about the place again, I'm sure.'

Roger nodded politely, Susan smiled, but Benjy clung to her side, half-hiding behind her coat.

'We were just about to go play outside,' Roger said, a little too quickly.

Carol gave him a look that said 'thanks-for-the-help' but said nothing.

'Of course, of course,' Reverend Atwell said, stepping aside. 'Fresh air is the best tonic, as they say!'

The children vanished, leaving Carol alone with the reverend.

'Would you care for a cup of tea, Reverend?' she asked, glancing towards Figgs who had appeared quietly on the scene.

'Oh, yes, thank you, that would be lovely. Just milk, no sugar. Unless it's brown sugar, then I might be persuaded,' he chuckled.

Carol smiled politely and raised her eyebrows to Figgs who disappeared noiselessly. Mrs Parker arrived a few minutes later with a trolley to the sitting room, where the vicar was standing near the mantelpiece, admiring a sepia-toned photograph of Charles in his uniform.

'Your husband?' he asked, taking the teacup. There was a trace of disappointment in his voice mixed with hope that the good-looking man in the picture might be a brother.

'Yes. Charles is serving in the RAF.'

Atwell looked momentarily flustered. 'Ah. Brave man. Brave men, all of them. Terrible strain for the families, though. I look forward to meeting him.'

Carol said nothing.

'I've only just taken up my post,' Atwell continued. 'Reverend Standish retired due to ill health. Poor fellow's hands shook so badly by the end he couldn't hold the chalice.' She sipped her tea, nodding politely. Atwell forged on, 'I do hope we'll see you at the service this Sunday. The parish is small, but quite devout. Though I daresay a new face in the front pew might encourage the lapsed among us.'

'I'll try to attend,' Carol replied, noncommittally.

'Excellent, excellent.' He cleared his throat, then said, 'Strange times, aren't they? What with the bank robbery the other day. I hear it was quite serious.'

Carol stiffened. 'You've heard about that?'

He chuckled nervously. 'Oh, just what the baker said. You know how these things go; nothing stays secret for long. Dreadful business.' Noting the surprise on Carol's face, he added, 'I'm sorry. I hope I've not upset you.'

Carol composed herself. 'No, not at all. Thank you for telling me.' They sat in silence for a moment, the air still between them.

'Actually,' Atwell said, in a brighter tone, 'I also had occasion to visit Dartmoor Prison yesterday. They've asked me to consider becoming chaplain there.'

Carol raised an eyebrow. 'That sounds... challenging.'

'It certainly was. Quite a grim place, really. I felt quite out of place among all that stone and steel. The prisoners weren't exactly pleased to see a clergyman wandering about. Still, someone must do it.'

'I wish you luck,' she said, rising. 'Thank you for calling by.'

He stood hastily, his tea unfinished. 'Yes, well, thank you for the tea. Very kind of you. I shall be off. Must make a few more calls before evensong.'

She walked him to the door and stood back as he mounted his bicycle with only marginal grace. It was dark outside now. The disappearance of the sun had made the air sting.

'Reverend Atwell, are you sure we can't offer you a lift back to your house? It's awfully cold now. And dark. I'm sure it can't be safe.'

'Oh, I'm used to riding in all weathers and at any time of night. Thank you again, Mrs Sinclair. Lovely meeting you all.'

With a final nod, he pedalled down the path, coat flapping behind him.

Carol watched him disappear through the gate, then turned with a quiet sigh and headed to the library. She paused at the window and looked out.

The children were in the garden, climbing the great sycamore tree near the west wall. Susan had made it halfway up, and Roger was already in the upper branches. Benjy sat on a lower limb, legs dangling, laughing.

Their laughter drifted through the open window, and Carol found herself smiling. They were children, she reminded herself. Children trying to live in the middle of a war. Orphans now. Displaced, bereaved, flung into the care of strangers. For the moment, though, they were just children playing.

She watched Susan help Benjy navigate a higher branch and suddenly felt the sting of tears. She was responsible for them now. Not in any official sense, perhaps, but morally. Emotionally. She could not let them drift from house to house like luggage.

But was she the right person? What did she know of children? Her marriage to Charles had grown cold long before the war began. There had been no children. No prospect of any, despite two years of trying.

A barren house. A barren life.

She looked around the library, dark wood panels, shelves lined with books no one had opened in years, and a faint scent of polish and paper. This place was too big, too empty. And now, somehow, too full.

Perhaps she should find someone more suitable. In town, perhaps, a schoolmistress, or a kindly widow. Someone who knew what to do with grief and childish tempers. Someone who had the stamina to endure tears in the night, or bloody knees, or unanswerable questions about death and fairness. She pressed her hand to her forehead. It all felt too much.

Outside, the children climbed higher, and somewhere in the distance, the caw of a rook broke the stillness. Carol remained by the window a moment longer, her thoughts spinning, her heart heavy. She could not escape this new chapter in her life, nor the faces of those children who needed her, even if they did not yet realise it.

She would have to be enough, for now.

Behind her, the clock in the hallway began to chime five o'clock.

And still, the war dragged on.

Charles Sinclair sat on the rough wooden bench in the draughty mess hut, the bowl of thin, greyish soup steaming faintly in front of him. A few scraps of gristly meat floated among slivers of carrot and potato, and the slice of dense, dark German rye bread on the side seemed more like a punishment than a meal.

He stared down at the food with undisguised dismay.

'Blimey,' said a voice across the table, 'don't look so shocked, sir. It ain't the Savoy, I grant you, but it won't kill you. Least I don't think it will.'

Charles looked up to see a wiry man with a broad grin and a battered face that had known too many fights in too many pubs. His blue eyes were alight with mischief.

'Private Alf Watson,' he added, giving a little mock salute. 'Ex-Royal Fusiliers. Pleased to meet you.'

Charles gave a short nod. 'Flight Lieutenant Charles Sinclair. RAF.'

Alf winked. 'Thought so. Got that look about you. Bit thin, bit tired, bit posh.'

Major Martin Fletcher, seated at the end of the table, cleared his throat. 'That's quite enough, Watson. Let the man eat in peace.'

'I'm only trying to cheer him up, sir,' said Alf innocently. 'You lot from the flying circus ain't used to Army rations.'

Charles smiled despite himself and raised the spoon.

'I'll take it up with the head chef,' said Charles. This brought a laugh from the other men at the table and diffused a little of the tension. It did nothing to improve the taste of what they were eating. The soup was lukewarm, salty, and unpleasant, but he forced it down.

As the men ate, the conversation turned to the business of the camp.

'So far,' said Fletcher, 'we've counted three sentry posts. One by the main gate, another on the southern edge by the fence, and a rotating post near the eastern side where they're still building. That one changes every four hours.'

Charles leaned in. 'How many guards in total?'

'Between ten and fifteen, depending on the shift,' Fletcher replied. 'They're Wehrmacht, not SS, thank God. Professional, but not zealots. If they'd have been SS, then you wouldn't be here, Sinclair, trust me.'

'Do they carry out regular patrols?' asked Charles, keen to talk of escape.

Captain Richard Cowdrey, seated beside Fletcher, nodded. 'Yes. Every hour during daylight. Twice during the night. Roll calls around seven and again after supper. And sometimes random ones if they suspect anything.'

'We've suspended all escape attempts for now,' Fletcher added. 'We're lying low. Let them think we're broken or bored. In a month, maybe two, they'll relax.'

Charles frowned. This was far too long. How could they think in terms of months? It seemed to him to be defeatist. He tried to smile and look hopeful, 'But when the time comes...'

'We'll be ready,' confirmed Cowdrey. 'We've got people making notes. Counting steps. Noting routines. It's not much, but it'll build up.'

Alf piped up again. 'Problem is, sir, even if we did get out, what then? No civvies, no papers, no maps, no money. We ain't exactly spoilt for kit.'

'And hardly any of us speak German,' Cowdrey added.

'I do,' said Charles quietly. 'Well, a bit, anyway.'

They all looked at him.

'Studied it at school. I wouldn't say I'd pass for a German for very long, but I can certainly understand it well enough and get by. I wish I'd paid more attention now when I had the chance.'

Fletcher nodded approvingly. 'Good. You'll be useful. We've two others with some fluency. You'll work with them and help teach the basics to anyone willing to learn. Phrases, accents, signs to spot. Could make the difference.'

Charles nodded. He had never thought of himself as a teacher, but he would do what was required.

'We'll need to be clever,' Fletcher said, his voice low. 'We're not in a big camp. Yet. This place is small, new, and poorly built, but don't let that fool you. They're watching. They know men like us will try. It makes them all the more suspicious and careful.'

Charles looked around at the makeshift hut, its flimsy walls and hastily nailed rafters. No insulation, no glass in the windows, and only one stove at the far end, giving out barely any heat.

The bunk beds were crammed together; mattresses stuffed with straw. The smell was one of wet earth, unwashed bodies, and cheap tobacco.

'It's a fine balance,' continued Fletcher. 'Too little progress on building this place, and they'll stop trusting us. Too much, and they'll finish the camp before we're ready to make our move. But for now, our compliance earns us some freedom to move about. That's what we need.'

Charles finished the last of his soup and forced a bite of the bread.

'I've had better meals,' he muttered.

Alf chuckled. 'You get used to it, sir. After the third or fourth week, your stomach gives up complaining.'

'Mine might revolt altogether,' replied Charles, which prompted another few chuckles around the table.

'You'll be all right,' Fletcher said. 'You're RAF. You boys are made of strong stuff.'

He said it kindly, with no mockery. Charles appreciated that. And they were all in the same boat. There was nothing worse than a bellyacher. He would not be one of those. Yet, at the same time, he worried that the men were becoming too complaisant about escape. The bide-your-time approach was a concern to him. Was this really just an excuse to see out the war, relatively safe, within the confines of a prison? This would not do. Not for him. It would, inevitably, bring him into conflict with the others. There was no point in worrying about that now. The future would take care of itself.

Later, after the tin bowls had been washed, a few of the men had returned to their bunks, while others chatted in a corner and a couple of others played chess using a rudimentary board and pieces. Charles climbed up onto his bunk. He lay back on the thin mattress and stared up at the wooden beams above. It creaked with every gust of wind. Sleep would not come easily. His mind was still spinning with but one thought. Escape. That was all he could think about.

He would teach German to the men. He would learn every inch of the perimeter. He would bide his time.

Then, when the moment came, he would run.

And this time, he would not get caught.

Thursday 19ᵗʰ December 1940

The polished brass of the Exeter Bank nameplate was much shinier than the rather gloomy atmosphere inside the bank. Chief Inspector Hopcroft and Detective Inspector Winslow walked through the tall mahogany doors and were met by the tense faces of its staff. It was only eight o'clock, but the place was already half-buzzing with fear and curiosity.

They had set up in the bank manager's office, a tidy, formal room with an imposing desk and neat rows of filing cabinets. Chops perched on the edge of a leather armchair, fedora tilted back on his head, a look of perpetual amusement flickering behind sharp eyes. Winslow sat with a notepad, looking fresher than most despite the early hour.

'Right,' Chops said, adjusting his raincoat over the back of his chair. 'Let's begin with the chief clerk. Cedric Nelson, isn't it?'

Nelson was ushered in by a constable. He was a lean, angular man in his early forties, with carefully combed hair and an expression that suggested someone perpetually offended by the world's informality. His pinstriped suit was pristine, and he took his seat with an air of superiority.

'Good morning, gentlemen,' he said crisply, as though he were the one conducting the interview. The smile on Chops' face broadened. He was going to enjoy this. Winslow groaned inwardly. He could see the amusement on the face of the Chief Inspector.

'Mr Nelson,' said Chops smoothly, 'thank you for taking some of your valuable time to help us in this unfortunate matter. We're hoping you might help us understand a little more about Mr Morrison.'

Nelson folded his hands in his lap and gave a tight smile. 'Fred Morrison? Yes. The night watchman. Reliable, I suppose, in his own way. Quiet. Kept to himself.'

'Did you have much interaction with him?' Winslow asked.

Nelson shook his head. 'Not as such. He was a night man. I work during the day. We'd nod to one another on occasion if I happened to stay late after four when I leave normally.'

Chops tilted his head. 'What did the rest of the staff think of him?'

Nelson sniffed. 'I can't speak for the opinions of the more junior staff. He seemed to keep a low profile. I can't think of any reason they would have to interact with him, any more than I would have interacted with him.'

Winslow scribbled something in his notebook. 'We understand Mr Morrison had served in the last War. Did you know that?'

'Vaguely,' Nelson replied, glancing at his fingernails. 'He never mentioned it. I assumed it from his bearing. I suppose many of his type did.'

'His type?' asked Winslow, jumping in before Chops could form a more sarcastic version of this question. He ignored the sour look of a boss denied the chance to wield a scalpel on this martinet's ego.

'Oh, you know.'

'No,' said Chops, leaning forward, a grin on his face that resembled a tiger encountering a sleeping goat. Perhaps Nelson guessed he had sounded a trifle pompous. The expression on his face slowly changed from a delicate mixture of surprise and amusement to fear, rather in the manner of meeting a baby shark and then its mother.

'Well, I meant that, I suppose,' he began, 'well, he was of that age. Of that bearing. You know. Silent. Haunted.'

111

'I see,' said Chops. He, himself, had caught the end of the war and he understood all too well what Nelson meant by haunted. The carnage he had witnessed in his year in Flanders would haunt his dreams for the rest of his life.

Winslow watched him carefully. 'Would you have put him down for someone who might have been involved in the robbery? Inside job, perhaps?'

Nelson looked mildly horrified. 'Certainly not. That sort of behaviour would be completely out of character. He was reliable. If, as I say, morose.'

'Morrison didn't have keys to the strongroom?' asked Winslow.

'Oh no. Just Williams and I,' replied Nelson.

'Would he ever have had cause to go down to the strongroom?'

'No. Only Williams and I can do that.'

'You always lock the door behind you?'

'Of course,' said Nelson rather huffily.

There was a knock, and the constable entered again.

'That'll be all, Mr Nelson,' Chops said, offering a polite nod. Nelson gave them both a stiff smile and left.

The door closed. Chops turned to Winslow. 'He seems the sort who'd sell his grandmother for a promotion.'

Winslow chuckled. 'And would write a memo about it afterwards.'

Their next interviewee was Norman Bennett, a young man in spectacles and a slightly oversized jacket. He looked nervous, clutching a battered briefcase in front of him like a shield.

'Sit down, Mr Bennett,' Winslow said kindly.

'Thank you, sir. I hope I can be of some help. I only joined a few months ago.'

Chops smiled reassuringly. 'We're just trying to get a sense of Mr Morrison's character. Anything you can tell us is useful.'

Norman adjusted his glasses. 'He was always very nice to me, sir. Said good evening when I left. Never rude. Quiet sort of man. I knew he'd been in the war. My father served too. They spoke once or twice, when Dad picked me up from the station.'

'Did Mr Morrison ever talk about the war?' Winslow asked.

'Not much. Said it wasn't something for young men to envy. Said he'd seen enough of death.'

Chops exchanged a glance with Winslow. 'And did he seem... troubled? Nervous?'

'No,' Norman said. 'He seemed steady. Like he'd seen everything and nothing much could surprise him anymore.'

'Are you thinking of joining up?' Chops asked.

Norman flushed. 'I tried, sir. They turned me down. Eyesight. I'll try again, though. I want to do something.'

'Who had keys to the strong room?' asked Chops, changing tack.

'Mr Williams and Mr Nelson.'

'No one else?'

'No.'

Chops nodded, a rare flicker of sympathy in his eyes. 'Thank you, Mr Bennett. That was very helpful.'

As Norman left, Winslow murmured, 'Decent lad.'

'Wouldn't last five minutes in Nelson's shoes,' Chops replied dryly.

Next came Linda Geddis, all neat hair and purposeful step. She was perhaps twenty-two, with a calm, intelligent face and a no-nonsense air. She smiled at the officers and sat politely.

'Miss Geddis,' Chops began, 'you're Mr Williams' secretary, I believe?'

'That's right, sir. I also help out at the counter when things get busy.'

'Did you know Mr Morrison well?'

She hesitated. 'Not very. Just to say hello, really. He seemed kind. Opened doors, smiled. Sometimes I brought him tea if I was staying late.'

'Ever hear him speak about anything unusual?' Winslow asked.

'No. He was private. But I did once see him reading a very worn book of poetry. I remember that.'

'Poetry?' Chops raised an eyebrow.

She nodded. 'Something romantic. I found it sweet.'

'Thank you, Miss Geddis. That helps us build a picture.'

She rose, but before leaving turned back. 'Sir? I hope you find who did it. He didn't deserve that.'

Chops nodded. 'We'll do our best.'

The final interviewee was Herbert Williams, the manager. He looked exhausted, with dark circles under his eyes. His hands trembled slightly as he held a cup of tea brought in by a constable.

'Mr Williams,' Chops said kindly, 'thank you for seeing us again. We won't keep you long.'

'Of course,' he said, voice hollow.

'We understand you hired Mr Morrison?'

'Yes,' Williams said. 'Five months ago. He came with a recommendation from a friend who worked in the prison service. I liked him. Seemed solid. Quiet.'

'Did you suspect him of anything unusual?' Winslow asked.

'Never. I trusted him. He reminded me of my uncle, actually. Steady and serious.'

Chops let the silence linger. Then he leaned forward. 'Do you think it could have been an inside job, Mr Williams?'

Williams looked genuinely stricken. 'Good Lord, I hope not. He had keys to the front door but not to the strongroom.'

'And yet both the door leading to the strongroom and the vault door showed no signs of forced entry,' chuckled Chops as he lit a pipe. 'How do you suppose that was possible without keys? It seems to me if you were going to choose an inside man from the bank then the last person I would suggest would be the nightwatchman. I mean he would be perfect if you were going to blast your way in but otherwise...'

114

'What are you implying, Chief Inspector?' stammered Williams. He was perspiring now under the heat of Winslow's gaze and Chops' detached amusement.

Chops stood up suddenly, which made Williams take a step backwards. 'Thank you. That's all we need for now.'

But just as they reached the door, Williams, voice shaking with emotion, stopped the two policemen in their tracks.

'Wait. I want to confess.'

Carol was woken by the morning sun spilling softly through the tall sash windows of her bedroom, casting faint golden lines across the floral wallpaper. Rather than go down to breakfast, she decided to have it in bed. Fifteen minutes later, wrapped in a silken robe, Carol sat propped up against crisp pillows, a breakfast tray balanced neatly across her lap. A pot of tea, some buttered toast, and a folded copy of the *Exeter Morning Gazette* sat before her.

She lifted the cup and sipped absently, her eyes flitting down the front page of the newspaper. And then she saw it.

'MURDER AND ROBBERY IN EXETER: ONLY WITNESS IS A CHILD,' the headline screamed.

Her eyes widened. She dropped the toast, forgotten, onto the tray and hastily unfolded the paper. The subheading read: 'Police question three young evacuees staying at Ravenley Hall after reports of suspicious vehicle.'

Her name was printed halfway down the article.

'Mrs Caroline Sinclair, widow of RAF Squadron Leader Charles Sinclair, accompanied the children to Exeter Police Station where they met with detectives. A police sketch, based on a description provided by one of the children, appears below.'

And there it was. A black-and-white reproduction of the police sketch: the man with the dark moustache and the pale, cold eyes. Beneath it, a caption: 'Do you know this man?'

Carol sat frozen, the colour rising in her cheeks. Fury, disbelief, and fear surged through her in equal measure.

116

'How dare they!' she muttered aloud.

She shoved the tray aside and swung her legs over the edge of the bed, the toast clattering onto the floor. She reached for her clothes, yanked open drawers, pulled on a skirt and blouse with trembling fingers, and buttoned them clumsily. Within ten minutes, she was striding through the front hall of Ravenley, calling for Figgs to bring the car round.

'Where are you going, madam?' Mrs Parker asked, emerging from the morning room.

'Into Exeter. The *Gazette* has printed a story that names me and the children in connection with the robbery. I have to speak to Chief Inspector Hopcroft. This is outrageous.'

Mrs Parker looked stricken. 'The children aren't mentioned by name, are they?'

'No, but it's more than enough. Anyone who knows we've taken evacuees will make the connection.'

Half an hour later, Carol was behind the wheel of the Morris, tyres hissing over wet roads as she made her way into Exeter. Clouds hung low, and the streets were still damp from last night's rain. Her face was set, jaw tight, as she pulled into the car park by the police station.

Inside, she was met by a bored-looking desk sergeant.

'Chief Inspector Hopcroft? Or Detective Inspector Winslow?' she asked curtly.

'Neither of them is in, madam. They're out making house calls.'

She exhaled sharply through her nose. 'Very well. I assume you know how to take a message. Tell them Mrs Caroline Sinclair was here and that I am extremely unhappy about a leak to the press concerning myself and the children. They will know what I mean.'

She turned on her heel and marched out before the sergeant could respond.

Next stop: the offices of the *Exeter Morning Gazette*.

The *Gazette* occupied a Georgian townhouse on the High Street. Its brass plaque gleamed, and the front door opened directly into a

117

flurry of movement, men in shirt sleeves and braces smoking furiously over typewriters, women in sensible skirts ferrying coffee and carbon paper. She strode to the reception desk.

'I need to speak to Mr Dick Dalton. Immediately. And I will see the editor too.'

The girl at the desk looked alarmed. 'One moment, madam.'

Ten minutes later, Carol found herself standing in the oak-panelled office of Henry Montague, the long-serving editor of the *Gazette*. Behind the desk sat Montague himself, a man in his sixties with neatly combed silver hair, an old school tie, and the air of someone who took long lunches at the club and preferred things done with decorum. To his left, lounging in a leather armchair with one ankle perched on the opposite knee, was Dalton, a cigarette dangling precariously from his lower lip. He wore what could only be described as a smirk.

'Well, Mrs Sinclair, I do believe you've come to complain,' he said.

Carol stood stiffly, glancing between the two men.

'You printed the likeness of a suspected murderer and thief and accompanied it with an article clearly implying that my house and the children staying with me were somehow involved. Are you mad?' she asked coldly.

Montague held up a hand.

'I understand your concern, Mrs Sinclair. Please, won't you sit down?'

'I'll stand, thank you.'

Dalton chuckled. 'It's hardly a libel, madam. You were seen entering the police station with three children. That's a matter of public record. And the police sketch was cleared for publication.'

Carol's eyes flashed. 'Do you not understand what you may have done? Those men could come after the children. They saw the car, they saw the man. And now anyone reading your rag can deduce who they are and where they live.'

Montague cleared his throat.

'Dick, enough. Mrs Sinclair, may I say we were assured by sources in the station that the children were not at risk. The decision to publish the sketch was taken in the public interest.'

'Public interest?' Carol said icily. 'You call this journalism? Prying into police matters? Endangering lives? You should be ashamed of yourselves.'

Dalton shrugged. 'We have a duty to inform the public. That man is dangerous. If your children saw him, then perhaps putting his face out there will help catch him before he hurts someone else.'

Carol turned to Montague. 'Is this how your paper operates now? Sensationalism over responsibility?'

Montague sighed. 'Mrs Sinclair, believe me, I understand your anger. But the piece was handled within the bounds of law and with approval. We took care not to name the children or give precise details.'

'Precise details,' Carol shot back. 'You don't need to be Sherlock Holmes to work out who the children are and where they are living.' Carol was yelling at the two newsmen now. She composed herself for a moment then added in a chillingly calm tone, 'If anything happens to those children, I will hold this paper accountable. I have friends who could make life very uncomfortable for you both.'

Dalton smirked. 'Are you threatening us, madam?'

Carol gave him a withering look. 'Oh yes, I'm threatening you all right, you toad. You'd better pray that no harm comes to them.'

Without waiting for a response, she turned and stalked from the office.

Back in the car, she sat for a moment with her hands gripping the steering wheel, her knuckles white. Her breathing was uneven. Her mind raced through scenarios she dared not voice aloud.

They had seen Roger. The man in the passenger seat had looked directly at him. And now the likeness of this man was in every shop and sitting room in Devon.

What if they came looking?

What if she couldn't protect them?

She started the engine and drove home, her eyes constantly flitting to the rear-view mirror. Her mind was racing though. With the man's face in the paper, it would increase the chances that he would be caught. He would be forced to lie low. The last thing on his mind, surely, would be to extract revenge on any witness.

The journey back felt longer than it was. The trees lining the road to Ravenley seemed darker, the fields more still. When she pulled into the drive and brought the car to a halt outside the house, she sat for a moment, her forehead resting against the wheel.

Carol's temper had not cooled by the time the car crunched up the gravel drive to Ravenley. Her fingers gripped the steering wheel so tightly they had gone white at the knuckles, and her jaw ached from clenching. The entire affair at the *Gazette* offices had been infuriating, and she still hadn't decided whether it was the oily insolence of Dick Dalton or the smug diplomacy of Henry Montague that had enraged her more. The fact remained that the *Gazette* had published details—names left out or not—that should never have been made public. And now the entire county knew she had taken evacuees into the house, as if she were collecting stray dogs or ration cards.

She parked and swung open the car door, the July air thick and hot even in the early morning. The house stood imposingly still against the sun-dappled backdrop of the surrounding parkland, its grey stone face giving nothing away. As she made her way up the steps, her heels clicking sharply on the flagstones, Figgs met her at the door with an expression she recognised at once—pinched, anxious, and apologetic.

'Lady Cressida and Viscount Sinclair are in the drawing room, madam,' he said in a lowered voice, his eyes sliding briefly to the hall as if half-hoping she might reverse back down the steps.

Carol paused for the briefest of moments, her lips tightening. 'Of course they are,' she said. 'No doubt summoned by today's scandalous headlines.'

She peeled off her gloves and handed them to Figgs. 'I trust tea was offered?'

'Yes, madam. Though only the Viscount accepted.'

'Any post?' Carol asked, trying to keep her voice level.

'Just a note from the vicar, thanking you for your hospitality yesterday,' Mrs Parker replied. 'And the children are out in the orchard.'

Carol nodded but inside she felt desolate. Her mind was on Charles once more. No news was not necessarily good news. It just prolonged the agony. She realised that Figgs was looking at her. She added, 'Good. Let them stay there as long as they like. And can you let our guests know I will join them in a few minutes. I have a few matters to attend to.'

She left Figgs and went into the drawing room where she poured herself a brandy. It wasn't yet midday, but her nerves were frayed.

Then, with new determination, she walked into the study and pulled a piece of writing paper from the bureau. If the police couldn't protect them, she would find someone who could.

But the feeling remained, like a stone in her chest: a creeping sense that something had shifted. That something dangerous had been stirred.

And it was now looking their way. She drained the rest of the glass and steeled herself to see Cressida and Jason.

A minute or two later, she entered the drawing room with a confidence she did not entirely feel. The tension in the air was immediate, almost tangible. Lady Cressida was seated by the window, her frame as rigid as her starched cream blouse. She wore a wide-brimmed hat despite being indoors, and her gloved hands rested in her lap as if folded in prayer. Jason, dear Jason, stood awkwardly near the mantelpiece, his teacup trembling faintly in one hand, the saucer rattling in the other.

121

'Caroline,' Cressida said at once, her voice like sugar tipped in acid. 'How very... modern of you to be out so early. We were on our way to St Austell and decided to detour, having read the *Gazette*. Rather alarming news, wouldn't you say?'

Carol didn't rise to the bait. 'Cressida. Jason. Do make yourselves comfortable—though clearly you already have.' She sat with exaggerated ease on the nearest sofa and crossed her legs. 'Is this a social visit or an inquisition?'

Jason gave a short, uneasy laugh. 'Nothing of the sort, Carol. We simply wanted to... to see how you were.'

'How I am,' she repeated drily. 'I'm perfectly well, thank you. Though it appears the *Gazette*'s reach is wider than I thought.'

Cressida's eyes narrowed. 'It's all over Exeter and beyond. People are talking. The Sinclair name, dragged into the affairs of common evacuees. What were you thinking?'

'That they needed somewhere safe,' Carol replied coolly. 'And Ravenley has rooms enough to spare. Or do you object to children escaping bombs?'

'Don't be melodramatic,' Cressida snapped. 'That house is not a boarding school. It's ancestral. It carries the family name, its legacy. It was not meant to be overrun by—'

'By orphans?' Carol said pointedly. 'Because that's what they are, Cressida. Orphans. Their parents are dead, and someone needed to step in.'

'Someone else could have done it.'

'But I did.'

Jason cleared his throat. 'Now, now, let's not argue...'

'I'm not arguing, Jason,' Cressida cut in sweetly. 'I'm stating facts. And here's another one. The entire county also knows you've been married three years and have yet to produce a child. Perhaps you feel these evacuees fill a void, Carol, but it isn't appropriate.'

Carol flushed, her hands curling into fists in her lap. She stood slowly, her tone tight. 'You will not speak of that again. Not here. Not in this house.'

There was a long silence, broken only by the tick of the grandfather clock in the hallway. Then Cressida rose, brushing invisible lint from her sleeve.

'I would like to see the children. Now. I believe it is time they were placed elsewhere, with someone more suitable. The vicarage, perhaps.'

'You're not seeing them,' Carol said flatly.

'Excuse me?'

'I said no. You won't see them.'

Jason looked horrified. Cressida took a step forward, but Carol didn't move. A curious steel had settled in her bones, a certainty she hadn't felt in days. The children were hers to protect. Her decision to make.

'Where are they, anyway?' Cressida said suddenly, peering about as if they might appear from behind a curtain.

Carol blinked. 'They should be in the nursery or the garden. Figgs...'

But Figgs was already at the door, his brow creased.

'I've not seen them since before luncheon, madam. Nor has Mrs Parker.'

Carol felt her stomach tighten. 'Try the orchard. And the stables. Ask Benjy if he's seen them.'

She was already striding into the hall, heart thudding now in earnest. She knew children went missing for minutes all the time, and there were dozens of places on the estate for them to wander to—but something about the silence of the house, the growing presence of Cressida and her unspoken threats, made it feel different today.

Mrs Parker met her at the foot of the stairs, worry etched across her kind face. 'They're not in their rooms, and I asked Cook. She hasn't seen them since mid-morning. I thought they were in the garden, but...'

'Damn it all,' Carol muttered, pushing past. She turned at the door and barked, 'Figgs, get Benjy and two of the stable boys. Have them check the woods and down by the stream.'

Cressida appeared behind her, arms folded, a look of distaste on her face. 'This is precisely what I mean. Complete disorder. You've no idea what you're doing, Caroline. You've let sentiment cloud your judgement. It was bound to end in disaster.'

Carol turned slowly to face her, a terrible calm settling on her features. 'And yet, it's still none of your business. They are my concern now. Mine.'

Cressida held her gaze for a moment, then turned away with a dramatic sigh and glided back into the drawing room. Jason lingered a second longer, as if he wanted to say something comforting, but instead followed his wife without a word.

Carol looked out across the lawn, the sun now slipping westward behind the trees. Somewhere out there, three children were missing. And for the first time since Charles had gone missing, she felt a sense of fear so sharp it cut through her pride. If anything had happened to them... she couldn't finish the thought. Not now. Not when she had just realised she needed them as much as they needed her.

21 Roger, Susan and Benjy

Roger, Susan, and Benjy stepped through the side gate near the conservatory, a scuffed leather football tucked under Roger's arm. They had no idea of the stir their names, or rather their anonymous selves, had caused in the morning edition of the *Exeter Gazette*. They were blissfully ignorant of newspapers and headlines, of scandalised editorials and furious conversations taking place inside the house. What they knew was that they had fields to run in, trees to climb, with no homework, no school bells, and no air-raid sirens.

'Come on, lazybones!' Roger shouted over his shoulder, jogging ahead into the long grass. 'This pitch isn't going to mark itself.'

Benjy stumbled after him, his shirt already untucked and one sock bunched around his ankle. 'Wait for me!'

Susan followed more slowly, trailing a hand along the feathery heads of tall grass. She was not in the same high spirits as the boys. Though she hadn't spoken of it to them, she'd overheard a conversation between Mrs Parker and one of the kitchen maids the previous evening. Something about the robbery. Something about a man who'd been killed. She hadn't slept very well after that.

But the boys, particularly Roger, seemed to find it all thrilling.

'Bet it was a proper gang,' Roger said, dropping the ball and giving it a solid kick. 'Like in that book we read. Tunnels, disguises. Maybe even Tommy guns.'

'Tommy guns are American,' Susan replied, but he wasn't listening.

Benjy let out a cheer as the ball soared through the air and landed in a slight dip in the field.

They played for nearly an hour, tearing up and down the field, arguing over goals, fouls, and imaginary referees. Susan stood in goal for a time, though her heart wasn't quite in it, and Benjy, as usual, got distracted by insects and paused mid-chase to examine a beetle with unusual stripes.

Then Roger launched the ball skyward with an almighty boot, and it arced clean over the far hedge before lodging itself in the crook of a chestnut tree.

'Brilliant,' he said, hands on hips, squinting up. 'Now we'll never get it back.'

'You're the one who kicked it there,' Susan said, shielding her eyes.

'That's what Benjy's for,' Roger replied with a grin. 'Fetch the catapult, private! Operation Rescue begins now.'

Benjy beamed and dug into his trouser pocket, producing a rather battered wooden slingshot and a few small stones. He lined up his first shot carefully, squinting like a sniper. The stone missed the ball completely and pinged off a branch.

'That was just a warm-up,' Benjy said solemnly.

The second stone knocked a few leaves loose, and the third, after Roger shouted, 'Aim for the seam, not the branch!' struck the ball smartly. It shuddered, bounced once, and then tumbled down with a thud.

'Victory!' Roger shouted, holding the ball aloft.

Benjy looked very pleased with himself. Susan merely rolled her eyes. Boys were very different, no question. Still, they had their uses, she supposed.

They crossed the fields, following a narrow track that led to the far paddock where they'd met a group of farmworkers the previous day. The men were crouched, sleeves rolled up and hats askew, busy pulling weeds from a crop line. One of them, Toby, with the crooked nose, spotted them first.

126

'Morning again, little miss and lads,' he called out. 'Should've known you'd be back.'

'We found a dead man,' Benjy said at once, wide-eyed with enthusiasm.

Roger rolled his eyes. 'We didn't *find* him, stupid. We *saw* him. After the bank robbery.'

The men straightened, eyebrows raised.

'That right?' another said. 'Saw the robbers too, did you?'

'One of them,' Susan said, quieter than the others. 'And a car.'

'Well, you lot be careful,' said Toby, wiping his hands on his trousers. 'Real nasty business, that. Robbery's one thing, but killing a man...'

Roger looked unconcerned. 'I think we could take 'em.'

Benjy nodded solemnly. 'I've got a catapult.'

'Ah yes,' the older man chuckled. 'Well, mind you don't go starting a war with it. You lot get off back before your people send the Home Guard out after you.'

They laughed and turned back across the fields, stomachs beginning to rumble with thoughts of tea and jam sandwiches.

By the time they pushed open the side gate again, the sun was well into its descent. Roger was composing a story in his head; he'd decided they should form a club, like the Famous Five, except with better adventures, when he heard the raised voices coming from the house.

Carol burst from the drawing room like a thundercloud, skirts swishing and eyes flashing, just as the children appeared at the foot of the steps. She stopped dead, her face pale with relief and fury.

'Where have you *been*?' she cried. 'I've had half the estate out looking!'

Roger looked startled. 'We were just playing football. Then we went to see the field men.'

'And didn't think to tell *anyone*?' Carol snapped. 'Susan? You should have known better.'

Susan looked at the ground. 'I'm sorry. We didn't think...'

127

'Clearly not,' came a new voice from the doorway.

They all turned.

Lady Cressida stood there in full regalia, lips pursed and eyes narrowed in distaste, as if someone had spilled coal dust across her Persian rug. Then stamped on it. Behind her, Viscount Jason Sinclair hovered uncertainly, hands clasped like a schoolboy caught loitering.

'So,' Cressida said icily, 'these are the evacuees. One can tell by the shoes.'

Roger looked down at his scuffed boots, puzzled. Benjy stared at Cressida like she might turn him into a frog.

Jason stepped forward with a warm smile. 'Hello there. I'm your uncle Charles's brother. You may call me Jason.'

Susan offered a quiet 'How do you do?' Roger simply nodded, and Benjy gave a wave that might have been mistaken for swatting a fly.

'Well,' Cressida said, sniffing, 'they seem... spirited.'

Carol folded her arms. 'They've been fine until this morning, thank you. And they'll continue to be fine.'

Cressida raised an eyebrow. 'We shall see.'

Roger glanced at Susan, then at Carol, reading the tension with an instinct children often possess but rarely voice. He said nothing, but slipped closer to Susan as they were ushered inside.

Benjy tugged at Carol's skirt as they passed her.

'I'm hungry,' he said.

'So am I,' Roger added.

Carol sighed, her anger now spent, replaced by weariness. She gave a small, wry smile and put a hand on each of their shoulders.

'Then let's get you something to eat. But after that, we're going to have a very serious talk about *telling people what you've been doing.*'

The boys groaned in chorus, and Susan gave a small, relieved smile.

Later that evening, the children sat on the floor, their knees drawn up, watching the dial of the wireless as if the words themselves might emerge from the thin green glow. The announcer's voice came thin and metallic, yet with an authority that sounded so ridiculous they immediately began to laugh.

'*Good evening, my poor, deluded British friends. I trust you are enjoying your blackouts and your queues, while your so-called leaders, those tired relics in Whitehall, promise you victory from the comfort of their well-stocked cellars. And yet, what have they delivered you? More ration books, more air-raid sirens, and the faint hope that perhaps, just perhaps, your next cup of tea won't be brewed from something that once lined a rabbit hutch. But never mind, your masters assure you it's all in the name of glory. How comforting that must be, as you huddle in the damp and listen to the crumbling of your Empire.*'

Benjy stood up and put his fingers underneath his nose, made a Nazi salute and said in the same grating tones, '...listen to the crumbling of your empire.'

Roger and Susan immediately exploded into laughter. For those few moments, all thoughts of their life now were forgotten. Benjy tried to continue but was overcome with laughter also.

The sound of the merriment brought Mrs Parker hurrying to the room. She frowned initially when she realised what they were listening to but then a smile creased her face when she saw how they were reacting to the propaganda.

Benjy had regained his composure. He began goose-stepping around the room proclaiming that Arsenal would win the league and that Denis Compton would be Prime Minister. Mrs Parker, a lifelong supporter of Tottenham Hotspur, began to laugh also. The mimicry was cruel in the way only children can be—an instinctive, raw rejection of the enemy they were fighting against. She thought of the past months: the raids, the queues, the ration books, the funerals. All of it had worn the people thin, but not hollow.

Looking at the three children, she felt a sudden and irrational certainty that the country would not surrender, not while there was breath left in its lungs. Defeat, she realised, was not merely a matter of armies and treaties; it was a thing that first had to take root in the hearts and minds of the people. And here, in the morning room, watching the three children curled up in hilarity, she knew it would not grow.

'Dalton!' barked Chops. 'Get out here now, you irresponsible little runt!'

A young secretary, pale and clearly intimidated, scurried to the back of the office. Moments later, Dick Dalton emerged from a side room, his expression caught somewhere between smugness and concern.

'Ah, gentlemen,' he said, attempting joviality. 'What brings Devon Constabulary to our humble newsroom?'

Chops stepped forward, looming. 'You damn well know why we're here. That piece you wrote, naming Mrs Sinclair, referring to the children, describing the witness sketch, it was a disgrace. An outright risk to lives.'

Dalton opened his mouth to speak but was interrupted by the appearance of the editor, Henry Montague. He was a man of patrician bearing, silver-haired, and dressed in a waistcoat with an immaculately knotted tie.

'Chief Inspector, please, let us not cause a scene,' Montague said, his voice calm. 'Perhaps you'd step into my office and we can speak like civilised men.'

'So long as you listen like civilised men,' Chops growled. 'Because what you've done is put three children, potential witnesses to a violent crime, in the crosshairs of a gang we haven't yet identified. I hope that bloody sells newspapers.'

They entered Montague's office; a room lined with leather-bound books and smelling faintly of pipe smoke. Dalton followed but was silenced by a sharp glance from Montague.

Winslow took a seat stiffly. 'You released a witness sketch before it was cleared. And you published details linking Mrs Sinclair and her home to the investigation. Have you no sense of responsibility?'

Dalton leaned forward. 'The public has a right to know,' he said piously. He lit a cigarette and waved it around airily. 'Isn't part of what we are fighting, freedom. Freedom of the press and all that.'

'Other people are doing the fighting Dalton, observed Chops, archly. Rather gratifyingly, this remark hit its target.

'I do my bit,' said Dalton, shifting in his seat.

'No, Dalton, you use freedom of the press as an excuse for all manner of sensationalist reporting,' Chops interrupted, voice steel. 'And for your information, the public has a right to *safety*. You've jeopardised an ongoing investigation and the wellbeing of civilians, children included.'

Montague raised a hand. 'I agree we may have been... premature. I shall ensure there are no follow-up pieces until we have your approval. And the children's names will be omitted from the record, should they come up again.'

Chops stood. 'You'd better. If any harm comes to those children, it'll be your conscience that bears it.'

With nothing more to add, the two officers left the newsroom. Outside, Chops stopped to light a cigarette, drawing deeply.

'Bloody papers,' he muttered. 'Half the time, they do the criminals' work for them.'

Winslow nodded, adjusting his tie. 'Where to next, sir?'

Chops looked at his watch. 'Williams's house. I want to speak to him and his family.'

The Williams residence, a modest semi-detached house on a quiet road just outside town, was notably subdued when the detectives arrived. The front garden was neat, the curtains drawn. Chops rang the bell. A moment later, the door was answered by Mrs Vera Williams, a woman in her mid-thirties, pale-faced and tired.

'Good afternoon, madam. Chief Inspector Hopcroft and Detective Inspector Winslow. We'd like to speak to your husband again, if we may.'

She nodded silently, stepping aside. Inside, the house was quiet except for the faint sound of a radio murmuring from the sitting room.

Herbert Williams was in the lounge, seated on the edge of an armchair. His shoulders slumped and his eyes hollowed by lack of sleep. When the officers entered, he rose with difficulty.

'Gentlemen,' he said, voice strained. 'I rather thought you might return.'

'You're on leave, Mr Williams?' Chops asked.

'Yes. The board thought it best. All things considered.'

'And what *are* all things, Mr Williams?' Chops took a seat. 'We've been going over the details again. There are two issues to discuss. The matter you raised yesterday in your office and then there is the dead man. We understand you were the one who brought in Mr Morrison as night watchman. We're not saying that's suspicious in itself, but then again, most crimes begin with ordinary choices.'

Williams glanced towards his wife. She met his gaze and gave a small nod. He exhaled heavily.

Chops leaned forward. 'Mrs Williams, please take a seat. This obviously involves you, too. Go on.'

'On the night of the robbery,' Williams began, 'my wife and children were being held hostage. A man broke into the house hours before and made my wife call me at the bank. He said if I didn't co-operate, if I didn't open the strongroom and allow the gang access, he'd harm them.'

Mrs Williams spoke then, her voice trembling but firm. 'He came in through the back door. Must've been watching the house for

133

days. He waited until the children were asleep. Had a gun. Made me sit on the sofa and ring Herbert. Said I had to sound desperate. I was desperate.'

'He didn't take off his mask the whole time,' Williams added. 'But he was English. Londoner, I'd say. Cockney accent. He knew what he was doing. Told me exactly what to do. Said if anything went wrong, he'd know.'

'And once the robbery was over?' Chops asked.

'He received a telephone call. Then he locked us in the shed in the back garden and left,' Vera said. 'He didn't touch us. Just vanished into the night.'

There was a long silence.

Winslow took notes. 'We'll need a full statement. Both of you. And anything you can remember about the man, the voice, his size, height, clothes.'

'Will I lose my job?' Williams asked quietly.

Chops didn't answer immediately. Then he said, 'That's not our decision. But you did the right thing coming forward. We'll do everything we can to help.'

Outside, back in the police car, both men sat in silence for a moment.

'Blackmail and coercion,' Winslow muttered. 'Poor devil. We'll have to inform Scotland Yard. Do you think Williams might've been in on it? They probably needed someone inside to help smooth the job. And someone to help justify opening the bank out of hours.'

'Yes, I still haven't discounted Williams,' said' Chops, starting the engine. 'But the murder of Morrison also means this gang is cold-blooded. They'll do whatever it takes. And that makes them dangerous. We need to catch them before they hurt anyone else.'

The drive back from Mr Williams's house was a quiet one at first. The sun had begun its slow descent behind the Devonshire hills, casting long shadows over the hedgerows and dry-stone walls that lined the country roads. In the passenger seat of the Morris, Winslow sat with his arms folded, gazing out of the window, brow furrowed. Chops drove, silent, his face bearing its usual expression of faint amusement — though today, it was tinged with something grimmer.

'We've got a problem, haven't we?' Winslow said at last, breaking the silence.

'Only one?' Chops murmured, shifting down a gear as they took a bend.

'You know what I mean. The children. That blasted article has put them in the line of fire.'

'Yes,' Chops replied, his tone suddenly serious. 'And it wasn't just idle gossip, was it? Their presence at the scene, the artist's impression. It's all in print now. Which means it's in the hands of anyone who bought the Gazette this morning. Including our robbers.'

Winslow turned towards him, eyes sharp. 'You think they'd go after them?'

'I think,' Chops said slowly, 'that desperate men do desperate things. And we now know this gang are more than just robbers. They're killers. Morrison's death proved that. They've got at least one cold-blooded murderer among them. And if they think for a moment that those children could identify one of their number, they might well decide it's safer to silence them.'

Winslow exhaled, rubbing his temples. 'God help them. And Mrs Sinclair. She's already under enough pressure without this.'

Chops glanced sideways at his junior. 'She's stronger than she lets on. But yes, she's in a difficult spot. And she's not the only one. There's Mrs Parker, and the staff. Anyone in that household could be at risk now.'

They were quiet again for a moment before Chops added, 'We'll make a virtue of necessity.'

Winslow raised an eyebrow. 'Meaning?'

'We'll station a constable at Ravenley for the next few days. In plain clothes, preferably. Someone competent who won't alarm the household but will keep an eye on things. Protection for the

135

children, and perhaps a net to catch any fish foolish enough to swim back.'

'You think they might come to the house?'

Chops gave a small, wry smile. 'I think if they're careless, or confident, or paranoid enough. But more likely, they'll be watching. And if they are, I want to know about it.'

Winslow nodded. 'I'll arrange it as soon as we get back to the station.'

'Good lad,' Chops murmured. 'And get someone to check with the post office — telegrams, phone records. See if anything odd's been reported from the Ravenley exchange. It's a long shot, but they may have tried to contact someone in that house.'

'Understood.'

The Morris bumped slightly as it turned off the country lane onto the smoother tarmac of the Exeter road. In the distance, the spires and rooftops of the city came into view, bathed in the amber glow of evening. Chops adjusted his fedora slightly on the back of his head, his mind already ticking forward.

'We'll need to move quickly, Tommy. This gang's already a step ahead.'

'What now, Chops?' asked Winslow.

'I'm off to Ravenley to break the good news to Carol that she'll have a guard.'

Carol sat with Susan in the library trying and failing to read a book in front of a fire glowing in the hearth, when Figgs stepped into the room and murmured, 'Chief Inspector Hopcroft is here to see you, madam.' She rose from the armchair and smoothed her skirt. She looked at Susan, who understood. She rose from her seat and left the room.

While the visit was not unexpected, she had been dreading it in a way but also welcoming the comfort of Chops' level-headedness. Her nerves had been taut since the Gazette article. The house had quietened after yesterday's commotion, but a shadow of unease still lingered.

She reached the entrance hall just in time to see Chops being greeted by Lady Cressida Sinclair and her husband Jason. Chops was removing his hat as he stepped inside, stamping his boots against the cold and brushing a few flakes of frost from his coat.

'Good morning, Chief Inspector,' said Cressida, icily formal, as though addressing a tradesman who had turned up at the wrong door. 'How... unexpected.'

'Good morning, Lady Cressida,' Chops replied with a dry smile. 'Always a pleasure to step into the warmth of a Ravenley welcome.'

Jason extended a hand with a joviality that felt almost comic beside his wife's frostiness. 'Chops, old man! What brings you out this far? Beastly weather for it. Come in and have a snifter, unless duty forbids, of course.'

'I might take you up on that, Viscount. But business first, I'm afraid.'

Carol appeared in the corridor, her short-lived escape from Cressida's disapproval now over. She stepped forward to greet the detective.

'Come in, Chops. We can talk in the drawing room. I daresay you need warming up.'

He gave her a quick nod, his eyes scanning her face with a brief flicker of concern. As they began to move away, Cressida's voice cut through the air like the edge of a knife.

'I do hope your visit isn't in connection with the recent... publicity, Chief Inspector. One might expect better from the police than to parade children through the headlines like some sort of music hall act.'

Chops turned slowly, his face composed but his eyes glinting. 'Indeed, Lady Cressida. If you're concerned, I'm glad to say I've already paid Mr Dalton at the Gazette a visit. Gave him a few thoughts on journalistic responsibility he'll remember.'

Carol's eyes widened slightly. 'You did?' she asked, leading him into the morning room. 'Good for you.'

'My only regret is that you beat me to the punch, Carol. Anyway, he won't be using children's names again, or I'll have his head on a platter, or worse' said Chops, who stopped short of expanding on what might be worse. Carol's smile suggested she might have a few ideas on that subject.

Cressida had followed them in, uninvited but clearly determined to make her presence known. 'Perhaps you'll also take the opportunity to reason with Caroline,' she said smoothly. 'Surely it isn't safe for the children to remain here now. The story has rather... exposed them, don't you think?'

Chops leaned on the back of a chair, regarding her with an expression of faux sympathy. 'I'm afraid the decision isn't yours, Lady Cressida. Nor mine. But as it happens, I came to inform Mrs

Sinclair that we'll be stationing a constable on the grounds for the next few days. Just in case.'

Carol blinked. 'A police guard?'

He nodded. 'It's a precaution, nothing more. But yes, with the children's identities out in the open, we can't rule out the possibility that the gang might consider them a liability. I would add that we think the possibility remote. The gang, particularly our friend with the moustache will want to put as much distance between themselves and Exeter. In fact, Scotland Yard have been in touch and will be paying us yokels a visit soon, no doubt to show us how it's done.'

Jason gave a low whistle and moved towards the drinks cabinet. 'The big boys. Sorry to hear that Chops. I'm sure you could've handled matters. All the more reason to join me for that brandy. Sounds as though you've earned it, old man.'

'Why not?' said Chops. 'Something to gird the loins against December's finest frost.' He cast his eyes in Cressida's direction and smiled. Carol despite the overwhelming sense of melancholy had to fight back the laughter. Jason, meanwhile, hot the cocktail cabinet like a sprinter out of the blocks working on the sound principle that even Cressida could hardly criticise him for being hospitable.

Cressida remained by the window, arms crossed, her eyes flicking between Carol and the Chief Inspector with open scepticism. 'One hopes this arrangement will be temporary. It's not seemly for children, particularly evacuees, to be billeted here indefinitely. It reflects poorly on the family. On the estate.'

'What reflects poorly on the family,' said Carol, her voice cold now, 'is a lack of compassion or an unwillingness to be seen to be helping the war effort. There is plenty of space at Ravenley. The children are staying, Cressida. I've made up my mind.'

'How noble,' Cressida replied with a delicate sneer. 'Let us hope such nobility does not come at too dear a price.'

Chops gave a short, sharp laugh. 'Well, if they are to be removed, it certainly won't be on Lady Cressida's say-so. The police consider them witnesses in an ongoing investigation. They'll remain close, under our protection. That's the end of it.'

Jason, who had handed Chops a glass of brandy, raised his own in a silent toast. To the war effort,' said Jason with a self-deprecating smile. Chop and he clinked glasses.

Cressida's lips thinned. 'If you'll excuse me, I find myself suddenly fatigued by all this civic virtue.' She turned and swept from the room, the train of her navy wool skirt brushing the edge of the rug as she exited.

Chops took a sip of his brandy and turned to Carol. He murmured 'Was it something I said?'

'She's right to be concerned,' said Carol, allowing herself a faint smile. 'It's a worrying situation.'

Jason chuckled and moved to refill his own glass. 'She was a debutante, you know. Daughter of an earl. Never lets anyone forget it. I know the mem sahib can let her battle axe tendencies get the better of her but she's not stupid. This is a rum situation and no mistake. Are you sure, Carol, it wouldn't be best to come and stay with us for a while? Bring the children. And for what it's worth, I agree, we need to be doing more. I'm sorry to say, Carol my dear, but this is not going to be over for any of us soon. I have my people at the ministry trying to find out about Charles.'

Carol looked at him gratefully. 'Thank you, Jason. For everything.'

'What's happening on the case, old fellow?' asked Jason.

Chops looked mournful. 'It'll be with Scotland Yard in a day. Then we'll be back investigating pickpockets and the like. But we'll continue in the meantime. Winslow's digging further into the background of the dead man, Morrison. There's more to him than meets the eye.'

'You don't say.'

Chops set his glass down and turned serious. 'I'm not discussing that outside the force. For now, it's enough to know that the gang is

140

dangerous, organised, and still at large. We'll get them, but we need to be careful. Keep the children close, keep them indoors if you can.'

Carol nodded, her brow drawn. 'I'll do my best. But they're children. They'll want to explore. And they've grown fond of the grounds.'

'Just don't let them wander too far. And keep an eye out for anything unusual. If anything feels off, anything at all, call me. Or have your constable do so.'

Jason walked Chops back to the front hall while Carol watched from the morning room door. He paused just before leaving.

'Thank you, really,' she said softly.

He gave her a nod, that same wry half-smile playing on his lips. 'Just doing my job, Carol. But you know I'd rather it be here than some dusty old office. Even with Lady Frostbite hovering around.'

Jason laughed as he opened the door. 'You're braver than I am, old chap. I simply retreat to the cellar when she's like this.'

'It's one approach,' Chops said as he stepped into the cold. 'But I prefer a good brandy and an argument.'

The door closed behind him with a satisfying thud, and Carol stood for a moment, the warmth of the fire behind her and the chill of unease returning to her heart. The children were safe, for now. But how long would that last? And what price would they all pay for being kind?

A keen wind scoured the exposed highlands as Chops and Winslow drew up at the grim stone gates of Dartmoor Prison. The bleakness of the landscape seemed to echo the mood in the car. They sat for a moment, eyeing the weathered stone walls, grim with centuries of damp and moss.

'Well,' Chops muttered, pulling his coat tighter about him, 'this is cheerful.'

Winslow smiled faintly. 'It does have a certain... historical gloom about it.'

They presented their credentials at the gatehouse, were ushered through with clipped formality, and soon found themselves walking the echoing corridors of the prison, escorted by a junior officer whose boots clicked on the worn flagstones.

Major J.C. Pannall, the Governor, awaited them in his office. He was a stiff, upright figure in his sixties, with a close-cropped moustache and a face lined by duty and disappointment.

'Gentlemen,' he said, rising. Major Pannall. Welcome to Dartmoor, though I'm not sure welcome is the word.'

Chops offered a firm handshake. 'Chief Inspector Hopcroft. This is Detective Inspector Winslow. Thank you for seeing us.'

Pannall gestured for them to sit. 'You're here about Morrison, I understand.'

'Indeed,' Winslow replied. 'We're trying to piece together his life prior to employment at the bank.'

Pannall nodded slowly. 'To be frank, I didn't know him well. He kept to himself. Morrison was one of many ex-servicemen who came through here. We're stretched, as you can imagine. Half my staff are off in uniform now. We've had to take on a lot of ex-soldiers. Morrison came with good references. A little too old for active service this time round, but he was reliable. Or so we thought.'

'Who supervised him directly?' Chops asked.

'Warden Clive Sheridan,' Pannall replied. 'I'll have him sent in.'

A few minutes later, Sheridan entered. He had the look of a man hewn from the very rock of the moor: tall, weathered, square-jawed, his grey uniform impeccable. He offered them a brusque nod and sat without invitation.

'Morrison?' he said, after a brief introduction. 'Difficult chap. Not one for idle conversation. Bitter as wormwood. Felt the country owed him more than he'd got. Which, to be fair, many of them do.'

'He served?' Winslow asked.

Sheridan nodded. 'As did I. So did Terry Roberts. We all went through the fire, one way or another.'

'Terry Roberts?' Chops asked.

'Senior warden. He's just doing the rounds at the moment but I've sent someone to get him in.'

A few minutes later, Roberts joined them. He was shorter and stockier than Sheridan, with a softer expression but watchful eyes. He had the air of a man not easily rattled. The detectives sat back and let the two men tell them about Morrison.

'Morrison,' Roberts said, after hearing the nature of their inquiry. 'He wasn't a pleasant fellow. Not cruel, just... lost, I think. Like a man who never came back from France, even if he was home. Didn't talk much, but he had this way of looking through you. Never raised his voice, but people listened. Even the lags. Especially the lags.'

'Feared?' Chops asked.

'A bit. He had a quiet menace to him. But he never crossed a line. Never gave cause for dismissal.'

'He ever mention financial troubles?' Winslow leaned forward slightly.

'Once or twice,' Sheridan said. 'He resented the pittance he earned here. Said it was no way to treat a man who'd fought for his country. But he didn't drink, didn't gamble. Just brooded.'

'Was he political?' Winslow asked.

Roberts frowned. 'Not overtly. Bit of a chip on his shoulder, but never heard him talk about any movements.'

'We're just trying to understand how a man ends up a nightwatchman at a bank, then part of a gang of robbers, and finally... well.'

'Did he have any friends among the guards, at all?' asked Winslow.

'No. Kept himself to himself, mostly,' replied Roberts.

'Can you provide us with his old duty rosters if you still have them?' asked Chops.

'Of course,' said Pannall. 'If it helps. We keep them for a couple of years then we clear space. Morrison kept to a tight routine. He was punctual, neat, and thorough. Never any trouble. Until now, of course.'

'Do you think that we could have them today? Asked Winslow. 'It will save us a trip back here.'

Benjy nodded at this. He was a military man to his toes.

'Could we speak to one of the inmates?' Chops asked.

'Who did you have in mind,' asked Pannall.

'Light-Fingered Lennie.'

Detective Inspector Winslow shivered beside Chops as they waited in a dim corridor that smelled of boiled cabbage and regret. A guard finally arrived to escort them to the visitor's room where one Light-Fingered Lennie Long was waiting.

Lennie had earned his moniker the honest way: by robbing everyone in South Devon at least once. He'd started as a pickpocket but graduated to bank robbery with the grace of a man moving up in the world. Five years ago, Chops had caught him red-handed attempting to crawl through the lavatory window of the West Country Bank dressed as a nun.

Despite that, Lennie held no grudge. In fact, he'd sent Chops a Christmas card every year since. Chops quite liked him. He was a thief, yes, but a professional thief. One with standards. No blood, no bodies. Just nimble fingers and a criminal mind sharp enough to slice fruit.

Lennie sat at the table now; his lanky frame poured into a prison uniform like whisky into a milk bottle. His hair was slicked back, face thin but somehow good-humoured.

'Chops,' he said, with a grin, 'you old ferret. Look at you. Still wearing that god-awful tie.'

'Nice to see you too, Lennie,' said Chops, pulling out a chair. 'Still a model inmate?'

'They let me lead prayer on Tuesdays. Not because I'm pious, just because I don't try to knife the others. It's all relative in here.'

Winslow sat across from Lennie, folding his long legs. His face was all sharp lines and reserve.

'This is DI Winslow,' said Chops. 'He thinks he's smarter than me, but he's not. Still, he's very good at sighing and looking disappointed.'

Lennie extended a hand, which Winslow ignored. Lennie chuckled.

'Chops says you were always the brains behind your operations,' Winslow said. 'That true?'

'Brains, heart, lungs. The full anatomy,' Lennie replied. 'So what brings you to the land of boiled carrots and bruised egos?'

Chops leaned forward. 'We're looking into a bank job. Morrison. You remember him?'

Lennie's smile vanished. 'The nightwatchman? Dead, isn't he?'

'Murdered,' Winslow said. 'Shot. Execution-style.'

145

Lennie let out a long breath. 'I never liked the man. Morose. Bitter. Always looking like someone had nicked his last smoke. But he didn't deserve that.'

'No one docs,' Chops said.

'Anything unusual about him?' Winslow asked.

Lennie scratched his chin. 'He weren't like the other screws. Most of them, they're either barkin' orders or ignoring you. Morrison... he'd look at you, and you'd think: 'He knows what it's like.' Quiet type. Walked like a man who had shrapnel in his soul. Sometimes I'd see him in the yard, watching us. Not like a screw. Like a man trying to remember what it was to care.'

'Anyone visit him? Anyone seem to be getting close?'

Lennie shook his head. 'He kept his distance. I think he wanted friends but didn't know how to make them.'

'You think he was capable of joining a gang?' Chops asked.

Lennie gave a short laugh. 'Capable? Maybe. But he weren't no leader. He'd follow someone, if they had the right pull. If they made him feel like he belonged. Like he mattered. That man was lost, Chief. You could see it in his eyes.'

Chops and Winslow exchanged glances. A silence fell in the room. The picture emerging of Morrison was clear. A man who had left something of himself in Flanders. A man who had been preyed upon by a gang smart enough to have taken advantage of the former prison guard's sense of resentment. Taken advantage of him and then cruelly disposed of him These were dangerous people.

'Was it a professional crew?' Lennie asked, eyes narrowing.

'If it was, they're not very good ones,' said Winslow. 'Left a mess. No clean getaway, they tripped the alarm or perhaps Morrison did. Too many risks taken. They held the bank manager's family hostage.'

Lennie blinked. 'Bloody hell. That's not a job; that's a war crime.'

Chops nodded. 'We thought the same. What do you think?'

'I had that idea once,' Lennie admitted. 'Kidnap a family, hold them hostage, force the bank to open up like a Christmas cracker. I even made diagrams. But then I thought: one twitchy hand, and someone ends up dead. Not my style. Never was. If I had a code, that'd be line one.'

'No one comes to harm,' said Chops.

'Right. You rob 'em. You don't ruin 'em. That's the difference.'

Winslow tilted his head. 'You know anyone still on the outside who'd pull something like this?'

Lennie scratched his chin. 'Old Tommy Greaves is in Dartmoor. Tony Withers got himself stabbed in Hull. Bertie 'No-Nose' is in the loony bin. Honestly, there's not many left. The war's either taken them or locked them up. Criminal class ain't what it used to be.'

'Would you do it again, if you were out?' Chops asked.

Lennie looked thoughtful. 'If you'd asked me five years ago, I'd say yes without blinking. But now... I'm thinking of joining the army. If they'll have me.'

Winslow raised an eyebrow. 'The army?'

'Why not? It's either that or another twenty years of porridge. I figure if I can survive Dartmoor, I can survive a few Germans.'

Chops laughed. 'What would your role be? Demolitions expert? Distraction specialist?'

'Field requisitions officer,' Lennie grinned. 'Unofficial.'

Winslow half-smiled, despite himself. He was quiet for a long time. Then he said, 'I've thought about it too. Joining up.'

Chops blinked. 'You? Really? You'd give up a badge for a uniform?'

'We all do our part, don't we?' Winslow said.

Lennie's eyes flicked between them. 'If you both sign up, who's going to catch the real crooks?'

Chops leaned back. 'Maybe there won't be any left by then. They'll all be in France nicking rifles.'

They stood. Lennie extended his hand again, and this time Winslow shook it.

'If I hear anything,' Lennie said, 'I'll let you know. There's always whispers. Even here.'

'Keep your nose clean, Lennie,' said Chops.

'I will. And if I do join the army, tell 'em not to give me anything too flammable.'

Back in the car, Chops lit a cigarette and stared out at the grey landscape. The prison walls were receding behind them.

'What do you think?' Winslow asked.

'I think Lennie's a crook, but an honest one. He tells it like it is. I believe him.'

'About going straight?'

'No. About the job. If he thought one of his old mates had done it, he'd have hinted.'

'What about this crew then?' Winslow asked. 'If they're not professionals, who are they?'

Chops exhaled smoke slowly. 'That's what worries me. They might be amateurs with delusions of grandeur. That makes them more dangerous. They don't know their limits.'

They drove in silence for a while, the rain starting up again, steady as ever.

'Think he'll really join the army?' Winslow asked.

Chops shrugged. 'If they'll have him. He'd probably end up stealing the colonel's boots and swapping them for whisky.'

Winslow allowed himself a smile.

'Think you'll go?' Chops asked quietly.

Winslow looked out the window. 'I don't know. Sometimes I feel like we're just rearranging the deckchairs on the Titanic. The war's getting bigger. Closer.'

'We do our bit here too,' Chops said. 'Don't forget that.'

'You ever think of signing up?' Winslow asked.

Chops blew out another plume of smoke. 'Once. Long ago. But I figure someone needs to keep an eye on what goes on at home. You go off and be a hero if you like. Just leave the villain-chasing to me.'

They drove the rest of the way back to Exeter without speaking, the windscreen wipers clicking rhythmically as the clouds thickened. There was work to do. And somewhere out there, men who had murdered an old nightwatchman were walking free. But for now, Chops was oddly comforted by the thought of Lennie Long, thief and philosopher, praying on Tuesdays and plotting his redemption.

Back at the police station, a worried-looking desk sergeant came rushing out to greet them. Chops smiled at the sergeant. He already knew what he was about to hear.

'Chops, I couldn't stop them,' said Harris the desk sergeant.

'Not to worry, I've been expecting our friends from London for some time now,' said Chops. He glanced at his watch and added, 'A bit later than I had imagined.'

Chops and Winslow climbed the stairs to their office. Inside they found two men sitting at their desks. Neither stood up when the two detectives entered.

'Scotland Yard, I presume,' said Chops, taking off his hat and throwing it onto the hat stand a few feet away. Much to Winslow's relief, Chops' aim was true, and the hat settled into its usual place.

The road to Exeter was unusually quiet for a weekday evening. Carol kept her hands steady on the wheel of the Morris Eight as the trees zipped past in a blur of leafless grey. The car heater was unreliable and barely emitted more than a wheeze of lukewarm air, so she'd wrapped herself in one of Charles's old woollen scarves. It smelled faintly of pipe tobacco and something else she couldn't quite place.

She drove with purpose, her lips pressed tightly together. The incident with Cressida had left her wound tighter than violin strings. Not even a steaming bath deep enough to house the Titanic, nor a brandy of such vintage it could legally vote, had helped soothe her nerves. Cressida's mean-spiritedness could inhabit into any room, and with one arch of an eyebrow reduce it to social rubble before the butler had time to announce her name. Carol had lain awake the night before, staring at the ceiling, fury burning in her chest. How dare Cressida swan into Ravenley with her pointed remarks and smug superiority, as if the house, the children, and Carol herself were all some unfortunate blot on the Sinclair nobility.

As she turned onto the road that led towards the city centre, she gripped the wheel a little tighter and allowed herself a small, dangerous smile. If Cressida wanted shock and scandal, then perhaps it was time to give her some.

She parked near the square and made her way briskly through the slush-covered pavement, nodding politely to a passing naval officer. The War Office auxiliary recruitment centre occupied a modest building off Sidwell Street. A faded Union Jack hung rather limply in the window, and the bell above the door gave a half-hearted jangle as she stepped inside.

The room was warmer than expected, filled with the hum of typewriters and the low murmur of voices. Two women in sensible wool suits stood behind a counter, one scribbling notes, the other folding a piece of paper with military precision.

Carol straightened her shoulders and stepped forward.

'Good morning,' she said. 'My name is Caroline Sinclair. I'd like to volunteer, if you've a need for anyone.'

Both women looked up, and the one holding the paper gave a small nod of welcome. She was in her forties, with the no-nonsense air of someone used to running things.

'Good morning, Mrs Sinclair. What sort of work were you thinking of?'

'I'm not trained as a nurse, I'm afraid,' Carol said quickly, anticipating the usual question. 'But I can drive. I've experience with motor vehicles, trucks, even tractors. When I was rather young, my father taught me. And my husband, Charles Sinclair, is with the RAF.'

At the mention of the RAF, the other woman, younger and with her hair pinned in a neat roll, looked up with interest.

'We're certainly short of ambulance drivers just now,' said the first woman, reaching for a clipboard. 'We've had three girls transferred to London this week and another sent to Plymouth. The raids have been frightful down there.'

Carol nodded. 'I'll do whatever I can. We're billeting three evacuees at our home in the country, a boy and his younger sister, and brother. Orphans, all of them. I can manage the hours around their care.'

'And you live where, Mrs Sinclair?'

'Ravenley. It's an estate a few miles outside Exeter. My husband's family has owned it for generations. My brother-in-law is the Viscount Sinclair.'

There it was. She hadn't intended to mention Jason, but the words had come out easily enough. She could picture Cressida's expression now if she ever caught wind of this conversation: her arched brows lifting in icy disbelief that her sister-in-law was careening around Devonshire in an ambulance, elbow-deep in other people's emergencies.

'Well,' said the older woman after a pause, her pencil now scratching across the form. 'You seem rather well-placed to help us, Mrs Sinclair. We'll need you to attend a short training session tomorrow evening. Usual stuff, driving protocol, handling the stretchers, first response. After that, we can put you on the rota. You'll be paired with a nurse or orderly and stationed at Royal Devon and Exeter Hospital unless otherwise directed. Uniforms are tight, I'm afraid you may have to sew your own.'

'I can manage that,' Carol said, trying to hide the flicker of doubt that passed through her. This was no social call or committee. This was real.

'Right, well, can you pop in at two o'clock tomorrow so that we can put you through your paces. You can meet some of the staff and perhaps whichever nurse who will accompany you.' The woman handed her a folded slip. 'Bring identification and warm clothing.'

Carol tucked the slip into her handbag and extended a gloved hand. 'Thank you. I appreciate the opportunity.'

As she turned to leave, the younger woman smiled at her. 'It's good of you to come forward. You'd be surprised how few of your... class... offer themselves in practical ways.'

Carol returned the smile, though her heart clenched a little. 'Well,' she said lightly, 'it's a new kind of war, isn't it?'

Outside, the wind had picked up, and the sky had darkened into a solid stretch of grey. Carol pulled her coat tighter around her and climbed into the driver's seat of the Morris, feeling a curious mix of nerves and exhilaration. She'd done it. Something real. Something for herself, and for the country. And best of all, something that would make Cressida positively choke on her morning coffee when she eventually heard.

She turned the key and the engine juddered to life, the vibration travelling up through her boots and into her bones. As she steered out onto the road, she caught a glimpse of her own reflection in the rear-view mirror. Her cheeks were pink with the cold, but her eyes looked different—more alive.

Yes, she thought, as she shifted into second gear. Let Cressida mutter and snipe. Let the gossip spread through the halls of Devonshire society. Let Jason sip his brandy and look helpless. None of it mattered. Not now.

Now, she had a war to help win.

The long winter dusk had already settled outside when Carol arrived back at Ravenley. She spoke with Mrs Parker and asked for dinner to be served at seven and that the children join her. Forty minutes later, Carol was pouring gravy from the porcelain jug onto Roger's potatoes, careful not to let it spill onto the white linen cloth.

'There we are,' she said, passing the jug to Susan. 'Make sure Benjy doesn't drown everything in it again.'

Carol allowed herself a small chuckle, though her mind was still weighted by the conversation she needed to have. She watched them for a moment, all three of them tucking in, chattering in their usual overlapping way, and she felt the sharp contrast between their energy and the knot of worry that had made its home just beneath her ribs.

She put down her knife and fork and folded her hands in her lap.

'I want to talk to you all about something,' she said, her tone just enough to hush the clatter of cutlery.

Roger glanced up first, a piece of bread halfway to his mouth. Susan, ever alert, straightened in her chair. Benjy looked disappointed to pause eating.

'I spoke with the police today,' Carol began, glancing from one to the other. 'You all know the situation with the robbery and the man who... the man who was killed.'

Susan nodded slowly. Roger's eyes flicked to hers before returning to Carol.

'We haven't forgotten,' Roger said quietly.

'No, and I know you haven't. But there's more. Because of the newspaper article, and don't get me started on how furious I am about that, we now have a police guard.'

There was a moment of silence. Even Benjy stopped chewing.

'Do you mean... the police fear that they might come here?' asked Susan, her voice small.

'We don't know,' said Carol. 'But Ch— Chief Inspector Hopcroft thinks we shouldn't take any risks. That's why there'll be a policeman watching the estate starting tomorrow morning. His name's Constable Talbot, and he'll be keeping an eye from a distance. But for the next few days, I need you to promise me something.'

'Anything,' said Roger quickly, leaning forward. 'What is it?'

'I want you to stay within the grounds. No wandering off to the fields, no visiting the men working at the far end of the estate, and definitely no sneaking off down to the village. I need to know where you are at all times. Do you understand?'

Roger opened his mouth, likely to protest, but stopped when he caught the expression on Carol's face.

'Yes, ma'am,' he said instead, a little stiffly. 'We'll do as we're told.'

Carol turned to Susan and Benjy. 'All of you?'

Susan nodded solemnly. 'Yes, Mrs Sinclair. We'll be careful.'

Benjy looked unhappy but mumbled, 'Yes,' around a mouthful of potatoes.

Carol smiled at Susan and took her hand. 'Perhaps we could be a little less formal when we are alone like this. You can call me Carol.

154

Perhaps when Lady Sinclair is here you revert to Mrs Sinclair. It can be our secret.'

This brought a few smiles from the children. Yet, behind the smiles Carol could see the fear and also the sadness. The pain of losing their parents would be with them for a long time to come.

'And one more thing,' Carol continued, forcing a lighter note into her voice. 'Constable Talbot is doing his job. I don't want you pestering him with questions or trying to spy on him. Let him be.'

'Spoilsport,' muttered Roger, but he gave her a cheeky grin, which she returned despite herself.

'Now,' she said, placing her napkin beside her plate and drawing in a steadying breath, 'there's something else I wanted to tell you. I've... decided to help with the war effort.'

'You're joining the Army?' asked Benjy, eyes wide.

'Not quite,' she said, smiling. 'But I've volunteered as an ambulance driver. Only part-time. I'm going into Exeter tomorrow evening for my first bit of training.'

Susan's eyes shone. 'That's wonderful!'

'Really?' asked Roger. 'You'll be driving ambulances and everything?'

'That's the idea,' she said. 'It's something I can do. I've been feeling a bit helpless lately, and I thought, well, why not put myself to use? Plenty of women are doing their bit. It's time I did mine.'

'We're proud of you,' said Susan firmly, her tone more grown-up than usual. 'Aren't we, boys?'

Benjy nodded enthusiastically. Roger hesitated, then nodded too, his earlier sulkiness forgotten.

'That's the nicest thing I've heard all day,' said Carol softly, her voice catching despite herself. She looked at each of them in turn, her heart brimming with both affection and fear. 'Thank you.'

She rose, beginning to clear the plates. Susan stood to help, as she always did, while the boys began scraping the last bits from their dishes.

'Are you scared?' Susan asked as they took the dishes into the kitchen.

Carol paused, setting a stack of plates on the counter.

'Yes,' she said simply. 'Sometimes I'm terrified. About Charles. About you children. About what's going to happen next. But I've found that the best way to stop fear taking over is to get busy doing something useful.'

Susan nodded, and Carol saw again just how much the girl was having to grow up too fast.

'Thank you for being proud of me,' she said. 'I needed that.'

'I meant it,' said Susan.

That night, after the children had gone up to bed and the lamps were extinguished one by one, Carol stood for a while at the window of the library, looking out into the frosted dark. Somewhere out there was the constable, tucked into some sheltered spot with his torch and his flask. Somewhere else, London, maybe, was a gang who might or might not be thinking of this place. And somewhere further off again, in France or Belgium or even Germany, was Charles.

She wrapped her arms around herself, but the chill that gripped her wasn't just the December air. It was uncertainty. It was the feeling of not knowing what would come tomorrow.

Still, she thought, I'm not alone. That, at least, gave her comfort.

Detective Inspector Basil Blaney and Detective Sergeant Ken Wilkins eyed the new arrivals with barely disguised apathy. Blaney was lanky and pale, with a thin moustache that looked as though it had been drawn on in pencil. Wilkins was shorter and broader, his hair slicked back like a film star but his eyes sharp and humourless.

'Ah, Chief Inspector Hopcroft,' Blaney said, standing. He spoke with an educated accent and offered a limp hand. 'And this must be your sergeant. Winslow.'

Chops shook the offered hand with a perfunctory grip. 'You've had a long journey, gentlemen. Would you like some tea before we begin?'

Blaney gave a slight sniff. 'We had tea on the train. I'm sure you can imagine how vile that was. No, thank you. Let's get to it, shall we? You've had a robbery, a murder, and a great deal of excitement, I gather.'

Winslow bristled, but Chops gave him a warning glance. He laid out the folder of statements and handed over the typed summaries, maps, and photographs.

'You'll find statements from all the bank staff and the children who encountered one of the gang. The victim, Morrison, was a former prisoner and nightwatchman. Shot in the chest from close range. Clearly, wasn't expecting it.'

'Clearly,' nodded Blaney.

Blaney skimmed through a few pages with a look of evident disinterest. Wilkins didn't even bother.

'Well, this is all quite comprehensive,' Blaney said, tone suggesting the opposite. 'But I rather think you've gone down the wrong track.'

Chops raised an eyebrow. 'Have we, now?'

'Yes. This robbery bears striking resemblance to one in Battersea in August. Same *modus operandi*: strong room breached, insider assistance, and the use of threats against staff. In that case, we apprehended one of the men. He refused to speak, of course, so he was handed a full sentence. He'll be out inside ten years and be set for life if we don't catch these men.'

'Well, you are here now,' said Chops. 'How can we help you?'

'Can you take us to where Morrison lived, that is if you don't want to knock off for the day. This may be a bit late in the day for you country chaps,' said Blaney. He sounded like he really meant it.

Winslow was incensed by the increasingly patronising manner of the new arrivals. Just as he was about to give a piece of his mind to someone who was, technically, the same rank, he spied Chops gently shale his head. There was a hint of amusement in his eyes. Winslow didn't know whether to laugh or despair. Chops was clearly going to enjoy one of his favourite sports. Goon-baiting. It was a term he used to describe anyone who donned the uniform of puffed-up self-importance while possessing the mental agility of an anvil. Chops considered it a sacred duty to poke gentle fun at such individuals until the penny dropped and they began quoting protocol like a cracked gramophone.

Winslow sighed the sigh of a man who has just spotted a small fire developing in the corner of a powder magazine and knows precisely who lit the match. Chops was already advancing on the newcomers with lazy menace of a cat.

'It is rather late, I grant you. However, we're never too old a thing or two from you boys from the Yard. We'll take you to his flat.'

Blaney wasn't quite sure if he was being taken for a fool but Chops' guileless smile suggested not. He nodded to the chief

158

inspector. The men departed the office and went down to the car park at the front of the police station.

'You spoke to the other people in the clock of flats where Morrison lived?'

'Oh yes, well all except one. One person was away. Can you remind me who that was?' asked Chops.

'A Mr Thorpe. Cyril Thorpe.'

'Interesting fellow, if I remember. Has a prison record,' said Chops.

The two Yard men turned to Chops and looked askance at the detective.

'Why wasn't he brought in for questioning?' snapped Wilkins. 'Damn shoddy, if you ask me.'

'I wish we had, Detective Sergeant Wilkins,' said Chops, nudging Winslow and nodding towards Wilkins. 'What wisdom might have been bestowed upon us if we had, eh, Winslow?

Blaney frowned. The suspicion that Chops was taking the rise was now firming in Blaney's mind but it was difficult to be certain such was the open nature of Chops' smiling countenance.

'Apparently he was in London for the last few days,' said Winslow. 'We traced his whereabouts and sent him a message and asked him to return immediately. He may be back by now.'

The four men were soon in the car driving to the outskirts of Exeter. The drive took them along the coast.

'Nice views but I'd get bored here pretty quickly,' said Wilkins staring out at the sea.

'Yes, I imagine Exeter would same rather tame by comparison,' agreed Chops. 'The opera, the ballet, theatre, art galleries – we have so little and you have so much.'

He fixed his eyebrows on Wilkins and raised his eyebrows. The sergeant's idea of culture was a sing song down at the Dog and Duck. Blaney looked horrified at his sergeant. By now, he was fully convinced that Chops was taking them for fools. This was a rather delicate matter. He could hardly say anything as he was subordinate to the chief inspector. However, Scotland Yard had primacy now in the investigation. He would deal with Hopcroft in his own way. Let him know where he stood.

They pulled up outside a block of flats that inspired nothing more than a desire to have done with the interview and get away. Thorpe was on the second floor.

'Do you mind waiting in the car?' asked Blaney.

'I do mind, dear fellow,' said Chops.

'We can't all of us go.'

'I agree. Wilkins and Winslow, my, they sound like a music hall duo, they can stay in the car while we speak to Mr Thorpe. Thereafter, I think we can happily hand over the responsibilities to Scotland Yard. I think you may find having local knowledge may be a benefit to you right now.'

Blaney looked like he might argue the point on this but, upon reflection, accepted the sense of Chops' suggestion. He nodded his head and said, 'Right, well, let's go and see if this chap is in or not.'

They walked up the stairs together. It occurred to the London man that he had not asked Chops yet why the man had spent time in prison. He did so now.

'He was a conscientious objector in the last war,' said Chops. 'I believe he spent a month in prison, hard labour, I understand.'

'Good,' murmured Blaney.

'Then he began his hunger strike.'

'Good Lord,' exclaimed Blaney. 'What an awful fellow. What happened then?'

'He went out to France in the end.'

'Quite right too. To fight?'

'He was a male nurse,' said Chops. This revelation stopped Blaney in his tracks. The frown he wore suggested that he didn't quite know what to make of the man they were about to meet.

They arrived at the door and were greeted by a man in his early forties. Cyril Thorpe was not the sort of man who entered a room unnoticed. He had the theatrical grace of someone who had long

160

since accepted he would never be able to announce himself the way he wished, so instead he made do with the rustle of a tailored scarf and a moustache so immaculately combed it could have had its own army rank.

'Gentlemen,' he said, as he showed them into the warm front room of his flat. Evidently he had only just returned from his week in London as he was still wearing his gloves indoors like someone auditioning for a Noël Coward revival.

Blaney stood awkwardly, as if unsure whether to offer a handshake or check the man for contraband. Chops, who had elected to stay seated in Thorpe's armchair like he owned the lease, offered a curt nod and a dry smile.

'Mr Thorpe, thank you for seeing us,' said Blaney, finally settling on standing stiffly by the fireplace, like a suit of armour lacking polish.

Thorpe unbuttoned his overcoat with elaborate ceremony. 'Well, I hardly had a choice, did I? It was something between an invitation and a conscription.'

'We were hoping,' said Blaney, a little less confidently now, 'that you might be able to help us with some background on a Mr Morrison. He was your...'

'Neighbour, yes. Although 'neighbour' suggests a degree of friendliness that would, I think, misrepresent our relationship rather wildly.' Thorpe lowered himself onto a small settee with the poise of a man who'd once read a book about posture and taken it personally.

'What was your relationship with Mr Morrison, exactly?' asked Blaney, pulling out his notebook and preparing for disappointment.

'We cordially detested one another,' Thorpe said matter-of-factly. 'Which is really the best you can hope for in some rural towns.'

Blaney looked to Chops for help, but the Devonshire man merely tilted his head and said, 'He's not wrong, you know.'

Thorpe smiled thinly and crossed his legs. 'Morrison and I had what one might call an understanding. He didn't talk to me, and I didn't tell him what I thought of his trousers.'

'Did you see much of him in the days before the incident?' Blaney asked, trying to steer things back to police work.

'No. I was in London, darling—er, Detective. You know that place with electricity after midnight and people who know how to pronounce 'Risotto'.'

There was no argument from Blaney on this but it was rather off topic.

'What took you to London?' Blaney asked, eyes narrowing in a way that suggested he thought the capital was where all sins were manufactured and exported.

'Why, I was there for a small exhibition,' Thorpe said airily.

'Art?' asked Chops, who was enjoying this more than he should.

'Something like that,' Thorpe replied with a wink.

Blaney didn't look amused. 'So you weren't here the night Morrison was murdered.'

'Correct. And before you ask, yes, there are people who can verify my whereabouts. I even have a hotel receipt, if you're the sort of man who enjoys that kind of thing.'

'We'll want to see it,' Blaney muttered, scribbling furiously.

'Of course you will,' Thorpe purred.

Chops cleared his throat. 'Mr Thorpe, did you ever have any dealings with Morrison outside your mutual contempt?'

'Hardly. We coexisted, barely. He once threw a dead squirrel into my bin and I responded by placing a well-chosen quotation from Oscar Wilde on his window. The man believed literature was a Communist invention, so I imagine it unsettled him.'

Blaney blinked. 'Did you ever see anyone suspicious around his place? Any unusual visitors?'

Thorpe raised an eyebrow. 'Define 'suspicious'. We're in the middle of a war. If I reported everyone who looked like they didn't belong, we'd have to set up a local branch of MI5 in the village hall.'

162

Chops leaned forward, elbows on knees. 'Even so. Anyone stick out? Unfamiliar face, odd car, strange hours?'

Thorpe considered this for a moment, then shrugged. 'He did receive a parcel about a fortnight before I left for London. Rather large. Delivered by a man I didn't recognise. Wearing a cap far too jaunty to be legitimate. Beyond that, no. Nothing worth writing to *The Times* about.'

'Could have been supplies,' Chops said, glancing at Blaney.

'Could have been anything,' Blaney replied.

Thorpe was watching them with a faintly amused expression. 'Are you hoping I'll break down in a fit of guilt and confess to doing him in with a pair of fire tongs?'

'No,' said Chops. 'I think if you'd done it, it would've involved something far more dramatic.'

Thorpe inclined his head. 'Now you're just flattering me, although you don't know how I might have used the fire tongs on Mr Morrison.'

'I think I can guess,' suggested Chops, eyes smiling, mouth serious.

Blaney bristled. 'We're simply gathering statements, Mr Thorpe.'

'Yes, yes,' Thorpe replied, waving a hand. 'I'll make you tea if you like. Or would that frighten the Yard too much?'

It was all too much for Blaney. The arrival of a Yorkshire Terrier into the room wearing a small pink bow was the signal for the detective to cut his losses. Thorpe did not strike him as a man with links to the underworld. In fact, Thorpe did not strike him as much of a man at all.

'We'll be in touch if we need anything further,' Blaney said, already closing his notebook and rising to leave.

Thorpe stood as well, eyes twinkling. 'Do take care out there, Inspector. There are all sorts of disreputable types about these days. One never knows what foul villainy may be afoot.'

'Thank you,' Blaney said shortly, already making for the door. At pace.

163

Chops lingered a moment.

'Mr Thorpe,' he said. 'Do you think Morrison had enemies?'

Thorpe's smile slipped just slightly. 'I think Morrison was the sort of man who saw enemies in every reflection. It wouldn't surprise me if he made some. But whether any of them were real... well, that's your job, isn't it?'

Chops nodded slowly. 'That it is. Thank you for your time.'

As they stepped back out into the cold air, Blaney muttered, 'Bloody locals.'

Chops chuckled. 'He rather enjoyed making you uncomfortable, I think.'

'That was mutual.'

'Still,' Chops said, glancing back at the house, 'he's sharp. If he knew something, I think he'd have told us. If only to be contrary.'

'Let's hope our next interview is less of a pantomime,' Blaney muttered, already turning up his collar against the wind.

But Chops wasn't so sure. Out here, pantomime and murder walked hand in hand. They hurried down the stairs to the entrance.

'By the way, where is this fellow Finch serving his time?' Chops asked.

'Dartmoor,' said Blaney

'Then you'll want to interview him,' said Chops. 'Who is he?'

'Name's Jack Finch. Nasty piece of work, though clever. We believe he was part of a larger outfit, perhaps travelling between counties.'

They reached the car and climbed in. Chops updated the two men on the interview, as they drove back to the police station. Along the way, Chops informed Winslow that they had one of the gang who had robbed the bank in Battersea residing at His Majesty's pleasure in Dartmoor.

'Can we come with you?' asked Winslow.

Blaney hesitated. 'We have our procedures. You and Winslow have been helpful, but this case now falls under our jurisdiction.'

Winslow's voice was bristling with barely contained anger. He said, 'With respect, sir, we know the area, the people. If the gang left any trace here, we're your best chance at finding it.'

Blaney sniffed again. 'Local knowledge is all well and good when you're dealing with poachers and sheep rustlers, Winslow. This is organised crime.'

There was a tense silence. Chops leaned forward, his voice calm but firm.

'Let me come to Dartmoor with you. Just to observe. If this Finch fellow is involved, it might help if someone local asks the questions. He may have let something slip before.'

Blaney looked as if he might refuse, but Wilkins murmured something under his breath. Blaney gave a curt nod.

'Very well. But your role should be to observe, Chief Inspector. We run the interview.'

'Perfectly,' Chops said, smiling insincerely.

They decided to travel the next morning. As the Yard men departed to find their lodgings, Winslow turned to Chops.

'Observe, he says. I can hardly wait.'

Chops chuckled. 'Let him do his strutting. We'll find our answers yet.'

165

Friday 20ᵗʰ December 1940

Carol was beginning to dread the sound of the telephone. Each time it rang, her breath caught in her throat and her hand froze midway to the receiver, as though some final, terrible truth were about to be revealed. This morning was no different. The shrill ring broke the silence of the drawing room where she'd been attempting to sew a torn button back on Benjy's cardigan. The thread slipped from her fingers.

She crossed the hall slowly, the floorboards cold under her feet, and lifted the receiver.

'Lady Sinclair?' said the clipped voice on the other end. 'This is Station Commander Bill at RAF Headquarters. I'm afraid we have no further news at present about your husband. We're still working through all the usual channels. These things can take time.'

Carol murmured her thanks, though the words scraped her throat dry. After she hung up, she leaned for a moment against the hallway wall, allowing the chill of the plaster to cool her skin. She had hoped that today might bring better news. The knock at the door came five minutes later.

She pulled herself upright and opened it to find a young man, perhaps not yet twenty, in a police uniform, shifting nervously on the step. His cheeks were ruddy from the cold, and his cap was slightly too large for his head.

'Good morning, ma'am,' he said. 'I'm Constable Talbot. Chief Inspector Hopcroft sent me to patrol the estate grounds. I'll be

166

staying out of sight mostly, but I'm to keep watch for anything unusual.'

Carol blinked, the fog of fatigue and worry slowing her reaction. Then she nodded and opened the door wider. 'Come in, Constable. You'd better meet Mrs Parker and Mr Figgs. They keep the house running, and they'll make sure you're fed properly while you're here.'

Figgs emerged from the kitchen wiping his hands on a tea towel, and Mrs Parker followed close behind, her expression unreadable. Carol explained the situation quickly.

'You'll be patrolling outside,' she said, turning back to Talbot. 'But every few hours, I'd like you to check in. Have something to eat. Keep warm. This place gets bitterly cold by late afternoon.'

'Yes, ma'am. Thank you. That's kind.'

His eyes darted about, taking in the high ceilings and polished wood of the entrance hall. Carol noticed that despite his youth, his bearing was earnest. He seemed to understand the weight of what he had been tasked with, even if he wore it with a touch of uncertainty.

'Come along, I'll introduce you to the children,' she said.

They found Roger, Susan and Benjy in the morning room, sprawled out on the rug with a jigsaw puzzle that looked only half attempted. Roger looked up at the sound of the door and narrowed his eyes when he saw the uniform.

'Is something wrong?' he asked.

'No, nothing's wrong,' Carol said quickly. 'This is Constable Talbot. He'll be keeping an eye on things around the estate for the next few days, just to be safe.'

The children stared at him. Benjy gave him a gap-toothed smile.

'Are you going to arrest someone?' he asked hopefully.

Talbot flushed and chuckled nervously. 'Not unless I have to.'

Carol smiled faintly. 'He's here for your safety. That's all. Roger, Susan, don't you show him where the stables are? He'll need to get a sense of the grounds.'

As the children trailed out with the young constable in tow, Carol returned to the morning room. She paused by the window, watching them go. A brittle gust of wind fluttered the bare branches of the trees. December was fully upon them.

She stood for a moment longer, her hand resting against the glass. She had meant to steel herself this morning, to push away the grief and fear that had haunted her for days. But now, standing in the quiet of the room, she could feel it rising again like a tide.

She hadn't slept properly since the RAF had first called. She was still reeling from Cressida's visit the previous day, that awful scene in the parlour—her sister-in-law's clipped, sneering tones, and the venom thinly veiled by civility. And now, there was Roger.

That boy. That brave, clever boy who had seen something. Something the gang would rather no one had seen. And they had already murdered once. Carol wrapped her arms around herself. The thought of Roger's face, so composed, so adult at times, flashed in her mind. He didn't yet understand the danger he was in. And perhaps that was a blessing.

She moved to the writing desk and sat down heavily. She opened the drawer and pulled out a sheet of paper. For a moment, she simply stared at it. Then she took up a pen and began to write. The letter was to Charles.

She hadn't written since the day he'd gone missing, but something inside her now demanded it. It took her a few seconds to think of what she could write. There was so much to tell him and yet the words would not come. She started with the obvious. Then after a few moments she began to write slowly and then with a rush.

My dearest Charles,

I do not know whether this letter will ever reach you. I do not know whether you are alive or lost to me. But I must write, if only to feel closer to you.

There is a young constable now posted at Ravenley. Chops sent him. You remember Chops, of course—always looking as though he's just heard the most amusing joke, even when he hasn't said a word. He has been kind to me. Steady, reliable. He still makes you laugh.

This will all sound terribly confused but really a lot has happened and I'm getting ahead of myself.

We have three orphan siblings billeted with us at the moment. Roger is thirteen and a very mature for his years. Susan is a year younger and a dear girl. She is desperate to help. Little Benjy is nine. He is very frightened and missing his mother. She was killed in the bombing of London.

But I am frightened, Charles. The children, Roger especially, are in danger. There was a robbery at the bank in Exeter, and a man was murdered. And Roger saw one of them. The police think the gang may come back. It's unthinkable, and yet I cannot dismiss the possibility.

She paused, her hand trembling slightly. Outside, she heard a gust of laughter—the children and Talbot, no doubt, now examining the stables.

Mrs Parker has been a rock. So has Figgs. But I find myself adrift. There is no one here I can lean on. No one who knows me. Knows us.

Cressida came. She was as poisonous as ever, full of her own righteousness. She wanted me to send the children away. And for the first time, I found that I didn't want to. I felt something—anger, yes, but also a kind of pride. A determination I didn't know I possessed.

I want to keep them safe, Charles. I want to do right by them.

She lowered her pen and folded the letter. She wouldn't send it. But the act of writing it had calmed her. She placed it in the drawer and rose from the desk.

The front door opened and closed again, and a few minutes later, Roger's voice rang down the corridor.

'He's all right, you know!' he called. 'The constable. He's not as stuffy as I thought.'

Carol moved to the hallway, her hands smoothing down her skirt. Roger was hanging up his coat, cheeks pink from the cold.

'Thank you for showing him around,' she said.

Roger nodded. 'He says he used to play football for his school. I said we might have a game if he's off-duty tomorrow.'

Carol smiled. 'That sounds like a good idea.'

She didn't say what she was really thinking. That Talbot might not be off duty tomorrow. That the situation was still far from safe. That they were all clinging to a thread and pretending it was rope.

But for now, it was enough. The children were safe. There was a policeman at the house. And she had remembered, if only briefly, what it felt like to fight for something she believed in.

And somewhere, in some cold barracks or unfamiliar town, she hoped Charles was thinking of her, too.

Just after lunch, Carol drove to Exeter Hospital. It had been years since she had felt this particular kind of nervous anticipation, it was the sensation of taking one's future by the shoulders and giving it a firm shake. She had promised herself that this was not simply about defying Cressida. That had been the spark, perhaps, but now the commitment had taken root and grown into something larger, something she felt proud of.

The Royal Devon and Exeter Hospital came into view just after midday, a broad red-brick building with wide white windows and an austere façade. Carol manoeuvred into a narrow space near the side entrance reserved for hospital vehicles, then paused for a moment, hands still resting on the steering wheel.

Right, then, she told herself. No turning back now.

Inside the reception, she was directed to a side wing where the ambulance service was based. She presented herself at the desk to a tall, sandy-haired man in his thirties wearing an orderly's uniform. His tunic sleeves were rolled to the elbows and he had the practical, no-nonsense air of someone who had seen more than his fair share of wartime chaos.

'I'm here to see Mr Elgood. I've volunteered to join the ambulance service,' Carol said, adjusting the collar of her coat.

'Ah, yes, Mrs Sinclair, isn't it?' he said, extending a hand. 'You're expected. I'm Corporal Danvers. Mr Elgood's just stepped out for a moment, but I'll take you down to the yard. You'll be meeting the rest of the shift crew there. Hope you can handle a motor with a bit more weight than that posh little thing you parked outside.'

Carol smiled. 'You'd be surprised what I've had to handle in recent weeks, Corporal.'

The ambulance yard was bustling. Two vehicles were being hosed down by a pair of grim-faced orderlies, and another was reversing into a bay with a grating whine. The scent of petrol, bleach, and damp wool hung in the air.

Mr Elgood turned out to be a thin, pale man with glasses too large for his face and the clipped, precise manner of a schoolmaster. He wore a medical coat stained faintly with iodine, and he examined Carol with a gaze that felt as though it might see straight through pretence.

'Mrs Sinclair,' he said, shaking her hand. 'You understand this isn't a glamour post, I hope.'

'I'm not looking for glamour,' Carol replied, meeting his eyes. 'I want to help. I can drive, I can follow instructions, and I can keep calm.'

'Can you?' He raised one sceptical eyebrow. 'Then let's see what you can do. Danvers, give her the keys to Unit Four.'

Danvers tossed her the keys with a lopsided grin and led her over to a slightly battered Austin K2 ambulance. It loomed much larger than her saloon car, and the paint was chipped along the doors, but it had the solid look of something built to endure.

Carol climbed into the driver's seat and adjusted the mirrors. The gear stick was clunky, and the clutch felt a bit stiff, but nothing she couldn't manage.

'Take her round the yard,' Danvers called. 'Then out through the gate, round the block and back. Don't be shy, we need to know you can handle her in town. In an emergency.'

Carol nodded and started the engine. It caught with a reluctant grumble, and she coaxed it into gear, easing the vehicle forward with a cautious confidence. The turning radius was tighter than she'd anticipated, and the weight took a moment to adjust to, but she kept the speed steady and gave herself extra room at corners.

As she turned back through the gates five minutes later, she saw Danvers and Elgood watching her from the kerb, their arms folded and expressions unreadable.

She parked neatly in the bay, set the brake, and climbed out.

'Well?' she asked, brushing a wisp of hair from her cheek.

'You didn't hit anything,' Danvers said, looking grudgingly impressed.

'And you didn't stall,' Elgood added. 'Not bad.'

'I told you I could drive.'

'We've had all sorts turning up since the war started,' Elgood said, leading her back towards the main building. 'One woman drove straight into a goose. Claimed it was sabotage.'

'Was it?'

'Hard to say,' mused Elgood. 'The goose survived. Look, I think we should do one more trip accompanied by Danvers. I want you to go into town and back. If you find a quiet stretch I want you to drive as if your life depended on it. Someone's may.'

'Drive quickly?'

'Quickly,' confirmed Danvers, who looked a little nervous.

They climbed back into the ambulance. The ambulance, a noble but rather lumbering creature by nature, had scarcely rolled beyond

172

the hospital gates when Danvers, with the air of a man seeking amusement on a rainy afternoon, said, 'Let's see what she can really do, shall we?' and directed Carol towards a quieter road on the outskirts of Exeter.

Once there, Carol gave the K2 a knowing pat on the dashboard, downshifted like a woman possessed, and sent the great beast hurtling along the tarmac with a surprising degree of verve. The hedgerows blurred, Danvers turned slightly green about the gills, and Carol, eyes alight and cheeks flushed, looked positively radiant. She had, after all, once terrified a succession of pre-war beaux by hurtling their Lagonda's and MGs round country bends at speeds more suited to Brooklands than Bridport.

As they screeched, more or less sideways, back into the hospital yard, Danvers extricated himself from the passenger seat with the reverence of one disembarking a Sopwith Camel post-dogfight and muttered to Elgood, as he straightened his jacket, 'She'll do.'

They returned to the break room, where two other women sat sipping tea from chipped mugs—one in her forties with a brisk manner and hair in tight curls, the other younger, perhaps twenty, looking pale but determined. Carol was introduced, and there was a general murmur of approval when Elgood informed them she'd passed the driving trial.

'We need more drivers,' the older woman said, whose name was May. 'They've taken four of the lads for conscription this month alone. We're down to half strength on night shifts.'

'Can you start tomorrow?' Elgood asked. 'We'll give you a six-hour evening shift to start with. Eighteen hundred to midnight. You'll ride with May here. She knows every cobbled street and ditch in this city.'

'I'll be here,' Carol said. 'Thank you for the opportunity.'

She left the hospital a little after one o'clock, her nerves slowly giving way to a warm flush of purpose. There was something grounding about being part of a system that had no time for snobbery or social standing. You were either useful or you weren't.

173

And Carol Sinclair, she now realised with some quiet pride, had been deemed useful.

As she pulled away in her own car and turned back onto the High Street, she felt a small spark of something she had not felt in days: the beginnings of hope.

The winter air had a crispness to it that stung the cheeks but made everything feel fresher, cleaner somehow. Roger, Susan, and Benjy trudged through the thin frost that crackled under their boots as they wandered beyond the familiar hedgerows and across the wilder edges of the Ravenley estate. The trees stood bare now, their branches etched black against the pale sky, but it only added to the sense of mystery that accompanied exploration.

'Let's go that way,' Roger said, pointing past a low wall covered in ivy. 'I think there's something down by the copse. I saw a chimney once, when we came this way before.'

Susan hesitated. 'Should we? Carol said not to stray too far.'

Roger rolled his eyes but didn't argue. Benjy, of course, was already halfway over the wall. The frost still clung to the grass as the children picked their way through the woodland path that led to the cottage. Roger was out in front, full of purpose, with Susan close behind and Benjy scampering at their heels, hopping from one mossy stone to the next like a particularly energetic squirrel. The air was crisp, the kind that made your nose tingle and your breath rise in plumes, and every sound—the crunch of boots, the caw of a distant crow seemed to echo more loudly than usual.

It was Roger who heard it first, a strange, frantic rustling ahead in the undergrowth. He stopped sharply, holding out a hand.

'Did you hear that?' he whispered.

Susan nodded. 'Something's caught.'

They crept forward carefully, pushing through low-hanging branches and brittle ferns until they came to a small clearing. There, lying on its side and struggling pitifully, was a young deer. Its hind leg was caught in a snare, the cruel wire digging into the flesh, now raw and bloodied from its desperate attempts to escape.

Benjy gasped. 'Oh no! Look at its leg!'

The deer twisted its head, eyes wide with fear, chest heaving in panic. Susan knelt down instinctively, murmuring softly.

'It's all right... we're not going to hurt you...'

Roger's heart was thudding. He dropped to his knees beside the creature, his fingers already reaching into his coat pocket.

'My knife,' he said urgently. 'I've got my knife.'

He pulled it free: a red Swiss Army penknife, well-polished and clearly loved, its blade already flicked out and ready. He glanced at the snare, then at the deer.

'Hold its head, Susan. Gently. Just so it doesn't thrash.'

She obeyed, stroking the deer's neck with one hand, murmuring nonsense in a soothing tone. Roger leaned in, steadying the snare with one hand while he worked the blade under the wire with the other. It was tough going; the wire was tight and the angle awkward.

'Hurry, Roger,' Benjy said anxiously. 'It's shaking.'

'I'm trying,' Roger muttered, teeth gritted.

Finally, after what felt like an age, the wire gave way with a metallic twang, snapping back into the underbrush. The deer kicked once, wildly, then scrambled to its feet. For a moment it stood frozen, staring at the three children. Then, without a sound, it bounded off into the trees, its white tail flashing once before it vanished from sight.

They sat back on their heels, breathless.

'Well done, Roger,' Susan said. 'That was brave.'

Roger flushed but said nothing, running his thumb along the blade before folding the knife away and tucking it back into his coat. It was his proudest possession, given to him by his father the Christmas before he disappeared, and now more valuable than ever.

176

'I hope it'll be all right,' Benjy said quietly.

'It'll be sore,' Roger replied. 'But it'll run. That's the main thing.'

The three of them stood in silence for a moment, the forest calm again around them. Then Roger turned and nodded towards the path.

The cottage came into view a few minutes later, nestled at the edge of the woods, its thatched roof mossy and sagging slightly, but still neat and clearly tended to. Smoke curled from the chimney in a steady plume. A dog barked once from inside, then quieted.

Roger knocked on the weathered wooden door, and after a moment it opened to reveal a man of about seventy, stout and broad-shouldered, with a shock of white hair and bright blue eyes. He wore a heavy woollen jumper, corduroy trousers and smelled faintly of pipe tobacco and earth.

'Well, now. You must be the young 'uns up at the big house,' he said, squinting at them. 'I'm Ned Turnbull. Come in, come in. It's too cold to be standing on doorsteps.'

The children stepped into a warm, cluttered room filled with books, boots, a cast-iron stove humming in the corner, and the comforting scent of something stewing. A collie raised its head from a rug and wagged its tail lazily.

'We didn't mean to bother you,' Susan said, suddenly shy.

'Nonsense,' Ned replied. 'Always glad of company, me. Besides, I've heard all about you three. Talk of the estate, you are.'

Roger flushed slightly but said, 'We were just exploring.'

'As you should,' Ned said, handing them each a mug of warm apple cider. 'Exploring's how you find things worth knowing.'

'We found a deer,' Benjy blurted, unable to contain himself.

Roger stepped forward. 'It was caught in a snare, just off the lower path near the birch grove. Its back leg was stuck, tight. I cut it free with my knife.'

Ned's expression changed in an instant—his brow darkened, and he set the kettle down with a decisive thump. 'A snare, you say. On Ravenley land?'

177

Roger nodded. 'Yes. Looked new. Not rusted or anything.'

'Blasted poachers,' Ned muttered. 'Thought I'd chased the last of them off last winter. Still one or two slippery enough to creep in from the edge of the common, I suppose. Vultures, the lot of 'em.'

He straightened up, eyes sharper now. 'You did right, lad. Brave thing to do—those wires can bite if you're not careful.'

'I used my penknife,' Roger said, a hint of pride in his voice.

'Aye,' Ned replied, and this time there was approval in his tone. 'A good knife's a useful friend. And a kind hand's rarer still. That deer owes you its life.'

Susan laid her gloves on the windowsill. 'Will it survive, do you think?'

'If it can keep weight off that leg for a bit, and the wound doesn't turn bad, it's got a chance,' said Ned. He shook his head and looked grave. Then he added, a trace of guilt in his voice, 'That's how I came to be here. Used to be a poacher, believe it or not. Mr Sinclair's father, the Viscount, caught me, tried to scare me straight. Talked me into putting my skills to good use.'

'You were a poacher?' Benjy said, eyes wide.

'And a good one,' Ned said with a chuckle. 'But they turned me gamekeeper. Never looked back. Fifty years ago now. Fifty years. Where did the time go?'

The children sat on stools and listened as he spoke of his work on the estate, his careful tracking of deer and foxes, his quiet war with poachers who weren't quite as honourable as he had been.

On the mantel above the fire was a sepia photograph of a smiling woman with kind eyes.

'Is that your wife?' Susan asked gently.

Ned's face softened. 'That's Elsie. Lost her in the Spanish flu, back in nineteen. Never remarried. She was the love of my life.'

There was a pause, the silence respectful.

'Our mum was called Daisy,' Benjy said. 'She died in the bombing.'

178

Ned looked at him with quiet understanding. 'I'm sorry, lad. That's a cruel loss.'

Susan nodded. 'She was beautiful. She had red hair and laughed all the time. She made up stories for us at bedtime. Silly ones, with elephants and typewriters and flying umbrellas.'

Roger looked down at his cider. 'We miss her a lot.'

Ned stood slowly, walked to the fire, and took a long breath.

'It never stops hurting,' he said, stirring the logs with the poker. 'But it changes. You find the good bits in the memory, and those bits stay with you. You three—you're young. You've got life ahead of you, full of all sorts of things. It won't always be like this.'

They were quiet after that, and Ned let them sit with their thoughts. The collie stretched and thumped its tail gently.

'Carol says we're to stay close to the house for now,' Roger said after a moment. 'Because of the robbery.'

Ned raised an eyebrow but he was smiling too. 'Carol? Well, sounds like you've become firm friends if you can call Mrs Sinclair, Carol.

'She asked us too,' said Benjy defensively.

'I don't doubt it lad. Modern ways. I don't hold with all of them. Anyway, you were saying about the robbery. I heard about that. You were the one who saw them, weren't you?'

Roger nodded. 'One of them saw me too.'

Ned rubbed his chin. 'Then you'd best be sharp. Not scared, mind—but sharp. If something doesn't feel right, it probably isn't. There are bad men in the world. Seen 'em. Fought 'em.'

'You were in the war?' Susan asked.

He gestured to a sideboard. On it was a framed photograph of a young man in a First World War uniform, smiling with an easy confidence. Next to it, a small bronze medal in a case.

'That was me,' Ned said, his voice thickening slightly. 'Long time ago.'

There was silence again, and the children sensed this was something important.

Eventually, Ned stood. 'Well, I best get back to checking the fences. You three mind what Mrs Sinclair says. And if ever you want to come back, the door's always open.'

They rose and thanked him, the collie following them to the gate and watching with a solemn expression.

When they had gone, Ned closed the door softly and walked back into the warm, silent room. He looked at the photographs on the sideboard.

'They're good kids, Elsie,' he murmured, brushing his fingers along the frame of her picture. 'You'd like 'em. Remind me of us, a little. The way we used to dream.'

Ned reached for the photograph on the sideboard, his weathered fingers brushing the edge of the simple wooden frame. Inside it, a young man in World War One uniform smiled out at the world, his eyes full of mischief and promise. Beside the photograph sat a single medal, polished until it gleamed. 'Frank,' Ned said quietly, almost to himself. 'My boy.' He held the picture a moment longer, then bowed his head. The tears came without sound, slipping down the creases of his cheeks. He didn't bother to wipe them away. Whatever else the day had brought, this was the moment that stilled everything—the ache of love and loss, that would never leave him. That he never wanted to leave him. When he felt the sting of tears, he knew they were with him still.

And always would be.

The next morning, the four men drove in stiff silence through the bleak Dartmoor landscape, mist clinging to the ground like a living thing. Dartmoor Prison loomed ahead, grim and hulking, its high stone walls as forbidding as any fortress.

Inside, they were met by Governor Benjy, who remembered Chops from a previous visit. He led them to an interview room, where Jack Finch sat at a table, manacled but looking perfectly at ease. He was younger than expected, with bright, calculating eyes and a crooked grin.

Blaney cleared his throat in a manner that suggested this was a distasteful business, best gotten through quickly and with minimal fuss.

'Mr Finch,' he began, crisply, 'I trust you understand why we're here.'

Finch, whose eyelids moved only just enough to indicate he'd heard, offered a smile of such irritating indolence that Sergeant Wilkins, standing in the background with his notebook at the ready, twitched involuntarily.

'Oh, I daresay I do, Inspector,' Finch drawled. 'You're here to try your hand at wringing information out of me. Thought, perhaps, a change of scenery from Scotland Yard might inspire some fresh confessions?'

Blaney ignored the jibe. 'We're revisiting the circumstances of the recent Exeter bank robbery. The methods used then bear certain striking resemblances to the present case.'

'Yes, I heard about your little country caper,' Finch said, his eyes glinting. 'Rather unfortunate about the nightwatchman, wasn't it? Messy. Definitely not my style.'

Blaney narrowed his eyes. 'Are you denying you had any involvement?'

Finch spread his arms out wide and said, 'A bit difficult, isn't it?,' Finch said smoothly. 'I've been here, in this charming establishment, for some months now. Bit difficult to knock off a bank while one's locked up, wouldn't you say?'

'You had associates, Mr Finch. We have reason to believe you were part of a larger organisation, and it's not inconceivable that they've taken up where you left off. A word from you might go some way toward easing your circumstances.'

Finch laughed, a dry, derisive sound that echoed unpleasantly in the stone-walled chamber. 'Spoken like a man who hasn't spent much time in Dartmoor. Let me save you some breath, Inspector. There's nothing for you here. No names. No useful scraps. Nothing. I mean it. I know nothing and even if I did know something, you'd be the last to know.'

Blaney leaned slightly forward. 'You're facing a full sentence, Finch. One might think you'd welcome an opportunity to shave something off it.'

'And in exchange I give you what?' Finch cocked his head. 'A vague hint? A convenient scapegoat? You'll run off to your superiors with a scrap of tittle-tattle and I'll have bought myself a few miserable months in a different cell with a better view and a lifetime looking over my shoulder? No, thank you.'

Sergeant Wilkins shifted awkwardly, glancing at Blaney, who remained as still as a marble bust.

'Let me put it plainly,' Blaney said at last. 'A man was killed in this latest robbery. A nightwatchman. If your people, if your former associates, have taken to murder, the charge sheet will look rather different than it did before.'

Finch's smile vanished for the first time, but it wasn't replaced by fear, rather by something that looked suspiciously like contempt.

'Oh, I've no doubt it will,' he said. 'But I've told you, I'm not involved. And I've nothing to say about men I haven't seen in nearly half a year. If you can't manage to catch them yourselves, Inspector, I shouldn't think you'll find it easier here behind these walls.'

Blaney rose, smoothing the front of his coat with studied precision. 'I see. Very well, Mr Finch. Thank you for your... candour.'

Finch grinned. 'Any time. Do pop back again if you're ever in the area. The conversation's simply riveting.'

As Blaney turned to go, Finch called out, his voice echoing with deliberate cheer. 'Oh, and Inspector? Do send my love to the countryside. I've always said robbing banks among the hedgerows and haystacks had a certain rustic charm. Shame about the blood, though. Spoils the landscape.'

Blaney paused, only for a moment, then strode from the room with Wilkins close behind, his lips pressed into a thin, bloodless line.

'Thinks he's clever,' Wilkins muttered once they were out of earshot.

Blaney did not reply. He was already considering his next move.

Finally, Chops leaned forward.

'How's the food here, Jack? They still do the boiled beef Tuesdays?'

Finch smirked. 'Still as grey as ever.'

'Did you know him?' asked Chops conversationally.

The smile on Finch's face faded, 'Who?'

'Morrison. Nightwatchman. Ex-army. Ex-Dartmoor. Your paths must have crossed.'

Finch said nothing.

'They held the bank manager's family hostage. Wife, two children. Put a gun to their heads while they cracked the safe.'

Finch's face hardened.

'That wasn't me. Never touched women or children. Never will.'

183

Wilkins leaned forward. 'Names, Finch. We need names.'

Finch snorted. 'Even if I had one, I wouldn't live to see breakfast tomorrow.'

The interview yielded no names, but Chops noted the tension in Finch's voice when he spoke of the murder. The man was a thief, but he had a code. Someone out there had broken it.

As they left the prison, Blaney was tight-lipped, but Chops caught Wilkins glancing back over his shoulder, brows furrowed.

Back in the car, Blaney sighed. 'Complete waste of time.'

'I'm not so sure,' Chops said quietly.

Wilkins looked out at the moor. 'Someone out there scares Finch. That might be the break we need.'

Blaney scoffed, but Winslow caught Chops' eye and gave a subtle nod.

It wasn't much, but it was something.

And sometimes, Chops knew, that was all you needed to keep going.

Carol had just hung up her coat when she heard the knock at the back door—a brisk, familiar rap that could only belong to one man. She opened it to find Chops standing there, his overcoat damp at the shoulders and a faint smile playing about his lips.

'Heard you've been whizzing about in ambulances,' he said without preamble, stepping into the warmth of the hallway. 'Rather impressive, if I may say so.' Carol, flushed from the wind and the nerves of her driving trial, managed a tired smile.

'I've been told I'll do,' she said modestly, brushing a loose strand of hair from her forehead. Chops nodded approvingly.

'That's good. The country needs more women like you.' He glanced at the clock. 'I've just come to say Scotland Yard will be paying a visit this evening. They'd like to speak to Roger, if you're agreeable.'

184

Carol stiffened, but only slightly. She said, 'Yes, of course. If it helps.' She hesitated, then added more softly, 'I'm sorry they're taking you off the case.' Chops met her eyes, the corner of his mouth quirking in what might have been amusement or regret—it was hard to tell with him.

'Comes with the job,' he said breezily. 'Just because I'm off a case doesn't mean I will stop investigating it. I fear these gentlemen are a little too certain they are right. They could do with practising a little humility.'

Carol looked at him with an arched eyebrow.

'Humility, Chops? Not a word I would have associated with you.'

'I hide my doubts behind a cloak of confidence, my dear.'

Carol's eyes narrowed as she smiled at the detective.

'No leads?'

'None. In fact, fewer than none. The gang have disappeared.'

'To London?' asked Carol, hopefully. The concern returned to her face.

'I wouldn't be certain of that,' said Chops, with a raised eyebrow. 'Let's not take any chances. In the meantime, Talbot stays. I'll continue to look. My sense is that this was more local than our friends from the Yards think. I might be wrong. I hope I am. Let's see.'

He took his leave soon after, the wind catching the door as he pulled it shut. Outside, he found young Constable Talbot circling the western hedge-line, his breath rising in pale clouds.

'Anything to report?' Chops asked.

Talbot shook his head. 'All quiet, sir.' Chops studied him a moment.

'Would you be willing to stay the night in the house? I'm afraid we've no spare men to relieve you just yet.'

The young man blinked, then nodded with quiet determination. 'Of course, sir. Happy to do my part.' Chops gave a grunt of approval and turned back toward the house; his shoulders hunched against the evening chill.

The morning mist clung to the barbed wire as Charles Sinclair rubbed his hands together against the chill. He adjusted his collar but this was a forlorn hope that it would combat the chill. The camp was quiet, save for the occasional bark of a German guard or the distant murmur of men shuffling towards the latrines. Another day in captivity. Another day closer to madness, or escape.

'Look alive, chaps,' murmured Lieutenant Pembridge, nodding towards the gates. 'Truck's coming in.'

Charles straightened, watching as the battered Opel lorry rumbled through the gates, its engine coughing like a lifelong smoker. Two German soldiers sat in the cab; their faces pinched with boredom. It brought supplies of food, blankets, medical provisions, though precious little of anything useful. The guards barked orders in clipped German, and the British prisoners obeyed without resistance. They knew better than to invite punishment over something as mundane as supply duty.

'You lot!' A guard jabbed his rifle towards the British prisoners. 'Help unload!'

Charles exchanged a glance with Fletcher. The Germans never let them near deliveries unless they were short-handed. Something was off. Still, orders were orders. He fell into line with the others, trudging towards the truck as the tailgate dropped with a clang.

'Right, easy does it,' Pembridge muttered as they hefted the first crate. 'No sudden moves. Don't give the bastards an excuse.'

The work was monotonous: box after box hauled into the dim storeroom, their contents a mystery. But then the Germans began shifting a separate stack towards the truck, their movements brisk, almost nervous.

Charles slowed, watching as a sergeant prised open one of the crates with his bayonet. Inside were tins. Bully beef, by the look of it. The German grunted, jabbing the butt of his rifle into the box to check beneath. Then it happened. The men heard a gasp of pain. The German sergeant leapt back, yelling as the lid burst open, and a man tumbled out, blinking in the daylight. A British soldier.

'Bloody hell,' breathed Fletcher.

The hidden man was thin, his uniform filthy, but his eyes were sharp with defiance. Before he could speak, the sergeant seized him by the collar, snarling something in German. Another guard swung his rifle butt straight into the man's ribs. The man grunted in pain.

A collective growl rose from the British prisoners.

'Oi! That's enough!' someone shouted.

The Germans ignored them, dragging the escapee to his feet. Another blow sent him sprawling. Charles' fists clenched. Around him, the air thickened with rage. The atmosphere was febrile. And then it exploded.

A burly Scotsman, McTavish, lunged at the nearest guard, wrenching the rifle from his hands. Another prisoner tackled a second German to the ground. Shouts erupted. Fists flew. The guards, outnumbered, scrambled back, bellowing for reinforcements.

Charles' pulse roared in his ears. This was it—the distraction he needed. While the brawl surged, he edged backwards, then bolted for the truck. The cab door creaked as he yanked it open. The keys were still in the ignition.

God, let this work.

He twisted the key. The engine sputtered—then roared to life. A German turned, eyes widening. '*Halt!*'

187

Charles slammed the gearstick into first and stamped on the accelerator. The truck lurched forward, wheels spinning in the mud before catching. Shouts erupted behind him. A shot rang out, then another.

Too late.

The gates loomed ahead. Two guards scrambled to close them. Charles gritted his teeth and *pushed the pedal harder.* Wood splintered. Metal shrieked. The truck burst through, careening onto the road beyond. Bullets whined past the cab. One shattered the side mirror. Another pinged off the bonnet. Charles hunched low, steering blindly as the camp vanished in the rear-view mirror. The forest rose ahead—thick, dark, salvation. Then the engine coughed.

'No—' He slapped the dashboard. 'Not now!'

Another splutter. A dying wheeze. The truck rolled to a halt just as the trees closed around him. Charles leapt out, heart hammering. Petrol. It had to be. He dropped to his knees, checking the tank, and swore.

Bullet holes. Three of them. The fuel had bled out onto the road. Shouts echoed in the distance. Dogs barked.

Run.

He plunged into the forest, branches whipping at his face. His lungs burned. His legs ached. But he didn't stop. The barking grew louder. Then, a new sound. A low, rhythmic *clack-clack* beneath his feet. Train tracks. Charles dropped to the ground, pressing his ear to the cold metal. A vibration. Distant, but growing.

The shouts were closer now. The dogs—*Christ, the dogs*—were nearly upon him. Then, like a miracle, the train appeared, rounding the bend in a cloud of steam. It was moving fast. Too fast?

There was no choice.

The soldiers burst through the trees just as the engine roared past. Charles sprinted across the tracks, timing his jump. His fingers caught a ladder. He hauled himself up, legs dangling for one terrifying second before he scrambled onto the carriage roof. Below, the Germans shouted, rifles raised. A shot zipped past his ear. Then

188

the train rounded another bend, and the camp, the dogs, the bullets, the war, vanished behind him. Charles collapsed onto the roof, gasping.

Now came the real question.

Where the hell was this train headed?

Around seven-thirty in the evening, the children heard the thud of car doors shutting at the front, followed by the heavy knock at the front door. Figgs answered, his usual unflappable manner perhaps a touch more rigid than usual, and moments later, two men were ushered in. They gathered by the door of the drawing room and listened as the two policemen were met by Carol. Roger opened the door of the room slightly and gazed out at the scene.

'Mrs Sinclair,' said the taller of the detectives, stepping forward with a crisp nod. 'Detective Inspector Basil Blaney. This is Detective Sergeant Wilkins.'

Carol extended her hand and offered a polite smile. 'Do come in.'

'Thank you for agreeing to meet with us,' Blaney said, consulting a small leather notebook as though this were a routine interview with a tradesman, not a grieving household in the middle of a crisis.

'I understand you'll want to speak with young Roger,' Carol said, her tone steady, though she could already feel a flush of protective indignation rising at the thought of her children being interrogated by such a man.

'Yes,' Blaney said briskly. 'We'll need to go over his statement again, in person. These matters often rest on the smallest detail.'

Carol's lips tightened. 'Of course. But I must ask that you proceed gently. Roger and the others are... well, they've suffered a recent trauma. Their mother was killed in the bombing raids. They've only been with us a short while.'

Wilkins, who had thus far remained silent, glanced up with a flicker of sympathy in his eyes. Blaney, however, merely made a note in his book.

'Yes, we heard that they're evacuees,' replied Blaney, without looking up.

'Not exactly,' Carol said, her voice cooling. 'They're orphans. From London. They were placed with us shortly after their mother's death. We've done our best to offer them stability and some sense of normal life, though I'm afraid there's no such thing anymore.'

Blaney nodded, businesslike. 'I see. And they've not been attending school?'

'No,' Carol replied, the faintest edge to her voice now. 'We've arranged for them to begin at the local school in January. In fact, they will visit the school tomorrow to meet the staff. For now, we felt it was best they remain at home. They need time to adjust. They've lost everything.'

There was a brief silence as Blaney made another note.

'Of course,' he said finally, though his tone suggested he thought very little of such sentiment. 'Children can be resilient, Mrs Sinclair. Often more than we expect.'

'Or far less,' Carol countered quietly, meeting his gaze.

Wilkins cleared his throat and looked out of the window, perhaps uncomfortable with the growing tension. 'It's a lovely place here,' he said. 'Must be a comfort to them, all this space. And quiet.'

Carol's expression softened slightly. 'I hope so. I want them to feel safe here. That's why I hope your investigation can be conducted with the utmost discretion. I don't want them frightened all over again.'

Blaney finally closed his notebook. 'We'll be as brief as possible.'

Carol inclined her head. 'Very well. But I'll be present for the interview. And I must ask—do you think the gang might return? Should I be concerned about their safety?'

Blaney stood. 'We're pursuing several leads, Mrs Sinclair. I wouldn't be overly concerned. If the gang believes they've been identified, they're more likely to flee the area.'

'That may be,' Carol said evenly, 'but we've already seen what they're capable of.'

Blaney hesitated, then gave a curt nod. 'We'll keep you informed.'

There was something about Blaney that unsettled Roger and the children, not merely his manner, which was brusque to the point of rudeness, but the way he dismissed everything that wasn't directly useful to the case. Seeing that their conversation had ended, Roger quietly closed the door and pointed to the seats. He stayed on his feet by the door as if he were a host about to greet visitors.

Blaney and Wilkins entered with the air of men ticking a box at the end of a long day. Blaney gave a tight-lipped nod, while Wilkins offered a kind if faintly awkward smile. Carol smiled and was oddly impressed when she saw Roger on his feet waiting for the detectives. Perhaps this would not be so bad. He was a young man who would have to grow up quickly. So far, in Carol's estimation, he had handled the situation with astonishing maturity.

'Good evening,' Blaney said, glancing at the children as though assessing a row of items at a market stall. 'I understand you're Roger.'

'Yes, sir,' said Roger holding out his hand. This surprised Blaney and delighted Carol. Blaney shook it as did Wilkins.

'No need to stand,' Wilkins said quickly. 'We just want to ask you a few things. Nothing to worry about.'

Roger sat again, his back straight.

Blaney held up a small leather notebook and a worn envelope from his coat pocket. 'We'd just like to confirm a few details about what you saw. This won't take long.'

He drew out a photograph, creased and faintly smudged, and handed it to Roger.

'Do you recognise this man?'

192

Roger took the photo and stared at it. It showed a man in a flat cap and dark coat, looking away from the camera, but his profile was visible, as was the set of his shoulders—thick, with a slight stoop.

Roger frowned. 'It looks like him. But it was dark, and I only saw him for a second.' He stared at the photograph a little longer. Then he shook his head. 'No, I don't think it is him. The man's face I saw was longer. This is not him. The moustache is similar. And same colour too. Also, this man's eyes are dark, unless it's the photograph. The man I saw had clear eyes.'

The look on the faces of the two men suggested this was not the answer they wanted never mind anticipated.

There was a trace of irritation in Blaney's voice when he said, 'Are you sure? You said it was dark.

'I'm sure,' said Roger uncowed. Carol desperately wanted the man in the photograph to be the robber but just at that moment she could not have been any prouder of the young man who was evidently not going to tell a lie just to avoid upsetting the detective.

Blaney tried again. He said, 'Look at the photograph then close your eyes and try and recall the moment the car went past you. At speed.'

Roger corrected him, 'It slowed down at the corner before speeding off, sir. I saw him when it slowed down so I did have time. Not much but time. We looked at each other. Just looked. He had pale eyes. Cold-looking.'

Blaney sighed audibly which caused Wilkins to look up sharply. Carol was incensed by the detective's undisguised frustration.

'Detective Inspector Blaney, I believe that Roger is quite clear on the matter. The man in the photograph is not the man he saw in the car.'

There was a crispness to Carol's tone, a crispness that only be cultivated through generations of ancestors who've never had any doubts about rank and their position in the natural order of things: at the very top.

193

'Cold,' Blaney repeated, writing it down. 'Did he have a scar? A limp? Anything like that?'

'No,' Roger said again, frustration and anger rising in his chest. 'I'm sorry. I'd tell you if I could.'

Wilkins spoke more gently than Blaney who had more skills in breaking down suspect's alibis than dealing with children. 'You've done very well, Roger. And you too, Susan and Benjy. It's not easy, what you've all been through. We're very grateful.'

Benjy beamed, thinking it was praise for sitting still, and Susan gave a polite nod, her eyes never leaving Roger's face. Like Carol, she felt desperately proud of him.

'You didn't see anyone else?' asked the detective sergeant.

'No, sir. Just this man.'

'Susan, Benjy, did you see anyone?' asked Wilkins.

'No, sir,' chorused the two children.

Blaney closed the notebook with a snap. 'That's all, then. Thank you.'

The children stood politely. Roger handed the photograph back, feeling as though he'd failed some invisible test.

Carol rose and crossed the room and put her hand on Roger's shoulder which made him feel better. Then she stepped forward and offered her hand to each man in turn.

'I trust you found that helpful,' she said, her tone light but edged with faint irony.

Blaney gave a noncommittal grunt. 'It's something.'

'I'll see you out,' Carol said, leading them through the dimly lit corridor to the great front door. As Figgs moved to open it, she paused.

'If you need anything further,' she said coolly, 'you'll come to me first.'

Blaney gave the barest nod, already halfway through the door. Wilkins offered a more sincere parting. 'Good evening, Mrs Sinclair. Thank you.'

194

As the door closed behind them and the sound of their motorcar faded into the frosty night, Carol stood for a moment in the silence of the hall. Somewhere deeper in the house, a floorboard creaked. A log cracked in the hearth.

She let out a long breath and turned back to her drawing room, where the children waited. Roger looked up at her, uncertain.

'You did very well,' she said, sitting beside him. 'Truly. Your mother would have been very proud of you. I feel proud of you, too, for what it's worth.'

He nodded, but there was still a worried frown on his face. He said, 'I wish I could remember more.'

'You remembered what you could,' she said gently, brushing a hand across his hair. 'And that's enough.'

She glanced over at Susan and Benjy, both silent now in the warmth of the firelight.

'We're going to be all right,' Carol said softly, more to herself than to them.

Susan switched the radio on. Almost at once the roof filled with the warm, romantic voice of Al Bowlly singing *The Very Thought of You*. It was one of Carol's favourite songs. By the dreamy look in Susan's eyes, she suspected that young girl shared her view of the singer. They exchanged glances and both smiled.

Outside, the frost deepened across the lawns, and the darkness wrapped itself around Ravenley once more.

The pub had no name that Chops could see, or ever remember. It was simply known as *The Gravedigger's* due to the proximity of a place that a few of its former, frequent customers probably resided. He walked through a door with a peeling sign that once may have borne the image of a boar or stag, now so faded by smoke and time that only a few curled remnants of paint clung to the wood. The pub stood at the corner of a narrow, slanting street near the river, the sort of place honest folk avoided after nightfall. The air outside was damp with fog, clinging to the cobbles, and the glow from the windows cast a jaundiced light onto the pavement.

Inside, the atmosphere was thick with pipe smoke, the sour tang of spilled beer, and something vaguely medicinal that might have been a bad cologne or floor polish. The low ceiling seemed to press down on the assembled clientele, most of whom turned to glance as Chops stepped in, then quickly turned back.

He paused, taking off his gloves and shaking the damp from his coat. He saw the way shoulders stiffened and glances were exchanged. They recognised him.

It was clear that many in the pub recognised among whom, opinions were divided between amused loathing and amused respect.

He walked in slowly, not looming, not threatening, just steady. He had a way of moving that suggested he knew exactly how much space he took up and wasn't in the habit of apologising for it. The men at the nearest table muttered and made a quiet exodus to the far

196

side of the room. But not all of them backed away. A few lingered, curiosity or old grudges flickering in their eyes.

'Lefty,' Chops said amiably, tipping his head to a wiry man with a crooked jaw and an old scar above his eyebrow.

Lefty Cartwright blinked, then grinned. 'Well, well. Look what the cat's dragged in. Thought you were chasing robbers in the country.'

'Thirsty work,' Chops replied mildly. 'I hope this place still does that.'

Lefty laughed, showing a gold tooth. 'Just about. You want something that won't rot your guts, ask for the bottled stuff.'

'Noted,' Chops said, moving toward the bar.

Another figure leaned against the end of the counter, sharp suit long past its prime, a silk handkerchief wilting in the pocket. He raised a glass without enthusiasm.

'Giles,' Chops said.

'Inspector,' murmured Giles 'The Gent' Munnings with mock courtesy. 'You're far from Belgravia.'

Chops allowed a faint smile. 'Just keeping my feet on familiar ground.'

The barman was a squat man with a neck like a ham joint and a habit of wiping glasses that were already clean. He glanced up as Chops approached.

'What can I get you?'

'Bitter. In a clean glass, if that's not too revolutionary.'

The barman gave him a look but complied. Chops waited until the pint was in front of him before speaking again.

'I'm looking into someone. Morrison. Bit of a loner. Used to come in here now and then.'

The room didn't exactly fall silent, but the atmosphere became oddly tighter, expectant, like a gunfighter walking into a saloon, clad only his holster and gun.

The barman's expression didn't change. 'Screw, wasn't he?'

'That's right,' Chops said evenly. 'Dead now.'

'Yeah. I heard.'

'You ever serve him?'

The barman shrugged. 'Now and then. Always kept to himself. Drank bottled stout. Didn't talk much. Didn't seem to like company. Which is just as well, since no one liked him much either.'

Chops sipped his drink. 'Was that because he was a prison officer? Or because of something else?'

Lefty chimed in from his table. 'Bit of both, I reckon. He had a way of looking at people. Like we was bugs on a pin. One of those fellas who made you want to get up and leave when he walked in. Still, wasn't right what happened. You don't do that, do you?'

'I wouldn't know,' grinned Chops. He moved away from Left towards the bar. A couple of men moved out of his way to let him through. Chops thanked them with a smile.

The barman moved over to him.

'Hello, Chief Inspector. Haven't seen you in a while.'

Chops shrugged and said, 'I've been busy. How are things here? You don't seem to be short of customers despite the Germans and their occasional efforts to deny a man his pint.'

'They usually come after last bell,' laughed the barman. Chops laughed too.

'I'm looking to find out more about Morrison, the man that died in the bank raid. I hear that he occasionally drank here.'

'From time to time.'

'Anyone come in with him?' asked Chops. 'Or talk to him regular?'

'Not that I saw. Sometimes he'd sit in the back. Read the paper. Drink slow. Once or twice he met someone, I didn't catch a name. Bit posh for this place. Slick hair, overcoat. The kind of chap who smells like he owns half of Devon.'

Chops raised an eyebrow. 'He talk to Morrison like they were friends?'

'Didn't seem friendly. More like business. Quiet talk. Never stayed long. Morrison left first, usually.'

Chops looked thoughtful. 'You see that man again of late, or tonight even?'

The barman shook his head. 'Not that I recall.

'I don't suppose you might ask round?' said Chops in a low voice.

One might be forgiven for assuming that a chap in the barman line wouldn't go out of his way to do a favour for a member of His Majesty's constabulary. And, broadly speaking, that assumption would be sound. However, our man behind the bar was possessed of a finely tuned survival instinct and a keen sense of which way the wind was blowing.

When Inspector Chops asked him, ever so politely, to 'ask around,' Alf understood this to mean something quite specific. It meant: 'Be helpful, or life might get sticky.'

'Okay,' said the barman.

'I'd appreciate it.'

Chops finished the last of his pint, left a few coins on the bar, and stood. 'If anything comes back to you...'

'You'll be the first to know,' the barman said.

As Chops turned to go, Lefty called out, 'You think someone in here did him in, Inspector?'

Chops paused, adjusting his hat to the back of his head.

'I think someone did. And I think Morrison knew something he shouldn't.'

The pub watched him leave; the door swinging shut behind him with a soft thud. Outside, the fog had thickened, blurring the lamplight into golden pools on the cobbles. Chops pulled on his gloves, turned up his collar, and walked over to his car.

Chops let himself into the flat with the same deliberate quietness he used when entering a suspect's lair. Old habits. The lock clicked behind him with a finality that echoed in the stillness. No lights were on, but that suited him fine. He didn't need to see the peeling paint

199

in the hallway or the stack of unwashed dishes in the sink. The air had that faint, sour tang of a place left too much to its own devices — like the rooms had given up on ever being lived in properly.

From the shadows emerged a sleek black shape, padding silently across the floor with the dignity of a creature who had never doubted its right to exist. The cat wound itself around his ankles, tail like a question mark. Chops glanced down.

'All right, Moriarty,' he muttered. 'Still breathing, are you?'

The cat gave a low, rasping purr. Chops stooped stiffly to scratch behind its ears, then stepped around the animal and into the main room. There wasn't much to see. A battered armchair. A bookcase with more empty shelves than books. A half-drunk bottle of scotch beside an ashtray full of pipe ash. The room wasn't designed for comfort, only for function — and even that, grudgingly.

As he crossed towards the kitchen, he passed the small side table where the only framed photograph in the flat stood like a forgotten relic. A younger Chops stared out of it, straight-backed and hopeful in a suit a little too smart for him, beside a woman with auburn hair and a smile like a loaded gun.

He stopped. Looked at it for a moment. Long enough to feel the prick of memory, short enough to avoid dwelling in it.

'Cow,' he said with some venom before placing his fedora over the picture to cover her face. And then, with a breath like a shrug, he moved on.

In the kitchen, he opened a cupboard, extracted a tin, and upended it into a chipped bowl. Moriarty leapt onto the counter in a single fluid movement, ears forward, eyes gleaming with interest.

'There you go, professor,' Chops said, setting the bowl down. 'That's the closest either of us gets to a hot meal tonight.'

The cat ate without thanks. Chops watched him for a moment, then turned away and opened the scotch.

Some company, after all, was better than none.

The jolting of the truck was enough to jar teeth loose. Charles Sinclair sat on the cold wooden bench, his wrists still aching from the tightness of the restraints. He'd lost count of how long he'd been running before they'd caught him again. Somewhere in the forest, after the train had vanished and he'd thought—foolishly—that perhaps he had a real chance. That he was going home.

He wasn't.

The truck smelled of petrol, damp canvas, and the faint coppery tang of blood. He wasn't sure if it was his or someone else's. There were three others in the back with him: two Dutch soldiers, with grim, tight mouths and a habit of glancing side-eyed at anyone who moved too quickly, and a Frenchman with a trim moustache and a face so gaunt it looked carved. They hadn't been introduced, and the German guards made it clear—no speaking.

The truck bounced again, lifting them momentarily off their seats. The Dutchmen grunted but said nothing. The Frenchman raised his brows at Charles, then gave a small, rueful smile.

Charles had time to think. Too much, in fact. Every mile that passed, every lurch of the tyres against the pitted roads, ratcheted his nerves tighter. Was this it? A quiet road, a bullet to the back of the head, and the problem of a recaptured British officer would be conveniently resolved.

He could run, he thought. Wait for the truck to slow on a turn, hurl himself out, take his chances again. But his legs still ached from the last sprint, his ribs bruised from where the butt of a rifle had met

201

them. And the odds of getting far before they caught him again were laughable. Still, he couldn't shake the thought.

After nearly two hours, they began to slow. The engine grumbled into lower gears, the road surface smoother now, the rattle of cobblestones giving way to tarmac. Charles dared a glance through a small tear in the canvas. Buildings. Houses, a church spire, distant smokestacks. A town. That was something.

The truck drew to a halt, brakes hissing. Boots scraped on gravel. The tailgate dropped with a clatter and the guards barked orders in clipped German. The prisoners dismounted one by one, blinking against the wan afternoon light.

Charles looked around quickly. A square. Trees stripped bare by winter, children watching from behind doorways, curious but silent. No sign of where they were. Not France. Possibly Belgium. Maybe still Germany. Impossible to say.

They were herded into a stone building, heavy with the smell of coal smoke and boiled cabbage. A police station, by the look of it. Cells lined the corridor. Charles was shoved into one with the Frenchman. The Dutchmen were taken separately.

Inside, there was a narrow bunk, a bucket in the corner, and a tiny, barred window too high to reach. It wasn't the worst cell he'd seen. But it wasn't freedom, either.

He sat heavily on the bunk, and only then realised how bone-tired he was. Every muscle in his body throbbed. His stomach grumbled angrily, and he remembered that he hadn't eaten since the crust of bread he'd swiped before the escape.

The Frenchman sat opposite, watching him with a keen interest.

'They did not break you, then?' he asked in quiet, accented English.

Charles looked up. 'Not yet.'

'Good. They like to think we are weak. Sometimes they are right.' He extended a hand. 'Sergeant Justin Leclerc.'

'Charles Sinclair. RAF. Formerly.'

202

They shook hands. Leclerc leaned back, folding his arms. 'I was taken near Paris last week. I have no idea where we are now. You?'

Charles shook his head. 'Somewhere east, I think. Maybe Germany. Maybe still in Belgium.'

Leclerc sighed. 'They moved me three times in five days. Always at night. No questions. Just orders. They keep us guessing.'

Charles glanced at the door. 'Do you know those two Dutch chaps?'

'No. They are not talkers. They look at us as though we might be spies.'

'They could be,' Charles muttered. He'd met plenty of infiltrators dressed like allies.

Silence settled between them. The cold began to creep in. Leclerc stood and knocked on the door.

'They won't come,' Charles said. 'Not unless they're shouting.'

He was right.

They waited. The light outside dimmed. The noises of the town died away. Somewhere, a dog barked. Charles sat on the bunk and rested his head against the wall, fatigue finally overtaking his nerves. Just as he began to drift, footsteps approached. The door clanged open. A German officer stepped inside. He was tall, slender, with the glacial expression of someone who enjoyed his job. His uniform was impeccable. Not a speck of dust.

He switched to English without preamble.

'Gentlemen. I hope you are comfortable. I regret to inform you that you are considered problematic prisoners.'

Leclerc's eyebrows lifted. Charles remained silent but oddly pleased to be considered a problem. He had been a problematic schoolboy at Eton. It was nice to feel that he'd not grown up very much since then.

'Escapes. Disobedience. Refusal to cooperate. We do not appreciate such behaviour. And we do not reward it.'

'What is this place?' Charles asked.

203

'A temporary holding. You will be transferred tomorrow to a facility where... discipline is better enforced. You have left me no alternative, but to pass you on to Oflag IVc.'

'Off What?' said Charles. However, rather worryingly he noticed that the Frenchman's head shot up upon hearing the name of the new prison.

The officer smiled, a thin, humourless curve of the lips. 'Let us say it is a place from which no one escapes. It is a *Sonderlager*. A special prisoner-of-war camp in Saxony, from which there is no escape. It has another name.'

Leclerc chuckled, but it held no amusement. 'I have heard that before.'

The officer ignored him. 'You will be allowed to rest tonight. No talking. No noise.' He turned on his heel and left. The door slammed. The lock clicked. Charles exhaled slowly.

'You believe him?' asked Charles, turning to Leclerc.

Leclerc was already on the floor, trying to get comfortable. 'He believes it. But I do not plan to stay long enough to find out.'

Charles lay back and stared at the ceiling. His muscles throbbed. Hunger gnawed at him. But beneath it all was a pulse of fear he couldn't shake. It sounded as if this wasn't going to be like the last prison. The rules were changing.

'Fortress?' asked Charles. 'You know where they are sending us.'

Leclerc nodded at this.

'It is a place called Colditz.'

Saturday 21st December 1940

The morning was crisp and frost-laden as Carol guided the car down the winding lanes towards Belsaw-on-the-Moor. The heater in the car had long since given up any pretence of working, and she could see her breath curling in the air as she drove. In the back seat, Roger, Susan, and little Benjy huddled together under a tartan blanket, their faces a mixture of excitement and apprehension.

'Are we nearly there?' Benjy piped up for the third time in as many miles.

'Nearly,' Carol replied, glancing at him in the rear-view mirror. His round cheeks were pink with cold, his dark hair sticking up in tufts where he'd pulled his woollen hat off. 'Just over this next hill, I should think.'

Susan, ever the practical one, leaned forward. 'What if the other children don't like us?'

'You'll make friends quickly enough,' Carol assured her. 'And I'm sure there'll be others from different villages. It's a small school, but that just means you'll get more attention from the teachers.'

Roger, who had been uncharacteristically quiet, finally spoke. 'What's the schoolmaster like? The one who wrote the letter?'

'Mr Darby? I've never met him, but he seemed very polite in his correspondence,' Carol said. 'And Mrs Adams, the headmistress, sounds perfectly kind.'

The car crested the hill, and there, nestled in the valley below, was Belsaw-on-the-Moor. The village was little more than a cluster of stone cottages, a church with a squat tower, and a long, low building that could only be the schoolhouse. Smoke curled from its chimney, a welcoming sight against the winter sky.

As they pulled up outside, a tall, broad-shouldered man in a tweed jacket emerged from the schoolhouse, his dark hair slightly windswept. He waved as Carol stepped out of the car.

'Mrs Sinclair?' he called, walking towards her. There was just a hint of a limp in his gait. His voice was warm, his smile genuine.

'Yes, and you must be Mr Darby.' She extended her hand, which he shook firmly.

'Jonathan Darby, at your service,' he said, then turned his attention to the children, who had clambered out of the car and now stood in a nervous huddle. 'And these must be Roger, Susan, and Benjy.'

Benjy, emboldened by Mr Darby's friendly tone, stepped forward. 'Hello, sir.'

'No need for *sir*,' Mr Darby said with a laugh. 'Mr Darby will do just fine. Come along inside—Mrs Adams is waiting to meet you, and we've got the kettle on.'

The schoolhouse was cosy, the scent of woodsmoke and chalk dust mingling in the air. Mrs Adams appeared like a cavalry general on a hill overlooking the battlefield.

Having spent the better part of her sixty-odd years in India, where she had ruled a household and, it was whispered, an army compound, with fierce efficiency, a similarly disciplined approach would now be now applied to the Belsaw-on-the-Moor village school. She had returned to England a widow, but by no means a spent force. The subcontinent's loss was England's gain.

Her attire was a declaration of principles: stout shoes, the sort that could march unflinching through monsoons or Scottish bogs; tweeds that seemed to have been woven from the very fabric of British resilience; and a hat that suggested she was always, in spirit if not in fact, on her way to inspect something.

206

'Welcome, my dears,' she said, her voice authoritative and military-like but oddly, reassuring too. Her father had been a colonel, her husband a Brigadier. She eyed the children like they were on parade. Roger, Susan and Benjy seemed to divine this and stood a little straighter than normal. 'We're so pleased to have you join us. The other children are on their Christmas break just now, but you'll meet them in January.'

The inspection seemed to pass without any issues and Mrs Adams returned to her classroom.

Susan, ever observant, whispered to Roger, 'She talks like someone from an old book.'

Roger stifled a laugh, but Mr Darby caught the exchange and winked at them. 'Mrs Adams is a traditionalist, but don't let that fool you—she's sharper than any of us.'

Over tea and slices of seed cake, they discussed the school routine. There were two classes—the younger children taught by Mrs Adams, the older ones by Mr Darby. Lessons ran from nine until half past three, with a break for lunch, which the children would bring themselves unless they lived too far, in which case the school provided soup and bread.

'And what about games?' Roger asked, trying to sound casual, though Carol could see the eagerness in his eyes.

'Plenty of those,' Mr Darby said. 'Cricket and rounders in the summer, football in the winter, and we've even been known to organise a treasure hunt or two across the moors.'

Benjy's eyes lit up. 'Real treasure?'

'Well, perhaps not gold doubloons,' Mr Darby admitted, 'but I'll make sure there's a prize worth having.'

'May I speak to you a moment?' asked Carol to Jonathan. He nodded and they walked a little away from the children who were now with Mrs Adams getting acquainted.

'I wanted to bring you up to speed with their circumstances. I think it's only fair you understand where they're coming from.'

'Yes, of course,' Jonathan said, his expression softening. 'I've heard bits and pieces, but I'd appreciate the details.'

Carol gave a small sigh, staring down at her tea for a moment before beginning. 'Roger, Susan, and Benjy arrived in early November. They're from the East End. Their home was bombed. Their mother, Daisy, was killed during a night raid. Their father... well, he had disappeared some years earlier. So they've come to us with no family to speak of. Orphans, I'm afraid.'

Jonathan's brow furrowed. 'I'm so sorry. That must have been...'

'Yes, quite,' Carol said, brisk but not unkind. 'They've adjusted well, all things considered. But it's important to remember that they are grieving. Roger, the eldest, tries very hard to be grown-up about everything, but the weight of responsibility shows. Susan is a bright girl, thoughtful, perhaps a little too sensitive. And Benjy... he's still a baby, really. Ten years old. He cries for his mother sometimes, though he tries not to let the others see.'

Jonathan nodded, absorbing every word. 'I'll bear that in mind. I've taught children who've lost parents before, though not in quite such tragic circumstances. The war leaves little untouched, doesn't it?'

Carol's eyes met his. 'No. It doesn't.'

A moment passed between them, quiet, respectful.

'We've kept them away from school for the time being,' she explained. 'They needed time to breathe. To settle. They've had quite a shock, and I didn't think plunging them into a new environment with a whole new set of expectations would serve them well.'

Jonathan tilted his head. 'That seems entirely sensible. And frankly, I think most of the other children will be away with relatives or picking up measles until mid-January anyway. They'll have time to ease in.'

Carol gave a small smile. 'Good. I want them to feel that they're safe. That they can begin to build something again, even if it's only a normal school day with a lesson on fractions and a muddy game of football.'

'Football, yes,' Jonathan said with a grin. 'Roger already asked if we played regularly.'

Carol chuckled. 'That sounds like him.'

There was a pause then, not uncomfortable, but reflective. Jonathan leaned forward slightly, his elbows resting lightly on his knees.

'May I ask something, Mrs Sinclair?'

'Of course.'

'Why did you take them in? I know many families have done their duty with billeting, but three children is no small undertaking.'

Carol's smile faded a little, replaced by something softer. 'My husband, Charles, is in the RAF.' She stopped for a moment, not sure about how much to reveal. 'And my house... well, it was empty in all the wrong ways. Or to be entirely honest, it was my housekeeper's idea, Mrs Parker. It was a good idea, I now see. I'm glad she insisted.'

Jonathan looked at her, his expression unreadable but kind. 'You've done a good thing.'

Carol gave a small shrug. 'I only hope it's enough.'

'Well,' said Jonathan, standing, 'thank you for coming by. I'll look forward to seeing the children in January. I'll make sure they have a gentle start.'

Carol smiled. 'That's all I ask.'

He turned at the door, hesitating just slightly. 'You know, I think they're rather lucky. Not every billet turns into a home.'

Carol stood still for a moment after he'd gone, the warmth of his words lingering in the quiet. Then she sighed, brushed a lock of hair from her brow, and returned to the fire.

They were good children. And Jonathan Darby, she thought, might just be the right person to help them find their feet again.

By the time they left, the children's nerves had melted away, replaced by excitement. Even Roger, who had been determined to remain stoic, admitted, 'Mr Darby's all right. Better than old Mr Higgins at the last place, anyway.'

As they drove back to Ravenley, Carol felt a quiet satisfaction. The school was perfect, small, friendly, and far enough from the city to be safe from air raids. And Mr Darby... well, he was certainly a reassuring presence. Handsome, too, though she chided herself for noticing.

Her thoughts drifted, as they often did, to Charles, somewhere in a POW camp. She wondered if he was cold, if he was hungry. If he knew how much she missed him.

But for now, she had these three to look after. And as Benjy chattered excitedly about the school and Susan debated whether she'd be allowed to join the football games, Carol allowed herself a small smile.

They would be happy here. She was sure of it.

The police station in Exeter was not what one would call a hive of activity that mid-December afternoon. Rain fell in a half-hearted fashion against the windowpanes, as if the clouds themselves couldn't quite be bothered. Inside, the little station office hummed with the creak of an old wooden chair, and nothing more exciting than the occasional clink of a teaspoon stirring in chipped enamel mugs.

Chops leaned back with a grunt, rubbing a hand over his jaw and stretching his lanky frame across half of the room. He stared at the crime report for the previous day with a distinct lack of enthusiasm. Winslow, was altogether more resigned to the grind of daily police work, sat across the desk from him, scanning the list.

'Shoplifting in Sidwell Street,' he muttered. 'Two tins of condensed milk and a bar of carbolic soap. Caught in the act.'

'Daring,' Chops said flatly.

Winslow gave the faintest twitch of a smirk. 'Followed by... another domestic disturbance in at Moorings. Husband claims his wife hit him with a broom. She says he's a lazy good-for-nothing idler. He was asking for it.'

'Poor man. Can we lock her up?'

'No, Chops.'

'Very well, let's mark that one under 'mutual hostility' and move on.'

Chops reached for the remaining papers, but already knew the rhythm: one petty theft, one squabble, one pointless complaint from a nosey neighbour. The war had changed many things, but not the nature of day-to-day crime. A fellow still wanted his tobacco, even if he couldn't afford it, and a marriage was still capable of turning sour no matter how many bombs were falling overhead.

Winslow turned the page with something close to despair. 'Pickpocketing in the market square. Victim lost a ration book and a packet of Woodbines. Likely never see either again.'

'Let's just hope the thief doesn't start taking liberties with his egg coupons,' Chops muttered, rubbing at his temple. 'Is it just me, or are we wasting our time today?'

'Where are friends from the Yard?' asked Winslow.

'With the bank manager Williams and his family. Taking another statement which I have no doubt they will ignore. I mean, the poor lady was held at gunpoint by a man in a balaclava of average height with a cockney accent. Not exactly a narrow field is it?'

Before Winslow could reply, the telephone rang. They both looked at it as though it had just barked at them.

Chops reached for the receiver. 'Chief Inspector Hopcroft.'

There was a burst of noise on the other end; murmured voices, the clink of glasses, and what sounded distinctly like the beginning of a pub brawl being nipped in the bud.

A man's voice came through, low and wary. 'Chief? It's Alf. From *The Gravediggers.*'

Chops sat up a little straighter. 'Alf. Good to hear from you. Have you something for me?'

'You asked me to keep my ears open,' Alf said, clearly keeping his voice down. 'That fellow, Morrison, the screw who got himself done in, well, one of his drinking pals is here now. Big lad. Name's Crockett.

'Davy?' asked Chops, semi-amused.

'No. From what I can hear. He's on his second pint and getting chatty.'

Chops straightened further. 'You're sure?'

'Positive. He's been here before, usually by himself, but sometimes with Morrison.'

212

There was a pause, and Chops could almost hear Alf raising an eyebrow through the line.

'Thought you might want to nip over before he has his fourth pint and gets less helpful.'

'Quite right,' Chops said. 'Keep him there, will you? Offer him a fifth if it comes to it. Say it's from a friend. We'll be there in fifteen.'

He hung up with a satisfying clack and turned to Winslow, who was already rising from his chair and straightening his uniform.

'What's the word?'

'That's the barman at *The Gravedigger's*,' said Chops. 'He says there's a man there at the moment that used to drink with Morrison.'

Winslow raised a brow. 'Could be nothing.'

'Could be something. And frankly, I'd rather take my chances with a proper line of enquiry than another row over missing jam rations.'

They grabbed their coats, hats, and headed into the rain.

Ten minutes and one near heart attack later for Chops brought on by Winslow's penchant for driving like a maniac, at least according to the estimable Chief Inspector, they pulled up outside the pub.

Alf nodded from behind the bar, jerking his chin towards the far end of the room where a red-headed brute of a man was hunched over a pint, his cheeks florid and his coat damp with rain. Chops followed the eyes of the barman to the lone figure.

Winslow nodded. 'Shall we?'

They approached slowly, not aggressive, but with that unmistakable air of purpose that came from two men who had long since given up pretending they weren't coppers.

The man known as Bill looked up, frowning at the two men joining him at the table.

'Merry Christmas,' said Chops with a disarming grin he used when he was at his deadliest.

Crockett looked up and immediately understood that he was in the presence of two policemen. Surly was his natural expression and

213

it was on display to its fullest just then, aided and abetted by the five pints he'd consumed. He pointed to the pint in front of him.

'From you?'

'With our compliments for the season,' replied Chops.

'You're Chops, ain't you?' he said with a sniff.

'How ever did you guess, old fellow. Perhaps you should be in our line of work,' replied Chops amiably.

Crockett glanced up at the bald pate, half disguised by the fedora sitting at the back of his head.

'Bad luck on the hairline,' said Crockett, a mirthless grin revealing a set of teeth that wouldn't have looked out of place on a mule.

Chops gave a faint smile. 'You can help us if you only but knew it.'

Crockett shrugged. 'Depends on what you want to know.'

'We heard you used to drink with a Fred Morrison,' Chops said calmly. 'You know that he was killed in bank raid?' Chops did not add that Morrison was part of the bank raid. This detail had not been released to the press.

Cockett's face clouded for a moment, though whether from grief, guilt, or beer it was hard to say. 'Just hadn't seen him, that's all. Heard he got himself killed. Thought it was a robbery or somethin'.'

'Or something,' Winslow said mildly. 'You two were friendly?'

Crockett gave a harsh laugh. 'Friendly? He was a screw. I did eighteen months in Dartmoor. Never called that 'friendly.' But we had a drink now and then. He didn't talk much.'

'Did he say anything recently? Anyone he was afraid of? Worried about?'

Crockett took a long pull of his pint and then set it down with a dull clink.

'He said he'd made a mistake. Said he'd got involved with people he shouldn't've. And he was trying to get out. That's all.'

Chops leaned in just a touch. 'Did he say who?'

'No names. But he looked spooked. Said if anything happened to him, I should keep my mouth shut.'

Chops nodded slowly. 'And yet here you are.'

Crockett gave a lopsided grin. 'Yeah. Well. Maybe I liked him more than I let on. We were both over there.'

Chops did not have to ask what he meant. The man before him, like Morrison, had fought in Flanders. Lord only knows what they had left out there. One way or another, everyone who had come back was wounded.

Chops studied the man for a moment longer. He asked quietly, 'All the more reason to catch the men that killed him, don't you think. He came through all of that didn't he just to have some coward shoot him dead.'

'What would you know about all of that Chief Inspector?'

Despite nearing forty at the end of the war, Chops had spent the last six months working in the military police. He had seen first-hand the impact wrought on body and mind in those awful months.

'Enough,' said Chops. 'Perhaps not like you and Morrison, but enough to do me a lifetime. He deserved better didn't he? You all did. You weren't looked after well. A couple of quid and a civvy suit for risking your lives for years at the front. It wasn't right.'

'It wasn't,' agreed Crockett. He looked at Chops and saw that he was, for once, in earnest.

'Look, I don't know what Fred was involved with but he was worried. He had debts. Gambling debts. He was always trying to earn an extra quid here or there.'

'Who were the debts with?'

'He never said. I didn't ask.'

Chops and Winslow exchanged glances. Then Winslow chipped in with a question.

'Did he ever mention a man called Jefferies at all?'

Crockett shook his head. He said, 'Means nothing to me, that.'

The detectives tried a few other names that they associated with gambling activities in the county. None registered with him. They

215

decided to end the interview and return to the police station. They now had a potential lead as to why Morrison might have had a role in the robbery. There were many criminal gangs who were involved with gambling. It was a lead that they would follow up with or without the help of Scotland Yard.

Chops and Winslow returned to the station in a slightly better frame of mind but they still felt frustrated by the glacial rate of progress.

Chops slumped into his chair with a long sigh and removed a pipe from his pocket and began to light it.

'I'll say one thing,' he muttered. 'I miss the days when people just robbed post boxes or stole sheep.'

Winslow gave a grunt of agreement as he shrugged off his coat and hung it on the peg behind the door. He was reaching for the lukewarm remains of the tea in his chipped enamel mug when the telephone on the desk rang sharply, slicing through the peace like a blade.

Winslow reached for it with the air of a man bracing for bad news. 'Winslow.'

A voice answered—high, breathless, frantic.

'Inspector! It's—oh God—it's Vera. Vera Williams. My husband's been taken.'

Winslow blinked, straightening. 'Mrs Williams? Taken by whom?'

'The police!' she cried. 'The London men. The ones you said were helping. Scotland Yard, they said! They came to the house not twenty minutes ago and said they needed to speak to him about the robbery. They were so cold, Inspector. So official. They said they had questions and they needed to take him under caution. They just took him!'

Chops motioned quickly to Winslow, who held out the receiver so that they both could hear.

'Where did they take him, Mrs Williams?'

216

'They said they were taking him to the station. Yours. But I don't understand—he hasn't done anything. Herbert wouldn't—he *couldn't—*'

Her voice cracked then, and Winslow held the receiver slightly away from his ear as the sound of sobbing filled the line.

'I understand, Mrs Williams. I'll look into it straight away. Sit tight. And try not to worry until there's something to worry *about*, all right?'

She gave a broken sob in reply, then the line went dead.

Winslow replaced the receiver with a slow, deliberate motion. He stood still for a moment, jaw working.

Chops nodded grimly. 'So, Blaney and Wilkins have gone and hauled him in.'

'On what charge? It's absurd.'

'They're Scotland Yard. They don't always feel the need to explain themselves. I heard that right. They are in the station?' Winslow nodded, rising to his feet along with Chops. 'Come on. Let's see what our colleagues from London are playing at.'

They found Blaney and Wilkins occupying the interview room, the largest one in the station, naturally. It had been commandeered by the Yard men since their arrival, and the other officers had quickly learnt to steer clear of it. Chops and Winslow ignored the closed door and strode straight in.

Inside, Herbert Williams sat at the end of a wooden table, his face pale and his hat clenched tightly in both hands. He looked like a man caught in the middle of a particularly cruel joke. Blaney, meanwhile, stood over him with a self-satisfied air, while Wilkins leaned against the wall, notebook in hand.

'Good afternoon,' Blaney said with the faintest trace of sarcasm.

Chops didn't return the pleasantries. 'What's this about, Inspector?'

Blaney raised a brow. 'We're pursuing a lead. Mr Williams here was working at the bank on the day of the robbery. The vault room. Isn't that right, Mr Williams?'

217

Herbert gave a miserable nod. 'Aye. I check the secure door each morning and again at close.'

'Exactly,' Blaney said. 'A man with routine access. Who would know when the guard changes, who would see the van arrive...'

Chops narrowed his eyes. 'You brought him in under *caution?*'

Wilkins glanced up from his notebook. 'Given the timeline, we feel it's appropriate.'

'You *feel?*' Chops repeated, voice tightening. 'We've been through all this with Mr Williams already. His alibi's solid, and Morrison himself signed the check sheet confirming the vaults were sealed that evening. And now Morrison's dead.'

Blaney's tone sharpened. 'Exactly. The only man who could confirm Williams' story is no longer available.'

'You think *he* had Morrison killed?' Winslow said in disbelief. 'Come off it.'

'We're not saying this,' Wilkins replied coolly. 'We're simply saying the circumstances warrant a proper look. Something that wasn't carried out thoroughly enough when the case was local.'

Chops' jaw set. 'We've worked this from every angle. I'll remind you this is *our* station, Inspector Blaney. We're not here to be patronised.'

There was a charged silence, broken only by the ticking of the station wall clock.

Chops turned to Herbert, his tone softening.

'You've said nothing wrong, Mr Williams. You're not under arrest. These men are asking questions, and you're free to leave if you choose.'

Williams looked at him, eyes wide. 'I can go?'

'You can,' Chops said firmly. 'Unless they want to place you under arrest. And I don't think they've got the cause.'

Blaney looked at him coolly but said nothing.

Herbert rose from his chair, still clutching his cap like a lifeline. 'Thank you, Chief Inspector. I didn't know what was happening. My wife—she'll be in bits.'

Chops nodded. 'Go to her. We'll call if we need anything else.'

Herbert nodded gratefully and hurried out, his boots echoing down the corridor.

Blaney remained by the fireplace, unmoved.

'You're letting sentiment cloud your judgement,' he said.

'And you're forgetting we *live* in this community,' Chops said tightly. 'These aren't just names in a ledger to us. He's not your man.'

'We'll see.'

Chops and Winslow turned and left the room. In the corridor, they met a large ungainly man who brought to mind a walrus. To his bulk, was added height, he scaled at least six feet five. This was Superintendent Fergus McDaid. The Northern Irishman had been superintendent at the police station for the last five years. There was little love lost between him and Chops. They tolerated one another at best. He motioned to Chops to follow him to his office.

Chops rolled his eyes to Winslow. He knew what was coming. Moments later he was shutting the door behind him and sitting down in front of McDaid. The Ulsterman was known neither for being loquacious nor for having a sense of humour.

'You're off the case. So is Winslow. And Talbot.' Chops opened his mouth to protest but McDaid waved him away. 'This isn't for discussion. Off you go. Bring Talbot back in. Immediately.'

It was a grey afternoon with the promise of rain when Carol called the children into the drawing room. The fire crackled gently behind her, lending a warmth to the room that contrasted with the sharp bite in the air outside.

'Children,' she began, clasping her hands in front of her, her expression carefully composed, 'As you know, I'm going to have to go into Exeter for the afternoon and the evening as well. It's my first night on ambulance duty. Well, it's more of a test really. I'll still be on probation. The best way seeing is to throw me in at the deep end.'

Susan, smiled up at her and said, 'I'm sure you'll do well.'

Carol smiled. 'Thank you Sussan. Let's see. I'm really quite nervous.'

Benjy was fiddling with a model aeroplane. He seemed a little more worried than the Roger or Susan. He asked, 'Will you be gone long?'

'Not too long, I hope. I'll be back after bedtime, but Mrs Parker will make your tea. And I want you all to stay close to the house. You can play in the grounds, but don't go far. Is that clear?'

Roger and Susan exchanged a glance, then nodded.

Carol crouched beside Benjy, her voice softening. 'Can you keep your older brother and sister under control, Benjy?'

He nodded solemnly which brought a smile from the two older siblings.

Carol studied the three of them for a few moments. She said, 'I know things have been different lately. And I know it can be difficult. But I need to be able to trust you when I'm gone. Can I?'

Three solemn heads nodded.

'Good,' she said briskly, rising. She kissed each of them in turn and then reached for her coat. 'Wish me luck.'

'Good luck!' they all chorused.

It took less than ten minutes for the children to agree what they would do.

'We could go back to Ned's cottage,' Roger said, already slipping into his coat. 'We promised him we'd visit again.'

Benjy was lacing his boots. 'We could take him those apples Mrs Parker gave us. Everyone likes apples.'

Susan hesitated. 'We're not meant to go far.'

Roger looked at her with mock solemnity. 'The cottage is barely out of sight of the house. Almost.'

'Come on, Susan,' Benjy coaxed. 'We'll be back before anyone notices.'

That decided it. Susan grabbed her scarf and followed the boys through the side door and into the chill of the afternoon. The woods were quieter than usual. A damp mist clung low to the ground, curling around their feet as they made their way along the familiar path. Birds called intermittently from the trees above, and now and then the dry crunch of leaves broke the stillness.

It was Benjy who spotted it first.

'Look!' he hissed, pointing to the base of a tree where something glinted dully in the undergrowth. The three of them moved closer, treading carefully.

'Is that a trap?' Susan asked, peering at the strange contraption.

'A snare,' Roger confirmed grimly. This was not the sort they'd encountered before. The one they'd found the week before had been crude, fashioned from wire. This one was metal, with sharp teeth.

'How awful,' said Susan studying it more closely. She felt Benjy's hand on her arm, so she did not go too close.

The clack of the trap snapping shut made Susan jump.

'That could break someone's leg,' Roger said, awestruck.

'Or worse,' Susan agreed.

'Private Benjy,' said Roger.

'Yes, sir,' said Benjy saluting with a grin.

'Ready catapult.'

Benjy took out his catapult and found a stone to place in the holder. Then he said, 'Catapult armed, sir.'

'Fire when you are ready,' came the order.

Benjy fired at the teeth of the snare. With a chilling crunch, the jaws snapped shut.

Roger picked up a stick and began to prod the snare to make sure it was safe. He bent down and said, 'We should take it to Ned. He'll know what to do.' He was just about to attempt picking it up when they heard the sound.

A twig snapped. Then another. And another. Slow, deliberate steps. Susan's breath caught in her throat. Roger dropped the stick.

'Who's there?' Benjy called, trying to sound braver than he felt.

The woods fell silent. Then, from behind a thick oak tree, a man appeared.

Susan screamed.

He was tall, thin, and stooped slightly as though trying to blend into the trees. His coat was tattered and hung off his frame like a scarecrow's, and a flat cap was pulled low over his forehead. His boots were muddied, and his face was shadowed by the brim of his cap.

'Well, well,' he said, his voice raspy but oddly amused. 'What have we here?'

Roger instinctively stepped in front of Susan. Benjy, though clearly frightened, bent to pick up the stick Roger had dropped.

'We're not doing anything wrong,' Roger said stoutly. 'We were going to show this to our friend. He's the gamekeeper.'

The man cocked his head. 'That so? And what would Ned Turnbull want with a bit of old iron like that, eh?'

He took a step forward. Benjy raised the stick slightly, his knuckles white.

'Don't come any closer,' Roger said.

The man held up his hands, though not in any way that suggested true surrender.

'No harm meant,' he said. 'Just wondering what a few children are doing poking about in other folk's business.'

Roger's heart pounded in his chest. 'We'll be going now.' He turned, gently tugging Susan's hand. Benjy backed away; the stick still raised. The man didn't follow. He simply stood there, half in shadow, watching them go.

It wasn't until they'd cleared the next bend in the path and were running full tilt towards Ned's cottage that any of them spoke again.

'Who was he?' Susan gasped, clutching Roger's arm.

'I don't know,' Roger said, breathless. 'But I don't like him.'

Ned Turnbull opened his door with a surprised expression.

'You lot again? And in a bit of a state too. Come in, come in.'

Once they were inside, warmed by the fire and given mugs of sweet tea, they told him what had happened. About the trap. The man. The strange way he'd watched them. Ned's brow furrowed deeply. He stood and paced the hearth.

'You say it was a metal trap? That's no rabbit snare, that's for sure. That sort of thing could cripple a deer. Or worse.'

'We think he set it,' Benjy said quietly.

'Aye, I expect he did. Sounds like one of them poachers who think they've more right to the land than the folk who live on it.'

'But we thought you were a poacher once,' Susan said, then blushed. 'I didn't mean—'

Ned smiled faintly. 'I was. Long time ago. But I never set anything like that. Not something that'd tear a leg in two.'

He looked out the window towards the woods.

'You did right to come to me. And right to be scared. That sort of man doesn't like being watched.'

'Do you know who he was?' Roger asked.

Ned hesitated. 'I've a few ideas. But none I can prove. Don't you worry about that. I'll take care of it.'

He turned back to them. 'But I want a promise. No more wandering. Not without an adult. Not until we know who's setting traps on the land.'

They nodded solemnly. Susan clutched her tea as though it were a lifeline.

'I didn't like the way he looked at us,' she admitted.

They trooped home later, Benjy clutching his prize, the snare, which Ned let him keep. They saw Constable Talbot and told him about the man they met in the forest.

As the sky darkened outside and the fire crackled in the grate, the children sat in the warmth of the kitchen at Ravenley. And though none would say it, they all felt it; the forest wasn't quite so friendly anymore.

The December evening settled in with a damp chill that clung to the stone streets of Exeter and seeped through even the thickest coat. Carol Sinclair pulled her scarf tighter about her neck as she hurried through the narrow entrance, narrower thanks to the sandbags protecting the doorway to the hospital courtyard. More and more she was seeing entrances so protected.

Tonight she was to take up her post behind the wheel of one of the hospital's ambulances. The thought filled her with immense apprehension. This sight of Corporal Danvers, waiting just inside the doors, was reassuring. He gave her a brisk nod.

'Mrs Sinclair. Good to see you again. You're early. I like that in a driver.'

'I thought it best,' Carol replied. She was trying for brisk and capable, though her heart was hammering rather harder than she would have liked.

Danvers led her through the echoing corridor, the smell of carbolic and steam drifting from the wards. 'I'll introduce you to your partner for the evening. We always send drivers out in pairs — one to steer, one to tend to the poor souls we collect. Makes the work smoother. He's probably our most experienced nurse.'

'He?' exclaimed Carol.

Corporal Danvers did not quite get the question. He said 'Yes, your man tonight is Cyril Thorpe.'

'Your man?' she repeated with a faint smile.

Danvers grinned. 'Figure of speech, ma'am. Thorpe's one of our best. Knows the city like the back of his hand and has a steady way about him. Nothing flusters him.'

A male nurse, whatever next. She supposed it was no odder than a female ambulance driver. War changes things. Barriers, once insurmountable, fall away. It's a pity that it took a war for this to happen.

They emerged into the garage, where two ambulances sat side by side under the electric lamps, their paintwork dulled by winter grime. A tall figure in a heavy overcoat was checking the contents of a medical satchel by one of the vehicles. He looked up at their approach.

'Thorpe, this is Mrs Sinclair. You'll be out together tonight.'

Cyril Thorpe extended a hand, his grip firm but not crushing. She estimated that he was perhaps in his mid to late forties, with a lean face, a strong jaw, and eyes that seemed to take in more than he ever said aloud. His cap was pushed back slightly, showing dark hair touched with silver at the temples.

'Pleased to meet you, Mrs Sinclair. I hope you're a steady driver. Danvers here says you're fresh to the job.'

Carol found herself smiling despite her nerves. 'Fresh, yes, but I promise not to take any corners on two wheels.'

'Shame,' Cyril said mildly. 'Those are the most fun.'

Danvers chuckled. 'I'll leave you two to it. Thorpe will see you right.'

When Danvers had gone, Cyril climbed into the passenger seat, nodding for Carol to take the wheel. 'Let's take her for a short spin before we start proper. Better you get the feel of her before the first call comes in.'

The ambulance was older than the one she had driven the previous day. It felt heavy under her hands but obedient once she understood the clutch and the way the engine wanted to be coaxed rather than bullied. Cyril gave directions around the quiet streets, occasionally pointing out shortcuts or hazards.

'It's mostly about keeping your wits about you,' he said as they pulled back into the hospital yard. 'You'll get the odd motorist who won't give way, no matter the siren. And children — they'll dash into the road without a thought.'

Their first hours passed quietly. They waited in the garage, the radio silent, the night broken only by the muffled sounds of the hospital at work: footsteps on tiled floors, the clink of metal basins, distant voices in low, urgent tones.

Carol learned that Cyril carried a small notebook in which he sketched in spare moments — streets, buildings, faces caught in profile. He showed her a page of rapid pencil strokes capturing a nurse at her desk, head bent over a ledger.

'It passes the time,' he said. 'And it keeps the hands busy while the mind... thinks.'

They attended a few incidents between seven and nine but none that Cyril deemed required hospitalisation. It was nearly ten when the first real emergency call came. Danvers appeared in the doorway, his voice brisk. 'Emergency in St Thomas Street. Woman in labour. Neighbours say it's coming fast. There are no doctors available and the midwife is on another delivery. We'll have to bring her in as there may be complications.'

Carol was behind the wheel in seconds, Cyril at her side with the satchel. The streets seemed narrower than ever in the darkness, and the fog that had rolled in made the lamps blur and smear. Cyril guided her unerringly through the twisting lanes until they reached a small, terraced house, its doorway crowded with anxious neighbours.

The woman was pale and sweating, her breath coming in shallow gasps. Between them, Carol and Cyril eased her onto the stretcher.

'Nice and steady now, love,' Cyril murmured, his voice low and reassuring.

Carol took the corners smoothly but swiftly, the engine purring, her eyes flicking constantly between road and mirrors. The hospital loomed up ahead, and she drew up at the entrance in what Cyril later declared was record time. The midwife was waiting. Within moments, the woman was inside, and the street was quiet again.

Back in the ambulance, Carol let out the breath she'd been holding. 'Well. That was...'

'Textbook,' Cyril finished. 'You've got the makings of a fine driver...for a racing team.'

Carol exploded into laughter at this. It was just the right comment at the right moment and any tension she felt related to the job disappeared.

As the night wore on, conversation came more easily. Around eleven, Cyril told her, without drama, about his time in France.

'I was a conscientious objector at the start,' he said. 'Didn't believe in taking life. Thought I'd serve my time in prison if need be. But they sent me to the front anyway; said they needed stretcher-bearers and nurses as much as riflemen.'

'And you went?'

He shrugged. 'Seemed the right thing. Spent two years patching up boys younger than I was. Saw more blood than I care to remember. Got this.' He tapped the small ribbon on his lapel. 'I pulled three men out of a shell crater under fire.'

Carol hesitated, then asked, 'Did you know many of the local lads?'

Cyril's eyes flickered, just for a moment. 'Some. One in particular. James Turnbull. You might know his father, Ned. Gamekeeper out at Ravenley. Your *that* Mrs Sinclair, aren't you?'

'Yes, I am that Mrs Sinclair,' laughed Carol. 'I won't ask how you guessed and, yes, I know Ned. Not well. Charles introduced me after we were married. I haven't seen a lot of him, I confess.'

Cyril was silent for a long moment, then said softly, 'James was... a fine man. Good with his hands, good with people. We were friends. You know, school.' His tone made the words carry more weight than they appeared to on the surface. 'He went to war the year before I did. Never came back.'

Carol heard the finality in his voice and knew better than to press. The remaining hour passed quickly. No further calls came aside from delivering a few patients back to their houses. At midnight, Carol drove Cyril back to his flat. She declined his invitation for a cuppa.

Cyril said, 'Not every night is this quiet. Some nights... well, let's just say you'll earn your sleep.'

'Thank you,' she said to Cyril. 'For making my first night an easy one.'

He smiled faintly. 'Don't thank me yet. Wait until you've had the other sort of night.'

As she walked back to the car that would take her home, Carol thought about the things she had learned about Cyril, about the work, and about the unseen threads that linked people in unexpected ways. Ned, Cyril, James... stories woven together, some finished, some still being written.

She was beginning to realise that her new role was not just about driving an ambulance. It was about carrying fragments of people's lives, sometimes from one place to another, sometimes only for the briefest stretch of road, and knowing that each journey mattered.

The night sky was black as she drove and frost was thickening on the hedges while the fields silvered in the moonlight as she headed back to Ravenley.

Carol let herself in quietly, not wanting to wake the children. The hallway was dark, the only light coming from the moon spilling pale silver through the fanlight above the door. She shut it gently, leaning her back against the wood for a moment, letting the stillness wash over her after the hum and urgency of the hospital.

Her legs felt heavy, and her shoulders ached from the hours of tension, yet there was an undeniable lightness within her too. A sense of having done something that mattered. She had driven, kept her head, helped bring a woman in labour to safety, and earned the quiet approval in Cyril Thorpe's eyes. She had been useful, capable, more than just a figure on the margins.

She set her bag on the hall table and began unfastening her coat, moving slowly, as if savouring each step. She was smiling to herself without realising it. Then the smile faltered. The truth struck her in the gut, sudden and sharp.

Charles.

Somewhere, perhaps in a German prison camp, perhaps lying cold in a nameless grave, her husband was enduring the war in ways she could hardly bear to imagine. And here she was, warm and safe, with the faint thrill of pride still humming through her veins because she had done well behind the wheel of an ambulance.

She pressed her hands to her face, the tears coming before she could stop them. They were hot and urgent, spilling down her cheeks, a tangled mess of relief, pride, exhaustion, and guilt. What right had she, to feel this way? To take pleasure in proving herself, when Charles might be suffering or dead felt like a betrayal, not the sort that others could see, but one that gnawed quietly at the edges of her heart.

She dropped into the armchair by the fire, not bothering to light it. The cold crept in, but she barely noticed. She sat there, head bowed, letting the tears run their course, until her breathing steadied. She wiped her face with the edge of her sleeve.

She was free, in a way she had never been before; free to work, to take decisions, to be judged on her own merit. And yet that freedom came at the cost of the man who had once been her world.

At last she rose, moving softly upstairs to her room. The children were asleep, their breathing steady in the quiet house. She stood for a long time at her own window, looking out over the frost-silvered garden to where the dark line of the woods met the sky, wondering if Charles could see the same moon.

Winslow hunched over the wheel of the Wolseley as if attempting to throttle it into greater speed, peering through a windscreen mottled by the fine drizzle. Beside him, Chops wore the expression of a man resigned to the prospect of seeing his life end in a car wrapped around a tree like moss.

They had taken a narrow turn off Exeter's high street, plunging into streets with names the cab drivers avoided, where the shops were either shuttered or sold things that came without receipts. Winslow eased the car to a stop outside a fish and chip shop whose paint was flaking in long, tired curls. The window was hazed with steam, behind which a faint shape moved briskly about.

'Well, we're still alive,' Chops said sourly, watching Winslow switching off the ignition.

Winslow gave the façade a doubtful look. 'Not exactly the Ritz, is it?'

'The Ritz doesn't fry cod the way Big Jim does.'

Winslow sniffed, half from the damp, half from scepticism. 'Are you a regular?'

'With Jim, you don't just ask. You show your face, you let him remember you're still in the game, and maybe, if the stars align, he throws you a scrap. In this case, it can be wrapped up in *The Gazette*.' Chops pushed open his door. 'Best keep your eyes open. And your mouth shut.'

Inside, the heat hit them like a slap, thick with the smell of hot oil and vinegar. A girl in a white apron, hair tied back in a scarf, stood

231

behind the counter. She didn't need to be told who they were. She gave Chops the barest nod and jerked her head towards a side door.

The corridor beyond was dim, smelling of frying and yet more frying. The stairs were steep and narrow, creaking in protest under their weight. Halfway up they were met by Ronnie Richardson, a thin, weaselly man with slicked-back hair and a moustache that looked like it had been drawn on in a hurry. His narrow eyes took in Chops and Winslow. There was a brief flicker of calculation, followed by the sort of wary distaste one might reserve for policemen, Brussels sprouts, and surprise visits from the mother-in-law. Chops had disliked him for years—ever since Ronnie had tried to give evidence in a case by swearing on the life of a grandmother who, it later transpired, had been dead a decade. Ronnie grinned without warmth. 'Jim is expecting you.'

Big Jim Jefferies was behind a battered oak desk the size of a billiard table. The man himself had been named after the former heavyweight champion of the world. His dad had been a prize fighter, and his dad before him. Big Jim had tried it for a few years but decided that low-level crime paid better.

It did.

Jefferies had the physical attributes of the man he had been named after, only the years had softened the lines. He still had the height and the shoulders, but there was more belly now, more ease in the way he sat back, lacing thick fingers over his middle as though he had all the time in the world. His scalp was shaved, his broken nose long since set in its new, perhaps even more crooked direction, and his pale blue eyes could make you feel as if you'd been weighed, measured, and filed away in the first second of meeting him.

A cigar smouldered in the ashtray, its smoke curling lazily towards the low ceiling.

'Well, well,' Jefferies said in that low, rolling voice of his. 'If it isn't Chief Inspector Hopcroft. Thought you'd have taken up bee keeping by now.'

232

'Not my style,' Chops said, stepping forward to shake the big hand. 'Bees don't pay out like you do. But nice touch on comparing me to Sherlock. I didn't know you could read.'

This produced a deep-throated laugh that was genuine. He replied, 'And I didn't know you could string two thoughts together without stopping for a lie-down and a cup of tea.'

Winslow got the briefest introduction and a measuring glance, then was forgotten.

Jefferies gestured at the chairs opposite. 'Sit yourselves down. Tell me what brings the law to my little corner of the world. Can't be betting, surely? You've never managed to catch me on that.'

Chops lowered himself into the creaky chair. 'I'd hate to spoil your perfect record. We're here about a man called Morrison. Worked nights at a bank. Found dead last week. Bad business. I'm sure you read about it.'

'Yes, I heard. Bad Business. I hope you don't think I'm branching out, Chops. Not really my style, is it?'

'No,' agreed Chops. 'Not the angle we are looking at. He owed money. We don't know who to.'

'You think the geezers he owed money to, topped him while they were robbing the bank?'

'You should be a detective,' said Chops.

'You should try it, too, Chops,' laughed Jefferies.

Chops had the gave to laugh at this. He pushed the back up to the back of his head like centurion preparing for battle. From Winslow's vantage point, viewing the exchange, the two men seemed to be enjoying the jousting.

'Short, wiry, liked a drink. Spent a few here and there, maybe even here.'

Jefferies picked up the cigar, rolled it between his fingers without looking at Chops. 'Chief Inspector, I get dozens of punters through my doors. I can't be expected to remember every one.'

'I think you remember the ones who owe you money,' Chops said mildly.

The faintest quirk touched Jefferies' mouth. 'And I think you've been listening to street talk. You know how it is. Stories grow legs.'

Winslow leaned forward. 'So you never saw him. Never heard the name. Never took a bet from him.'

'You could repeat it another five ways and the answer would still be the same.' Jefferies puffed a cloud of smoke that hung stubbornly in the air. 'If he'd owed me, he'd have paid. I don't let debts get messy.'

The two men looked at each other over the desk, a long, quiet measure of wills. There was history in the air—past race days when Chops had been on the same turf, watching Jefferies work his quiet magic; investigations where names had been whispered only to recant the next day, a little richer but also more afraid. No one messed with Jefferies twice and few dd so even once. He wielded his power, like America, with a laugh and joke and a big stick if the need arose.

'Word is,' Chops said finally, 'Morrison had serious gambling debts. If not with you, then with someone you know.'

'Word is,' Jefferies said smoothly, 'that Morrison is dead. And you're asking the wrong man about him.'

There was nothing more to be had—not now. Chops rose, tugging his coat straight. 'Thanks for the hospitality, Jim. If you should happen to hear anything, though, it would be in your interest to tell us. Kill two birds with one stone. We catch our killers and you stop a rival in his tracks.'

Jefferies nodded thoughtfully at this. He replied, 'You're always welcome, Chops,' 'Bring your lad here again, I'll give him the proper tour. Have a fish supper on me, on the way out. You'll be tired of cooking for yourself Chops, I'm sure.'

'I never liked Dora's cooking anyway,' said Chops, ruefully. 'Don't miss it or her in the slightest.'

Winslow gave a polite nod, though it was clear the idea of a 'tour' filled him with no delight.

Ronnie Richardson was waiting for them at the bottom of the stairs. He swung the door open with exaggerated courtesy. 'Always a pleasure, Inspector,' he said, tone as sour as old vinegar. Chops gave him a look that conveyed exactly what he thought of Ronnie's pleasures. 'Try to keep out of trouble, Ronnie,' Chops said. 'One day your luck'll run out.' Ronnie's grin widened, showing teeth that looked like they'd been assembled from the remains of several dead bodies. 'Not before yours, copper.'

They left the office, the hot smell of frying hitting them again on the stairs. Outside, the wind cut through them afresh, cold and clean.

'Friendly sort,' Winslow muttered.

'Friendlier because he needs to be,' Chops replied. 'He won't be any happier than we are if there's a new player in town.'

'What are you getting at?'

'It's one thing to have a robbery. It's another to have a second gang setting up shop in town. I'm wondering if the two things are connected.'

'You mean that the robbery was seed capital?'

Chops nodded. He stared through the drizzle-streaked windscreen window in the direction of the sea.

'Does this sound strange? A gang hears about the robbery that took place in Battersea. They think isn't-this-a-good-idea? They copy the method. They use our friend Morrison as the inside man but dispose of him immediately. He's not really a gang member, just some poor idiot who's probably gotten into debt playing with card sharks that the gang have put up against him.'

They climbed into the Wolseley, Chops staring. Winslow waited, knowing better than to fill the silence. Finally, he turned the key, the engine rattling to life. 'You could be right, Chops. Jim looks like he's thinking along similar lines.'

'Sometimes, it pays to plant the odd seed yourself. *My enemy's enemy is my friend.*'

The city closed in around them again—wet pavements, dim shop windows, the hiss of tyres on rain-slick roads. Chops drove with his usual steady purpose, but his mind was somewhere else, turning over the shape of the thing. Morrison's debts made sense. Men got themselves killed over less every week. But whose books had his name in them? And how many more would clam up before they got close?

Sunday 21st December 1940

From the drawing room window, Carol had watched the morning shadows creep across the garden, swallowing up the last of the autumn leaves as though the world beyond were being erased. Inside, the house was warm with the smell of coal smoke and baking bread, the kind of comfort that could make a person forget there was a war on—until the wireless sputtered out another casualty list.

She was at a desk writing a letter that wouldn't write to Charles. Her fountain pen scratched in irritated bursts, when the front door banged. Muffled voices tumbled in from the hallway, high and urgent, and a moment later Susan came flying into the room, cheeks pink from the cold, dark curls slipping from her ribbon.

'Carol! Carol! We've something to show you!'

Benjy was right behind her, clutching something between both hands as if it might wriggle away, and Roger followed last, hanging back in the doorway, eyes flicking towards the windows as though still half in the wood.

'What is it?' Carol shut the ledger with a snap and rose, brushing a crumb of eraser from her skirt.

Benjy stepped forward and laid his find in her hands—a jagged, rust-pitted contraption with steel jaws and a coiled spring. The chill of the metal bit into her skin.

'We found another one,' he said, his voice carrying both pride and disgust. 'In the wood. Not like the string one from before. This one's nasty—it could take the leg off a fox. Or worse.'

237

Carol turned it over, mindful of the teeth. Even dulled by age, they were still sharp enough to tear through fur—or flesh. She placed it carefully on the table, away from exploring fingers.

'Where exactly did you find it?'

'Near Ned's place,' Susan said, eyes widening for emphasis. 'We were going to take it to him, but then...' She broke off, glancing at Roger.

'Then what?' Carol prompted.

Roger hesitated, rubbing a thumb along the seam of his pocket. 'We saw someone. A man. He came out from behind a tree, just like that.' He snapped his fingers. 'Didn't hear him until he was right there.'

'Describe him.' Carol kept her voice level, though her heart gave a small, unwelcome kick.

'Tallish,' Benjy began, 'with a beard. Scruffy. Hair sticking out everywhere. He had an old coat with patches. And—' He frowned. 'He looked at us funny.'

'Like we didn't belong there,' Susan added. 'And he smelled... odd. I don't know how describe it. Just funny.'

'Did he speak?'

Roger shook his head. 'Yes, he asked us what we were doing. We told him we'd found a snare and we were going to bring it to Ned. He didn't hang around. When we told Ned he said that it was a poacher. He thinks he knows the man but he's never caught him in the act.'

She took in their faces, Roger pale under his freckles, Susan twisting her cardigan buttons, Benjy trying for a nonchalant shrug and failing. 'Don't go back to that part of the wood. Do you understand me?'

Three nods, solemn enough for her to believe them. Yet Susan could not stop to think about Ned. She sensed he was lonely and he liked their company.

'What about Ned?' asked Susan.

Carol sighed audibly; if she barred them from the woods entirely, she would be leaving Ned to his own company in the dead of winter, when evenings stretched long and cold. Yet if she allowed them to keep visiting, she risked exposing them to danger from the poacher, or worse. It was a choice between the safety of three young lives and the loneliness of an old man who had already lost more than his share.

'If you go, make sure you tell Constable Talbot first. Then walk with utmost care because there may be other snares there. I'll tell Ned to keep an eye out for these.'

This seemed a sensible solution and they accepted it immediately.

In the kitchen, she set the snare on the draining board, the cold metal leaving a damp ring on the enamel. Then she went straight to the telephone in the hall. The cord twisted between her fingers as she waited for the operator, then for the inevitable crackle and hum before Chops' voice came on the line.

'Hello Carol, Chops here.'

'Sorry Chops, I know it's Sunday, but I just had to call you. The children found a metal snare in the wood, near Ned's. And they saw a man, tall, unshaven, patched coat. Does that ring any bells?'

He was silent for a moment, the faint murmur of voices in the background. 'Could be one of several local chaps.'

'Quite certain. He didn't speak to them, but they were frightened. I don't like it, Chops.'

'Let Constable Talbot know. If you see him again, ring me straight away.'

When the line went dead, she stood for a moment in the hall, hearing the tick of the clock and the faint shuffle of the children in the kitchen. The war had brought enough strangers to Devon; she didn't need any more.

Outside, the cold air was edged with the sharp tang of woodsmoke. She caught sight of Talbot between the bare branches as he patrolled the boundary. He met her halfway down the path.

'Everything all right, Mrs Sinclair?'

She told him quickly, and his expression hardened. 'I'll keep watch for him, and for more snares. If he's the man I think, he's a local poacher. Not dangerous to people, but no friend to the law.'

'Ned Turnbull thought the same.'

'We'll see,' Talbot said, pulling his collar up against the wind.

From there she took the path towards Ned's. The hedgerows were stripped bare, and puddles filled the ruts where cartwheels had passed. She found him in the yard, splitting logs with the unhurried rhythm of a man who had done it all his life.

'Afternoon, Mrs Sinclair,' he called, straightening and wiping a forearm across his brow. 'You've a look about you. Trouble?'

She held out the snare, and his brows rose. 'Nasty bit of work, that. You were right to bring it away.'

When she described the man, Ned's mouth tightened. 'Sounds like Ravel Briggs. Lives in a caravan by the old quarry. Been here years. Keeps to himself mostly, but I reckon he does a bit of poaching. Never caught him at it, mind.'

'Is he dangerous?'

'Not in the way you're thinking. Short temper, that's all. Still, keep the young 'uns away from him.'

As she followed him into the kitchen for a cup of tea, her eyes went to the small black-and-white photograph on the mantel, a young man in uniform, grinning at the camera.

'Your son?' she asked softly.

Ned's face fell a little. The desolation in his eyes was all too apparent. Before Carol could apologise, Ned replied, 'James. Lost him in Flanders.'

'I met someone the other night who knew him. Cyril Thorpe. He's a nurse at the hospital.'

For a fraction of a second, Ned's expression shifted; surprise at first, and something else she couldn't quite name. He looked away, busying himself with the teapot. 'Cyril. Aye, they were... good friends.'

The pause before 'good friends' was slight, but enough. Carol said nothing, merely sipped the tea when it came, yet a quiet certainty settled over her. Perhaps the bond between James and Cyril had gone beyond ordinary friendship, though neither man would have said so aloud in those days. Her days and nights in London as a young woman had exposed her to a world that would have been unimaginable in deepest Devon.

When she took her leave, Ned promised again to keep watch for the poacher. The walk back to the house was brighter, the clouds thinning to reveal a thin winter sun, but the image of the stranger—unshaven, watching—lingered, like a shadow in the trees.

Inside, the children were at the kitchen table, bent over their exercise books, the lamplight making a golden pool around them. Carol paused in the doorway, taking in the sight. Whatever prowled in the wood, whatever danger the war might yet bring, she would keep them safe.

Around midday Carol and the children went to the village church at Belsaw-on-the-Moor. The church sat modestly at the far end of the village green, a squat Norman affair of grey stone that looked as though it had weathered not only the centuries but the moorland gales with quiet obstinacy. Its square tower rose above a scattering of wind-bent yews, and the moss on its walls gave the impression that it was slowly being consumed by the landscape.

Carol had debated with herself that morning. The Reverend Atwell's visit earlier in the week, earnest, eager, and very much the young clergyman on probation brought with it the lingering suggestion that he expected to see her in the front pew. It was a gentle guilt-trip, but it had worked. If she was truthful, there was another reason she was setting out across the frosty green with the children. Jonathan Darby, the new schoolmaster, might be there. And if one couldn't admit that entirely to oneself, one could at least disguise it under the cloak of duty to God and community.

241

The children, less susceptible to such notions, trailed along behind her with varying degrees of enthusiasm. Roger, in his cap and slightly too-large Sunday jacket, seemed philosophical. Susan dragged her feet over the frosty grass, pulling her gloves on with exaggerated slowness. Benjy, at least, seemed content enough, humming to himself and kicking at the pale, frozen clods of earth that lined the path.

Sunlight filtered in through the narrow stained-glass windows, dappling the flagstones in colours that didn't quite brighten the gloom. The church was filling slowly with villagers, farmers' families , a few elderly widows in their black coats, a scattering of children who looked no keener than the three orphans.

Jonathan Darby was there. Carol saw him as they made their way up the aisle; a tall figure, his brown hair catching the dim light, leaning slightly as he spoke to one of the older parishioners. He glanced up, caught her eye, and smiled in a way that warmed the cold edges of the morning. She returned the smile, though she felt Roger's sideways glance and ignored it. He walked to his pew. Once again, she detected just the hint of a limp.

The Reverend Atwell began the service with a brisk intonation, his voice unexpectedly deep for such a slight man. Carol did her best to follow the prayers and responses, but her mind wandered. She glanced at the children: Roger was staring fixedly at a cobweb hanging from one of the arches; Susan was leafing through the hymn book as if searching for something better to sing; Peter's head was beginning to droop towards his chest.

Then came the sermon. Atwell was clearly earnest and gave a sermon bulging with sincerity. He spoke on the need for steadfastness in troubled times, for vigilance against temptation, for the importance of keeping one's eyes fixed on the higher purpose. Carol caught about one word in five. She found herself wondering how long a sermon was supposed to last here, and whether Jonathan Darby was listening with more interest than she was.

The children were fidgeting openly by the end, Roger shifting from one foot to the other, Susan sighing as though her very life were being drained away, Benjy spending more time looking around at the other children in the rows behind. Carol was just about to give Roger a warning nudge when Atwell said, 'Let us pray,' and she realised they were mercifully close to the end.

When the final hymn was sung and the last blessing given, the congregation began to trickle out into the thin winter sunshine. Carol felt her shoulders loosen; she wasn't sure if she'd been tensing them against the chill or the sermon. Outside, the yews offered a little shelter from the wind, and small knots of people stood chatting, stamping their feet on the frozen ground.

Atwell appeared, smiling warmly, and shook her hand.

'So glad you could come, Mrs Sinclair.'

'Yes,' Carol said, mustering her most convincing smile. 'We enjoyed the service very much.'

She could feel Roger hesitate almost imperceptibly before nodding.

'Yes, sir,' he said, in a tone that could pass for politeness if you weren't listening too closely.

Susan added, 'It was nice,' and Benjy, perhaps carried away by the sight of the farmer's dog nosing about behind him, said, 'I liked the singing.'

Atwell beamed as though they had just confirmed his vocation. 'Well, I do hope we shall see you here regularly. You'd be most welcome.'

Carol promised vaguely that they would, and they moved aside to allow others to greet him. She saw Jonathan Darby standing by the low stone wall, talking with one of the farmers. As they passed, he caught her eye again.

'Good morning, Mrs Sinclair. I hope the children are settling in well?'

'They are, thank you. Am I right in thinking there were many children from the school here today?,' she said, keeping her tone

243

light, though she was aware of Roger watching her with an expression she suspected was not wholly innocent.

'Yes, quite a few,' said Jonathan looking around him. 'It's good you brought the children today. It will help, I imagine, if they seem somehow, familiar.'

By now, Carol was aware that Susan was also staring at the two of them so she decided that the conversation should remain relatively brief. She thanked Jonathan again but could scarcely think why and then led the children to the car.

In the back of the car, the children had already begun discussing, in frank tones, exactly how boring the sermon had been, though Susan maintained the singing was worth the trip. Carol let them chatter, keeping her own thoughts to herself. Reverend Atwell was well-meaning enough, but she doubted he would ever set the village alight with his sermons.

Still, there was the matter of appearances, and appearances mattered—especially here, where tongues could wag as briskly as the wind. And, she told herself firmly, it was good for the children to be seen as part of the community. That Jonathan Darby's smile had brightened her morning was simply an incidental bonus.

Ravel Briggs walked into the smoky interior of *The Gravedigger's* just after midday. He looked around the gloomy interior but did not see anyone who interested him. A slight motioning gesture from one of the men in a distant corner caught his eye. He saw a man hunched over a pint near the back where the light from the lanterns barely reached. On the table before him lay a folded newspaper he hadn't read, serving as a mat for his glass.

He was a well-made man in an overcoat and still wearing his hat. It was as if he did not want to draw attention to himself but in dressing so, did just that. From underneath the brim of his fedora, Briggs could see that the man's eyes were fixed on him. They were clear blue and never seemed to move. Briggs was not someone of a nervous disposition normally but he felt a chill rise up his back that had nothing to do with the cold air from which he had just escaped.

Biggs paused just inside the door, letting his eyes adjust to the gloom. He nodded to the man before going to the bar. He ordered a whisky. Neat. Then he made his way towards the man's table with a confidence he certainly did not feel. The regulars glanced up briefly, then returned to their drinks.

He sat down without a word and set down his own glass.

Briggs studied the man opposite him, trying to convey that he was unafraid. The man had a strong jaw and was recently clean-shaven. There was a kind of precise stillness about him that made Briggs uneasy. The man looked around to see if anyone was listening. He spoke in a low voice.

'Any news?' asked the man quickly getting to the point.

Briggs sipped his whisky, weighing the question. 'Might be.'

The man ignored the challenge. 'You saw some children there, didn't you? Two boys and a girl.'

Briggs gave a dry chuckle, the kind that never reached the eyes. 'I see plenty of things in the woods. Rabbits. Deer. Folk as shouldn't be there.'

The man leaned forward just enough to make the space between them feel smaller. 'Answer the question. I told you to look. I've paid you.'

Briggs felt a prickle at the back of his neck. He was used to talking his way around nosy gamekeepers or villagers with too much curiosity, but there was something about this fellow's manner—calm, deliberate—that told him bluff wouldn't get him far.

'Aye,' Briggs said at last. 'Saw 'em. Yesterday. Off the main path.'

'Did they see you?' asked the man. Sadly, they had and Briggs felt his face redden. 'You damn fool. I told you to stay hidden. Are they definitely staying at Ravenley?'

'Yes,' said Briggs.'

The confirmation seemed to hang in the air for a moment, as though the man were testing its weight. Then the man asked, 'Who lives there?'

Briggs scratched at the stubble on his chin. 'Old fella. Some kind of butler and housekeeper, too. Stern woman, middle years, goes by Mrs something-or-other. And a younger one. Carol Sinclair. Husband's in the RAF. During the day and early evening a cook is there but she leaves at seven.'

'And the children.'

Briggs shook his head. 'They've the look of evacuees about 'em. Bit out o' place, if you ask me.'

The man's eyes narrowed slightly, though his tone stayed level. 'Does Mrs Sinclair live alone?'

'More or less. Just them three and the two staff. But...' Briggs took a slow sip of whisky, watching for a flicker of interest. 'I heard she's just been taken on by the ambulance service. Means she might be away nights. Don't know which ones, mind you. There's a copper too watching over the place. Patrols a bit. It's such a big place though you can easily avoid him.'

The man took this in without comment, swirling the whisky in his glass. He had the air of someone building a map in his head, marking details as they came.

'You've been in the woods since then?' he asked.

Briggs nodded cautiously. 'I keep my traps there.'

'Good.' The man stood abruptly, leaving his drink half-finished. 'If you see them again, you will tell me. And you will tell no one else that we spoke. Understand?'

Briggs bristled slightly. He didn't like being given orders, especially by strangers. 'And what's in it for me?'

The man reached into his coat and slid something across the table. Briggs glanced down—a folded banknote. Not much, but enough for a week's drink and baccy.

'I'll find you when I need to,' the man said. His voice was calm, but the steel underneath was unmistakable.

Without another word, he turned and walked towards the door, his steps unhurried. The latch clicked behind him, and the murmur of the pub swelled to fill the space he'd left.

Briggs sat back, the banknote resting under his fingertips. He didn't like the man, didn't like the way his pale eyes had seemed to look right through him, but money was money, and Ravel Briggs had never been known to turn down easy coin. Still, as he drained the tumbler, he couldn't shake the feeling that he'd just stepped into something bigger than a poacher's business had any right to be.

What did he intend doing to the children?

The rain had started again by the time the mysterious man stepped out of *The Gravedigger's*. He pulled his overcoat collar up and strode towards the far end of the lane, where a dark saloon car

247

waited with its engine running. The vehicle's dark paintwork dulled by road grime. The condensation on the inside of the windscreen suggested they'd been waiting some time. As the man approached, the driver leaned over and unlocked the back door.

He slid into the rear seat without a word, shutting the door firmly behind him.

'Well?' The voice came from the passenger seat, gravelly, impatient.

The man settled himself, brushing a bead of rain from his cuff. 'Briggs saw them. Two boys and a girl. Staying at Ravenley.'

The driver gave a low whistle, though whether from recognition or unease it was hard to say. 'Bit out in the sticks, isn't it?'

'Not enough to matter,' the man replied. 'Household consists of an elderly servant, a housekeeper, and a Mrs Carol Sinclair. There's a copper too, keeping watch. Husband's away in the RAF. She's just been accepted for ambulance work, so she's out some nights.'

The passenger shifted in his seat. 'Which nights?'

'Briggs doesn't know,' the man said curtly. 'Let's hope it's tonight otherwise we'll have to wait another week.'

There was a pause. Rain drummed against the roof and the sound of the idling engine filled the close space.

'Tonight, then?' the passenger asked at last.

'Yes.'

The driver glanced in the rear-view mirror, meeting the man's pale eyes. 'You sure about that? Place like that... people notice comings and goings.'

'We won't be noticed.' The man's tone allowed no room for disagreement.

From the passenger seat came a faint, uneasy cough. 'It's not just that,' he said slowly. 'He's only a lad.'

The man in the back didn't answer straightaway. Instead he leaned forward slightly, his voice dropping a fraction. 'Do you think I enjoy this?'

The passenger's gaze remained fixed on the wet road ahead.

'We have no choice,' the man went on. 'He saw me. He described me. If he remembers more...' He let the sentence hang, unfinished but heavy with implication.

'Couldn't we just...?' the passenger began, but the man cut across him.

'No. There's no 'just' about it. The longer he breathes, the greater the risk.'

Silence settled in the car again, save for the occasional squeak of the wipers across the misted windscreen. The driver shifted uncomfortably, as though the seat had grown harder beneath him.

The passenger's fingers drummed lightly on his knee, an unconscious rhythm of nerves. 'What about the others? The girl and the little one?'

'They'll be asleep. We won't disturb them.' The words were meant to be reassuring, but the flatness of the delivery did nothing to soften them.

The man in the passenger seat gave a short, humourless laugh. 'Doesn't make it any prettier.'

'No,' the man agreed. 'But we don't get to choose pretty. We choose what keeps us free.'

They drove off a few minutes later, the vehicle gliding through the slick streets with its lights kept low. From the outside, they could have been three tradesmen heading home late from a job. Inside, the air was thick with the unspoken—plans unvoiced but understood, and a single fact that pressed on them all: before the night was out, they would be standing in the dark outside Ravenley, and one small witness would not see another dawn.

249

Sunday mornings were made for lying in, and Chops intended to give the tradition a thorough work-out, at least until his brain decided otherwise. He lay sprawled in the half-light of his bedroom, the curtains still drawn against the pale winter sun. Somewhere outside, a milk cart rattled past, and the yelping keow of a few distant seagulls drifted in. Ordinarily, these were the sounds of blissful indolence, but today they only prodded at him as his wife once had when there were jobs to be done in the house. He missed this not a jot.

The murder of Morrison refused to leave him alone. It had followed him into his dreams the night before, turning up in a jumble of faces including the nightwatchman's own, shadowed and half-smiling; Big Jim Jefferies behind his desk with the smell of fried fish in the air; and that weaselly specimen Richardson, smirking like a man who thought he knew more than he did.

It was just after nine when Chops admitted defeat. He rolled onto his side and found himself staring at Moriarty, the cat, who had chosen to sleep directly against his ribs as though trying to fuse their body heat.

'Morning, professor,' Chops muttered.

Moriarty opened one eye in a slow, contemptuous blink, the feline equivalent of telling him to shove off. The tip of his tail twitched twice which was enough for the policeman to know that the cat was not to be disturbed further. Chops swung his legs out of bed, earning a disgruntled grunt from the cat as his warm perch was disturbed.

'Yes, yes, I know,' Chops said. 'I'm a cruel man. But duty calls.'

At the word 'duty,' Moriarty merely yawned, baring teeth that looked far too sharp for an animal who spent most of his days pretending to be asleep. But when Chops reached the kitchen and took down the tin of fish, Moriarty's attitude shifted in an instant. The cat was suddenly underfoot, winding in and out of his legs like a furry con artist who'd just spotted a mark.

'Utterly shameless' said Chops, spooning the meat into a bowl.

Moriarty didn't care. By the time Chops had filled the kettle, the cat was already crouched over his breakfast, tail held upright in triumph.

Chops let him be and drank his tea at the table, staring into the steam and thinking about Briggs. The man wasn't just setting snares for rabbits. Something about the way Carol Sinclair said the children had described him, shifty, evasive, too interested in the children, made the hairs on the back of Chops' neck prickle. Poachers didn't usually have conversations with kids unless they were trying to shoo them away.

He glanced at the clock. If Briggs was local, there was a good chance he'd still be somewhere on the moor this morning. And Sunday was as good a day as any to poke a stick in the hornet's nest.

Decision made, Chops went to the hallway, where his fedora sat on the sideboard. He lifted it up to reveal that it had been hiding a framed photograph. The picture showed a younger Chops, hair still thick and dark, standing beside a woman with sharp eyes and a smile that was all angles.

He paused, looking at her face for a moment. Then, almost without thinking, he said, 'Cow.'

This was said with genuine venom. It set Chops up for the day. He liked to start each morning with a little bit of resentment. Having this edge gave him the motivation to catch criminals. Coat on, hat settled, Chops stepped into the cold air. The street was quiet, most of the houses still shuttered up for Sunday lie-ins. Somewhere in the distance a church bell began its slow, deliberate calling, and Chops imagined half the parish groaning under their bedclothes at the reminder.

He walked with his hands in his pockets, tilted his hat to the back of his head, ready to work. His day off and all he could think about was thinking about how he'd find Briggs. The man was a shadow operator, kept to the edges of villages, spent most of his time in the rougher patches of the moor. A few questions at the right pub might do the trick, or maybe a word with the local gamekeeper.

The case was still just a series of bits and pieces that didn't seem to fit, but which Chops was sure would line up if he could just get the missing bit of picture. Morrison's gambling debts were the obvious thread, but to who? And why was Briggs in the woods? Was their more to it than just poaching?

It was the sort of tangle that kept a man from enjoying his Sunday. The cold air sharpened his thoughts, and by the time he reached the corner, he had a plan. First stop would be *The Gravedigger's* . If Briggs was drinking anywhere before noon, it would be there. After that, maybe a walk out past the edge of the common, see if he could catch the poacher in his natural habitat.

Behind him, back in the flat, Moriarty had finished his breakfast and leapt onto the bed again, curling into the warm dent left by Chops. The cat would sleep until Chops returned, and perhaps after that too.

It was almost midday when Chops finally turned his old Morris onto the gravel drive at Ravenley. The low winter light slanted across the parkland, catching the frost still clinging in the shaded hollows. Beyond the rise, the big house stood dark against a pewter sky, its chimneys sending up the occasional wisp of smoke like some ancient beast breathing in the cold.

He spotted Talbot near the south lawn, hands buried in the pockets of his heavy coat, the brim of his cap pulled low. He was studying a row of frost-burned hedges as if they'd committed some personal offence.

'How's the hypothermia settling in?' Chops said by way of greeting.

Talbot grunted. 'You're not wrong. Thought you'd be warm in the station, sipping tea.'

'It's my day off,' said Chops. 'You'll be downhearted to hear; this'll be your last night here.'

That made Talbot turn. His face didn't change much, but the slight narrowing of his eyes was enough. 'What's that supposed to mean? Is the case solved.'

'Superintendent thinks it is, in a matter of speaking. Says Scotland Yard's on it now. We're to step back.'

'Step back?' Talbot's voice had a hard edge. 'That's rich, after the nights I've spent freezing my proverbials off.'

'Aye, I know,' Chops cut in, tone steady. 'I don't agree with him. But I'm not in the business of crossing orders; at least not ones I can't get away with.'

Talbot laughed despite himself. Finally, he gave a curt nod. 'Can you give me a lift back?'

'I have to do a few things first,' said Chops, allowing himself the ghost of a smile.

They stood in silence for a few moments, breath pluming in the cold. Somewhere across the grounds a rook cawed, the sound flat and thin in the frosty air.

'Right,' Chops said at last. 'I'll see you back here in an hour or so.'

The Morris rattled along the narrow lane that skirted the edge of the estate, its tyres hissing on the damp tarmac. He'd been given Ravel Briggs's last known address by a constable who'd spoken of it with the sort of tone one might reserve for a wasp's nest on a hot day: a caravan pitched in a patch of scrubland just outside the estate boundary, half hidden by a stand of skeletal birch trees.

253

When Chops found it, the place looked as though it had been abandoned in a hurry. The caravan's paint was peeling in strips, revealing the grey tin beneath, and a line of washing with two shirts that didn't look any cleaner in Chops' view and what might once have been a pair of trousers, hung stiff and frozen from a sagging rope.

He got as far as the first step up to the door before the growl stopped him. It came from the left, low and deliberate, the kind of sound that didn't just warn you, it promised. Pain.

Out of the shadows beside the caravan slunk a pit bull, heavy-muscled, square-jawed, eyes like chips of wet slate. Its hackles were already up, and the thick leather collar round its neck looked as though it had seen better days and perhaps more than one unlucky ankle.

'Oh, marvellous, as if this case couldn't get any better,' Chops muttered. He'd never had much time for that breed. There was a little too much jaw, not enough sense, for his liking.

The dog gave another growl, this one accompanied by a slow advance that suggested it had all the time in the world to consider exactly which limb it would feed on that day. Chops with all of the courage and decisiveness one associates with a man of action such as he, immediately backed down the step, smiling nervously.

'Let's not fall out Fido. Just a few questions for your master.'

The pit bull stopped but didn't relax. It watched him with the intensity of a sentry guarding the crown jewels, the faint steam of its breath curling in the cold air.

Chops took the hint. He walked back towards the Morris, slow and steady just to show the pit bull that he had not been afraid. Only when he was in the driver's seat with the door shut did he allow himself to let out the breath he'd been holding.

Through the windscreen, the dog was still there, standing watching him with the barely disguised loathing he held for all humans.

254

'Charming,' he said, starting the engine. 'I must introduce you to Dora, sometime. On second thoughts, you don't deserve that.'

The road back to Ravenley wound between low hedges and over a small stone bridge, the water below running dark and quick. Chops kept one hand on the wheel and let the other drum absently against his knee. The visit hadn't yielded anything except a reminder of how unfriendly the countryside could be when it wanted.

By the time the house came back into view, Chops was feeling rather peckish. He hoped that he was in time to join Carol for lunch. He remembered that Carol's part-time cook, Mrs Givens was capable in ways that his errant wife, Dora, could only dream of being.

Even a cheese sandwich would have sufficed.

The truck's engine roared into life with a lurch that nearly pitched Charles from the narrow wooden bench. The canvas flaps at the back shuddered in the wind as they pulled away from whatever nameless police station they had spent the night in. His wrists were unbound, but there was a guard at either end of the truck bed, each with a rifle cradled loosely but never far from ready. The four prisoners—himself, the Frenchman, Leclerc, and the two tight-lipped Dutchmen—were seated on opposite benches, forbidden to speak.

The order had been given curtly when they were bundled aboard: *Keine Gespräche.* No talking. Charles suspected that the guard's real motive was to keep them from comparing notes, or perhaps from organising something foolish. Their reputation went before them, obviously. Charles felt a=oddly proud about this. It was a shaft of light in an otherwise miserable moment.

The truck jolted over cobbled streets, then settled into a steadier rhythm as it reached the open road. For the first half-hour, Charles tried to fix his eyes on the slit of daylight at the back, but the wind that whipped through the flaps was cutting, and the scenery, a blurred succession of grey fields and skeletal trees, did little to lift his spirits. One thing was now evident to him.

They were heading deeper into Germany.

He was tired in that way a man is after too many nights of poor sleep, his body aching for rest but his mind wound tight as wire. There was the dull throb of hunger too; breakfast had been a tin mug of something pretending to be coffee and a heel of bread so stale it might have been used for sandpaper.

More than that, there was the gnawing question of their final destination. His first thought had been a firing squad, but the presence of the other prisoners argued against it. If the Germans had meant to dispose of him quietly, they wouldn't have lumped him in with a French sergeant and two Dutchmen who barely looked at him.

Still, the road stretched on without explanation. Two hours, maybe more. The guards gave no hint, no change of expression, no word beyond the occasional barked instruction for them to sit straighter.

When the truck finally slowed, Charles braced himself. They rumbled through a gate; he could hear the clang of iron and the muffled shouts of sentries and came to a halt. Charels felt the first stirrings of relief. They hadn't stopped in a forest and been dispatched to that great aircraft hangar in the sky. However, their new home filled him with worry. There had been something about the manner of the German officer which worried him. It wasn't arrogance. That would be too easy an accusation to level at the enemy. No, it was something else. If Charles had to put a finger to it, he would have described it as a quiet confidence.

This new prison was escape proof.

'*Raus!*' shouted one of the German soldiers.

The four of them clambered down into a yard paved with uneven cobbles, ringed by high walls and patrolled by soldiers in field grey. Above, the sky was the colour of unpolished lead.

And there it was, looming before him: Colditz.

The name carried a faint, old-world menace. A medieval castle perched on a cliff above the River Mulde, its turrets and thick curtain walls looking as if they had been carved straight from the rock itself. In another life, it might have been a postcard sight, a fortress for a fairy tale, with red-tiled roofs and narrow windows. But here, in the bone-brittle cold of winter, with the grey flags of the Reich hanging limp from its towers, it looked every inch the prison it was.

The courtyard into which they had been herded was dominated by the massive keep. Windows were barred, the heavy oak doors reinforced with iron.

They were marched across the yard; past groups of prisoners who paused in whatever business they had been about to watch the new arrivals. Charles caught glimpses. There were French officers in worn greatcoats, Poles in patched uniforms, a handful of British-looking figures who gave him a quick, assessing glance before resuming their stroll.

Inside, the air was colder still, the thick stone swallowing what little warmth the day offered. Boots rang hollow on flagstones as they were led up a wide stair and along a corridor whose windows looked down into the grey churn of the river far below. Eventually, they were halted outside a heavy wooden door. A guard rapped once, opened it, and gestured them inside.

The room was large, with a desk positioned before a tall window, behind which a man in Wehrmacht uniform rose to his feet. His hair was clipped short, the colour of iron filings, and his eyes were a pale, assessing blue.

'Gentlemen,' he said in careful English. 'I am Hauptmann Reinhold Eggers, Security Officer for the camp.'

Eggers, as Charles was to discover, was a different breed of officer from the brutal SS men he had heard about. His manner was brisk but not overtly hostile; his uniform was neat without being ostentatious. Still, there was something in his gaze that told Charles this was a man who missed nothing.

'I will be brief,' Eggers continued. 'You are here because you have caused trouble in other camps. Here, you will cause no trouble. Colditz is a special prison. Escape from here...is impossible.'

The word hung in the air like frost.

'You will find the guards here are disciplined,' Eggers went on. 'We are soldiers, professional soldiers, not butchers. This is not the

258

SS. But do not mistake discipline for weakness. The rules are clear. Break them, and you will regret it. I suggest you take the opportunity to make your stay here... tolerable.'

Charles felt an unexpected rush of relief at the distinction between Wehrmacht and SS. The Wehrmacht were no angels, but there was at least a framework, a code. The SS were a by-word for brutality.

Eggers dismissed them with a nod to the guards, who led them out to be processed; papers taken, possessions recorded, bunks assigned. Charles found himself in a small, bare room with three other men, one of them Leclerc, who gave him a faint smile. The Dutchmen had been placed elsewhere, perhaps by design.

From the narrow window, Charles could see the castle walls and, beyond them, the town of Colditz itself, roofs huddled together against the cold. Somewhere down there, ordinary Germans were going about their Sunday, fetching bread, tending stoves, perhaps going to a church service, trying to ignore the fortress that loomed above them like a stone sentinel.

It was going to be a long war. Half an hour later, he was nursing a tin mug of ersatz coffee that tasted faintly of burnt acorns when the door to his room banged open. Two guards stood over him, rifles slung but hands near the stocks.

'*Mitkommen!*' one barked.

Charles set down the mug and rose. Leclerc shot him a questioning glance, but the guards clearly had orders for only one prisoner. He followed them out into the corridor, his boots striking cold stone. They took him across a covered walkway that linked two wings of the castle. From the high, narrow windows he caught brief glimpses of the courtyard below, a dusting of frost still clinging to the cobbles, and a few prisoners already pacing in pairs like gentlemen taking the morning air.

Eventually they stopped before a heavy door reinforced with black iron straps. One guard rapped on it, and it was opened from within by a British soldier in a neat but well-worn uniform. He was

259

tall, brown-haired, with a clipped moustache and the sort of brisk manner that suggested the army had been bred into his bones.

'Ah,' he said, his eyes running over Charles with practised speed. 'You must be Sinclair.'

'Guilty,' Charles said. He stepped inside the quarters reserved, as he was to find out later, for British officers. The guards turned and left.

'Captain Pat Reid. I'm the escape officer here,' said the man who had greeted him.

They shook hands. Reid's grip was firm, the sort of handshake that, even here, seemed to carry an unspoken promise: *You're among our own now.*

'Come on,' Reid said. 'Let's get you introduced.'

They were in what had once been a spacious drawing room, now turned over to the business of war in captivity. Tables were pushed together to form a communal space; a few battered armchairs huddled near a fireplace in which a grudging fire smouldered. Around the room, half a dozen officers were engaged in various occupations like sewing, reading, playing chess. A small wireless sat on a side table, its aerial jury-rigged from what looked suspiciously like bed-frame springs.

'Welcome to the British quarters,' Reid said, steering Charles towards the hearth. 'It's not the Ritz, but it's warmer than the yard.'

'That wouldn't take much,' Charles said.

Reid gave him a brief grin. 'You'll find the Germans are very proud of their castle. They call it escape-proof. Some of our chaps would like to put that to the test.'

'Is that so?'

'Quite. That's my role here—co-ordinate escape attempts, keep track of who's working on what, stop chaps tripping over each other's tunnels, that sort of thing. We've got some very clever fellows, but cleverness without organisation gets you nowhere but solitary.'

Charles took this in. The man had been at Colditz, he said, just over a month, yet he spoke with the easy authority of one who already understood the place and its rhythms.

'And the Germans? I'm sure they don't mind,' said Charles, dryly.

'They mind very much,' Reid said with a chuckle. 'That's why we do it under their noses. Look, you'll hear this soon enough: they've got the place sewn up like a drum. Multiple perimeters, sentries who actually pay attention, barred windows, guards who can spot a shirt that's gone missing before you've even thought of turning it into civilian clothing. If it weren't such a dashed nuisance it'd be almost admirable.'

They moved about the room as Reid introduced him to the other British officers. He called their names out one by one and they came over to shake Charles' hand.

'Lieutenant Michael Duncan, Captain Harry Elliott, Lieutenant Jock Hamilton-Baillie, Captain Rupert Barry, Lieutenant Tony Murray'

Chales looked confused. He turned to Reid and asked, 'Only officers?'

'No, the men have their own quarters. The Germans may be the enemy but they believe in rank.'

Charles was offered a place by the fire and a tin mug of tea. Real tea, not the German chicory substitute. It was weak, but it tasted like home.

'You'll want to find your feet first,' Reid told him. 'Learn the routines. Mealtimes, exercise periods, roll calls. The guards here are Wehrmacht, not SS, makes life a bit less precarious. That said, don't mistake them for pushovers. They've been told this place is unbreakable, and they mean to keep it that way.'

Charles thought of Eggers, with his pale eyes and measured tone. Yes, he could believe it.

'Have there been... successes?' he asked.

Reid's moustache twitched. 'No runs scored yet. It's difficult game.'

'And what game are we playing?'

'Ours? Simple. To be such an infernal nuisance that they wish they'd never brought us here.'

Charles smiled despite himself. 'Sounds almost enjoyable.'

'Some days it is. Others... not so much.' Reid's eyes met his, and in that brief glance Charles saw the unspoken truth: the cold, the boredom, the relentless grind of confinement. But there was also steel there, and it steadied something in him.

For the next hour Reid showed him around the British section of the castle. They passed through a narrow corridor into what had once been servants' quarters, now used as workshops of sorts—one room for tailoring, another for tinkering with improvised gadgets. In one corner a man was filing at a piece of metal clamped to a table, the rasp of his tool blending with the low murmur of conversation.

'We make do,' Reid said. 'Everything's a resource: old tins, wire, bed slats. The Germans inspect regularly, but we're usually a step ahead.'

From there they went out into the yard. The cold hit Charles like a slap. Groups of prisoners walked in slow circuits, their breath pluming in the air. Across the way he could see the French and Polish contingents, separated from the British by an invisible but well-policed boundary.

'We're not supposed to mix much,' Reid explained. 'Keeps things tidy for the Germans. But we do, of course, exchange the odd bit of intelligence now and then.'

They passed under the watchful eye of a sentry, who nodded to Reid. It struck Charles that the guards seemed to know him by sight—probably a testament to his role as escape officer.

Back inside, they paused near a narrow staircase that spiralled upward into one of the towers.

'Observation point,' Reid said. 'Good for spotting changes in routine, new sentries, that sort of thing. Always worth keeping an eye on.'

'Do you know how many guards?' asked Charles.

'We estimate between one hundred and fifty to two hundred.'

Charles took a turn at the window, looking out over the outer wall and the town beyond. From this height the river looked deceptively calm, winding away into the hills. Somewhere out there was freedom.

When they returned to the common room, Reid pulled out a battered notebook.

'Right. I'll note you down as newly arrived. Any particular skills I should know about?'

Charles hesitated. 'Fluent in French and German. Fair hand at mechanics, though I doubt we'll be servicing motorcars in here.'

'You'd be surprised,' Reid said, jotting it down. 'Languages are useful. And as for mechanics... you never know when we might need a working winch or an improvised lock.'

He closed the book with a snap. 'We'll talk more in a day or two. For now, get to know the place. And remember, whatever Eggers told you about Colditz being escape-proof, take it as a challenge, not a fact.'

Charles found himself smiling again, though the truth was he had no immediate plans to try anything as bold as scaling the castle walls. But it was a comfort to know that others were thinking about it, planning, refusing to let the Germans win by default.

By the time the house at Ravenley came into view, Chops was feeling the sort of gnawing hunger that makes a man begin to eye his shoelaces speculatively, like Charlie Chaplin, wondering whether they might, in a pinch, be made into spaghetti. It was a Sunday sort of hunger, sluggish yet insistent, and he quickened his pace along the gravel path with the keen instinct of a man who suspected lunch might already be underway.

The thought of Mrs Givens, Carol's Irish part-time cook, sharpened his step even more. She was a woman who, armed with nothing more than a frying pan and a few odds and ends from the larder, could turn out a dish that would make a bishop weep for joy. Armed with a wooden spoon, she could probably win the war. Cooking was, Chops reflected grimly, a quality in which his own errant wife, Dora, was catastrophically deficient. Dora's one serious attempt at a hot meal had ended with the saucepan having to be thrown out entirely, on the grounds that even the scrap men would refuse to take it.

Luck, for once, was with him. As he stepped into the hall, brushing wind from his coat, Carol's voice called from the dining room.

'Chops! You're just in time. Mrs Givens has made a shepherd's pie.'

The words sent a small shiver of joy down his spine. 'Mrs Givens,' he replied, striding in, 'is a saint. A culinary saint, at that.

264

Where she in my kitchen, I might have gained a several stone by now, but I should have gone to my grave smiling.'

Carol smiled faintly. 'Sit down before it gets cold.'

The table was set with the neatness one would expect from a household run, however loosely, under Carol's eye. Sunlight from the high windows caught the gleam of silver cutlery and the lazy spirals of steam rising from the pie. Chops took his seat opposite her, aware of the comfortable warmth of the room compared to the chill outdoors.

'I won't pretend this isn't the best part of my day,' he said, already ladling a generous helping onto his plate.

'That bad?' Carol asked, watching him with the practised sympathy of someone who had seen men return from less than inspiring mornings.

'You could say so.' He took a mouthful, sighed contentedly, and then got down to it. 'I went to Dartmoor yesterday to see a man who, a few months back, was part of a robbery that looked remarkably like the one in Exeter. No one had thought to tell me he was there. Anyway, the method, the timing, the whole thing was identical. The rest of his lot were never caught, and they're still out somewhere. Scotland Yard's thinking is that they've taken their talents west. They don't see how a local gang could have so closely matched what was done in London.'

Carol nodded slowly. 'And what did he say?'

'Nothing useful. They rarely do. Denied it all, naturally. I might have got more out of a brick wall, and the wall wouldn't have smirked quite so much. He knows his share will be waiting for him when he comes out and his family will be looked after. Being in prison during a war is probably no bad place to be for the likes of him.' He set down his fork and gave a short, humourless laugh. 'Not that it matters now. I'm off the case. Talbot too. Superintendent McDaid says it's Yard business from here on. Talbot's protection duty will have to end.'

265

Carol was silent for a moment, her gaze drifting to the window where the bare branches of the beech trees scratched at the glass. 'It makes sense,' she said at last, though without much conviction. 'If the gang is from London, then perhaps they've already gone back.'

'Perhaps,' Chops said, but his tone made it clear he thought otherwise.

She looked at him more closely. 'You don't sound convinced. What's worrying you?'

He reached for the mustard, fiddled with the spoon a moment, then set it down. 'Ravel Briggs.'

'The poacher?'

'The same. I don't like loose ends, and he's a loose end the size of Devon. I'm not going to feel right until I've found him and had a proper word.'

Carol poured them both a glass of water. 'Do you think he's connected to the robbery?'

'I think,' Chops replied slowly, 'that Briggs knows more than he should about what's been going in those woods. Whether that ties him to the Exeter raid, I don't know. But I'd bet my last shilling he's seen something, and the longer he's left alone, the harder he'll be to pin down.'

Carol nodded, but her eyes had taken on that faraway look again, the one Chops recognised from the weeks since Charles's disappearance. 'Still no word from the RAF?' he asked gently.

She shook her head. 'Nothing. Not a letter, not a telegram.' She paused, then added, 'It's the not knowing that's worst. If he's alive, if he's...' Her voice trailed off and she picked up her fork again, though she barely touched the food.

'How were things before then?' Chops asked, perhaps a little too abruptly.

She gave him a wry glance. 'That's a rather personal question.'

'I remember you as the girl in the gossip columns,' he said with a faint smile. 'Always some fellow or other hanging about. I wondered if life at Ravenley, waiting for letters that don't come, is quite what you imagined.'

Carol's lips twitched, but she didn't smile. 'I'm happy with Charles,' she said after a moment. 'He's a good man.'

'Hm,' Chops said, unconvinced but not pressing the point. 'I remember the time you helped me out on the Greenhill murder case. You were sharper than half the men in the department.'

Her eyes brightened slightly at the memory. 'That was different. There was an excitement to it. I was living in London then. Coming back to Exeter felt like a trip back in time to a simpler world. No one was expecting me to spend my afternoons sewing blackout curtains. This damn war.'

'Yes,' Chops said, settling back in his chair, 'you spotted the key detail before anyone else. That whole business with the umbrella stand.'

She laughed softly. 'The umbrella stand was obvious once you saw it.'

'Not to young Inspector Partridge, it wasn't,' Chops said with relish. 'He had it in his head that the butler did it. Was halfway to charging the poor chap before you pointed out the blood on the underside of the stand. Only place it could have got there was if it had been used to hide the murder weapon.'

'And then you found the knife in the coal scuttle.'

'Yes, because you insisted we search the scullery again. I've never forgotten that.'

Carol looked faintly pleased. 'That was fun,' she admitted. 'In a morbid sort of way.'

'Well, you saved us all from Partridge's butler theory, which was worth the price of admission alone. Heaven knows how many times I've reminded him of it since.'

They both smiled at the memory, and for a moment the heaviness in the room lifted.

'What do you think of this case, then?' he asked.

She leaned back, considering. 'I think it's dangerous to underestimate men who can plan a robbery with military precision. I also think you're not ready to admit that Scotland Yard might be right. It could be the same gang as London.'

Chops smiled thinly. 'It's the sort of thing they'd like to be right about. Fits their tidy picture. But life's not tidy, and neither's crime.'

They finished the meal in a companionable silence, the warmth of the fire making the room drowsy. Chops lingered over his second cup of tea, reluctant to go back out into the grey afternoon.

'So,' Carol said at last, 'what will you do now you're officially off the case?'

'Officially? Keep out of it. Unofficially? I'm going to find Briggs.'

Carol gave him a small, knowing smile. 'I thought as much.'

Chops rose, stretching his legs. 'Thank Mrs Givens for me, won't you? Shepherd's pie is a dish I've almost given up on at home. Dora once tried to make one by using lentils instead of meat. It had to be served with a hammer and a chisel. I still have the sculpture I made.'

Carol laughed, the sound soft in the big room. 'Mrs Givens would be horrified.'

'Mrs Givens,' Chops said gravely, 'could teach the War Office a thing or two about rationing. She makes a pound of mince go further than most generals could take an army.'

'That's quite an endorsement.'

'It is,' Chops said, pulling on his coat. 'Now I must go and do something Superintendent McDaid would disapprove of.'

Carol raised an eyebrow. 'Which is?'

'Find Briggs,' Chops said simply. 'Before he disappears into the hedgerows entirely.'

'One thing before you go,' said Carol, her eyes turned towards the window. Chops could see something was swirling around in her mind.

'What are you thinking about?' asked Chops, leaning forward.

'Ned Turnbull.'

'Go on,' said Chops. He was now very interested.

'What you said earlier about the modus operandi of the gang.

'What has Ned to do with this?' asked Chops, frowning, not disbelieved Carol but because he couldn't make the connection.

'He's our resident poacher turned gamekeeper.'

'Yes, I remember.'

'Anyway,' continued Carol, 'that the Exeter raid you said was closely matched. This may sound strange but I can think of at least one reason how it may have been done by someone local.'

'How?'

So Carol told him.

Detective Inspector Winslow was, on this day, merely 'Tommy' to his wife and 'Daddy' to his two children, Mark and Diana. Sunday lunch had been completed and he was washing the dishes wearing his wife's blue gingham pinny when he heard an urgent rap on the door. He heard his wife, Penelope, go to answer. Then he heard a familiar voice followed by footsteps in the corridor. Moments later Chops appeared at the kitchen door. He spied the pinny, raised one eyebrow.

'Very fetching, Tommy. Blue suits you.'

'Very funny Chops,' frowned Winslow. 'What gives?'

'I had an idea. Sorry, I'll rephrase that. Carol Sinclair had an idea for a lead which I think is worth pursuing. Now, if possible.'

'Carol Sinclair?' said Winslow in surprise as he dried his hands with a tea towel.

'Don't underestimate that lady. I once did and damn near let a murderer get away. She may be a beauty but there's a brain in there too. This country should be using women like her more.'

'A beauty you say,' said Penelope Winslow, joining the two men in the kitchen. There was a dangerous tone to her voice and her eyes were fixed on Winslow who became very uncomfortable.

Chops could not resist twisting the knife further.

'Oh yes, Penny. Absolute corker. She likes Tommy, here, a lot. You better be careful.'

'What?' exploded Winslow in shock. Then he saw that Penny was laughing, as was Chops.

'You need to come for dinner Chops, and soon,' said Penny. 'Hurry up Tommy. It sounds like you have a case to solve.'

As they exited the house towards Chops' car, the chief inspector turned to Winslow. His face was serious.

'You're a lucky man, Tommy. Penny is a woman in a million.'

'I know,' agreed Winslow.

Chops stopped and looked at the young man.

'I mean it Tommy. Don't do anything silly. This war can be won without you charging into German bullets. You have a job to do here.'

Winslow's discomfort was evident. As ever, Chops was able to reach deep inside his mind and understand the conflict raging there.

They walked to the car in silence.

The telephone rang just as Carol was debating whether or not to go out to the children. She picked up the receiver, half expecting it to be Mrs Givens announcing that she'd enlisted. In the infantry. Mrs Givens was a formidable woman. The voice on the other end was brisk and clipped.

'Carol, it's Simon.'

Her hand tightened on the receiver. The hallway seemed to spin.

'Hello Simon. Yes? What is it?' she said in as composed a voice as she could manage.

'There's been word from the Air Ministry. The Germans have broadcast confirmation of a crash. The crew of his Blenheim...' Dean's voice cracked for a fraction of a second, then steadied. 'Danny White and Ralph Bolton are confirmed dead. No word on Charles.'

The breath caught in her throat. 'No word? What do you mean?'

'That means...' He paused, choosing his words with deliberate care. 'It means he may have survived the crash. But if so, he's been taken prisoner. The Germans won't announce that right away.'

For a moment she stood frozen, hearing only the faint hiss of the line. The kitchen clock ticked with monstrous slowness. In her mind, images came in rapid flashes, Charles laughing in his uniform before boarding the train to his posting, Charles leaning in the doorway of Ravenley with that half-smile that always softened his eyes, Charles disappearing into the roar of an engine.

271

When she spoke again her voice was calm, almost unnaturally so. 'Thank you for telling me, Simon.'

'Carol...'

'I have to go. Thank you Simon.' She replaced the receiver gently, as though sudden movement might shatter whatever fragile chance of hope the news had brought. She picked up the phone again and made a call to Charles' brother but reached Cressida instead. She told her what Simon had told her. For once Cressida did not use the opportunity to make a point. The call was mercifully short. Carol put the phone down with some relief.

She went into the library and found Susan hunched over a book. Susan looked up and smiled. She said, '*Sense and Sensibility.*'

'One of my favourites,' smiled Carol. She sat down beside Susan and said, 'You know I have to go out later. I'm on duty again. They're a bit short on Sundays.'

Susan smiled again and said, 'I think what you are doing is wonderful.'

'Thank you, Susan,' said Carol, feeling her turn cartwheels.

For the next hour, Carol stayed in the library and read with Susan. It helped calm her because she didn't know whether to be relieved or tearful. If Charles was a prisoner of war, the danger would remain. Yet, he would be away from the fighting. Every so often, tears would sting her eyes as she thought of him.

Around five, she could take no more of staying in the house. She had to leave. The drive into Exeter was a blur. She was dimly aware of hedgerows flicking past, of the road narrowing between dark-browed cottages, of the distant shimmer of the river, but her thoughts remained marbled by fear and relief. By the time she pulled into the hospital yard, her hands ached from gripping the wheel.

At six o'clock sharp she was in the garage, checking the ambulance with Cyril Thorpe. This was their second shift together. She tried not to let her nerves show. Their first task was a short run, returning a few patients to their homes. Cyril, all wiry energy and easy humour, seemed to sense she wasn't in a mood for small talk. He confined himself to brief instructions, showing her the route and which patients they'd be dropping off first.

The hour passed in a subdued rhythm, the steady thrum of the engine, the occasional muffled cough from the back, Cyril's low directions as they wound through narrow lanes and into the small villages dotting the countryside. Carol focused on the work, grateful for its quiet simplicity. Towards the end of the hour, Carol opened up a little on the news she'd heard from the Simon.

'I think you would have taken this a day or two ago, Carol,' said Cyril sympathetically. 'There's still hope, evidently. Pity about the two other airmen.'

'Yes,' said Carol. 'I never met them. Charles said they were good men. Yes, I was thinking about that. Somewhere in the country, a father and a mother perhaps, or a wife or sweetheart is going to receive the news they've been fearing. It's awful, Cyril. Just awful.'

Cyril put his hand on Carol's hand as she drove. Just as they had just left the last patient at a cottage on the outskirts of a hamlet Cyril suddenly stiffened in his seat.

'Hear that?'

Carol tilted her head. She did. At first it was faint tremor in the air. Then it grew, deepening into a dull, rhythmic drone. The sound she had been dreading.

Planes.

Not just the warm, rolling hum of a Wellington or a Lancaster, but a shriller note that carried its own shadow. German. Bombers accompanied by fighters.

Cyril's eyes flicked upward, scanning the slate-grey clouds. 'I heard word earlier. I suppose I was hoping they would go somewhere else.'

Carol's hands tightened on the wheel. Somewhere beneath the fear, she registered the absurdity. Only hours ago, her greatest fear had been news of Charles's death; now she was driving under skies where death itself might come in a sheet of fire. The sound was

273

growing louder. They were getting close now. By the time they were entering the hospital, she felt it in her chest as much as she heard it.

'Keep her steady,' Cyril said quietly.

Carol nodded, but she could see how white her knuckles were as she pulled up to the back entrance of the hospital. In that moment she realised that the fear she'd felt for Charles was something distant and abstract compared to the sharp, immediate terror of being here, in the open, with the enemy's machines somewhere overhead.

The drone thickened, and she found herself glancing instinctively toward the hedgerows, as though they might somehow shield the ambulance. Above them, the sky was still empty—but not for long.

'Perhaps they'll miss us said Carol hopefully.'

The first thud came from far away. It was dull, muffled, like someone slamming a great door deep underground. Then another, closer this time, sharper, and carrying with it a faint tremor underfoot.

And then the sound changed.

From above came a long, shivering whistle, a hideous metallic scream that cut through the night like tearing cloth. It grew in pitch and urgency, rushing earthward until it ended in a blinding, concussive roar. The ground shuddered. Somewhere far off, glass shattered in a great tinkling cascade.

More whistles followed, some distant, some close enough to make the air itself feel thick and hard to breathe.

Out towards Exeter, the night sky was no longer black but smeared with orange and livid red, rising in great, sullen pulses each time another explosion landed. The clouds above caught the light, turning them into rolling, bruised masses that glowed and darkened in time with the destruction below.

Searchlights clawed at the darkness, sweeping the heavens in slow, desperate arcs, their pale beams criss-crossing like the bars of a giant cage. Between them, the silhouettes of enemy planes moved with cold purpose, dropping their loads before banking away into the shadows.

274

Even from miles away, there was the acrid tang of smoke on the air. It slid into the lungs, mixed with the faint scent of burning wood and something heavier—stone dust, perhaps, or the charred remains of what had once been home to someone.

The rhythm of the bombardment was erratic, unpredictable: a moment's quiet, and then another shriek, another flash, another concussion that rolled like thunder through the bones. It was a sound one felt as much as heard, an unholy marriage of rage and precision.

'What do we do?' asked Carol in a hushed tone.

'Wait,' said Cyril calmly. Carol's turned sharply to the man in the seat beside her.

Carol turned sharply to the man in the seat beside her, searching his face in the dim light. He was gazing out through the ambulance windscreen as if they were merely paused at a traffic light rather than sitting in the middle of an air raid. His hands rested loosely on his knees, the posture of a man who had seen worse, and possibly more times than he could count.

She found herself matching his breathing, slower now, in rhythm with his own. She realised she was no longer just afraid. The fear had been replaced by senses that had sharpened, were tingling in anticipation of what was to be done. Her thoughts passed briefly to the children. They would be fine with Mrs Parker and Figgs. They knew what to do. Carol was where she needed to be. Whatever the night ahead would bring, she was ready.

A fire crackled in the grate of the drawing room, casting warm light over the polished wood panelling and the old, somewhat threadbare Persian rug that stretched from the hearth to the grand piano.

Benjy was sprawled in the largest armchair, his knees tucked up under his chin, eyes fixed on the wireless cabinet. Susan sat cross-legged on the floor beside him, a half-finished embroidery project dangling forgotten from her fingers. Mrs Parker had positioned herself in her customary seat nearest the fire, her knitting needles flashing with quiet precision. Figgs was perched primly on the edge of a straight-backed chair, though his expression suggested he might rather be scrubbing a stubborn stain out of a hallway carpet than partaking in this 'entertainment.'

From the wireless, the clipped, nasal voice of Lord Haw-Haw, or one of his impersonators, drifted into the room, full of deliberate menace and absurdly mangled English vowels.

'*Britain is finished, utterly finished. Your armies are in retreat; your navy is nothing but a...*'

'—a rusty old sardine tin,' Benjy supplied, adopting a passable imitation of the man's drawl.

Susan clapped a hand over her mouth to hide a giggle. Mrs Parker glanced over her spectacles and pursed her lips, though the corners of her mouth twitched treacherously.

The broadcast continued: '*You may as well give up now, before your cities are flattened...*'

276

'Like Mrs Given's pancakes,' Benjy interrupted.

This time Mrs Parker did laugh, a short, sharp burst that she disguised by pretending to cough. Figgs rolled her eyes heavenwards, muttering, 'Honestly,' though he couldn't quite suppress the small smile tugging at his mouth.

Lord Haw-Haw went on about the 'inevitable collapse' of the British Empire, sprinkling in exaggerated Germanic consonants which suggested only a nodding acquaintance with his adopted country's language and odd pauses that made his pronouncements sound as though they'd been assembled from a phrasebook.

Benjy stood up and performed an elaborate mock salute to the fireplace. 'We shall invade next Tuesday, provided the weather is nice and our packed lunches don't get soggy.'

Susan collapsed into helpless laughter, dropping her embroidery entirely. Even Mrs Parker, whose dignity was a point of pride, shook her head and said, 'You're an imp, Benjy, a complete imp.'

'Can't help it,' Benjy said cheerfully. 'He sets himself up for it. I'm merely the delivery boy of truth.'

The absurdity of the broadcast and the warmth of the fire made the outside world feel far away, at least for a few minutes. Even Figgs looked faintly entertained, though he immediately busied himself as if to show by example that a man's work is never done.

Lord Haw-Haw's voice droned on: '*Your Prime Minister, the so-called Winston Churchill, is hiding from the German might...*'

'Hiding?' exclaimed Roger indignantly. 'He's probably down the pub. Far better class of people than you lot.'

Susan's giggles had reached the point where she was wiping her eyes. The whole scene felt deliciously irreverent, mocking the enemy from the safety of the drawing room, safe behind drawn blackout curtains and the solid stone walls of Ravenley.

And then, quite suddenly, the atmosphere shifted.

It began faintly, almost hidden beneath the hiss of the wireless: a low, steady hum, somewhere at the edge of hearing. Susan was the first to stop laughing. She tilted her head, frowning slightly.

277

Benjy was about to deliver another jibe when Mrs Parker stiffened in her chair. Her knitting needles stilled. The hum was growing louder. Mrs Parker rose at once and crossed to the wireless, flicking the switch with brisk finality. Lord Haw-Haw's voice cut off mid-sentence, leaving a silence that was instantly filled by the unmistakable drone of engines overhead.

Not British engines.

In that silence, the children could hear the subtle difference in tone—deeper, more aggressive, a vibration that seemed to settle in the pit of the stomach.

Susan swallowed hard. 'Is it...?'

Mrs Parker didn't answer directly. 'Away from the windows, both of you,' she said firmly. 'Now.'

Benjy obeyed, though he tried to keep his face nonchalant. 'Probably just passing over,' he muttered.

'The lights in the kitchen,' exclaimed Mrs Parker suddenly. There was real fear in her voice.

'Back in a jiffy,' said Benjy. He shot out of the room before anyone could stop him.

'Benjy,' shouted Mrs parker and shook her head. Yet, a part of her admired his initiative. With his youth, speed and a low centre of gravity, he would probably reach the kitchen and be back before Figgs was out of the chair.

But the sound was close now; close enough that they could imagine the shadow of the planes sliding over the fields beyond the house. Figgs had risen too, his eyes fixed on the ceiling as though he might see through it.

The drawing room felt smaller, the air heavier. The crackle of the fire was suddenly far too loud, competing with the gathering thunder in the sky. And too bright.

Roger immediately went over with some water and doused the flames. The blackout curtains would probably have kept the light from permeating through but there was no sense in taking a risk.

Mrs Parker stood very straight, listening. Her hand rested lightly on the wireless as if she might turn it back on, but she didn't. Instead she looked towards the children with a level gaze that said, without words, *We will wait. And we will see.*

'We'll go to the cellar. Up everyone. Mr Figgs can you go and fetch Benjy?'

Figgs responded immediately to Mrs Parker's instructions. He'd found over the last fifteen years, that life was easier if one did so.

'Follow me, children,' said Mrs Parker. Roger and Susan already knew the way because they had been shown on their first night at Ravenley. They headed immediately to a door that led to Charles' wine cellar that was twenty feet below ground and had been deemed safe during an air raid.

Benjy reached the kitchen in record time. He was just about to switch off the light when Germany's bombs did him a favour. The lights in the kitchen went out of their own accord. In the distance he heard the muffled crump of bombs exploding. He looked up at the kitchen clock. It read 7:10pm.

Just as he was about to turn back and re-join the others when he heard a noise that definitely was not a German bomb. It was the sound of glass breaking at the back door of the kitchen. Moments later he heard voices. Whispered voices. Then a hand covered in cloth was thrust through the pane of glass that had been broken.

Burglars.

Benjy's heart was racing now. He stayed for a moment more out of curiosity than courage. There was no question now, there were at least two men outside looking to gain entry. They still hadn't seen him. Holding his breath, he stepped back wards out of the kitchen as quietly as he could.

Moments later, he collided with a body. He gasped as two arms encircled him.

'Constable's gone,' said Ravel Briggs without preamble, leaning a hand on the car window. His voice was soft, conspiratorial.

'Are you sure?' said the man he'd met at *The Gravedigger's*.

'Saw it with my own eyes. She's gone, too. Left twenty minutes ago. Must be at the hospital. That means it's just them kids and the two old folk.'

They were on the narrow lane that skirted the marsh. The hedgerows were thick with frost, gleaming faintly in the moonlight, and their old Wolseley idled at the verge, shuddering now and then as though impatient. Briggs, his dark coat buttoned to the throat, his homburg pulled low stayed away from the window. He did not want to know too much about the men in the car. Plausible deniability but he knew full well what they intended.

The men in the back seat shifted. The smell of tobacco smoke and leather filled the close air. Their leader—Stocky, broad-shouldered, with that thick neck Roger had glimpsed from the lane a week before—gave a short nod. 'Good. Then it's time.'

Briggs held out a gloved hand. 'My trouble's worth something.'

A packet of notes was produced, folded small, and passed over without ceremony. Briggs weighed it, slipped it away inside his coat, and tipped his hat. 'Then you'll not see me.' With that, he vanished into the night, leaving only the sound of his boots crunching down the lane.

'What do we do now?' asked one man.

'We wait.'

For an hour and half the gang waited. The car's engine was stilled; its windows fogged with breath. One man muttered about the cold, another about his stomach, but was silenced by a glance from the two other men. They had patience drilled into them, bank jobs demanded it, and besides, there was a nervous edge to the evening, as though the whole countryside were holding its breath. Twice they made patrols to check no one else was around.

At last the sky deepened and the first stars blinked through.

'It's time.'

They climbed out, stamping their feet, pulling scarves higher against the chill. The woods that bordered Ravenley stretched dark and skeletal, branches black against the pale sky. They trod carefully over the frozen earth, the crunch of each step sounding treacherously loud. Somewhere a fox barked. One of the men swore under his breath.

'Steady,' murmured the leading man. 'It's only a fox. You want to jump at shadows, go back to your mother.'

'All right, Purdy. Keep your hair on.'

'No, Robbo, you keep your hair on,' said the man called Purdy. He glared at the stocky man alongside him.

They pushed on, until, at last, the trees thinned and the rear of Ravenley loomed before them—an imposing silhouette, chimneys clawing at the night. Light still showed faintly at one or two windows. The men crouched in the shrubbery, watching.

Then it came: the drone of engines overhead, distant at first, then swelling until the very earth seemed to tremble with it. Planes, a squadron of them, cutting across the clouds. The gang froze. Even Robbo tilted his head upward, teeth bared slightly in the dark.

'They're ours?' whispered the third man.

'Or theirs,' said Robbo. Both were nervous enough already without this.

'Shut it,' snapped Purdy. 'They'll help us, whichever side they're on. Noise like that'll drive the household to ground. You know

281

where they'll go.' He jabbed a finger toward the great house. 'Cellar. Shelter. And that's where the brats will be.'

The word *brats* hung in the air, and for a moment no one moved. Then the youngest, twitchy with nerves, broke the silence: 'We go in, then?'

Purdy pulled a small crowbar from beneath his coat, the steel dull in the moonlight. 'We go in.'

They crossed the final stretch of lawn swiftly, crouching low. The house seemed to grow taller with every step, its stone walls implacable, its windows like watchful eyes. At the back door, a heavy oak affair with black iron hinges, they paused. Stocky gestured, and the man with the crowbar jammed it between window and frame. With a grunt, the glass gave a sharp crack, splintering into glittering shards. Cold air rushed out, carrying the scent of coal dust and polish.

And then, almost on cue, the lights went out. The whole house plunged into darkness, leaving the gang crouched in the brittle silence, hearts pounding in time with the dying hum of the planes above.

The order had come just after seven, the deafening drone of fighter planes and bombers overhead. Carol and Cyril had been huddled by the radio, a lukewarm mug of tea balanced on the table between them, when the call reached the station. The radio crackled with the news. A residential street in the town centre. A direct hit. Casualties expected.

They set out at once, Carol gripping the wheel of the ambulance with both hands, Cyril braced beside her, his satchel of bandages and morphine at his feet. The journey through the blacked-out streets was terrifyingly surreal: every window sealed tight against the light, the only glow that of their headlamps dimmed to thin slits. Up ahead they saw the flickering light of the fires in the city and searchlights panning the skies. Carol was pushing the ambulance to its maximum speed. The acrid smell of smoke was already in the air. And the noise—German planes, fire engine bells and shouting.

When they turned into the street, Carol caught her breath. Two houses were ablaze, flames leaping from the upper windows as if some unearthly creature were trying to claw its way free. The fire brigade was already at work, hoses snaking across the cobbles, the jets of water hissing and steaming as they struck the burning timbers. People were everywhere: dazed men and women clutching children, old people being shepherded toward the corner by wardens in steel helmets. A dog barked wildly, pulling at its lead.

Carol pulled the ambulance in as close as he could. Cyril took everything in immediately. As soon as the ambulance stopped, he

283

said briskly, 'Right, let's get to it.' He was already out of the cab and moving toward a cluster of people by the pavement.

Carol followed, tucking her hair beneath her cap, adjusting her armband. The air was hot and restless, carrying sparks and fragments of ash. Somewhere glass shattered, and the crowd flinched as one.

'Sit yourselves down,' Cyril was saying to a couple with soot-smeared faces. 'You're all right. Just shock, that's all. Let me have a look at that cut.' He knelt, pulling a torch from his pocket. Carol bent beside him, passing bandages on his instructions.

So this was it. She was now part of the ambulance service—no more drills in the draughty hall, no more lectures about readiness, but the real thing. People's lives, their fears, their tears—all of it raw and pressing in on her with the heat of the fire still raging a few yards away. She could feel her pulse hammering in her throat, but her hands moved steadily, as if they knew what to do before her mind quite caught up.

'Hold that there,' Cyril told the man, pressing his hand over the bandage. 'Good. Keep pressure on it. We'll get you sorted proper at the post.'

The woman beside him gave a small whimper and clutched Carol's sleeve. 'My—my boy,' she stammered. 'He was upstairs...'

But just then, a shrill cry split the air, piercing through the roar of flames and the hiss of the hoses. Carol jerked her head upward. Her vision was obscured by smoke. The child screamed again, carrying even above the roar of the fire. Her heart seemed to stop. Through the swirl of smoke, she saw the small face at an upper window, pale against the darkness, mouth open in a cry of terror.

'Cyril!' she shouted, tugging his sleeve. 'There—look!'

He followed her gaze, and for an instant they both stood frozen, transfixed by the sight. The child pounded at the glass, though whether in appeal or panic it was impossible to tell. Flames licked along the roofline, the tiles glowing red.

'Fire brigade will get them,' Cyril began, but Carol was already moving.

She thrust her satchel at him. 'Take this!'

'Carol... wait...'

But she didn't. The world had narrowed to that single window, that single voice. Without a second thought, she pushed through the crowd and toward the burning house. Smoke poured from the doorway, choking, but she dragged the hem of her coat across her mouth and plunged inside before anyone could stop her.

She ran to the back of the ambulance and grabbed a blanket. Then raced over to the window. A man nearby saw what she wanted to do. He joined her, along with another man.

Carol gazed up at the little girl.

'You have to jump, my darling. Do you understand?'

The terrified child shook her head.

'Jump, please,' pleaded Carol.

The heat of the fire was growing more intense. Inside the house, Carol could hear the sickening sound of timber crashing. The inferno was raging and spreading along the street. The house would soon be fully engulfed.

'Jump,' shouted Carol. Others were shouting at the child to do so, including her mother.

The child jumped.

Chops and Winslow were at the police station waiting for a phone call when they heard it. A low drone at first, which gathered strength with each passing second until the very windowpanes hummed with the vibration. Both men lifted their heads at once, eyes meeting across the desk.

'We have to leave,' said Winslow.

'You leave,' said Chops. 'Take my car.'

Winslow shook his head, torn between staying or returning to his family.

'Go,' ordered Chops. He held out the car keys. Winslow stared at the keys for a moment, then shook his head again.

285

'I can be home in ten minutes on foot. You stay and wait for the phone call. But don't stay too long.'

Winslow was not gone two minutes when Chops heard the first of the explosions. It came just as his phone began to ring. Was it to do with the case or the raid? Right at that moment, the death of Fred Morrison seemed a minor consideration in what might be happening in the city.

'Hopcroft speaking,' said Chops.

'Chief Inspector, it's Senior Warden Sheridan. I have the information you were seeking. The men off duty from the prison last Tuesday were...'

A series of loud explosions rocked the police station.

'Good Lord, what on earth is happening there?' said Sheridan.

'A raid,' shouted Chops over the din. 'Go on, you were telling me who was off duty.'

'Yes, Terry Moss and Gus Saxon.' Chops repeated the names back to Sheridan for confirmation. Then Sheridan added, 'I'm not sure why you wanted this, but you should know one other thing.'

'Yes,' said Chops, ducking as another explosion shattered the window of his office.

'Both Moss and Saxon are off duty tonight.'

The line went dead, but Chops was already heading out of the office and down the stairs to his car.

Benjy almost cried out when the hand clamped down on his shoulder. He whirled round, eyes wide in the dim light, only to find himself staring into the familiar face of Figgs.

'It's only me,' Figgs hissed, his features drawn and anxious. 'Sorry, lad, didn't mean to startle you.'

Benjy's heart was still thundering, but he pressed a finger to his lips. 'Shush,' he whispered, barely more than breath. 'There are people breaking in. I just heard them.'

For a moment, Figgs froze, his eyes flicking toward the ceiling as though he too might hear the muffled scrape of boots, the faint rattle of glass. He leaned closer, his voice urgent but soft enough to be swallowed by the darkness.

'Then we've no time to lose. We've got to get to the cellar.'

Benjy shook his head violently, his hair falling across his forehead. 'No,' he said, his voice fierce in spite of the tremor. 'That's the first place they'll look. In an air raid, everyone goes to the shelter. They'll expect us there.'

Figgs drew in a sharp breath, about to argue, then stopped. He saw the sense in it at once, and the truth of the boy's words made his stomach tighten. The shelter might be protection from bombs, but against men—these men—it was little more than a trap.

'You're right,' he whispered finally, his hand still resting on Benjy's arm. 'Then we'll have to think of somewhere else. Somewhere they won't search straightaway.'

'I'll go upstairs,' said Benjy, 'and distract them. You call the police.'

This seemed like an eminently sensible idea.

In the pause that followed, the sounds from downstairs grew clearer—the creak of a door opening, the muffled thud of boots on linoleum, a low voice giving instructions. Both Figgs and Benjy held their breath, listening. Benjy pointed that he was going upstairs. Figgs nodded and went immediately to the small office that Charles used. It had a phone. His heart was thumping. This was not what a sixty-eight-year-old man should be doing. He locked the door behind him and dialled the number for the police.

The line was dead.

Benjy reached the top of the stairs in record time just as he heard footsteps in the hallway. He ran to the room that he and Roger shared. He found what he was looking for by his bedside table. He grabbed what he needed and went out into the landing. Down in the hallway, he heard the whispers of at least two men, perhaps three.

Benjy crept forward, carrying what he'd taken from the bedroom.

The animal trap.

He opened its jaws and put it on the landing, just above the top step of the stairs. Then he leaned over the balustrade and looked down. The men below looked up at him.

'What are you doing here?' asked Benjy.

'Get him,' ordered Purdy.

Roberts and Saxon looked at one another. Saxon was the younger by a couple of years and therefore deemed the most junior, despite having turned forty-two earlier that month.

'All right,' he said sullenly.

He started to jog up the stairs. To his surprise, the young boy did not move. Saxon frowned at this but kept moving up, two stairs at a time.

Still, Benjy did not move. Saxon didn't have time to question why. He suspected the boy, in his terror, was rooted to the spot.

This, as the prison guard was to find out, was not the case.

288

Saxon reached the final stair. He stopped and stared at Benjy. Benjy stared back at him. Then Saxon planted his foot on the landing. His boot hit the trigger of the trap, and the iron jaws exploded upward, clamping his leg with nearly over one hundred pounds per square inch of pressure. The scream that followed was high-pitched and unmanly, the kind of sound that would've gotten him laughed out of the prison yard where he usually pretended to be tough.

Benjy stared with no little satisfaction at the success of his ploy. He stepped forward towards Saxon, who was crying agonised tears at the pain in his leg. The prison guard was teetering on the top of the stairs when Benjy arrived.

Then Benjy pushed him.

As Saxon tumbled down the stairs, screaming like Fay Wray when she first met King Kong, his two accomplices, Purdy and Roberts, stared open-mouthed at the scene.

'What the f...'

'...was that?'

Roger and Susan stared at Mrs Parker. They had never heard her swear before.

'Sorry, children. It rather slipped out,' said Mrs Parker. Even in the dim light of the cellar, the children could see the shame etched over the housekeeper's face.

The underground cellar was colder than any of them expected, the kind of cold that seeped straight into the bones and made teeth chatter if you sat still too long. Along both walls stretched racks upon racks of wine bottles, their shoulders cloaked in a thick pelt of dust and cobweb, some labels so faded they were no more than ghosts of writing. A single bulb dangled from a wire overhead, its light weak and yellow, throwing long, shivering shadows across the floor.

'Was that Mr Figgs?' asked Susan, returning to the practical matter of establishing just what the... hell... had happened.

Mrs Parker had worked with the aged for nigh on fifteen years. That certainly was not Figgs. Her eyes widened in horror, and Roger immediately understood two things. Firstly, this was the gang. They had come to find him. Secondly, they had met Benjy. His ten-year-old brother could be evil incarnate when the mood took him.

'We must find Benjy and Mr Figgs,' said Mrs Parker, who had also quickly arrived at the same place as Roger on who had entered.

Roger was the first to the door. He opened it, and the sight that greeted him was terrifying. Coming down the steps was a man. Roger stared at the clear blue eyes and felt a chill that had nothing to do with the cold air.

It was the man he'd seen in the car.

The moustache was gone, but it was clearly the same man. Then Roger saw something in his hand gleam.

He was carrying an axe.

Roger slammed the door shut and bolted it.

'What are you doing?' exclaimed Mrs Parker, aghast.

'It's the gang. They're here,' said Roger, pulling a table over to the door. 'Help me make a barricade.' They started to pile empty barrels against the door. Within seconds, the cellar door shuddered under the first blow, dust sifting down from the frame. On the other side, the man snarled a low, guttural sound of effort and rage.

Another crash followed, the wood groaning in protest. The hinges rattled. He was using his shoulder now, battering again and again, each strike accompanied by the scrape of boots on stone as he braced himself for the next assault. Between blows came the ragged intake of his breath, harsh and determined, like a bull that had scented blood.

Mrs Parker, Roger and Susan pressed back against the racks, eyes wide, listening to the furious pounding.

Carol's arms ached from holding the blanket taut, but she gritted her teeth and kept her grip. The smoke pouring from the upper floor was so thick it stung her eyes and blurred her sight. Then the small figure appeared, framed for an instant in the window, silhouetted against the fire. The child's cry rang out, then she leapt.

For one frozen second Carol thought they'd miss. But the blanket billowed, caught the weight, and sagged almost to the cobbles before bouncing back. The men beside her shouted with relief. Carol dropped to her knees, clutching the child to her chest. The girl's face was streaked with soot, her hair singed at the ends, and blisters were forming on one hand, but she was breathing—alive, safe.

Cyril's voice cut through the din. 'Well done, Carol!' His face was blackened with soot, but his grin was unmistakable. He gestured urgently toward the ambulance. 'But we've got more; two burns cases need the hospital sharpish.'

Together they lifted stretchers, the injured moaning softly beneath blankets. Carol's back and shoulders screamed in protest, but adrenaline drove her on. They slid the stretchers into the rear of the ambulance, Cyril clambering in after them without hesitation.

'You take the wheel,' he barked. 'I'll tend to them on the way.'

Carol slammed the door and ran for the cab. Her hands trembled as she gripped the steering wheel, but she set her jaw and started the engine. The ambulance lurched forward, siren wailing into the night.

The streets of Exeter blurred past: rows of shuttered shops, blacked-out houses, people hurrying in ones and twos to the shelters as the drone of engines circled above. Carol pressed the accelerator harder, weaving between rubble and fire hoses. Her whole body vibrated with the engine, her eyes darting constantly for dangers ahead.

Then came the blast. A deafening roar tore through the night, the shockwave slamming into the ambulance like a giant's fist. The windscreen lit up with sparks and debris. Carol's hands were wrenched on the wheel, the vehicle veering violently to the left.

She fought it, heart hammering, but the tyres jolted up onto the pavement. The kerb juddered beneath them. Ahead, looming out of the dark, was the iron bulk of a lamppost, rushing closer with every heartbeat.

Chops, who regarded the motorcar as a necessary evil rather than a thing of joy, was at the wheel, and Exeter was falling to bits behind him. The Luftwaffe were enthusiastically levelling his hometown from above. Bombs were going off in all directions, and the general effect on Chops' nerves was beginning to tell.

Ordinarily, Chops drove at a pace which caused cyclists to ring their bells impatiently and pass him with rude gestures. On this occasion, however, he made Ravenley, usually a ten-minute jaunt, into a six-minute record breaker, clinging to the wheel with all the grimness of a drowning man grasping a lifebelt.

The countryside streamed past in a dark blur, hedgerows and signposts leaping aside in self-preservation. Every bump in the road produced a groan from Chops as if his own vital organs had taken the jolt, and each distant boom from Exeter prompted a twitch of the shoulders. By the time the great house loomed out of the blackout before him, he was trembling like a newly set jelly.

He brought the car to a halt with a jerk that threatened to rearrange his vertebrae, sat gasping for air, and allowed his heart to edge back down from his tonsils to its customary resting place. For the first time since leaving the city he permitted himself the thought that, yes, he had survived the journey.

Then, of course, came the second thought, creeping in like an uninvited guest at a dinner party: he was unarmed. Entirely, comprehensively unarmed. And if his suspicions about those two prison guards were on the mark, he was about to pit his unimpressive fists against a gang of the rougher sort.

Chops sat there in the dark of Ravenley, considering this fresh horror. Speeding through falling bombs had been bad enough; walking into a nest of cut-throats armed with nothing better than a weak grasp of jujitsu and a whistle was altogether another kettle of fish.

'Bugger,' he said with some feeling.

There was nothing for it. He stepped out of the car and walked to the front door. It was then he heard a man yell.

A man experiencing extreme pain.

He tried the front door. It was locked. He took a step back with the intention of breaking it down. Common sense came to his aid. He had no chance of succeeding. He skipped down the steps and stared at the windows. Perhaps he could break them and enter that way.

He picked up a large rock from the garden and walked towards the drawing room window. Just as he was about to launch it, he heard gravel crunch to his left and then a gasp.

Chops turned in the direction of the sound.

Arm raised.

Rock in hand.

Gus Saxon was unlikely to fight again, in Roberts' view. In fact, he might not walk again, given what he was looking at just then. The clue was the fact he was crying like a newborn despite the fact that he'd just pulled the terrifying trap off his leg. Roberts did not want to think about the kind of damage that had been done. Nor was he particularly looking forward to coming face-to-face with the devil child who'd inflicted such an injury.

Purdy, meanwhile, seemed to have taken the easier option which was to check out the cellar. Purdy also had the sense to bring an axe with him. Roberts wished, at that moment, he'd had a similar level of forethought. With Saxon almost fainting in pain, Roberts, rather guiltily, certainly unwillingly, had to abandon him to continue with his mission, which was to find the boy and deal with him. Quite what *deal with him* meant was open to interpretation. A smack on the bottom, given what he'd just witnessed, did not strike Roberts as sufficient punishment for the evil imp but nor, in his view, was murder.

It was with some trepidation that he began his ascent of the stairs, gripping the handrail tightly. Thankfully, the evil sprite was nowhere to be seen. Perhaps he'd locked himself in a room. Roberts hoped that he had because none of his options were good just at that moment. As he reached the top of the stairs he took his hand off the handrail to reach inside his pocket for his flick knife.

It was afterwards he realised that this was his mistake. Taking his hand away from the handrail presented a moment of vulnerability that the spawn of Satan had probably been waiting for.

Just as he looked up, knife in hand, Benjy jumped out from behind a suit of armour. He shrieked like one of Geronimo's braves. Roberts immediately stepped backwards. Who wouldn't? It was dark and an evil spirit was attacking him. As he was, like Saxon, on the landing, his first step was to tread mid-air. He lost his balance.

But Benjy hadn't quite delivered the knockout punch.

Yet.

Rather worryingly for Roberts, he'd seen Benjy with something in his hand that looked rather like a catapult.

It all happened in split seconds.

Toppling backwards, Roberts saw Benjy draw the elastic back and, to his horror, he saw him release it. The stone heading directly towards his head from a distance of twenty feet was travelling at a speed of fifty miles per hour. It connected with the top of Roberts' head causing him almost to somersault backwards and then tumble down the stairs to join his fellow casualty at the bottom. While Saxon was conscious and snivelling, Roberts was out for the count. Beside Roberts was the stone that had done all the damage. Benjy ran down the stairs to retrieve it just in time to see Figgs appear from the office.

Figgs took one look at the carnage, then glanced at Benjy.

'Well done, sir,' said Figgs. There was no mistaking the note of awe in his voice, even for a ten-year-old.

'Thanks, Mr Figgs. There's another one of them. He's gone to the cellar.'

'Try not to kill him,' advised Figgs, looking once more at the two damaged men. They parted company.

Benjy went to the stairs leading to the cellar while Figgs went to the front door. He'd spied the arrival of Chops from the office. He opened the door and moved as quickly as he could round to the side where he'd seen the policeman. As he was about to address the chief inspector, Chops spun around. He was holding a rock and was about to throw it when Figgs gasped in fear.

'No sir,' said the aged butler, holding his hands up.

'Figgs,' said Chops in relief. 'You frightened the life out of me.'

Not quite the words you want the US Cavalry to be saying when you're under attack but, no matter, the police were here. Figgs looked around for the others. They were clearly well camouflaged. Chops' next words were even less comforting than his first.

'Just me, I'm afraid.'

Figgs looked askance at the chief inspector.

'There are three men in the house.'

'Three?'

'Actually, just one.'

'Well, make up your mind,' snapped Chops a little more irritably than he'd intended.

'Come with me, you'll see,' said Figgs.

Figgs struck Chops as a little braver than he'd ever imagined given his willingness to enter the fray with between one and three thugs in the house. When they arrived at the entrance hallway, he saw the reason for the butler's vagueness.

'Good Lord,' said Chops, or something not very like that.

'Master Benjy, sir. I think one was hit by a catapult and one caught in a metal trap.'

'Young hooligan,' murmured Chops. 'The other man?'

Just then they heard a roar of pain coming from the door that led to the cellar.

The axe was making such rapid progress through the old door that the three terrified occupants of the cellar could see the man chasing them. It was no use, thought Roger. He would be through the door in no time. They had to find a weapon to fight back. He looked around him.

Mrs Parker saw what Roger was contemplating immediately and felt rather proud of the young man, despite her fear, that he had correctly apprised what she had. She saw him reach for a bottle off the rack. Horror gripped her.

'No sir,' whispered Mrs Parker, urgently. 'Not that one. That's a Chateau Lafite Rothschild. It's worth too much. Do you see the case over there?'

Mrs Parker was pointing to a box with four bottles of wine. Roger frowned his question.

'Mr Sinclair uses those for Christmas presents for the staff and field workers. They are a little less expensive.'

Roger rushed over to the side of the door bringing the box with him. From his position, their attacker would not see him until he entered the cellar. It was a slim chance but they had no other good choices.

Seconds later the door flew open, sending the table several feet away. Purdy strode forward, perspiration matting his dark hair. Of more concern to Susan and Mrs Parker was the axe in his hand.

Roger, standing to the side, still unseen, was holding two bottles of the cheap plonk. He swung the bottle in his right hand towards the crown of Purdy's head.

Something in Roger's movement must have attracted Purdy's attention. He jerked his head to the side, meaning that the bottle's brutal impact on the skull was averted. Roger did manage to hit Purdy's arm, his axe arm.

The axe fell to the ground.

Roger tried to club Purdy with the bottle in his left hand. Purdy was ready for the attack and, despite the pain in his left arm, he grabbed Roger's arm forcing him to drop the bottle. Then he flung the boy onto the ground. Roger grunted as he landed on the concrete.

Beside the axe.

Roger grabbed the axe but it was kicked out of his hand by Purdy. A slow smile of victory spread over Purdy's face. The boy had showed some fight. It would be a pity to kill him and the others, but they had seen his face. It was just business. Nothing personal. As he was contemplating his triumph, he heard a sound from behind him.

297

He turned around and saw the other young boy. He seemed to be holding what looked like a catapult.

Then everything went black for Purdy.

The lamp post loomed out of the darkness as Carol fought to keep control of the vehicle following the explosion. She gasped, tugging the wheel with such violence that the heavy vehicle slewed across the cobblestones. For a moment, the whole ambulance tilted at a sickening angle, its wheels grinding against the pavement. Carol heard a terrified cry from the back. She held her breath.

With a lurch that nearly threw her from her seat, the ambulance slammed back upright, bouncing onto all four tyres again. She could feel her heart thudding in her chest. She dreaded to think about what it was like in the back for the victims of the raid and poor Cyril.

Carol's hands trembled on the wheel, but she kept her foot firmly on the pedal. A lesser driver might have slowed, shaken by the near catastrophe. Carol found herself doing the opposite. Adrenaline surged through her veins, urging her forward. If she thought too long about how close they had come to tipping over, she might freeze. She had no choice but to keep the vehicle moving.

The hospital lights appeared at last through the haze of smoke, glowing with an almost holy intensity. Carol steered into the yard with a screech of brakes. She pulled the ambulance up against the steps in record time, her chest heaving as though she had run the distance on foot.

Even before she had switched off the engine, the back doors flew open. Orderlies rushed forward, pulling stretchers out with practised efficiency. A woman, pale and bleeding from the scalp, was lifted carefully onto a gurney. A man with a broken leg groaned as he was eased down, his face ashen in the lamplight.

Carol sat for a moment, her hands frozen on the wheel, realising she had been holding her breath. Cyril glanced at her, a brief look of approval, before springing from the vehicle to assist.

She climbed down stiffly, her knees weak, and tried to steady her breathing. The scene around her was a blur of motion; stretchers carried at speed, nurses shouting instructions, the acrid smell of antiseptic already mingling with smoke.

Then a voice cut through the chaos.

'Driver!'

Carol turned sharply. A doctor in a blood-spattered coat was striding towards her, his hair dishevelled, his face grim with urgency. He was clearly a man used to command, his eyes narrowing as he saw the ambulance still running.

'You! Yes, you! We've reports of more injured on the far side of the High Street. Several trapped in a cellar. I need an ambulance there at once. You're the nearest.'

Carol blinked, her mind still catching up with the sheer pace of events. She had imagined, foolishly, that she might have a moment to gather herself, to recover from the perilous drive. But there was no time, no pause, not tonight.

'Yes, sir,' she said quickly, her voice steadier than she felt.

The doctor waved an arm. 'Thorpe! You're with her again. Go!'

Cyril appeared at her side, already pulling on his gloves, his face grim but calm. He touched Carol lightly on the elbow as they turned back to the vehicle. 'Come on, Carol. We're not done yet.'

She climbed back into the driver's seat, her body still quivering with nerves, but she forced her hands to the wheel again. Her whole being cried out for a moment's rest, but the cries of the wounded, the insistent command in the doctor's tone, and the steady presence of Cyril pushed her forward.

The engine growled as she pulled away from the hospital yard once more, headlights cutting through the smoke-filled night. Every corner of the city seemed ablaze; sparks rising into the air, roofs collapsing with a dull roar, the drone of enemy aircraft still faintly audible overhead.

Carol swallowed hard and pressed her lips together. Fear could not be allowed to take hold. She had already proven to herself, and to everyone else, that she could do this. She would not falter now, not with more lives depending on her.

Beside her, Cyril glanced sideways, his expression unreadable in the dim light. But when their eyes met for the briefest second, Carol felt a surge of reassurance, as if his calm had somehow been lent to her.

'Just keep steady,' he said softly. 'That's all. One street at a time.'

She nodded, gripping the wheel more firmly. The ambulance roared on, a fragile hope against the devastation of the night.

'Where are we going?' asked Carol.

'A country house. It's called Ravenley,' said the doctor. 'The police have just called.'

Carol's heart was racing. Ravenley. She stole a quick glance at Cyril, who was already bracing himself in the seat beside her. His face betrayed no surprise, only the faintest tightening of his jaw.

'Ravenley?' she echoed.

'Yes. Do you know it?' the doctor asked, already half turned away, as if ready to dash back into the hospital.

'A little,' Carol said quickly, masking her unease. 'We'll get there.'

'Good. Then don't waste a moment. Lives are waiting.'

The doctor's figure vanished into the smoke and confusion of the hospital yard. Carol threw the ambulance into gear. With a grinding of wheels, the vehicle pulled out once more, its siren rising above the din of Exeter's burning streets.

The city behind them was a chaos of fire and collapsing buildings, yet the further they drove the darker the world became, as if the night had swallowed everything whole. The drone of aircraft faded. In its place was the strange, almost shocking quiet of the countryside. Carol found the silence unnerving after the cacophony of the raid.

301

'Ravenley,' she said aloud, if only to fill the air. 'Why would the police call for an ambulance there?'

'Could be stray bombs,' Cyril replied, steady and calm as ever. 'Blast damage spreads far. A house that size would be a good landmark. Not impossible they were hit.'

Carol nodded but said no more. The thought of arriving at the great house, the very house she had left only that afternoon, with its high windows and quiet lawns, and finding it torn open by bombs made her chest tighten. She thought of the children. Benjy's mischievous grin, Susan's sharp little eyes, Roger with his quiet solemnity. And Mrs Parker, who fussed over them all like a nervous hen.

Please let them be safe.

The road narrowed, hedgerows looming up black on either side. Carol kept the headlights low, though she longed to blaze the path before her. She had heard too many stories of enemy pilots strafing country roads, picking off whatever moved. Even the faint glow was enough to show her the frost on the grass, glittering faintly in the darkness.

'Are you all right?' Cyril asked quietly.

She nodded, eyes fixed ahead. 'Yes. Just... Ravenley. It feels strange, being called back there like this. I mean, it would be a one in a million chance it would be hit.'

'Life has a way of circling us back to places we think we've left behind,' Cyril murmured. His tone was philosophical, but Carol thought she heard something personal behind the words.

The ambulance jolted over a rut, and she tightened her grip. A turn in the road revealed the familiar outline of Ravenley's gateposts, their stone worn by centuries, standing like silent sentinels in the night.

Carol swung the ambulance through, the tyres crunching on gravel. The drive stretched ahead, moonlight catching on the frost that lay like a silver veil over the lawns. And then, her heart caught, the house itself came into view.

302

Outside the house she could see Chops; he was nervously smoking a cigarette. With him were Mrs Parker, Figgs and some policemen. The three children were sitting on the steps of the house.

What was going on?

The ambulance pulled up outside the house, Carol, Cyril and the doctor leapt out. Tears of fear were in Carol's eyes now but the scene seemed oddly calm. Chops looked up at her as she arrived.

'The three victims are inside.'

'Victims?' blurted out Carol in astonishment.

Chops turned to Benjy and then back to Carol. He lowered his voice and said, 'I need to have a word with you about that young man and his use of catapults.'

Just after midnight, Carol pushed through the heavy doors of the Exeter police station. The sound seemed louder than it ought to have been, echoing off the stone walls and jangling her already frayed nerves. Her body was running on little more than tea, fumes, and sheer willpower. Every muscle in her arms and shoulders screamed after hours at the wheel, after carrying stretchers through rubble, after bending over the wounded until her knees felt ready to buckle.

And yet, she was wired. Her heart hadn't slowed since the first siren had wailed earlier that evening. Every sense remained too sharp, every movement edged with the same restless, jittering urgency that had carried her ambulance through the firestorm.

The desk sergeant looked up as she entered. Carol was aware, even in her state, of the picture she must make—hair shaken loose from its pins, her ambulance uniform smudged with soot and dust, her face pale and drawn but her eyes alight with something closer to fever.

'Mrs Sinclair,' the sergeant said, his tone pitched carefully between respect and surprise. 'The chief inspector is expecting you. He's in his office.'

Carol gave the briefest nod, not trusting her voice. She walked down the corridor, her boots scuffing against the tiles. Each step felt oddly unsteady, as though she were still in the ambulance swerving through debris, half expecting the ground to lurch beneath her.

She reached the door marked *Chief Inspector Clarence Hopcroft* and paused, pressing her hand to the wood. A deep breath. Her hands were still trembling faintly. She told herself it was only the adrenaline, not the fear.

Inside, Chops sat at his desk, a lamp throwing a pool of yellow light across the scattered papers and his tired face. Moriarty, his cat, was absent, but his fedora lay tilted on a chair as though even it had given up for the night. He looked up at her entrance, his heavy features softening into something almost kind.

'Carol,' he said simply. His voice carried the weight of the night: gruff, low, a little ragged at the edges.

She closed the door behind her and leaned against it for a moment. 'I came as soon as I could,' she said. The words came out more breathless than she intended.

'So I see,' Chops muttered, eyeing her dishevelled state. He rose, pulled out a chair opposite his desk. 'Sit down, before you fall down.'

She managed a faint, humourless smile, and lowered herself into the chair. The wooden seat felt almost too solid beneath her, as though her body didn't quite believe the world had stopped moving.

'What happened at Ravenley?' she asked. The question burst from her, urgent, sharp.

Chops sank back into his own chair with a sigh, but there was just a hint of mischief in his eyes as he related in detail Benjy's series of violent assaults on the invaders in the house. Carol, despite her horror at the injuries the ten-year-old boy had inflicted, laughed despite herself.

Chops concluded, 'The boy is a hell child, but I hope we have a few like him to put up against Mr Hitler.'

Carol hoped so too and immediately thought of Charles. She imagined that he and Benjy shared a lot in common. He'd been a hell child too, according to Jason.

'You were right, you know,' said Chops, lighting his pipe.

'How do you mean?' asked Carol, who still had no idea who the men were.

'When you said about Ned being a poacher-turned-gamekeeper. How the only other men who knew how to commit such a robbery might be the prison guards watching Jack Finch, the man who robbed the bank in London.'

Carol's eyes widened in shock. She couldn't believe what she was hearing and yet she could, because it had been her idea, after all. Yet, when it had occurred to her, it was more like a cryptic crossword clue than anything else—more an intellectual proof that something could theoretically be possible than any real belief that it was likely. She laughed with the nervous exhaustion that had built up inside her.

'I'm not sure I really believed the idea myself,' she admitted.

'Don't say that, Carol. It was a brilliant deduction. Leave it at that if anyone asks.'

'Surely no one will, Chops. I mean, you and the children made the catch.'

'Technically, it was all Benjy's work, but I see no reason why I should not tell everyone that you made the connection. The superintendent knows.'

Carol shook her head and said, 'You're one in a million, Chops. Most men would've tried to claim the credit themselves.'

Chops waved the pipe airily and grinned. 'You're one in a million, Carol. I hope your family appreciates this,' said Chops. Carol was not going to hold her breath on this. She smiled wistfully, and it made Chops feel sad for her.

'Are you on duty tomorrow?' asked Chops.

Carol said no. There were presents to buy. Christmas was a week away.

'What are you doing for Christmas?' asked Carol.

'Oh, you know...' said Chops evasively. Carol's eyes narrowed but she didn't pursue it. 'You?'

'Jason wants me to come to the Grange but I just don't feel like I can celebrate much, what with Charles...'

'The children?'

'We'll do what we can, of course. I'm not sure they'll be in a mood for much either. Without their mum.'

The thought of the children made them both quiet. The silence lingered, broken only by the faint ticking of the police station clock. Carol folded her hands together in her lap, her knuckles white, her face turned away from the lamp so Chops couldn't see the glimmer in her eyes.

Chops cleared his throat, uncomfortably. He was a man used to awkward pauses, but this one cut differently. He shifted in his chair, his great bulk making it creak.

'Well,' he said at last, his tone gruffer than he intended, 'there'll be plenty of sprouts going spare, I daresay. Mrs Givens strikes me as the type who boils enough for a regiment.'

'Join us, Chops.'

'I couldn't.'

'Mrs Givens' cooking, Chops...' said Carol in a voice that would have had movie producers firing Rita Hayworth and holding a contract under her nose.

'Well... let's see.'

Christmas Day 25th December 1940

Carol was woken on Christmas morning not by the children's excited whispers outside her bedroom door, nor by the sound of Mrs Givens clattering about in the kitchen with her pudding preparations, but by the shrill ring of the telephone in the hall. For a moment she lay there in confusion, her mind muddled by sleep and the heaviness of the past few weeks. Then she rose swiftly, pulling her dressing gown about her shoulders, and hurried to the receiver held out to her by Figgs.

'Mrs Sinclair?' came the voice on the line, faint and crackling as though carried over some vast distance.

'Yes, this is she.'

'It's Simon. I'm ringing with wonderful news. We've received confirmation that Charles, survived the crash. He has been taken prisoner and is now being held at a camp in Germany. The name, let me see here, it's Colditz. Somewhere in Saxony. That's all we have at present. But he is alive.'

Carol's hand flew to her mouth. For a moment, the hall seemed to tilt around her. Alive. Her heart leapt with a wild joy, but just as quickly came the ache: alive, but a prisoner. Alive, but unreachable. She pressed her forehead against the receiver, her voice a whisper.

'Thank you... thank you so much, Simon. This is the best Christmas present I could ever have hoped for.'

She replaced the receiver and stood there in the dim light of the hall, tears running freely down her cheeks. Happiness and grief, hope and fear, all tangled together. She let herself cry for a minute, her sobs muffled against the crook of her arm, before she drew a long, steadying breath and wiped her eyes. The children would need her to be strong.

When she entered the drawing room, Roger and Susan were already sitting on the rug, their presents piled beside them, though unopened. Benjy was fiddling with the ribbon on his parcel, as though his small fingers couldn't quite resist, even though the mood had muted their usual morning frenzy. They looked up at her anxiously.

'Mummy?' Susan asked softly.

Carol sank to her knees between them and pulled all three into her arms. 'I've just had a telephone call,' she said, her voice trembling. 'It's about Charles, my husband. He's alive. He's in a prisoner-of-war camp in Germany.'

The children clutched her, eyes wide. Roger, who had been holding himself stiffly for weeks, let out a long breath, as though he had been holding it since the day Charles went missing. Susan burst into tears.

The presents were opened, but quietly, each gift unwrapped with murmurs of thanks rather than the squeals of delight she might once have expected. Roger turned a model Spitfire in his hands with a strange, almost reverent seriousness. Susan stroked the new dress she had received as though it were something fragile, not to be disturbed. Even Benjy's tin soldiers marched across the hearth rug with less noise and bravado than usual.

Carol watched them, her heart swelling with pride and sorrow. It was not the Christmas any of them had wanted or imagined it would be, but it was theirs, and they were together.

'Hurry up children, we have to go to the Christmas service.'

Carol ignored the groans that greeted this. She felt a deep well of gratitude and it seemed the right thing to do. Perhaps He had somehow intervened to save Charles.

The church, though modest, had been dressed with what the villagers could spare: sprigs of holly wound about the pulpit, beeswax candles glowing faintly against the pale stone, and the faint, mingled scent of greenery and old hymn books. Reverend Atwell, earnest and pink-cheeked despite the chill, greeted them at the door with his customary cheer.

'Merry Christmas, Mrs Sinclair! Children! How good to see you all.'

They found a pew toward the middle, and the children settled themselves with the solemnity of those who had been sternly warned not to fidget. The organ wheezed bravely into life, and the congregation's voices rose—thin in places, but strong in others—singing *Once in Royal David's City*.

Carol sang too, her voice clear, though her mind wandered. She thought of Charles—alive, yes, but far away in some cold stone castle in Germany. Perhaps, she told herself, he could hear a carol that very moment, carried faintly across the prison yard, and might think of her as she thought of him. The thought was bittersweet but sustaining.

Reverend Atwell's sermon was kindly but rather long-winded, full of exhortations to courage, to faith, to the light shining in darkness. The children shifted and sighed softly beside her, and Carol herself could not deny a certain relief when the final hymn was sung and the blessing given.

Outside, the villagers stood in little groups, stamping their feet against the cold and exchanging greetings. And there, standing by the lichgate, was Jonathan Darby.

He caught sight of her and came forward, his dark coat buttoned high, his breath misting in the evening air. His expression, as always, was grave, but his eyes softened when they met hers.

'Mrs Sinclair,' he said, inclining his head. 'And children. A very Merry Christmas to you.'

'Merry Christmas,' Carol returned, her cheeks warming despite the chill. 'I wasn't sure if you would be here.'

'I try never to miss the service,' Jonathan replied. 'Especially this year, when so many need reminding of what we still have to be thankful for.'

There was a pause, filled with the chatter of voices and the crunch of boots on frosted ground. Carol hesitated, then said quietly, 'I had news this morning. About Charles.'

Jonathan's gaze sharpened. 'Yes?'

'He's alive,' she said, her voice trembling slightly with the weight of the words. 'His plane came down, but he survived. He's... he's a prisoner of war, in a place called Colditz.'

Jonathan's expression shifted; relief, certainly, but shadowed with sympathy. 'That is good news,' he said softly. 'Not all wives hear such tidings, these days.'

'I know.' Carol swallowed, looking down at the children, who were tugging at her sleeve and clamouring about the biscuits promised them at home. 'It's a strange thing, to cry with happiness and sadness at the same time.'

Jonathan inclined his head, his voice low and steady. 'It means you still love him. That is never strange.'

Carol felt the words settle within her, both comforting and painful. She met his eyes, and for a moment neither spoke. Then Susan tugged harder, declaring she was cold, and the moment passed.

Jonathan smiled faintly. 'Go on, then. Take them home. And Mrs Sinclair, hold to your hope. It may yet prove your greatest strength.'

By midday the smells of roasting goose and potatoes filled Ravenley, Mrs Givens performing small miracles in the kitchen as though war rationing did not exist. At one o'clock, Chops arrived, hat in hand and cheeks red from the cold.

'Merry Christmas,' he said, his voice a little too formal, as though he had not quite decided whether he was intruding or not.

'Come in, Chops,' Carol said warmly. 'You're just in time.'

He removed his coat, and the children clustered about him, glad of the distraction. 'Did you bring us a present?' Benjy asked boldly.

Chops raised an eyebrow. 'I did,' he said, reaching into his coat pocket. He produced three enormous humbugs; each wrapped in crackling paper. 'Not much, mind you, but better than a lump of coal.'

The children laughed, delighted. Even Mrs Parker, bustling past with a tray, allowed herself a small chuckle.

Lunch was as cheerful as they could manage. Chops praised Mrs Givens' goose to the skies, declaring it 'fit to turn the head of any man foolish enough to attempt cooking for himself'. Mrs Givens sniffed but her cheeks pinked with pleasure. Carol caught Chops' eye across the table and allowed herself the smallest smile. It was good to have him there, to keep them steady.

Later, as the grey light of afternoon faded, Carol lit the lamps and the family gathered in the drawing room once more. At four, the wireless crackled into life. A rich, sonorous voice intoned, 'Germany calling, Germany calling...'

Carol's lips tightened, her hand already reaching for the dial. But before she could turn it off, Benjy leapt to his feet, puffed out his chest, and declaimed in his best imitation of the pompous accent:

'This is Germany calling, and I tell you that England is finished! You are all doomed, do you hear? Doooomed!'

The children shrieked with laughter. Roger snorted tea out of his nose. Even Susan, who had been quiet all day, giggled helplessly behind her hand. Chops slapped his knee, eyes crinkling, and said, 'By Jove, lad, that's uncanny. You'll have us all in stitches if you carry on.'

Benjy continued, strutting about the hearthrug as though delivering a sermon: 'Your little goose will never save you! Your potatoes are dust! Your stockings are empty! And as for Santa Claus—he's been shot down over the Channel!'

The room rang with laughter, louder and freer than it had for weeks. Carol leaned back in her chair, her heart aching but lighter all the same. In that moment, with the children's laughter mingling with Chops' rumbling chuckle, she felt, for the first time in a long time, that hope might yet endure.

The vicarage at Belsaw-on-the-Moor stood in solemn quiet that Christmas evening, its stone walls rimed with frost, the lane outside hushed save for the distant toll of the church bell and the muted carols of a few stragglers returning home. Inside, the house was cold and draughty. Reverend Lionel Atwell sat alone in his study, hunched over a heavy oak table that bore little resemblance to an altar, though his posture might have suggested prayer to a passer-by.

But he was not praying.

The curtains were drawn tight against the night, a single lamp hooded so that its glow would not betray him. Upon the table stood not the Book of Common Prayer, but a square black radio transmitter, its valves glowing faintly, its dials gleaming under his careful touch. His thin fingers moved with a practised ease, adjusting knobs, bringing the signal into clarity.

His face, so blandly earnest in the pulpit that morning, now seemed sharper, meaner. The kindly pinkness of his cheeks had faded into something taut and pale under the lamp. He leaned close to the microphone, clearing his throat once, then spoke.

The voice that slipped from his lips was transformed; affected, almost theatrical, with that peculiar drawl that so many British listeners had come to mock and fear. It was the same voice that, earlier that afternoon, had drifted into the drawing room at Ravenley, causing Mrs Parker to cluck, the children to laugh, and Benjy to parody.

Now it was Atwell himself.

His words rolled out with the same doom-laden cadence, predicting the fall of British cities, the futility of resistance, the inevitable triumph of the Reich. He spoke of rationing, of crumbling morale, of German strength poised like a hammer above England's fragile shield. Though he knew that the broadcast would be filtered and rebroadcast by more powerful stations elsewhere, he still gave his lines the care of a practised orator.

Every few moments his eyes flicked to the dials, to the faint quiver of the needle, as though he were keeping time with his own treachery.

When at last he finished, closing with the grimly familiar refrain, "Germany calling... until tomorrow", he switched off the microphone with a little click. Silence fell abruptly, heavy as a shroud.

For a moment he simply sat there, breathing hard, as though he had given a sermon to a packed church rather than a hidden message to an unseen enemy. Then he leaned back in his chair. A thin smile crept across his lips, smug and satisfied. Reverend Atwell, parish priest, shepherd of Belsaw-on-the-Moor, had done his work for the Reich.

And in the quiet of the lonely vicarage, he felt a thrill of importance.

Colditz Castle rose out of the white-dusted valley like some ancient brooding beast, its towers and battlements stark against the pale winter sky. The courtyard was rimed with frost, the cobbles hard and treacherous underfoot. Around its walls, sentries in Wehrmacht grey stamped their boots and pulled their coats tighter, rifles slung casually yet always within reach. A bitter wind wound through the narrow passageways, bringing with it the faint chime of a church bell from the town below—a reminder that beyond these grim walls, Germany was marking Christmas Day.

Into this fortress came three men. British airmen, their greatcoats patched, their boots worn, their RAF caps dented and travel stained. Their faces were pinched with cold and weariness, but their backs were stiff, their chins held at that peculiar angle of defiance that told of a pride unbroken. They had been brought in on the back of a German lorry that had wheezed up the steep incline, its tyres slipping on the icy road.

Now, with the clatter of keys and the echo of boots, they were marched through the great wooden gates and across the yard, past curious faces peering from barred windows above. Shouts rang down from unseen men, cheers, jeers, greetings in English voices that carried an odd mixture of humour and pity. "Merry Christmas, chaps!" someone bellowed. Another called, "Hope you brought the turkey!" Laughter followed, hollow but determined.

The airmen were led into the castle proper, up stone staircases worn smooth by centuries of feet. The corridors smelled of damp and smoke, and in places the medieval walls seemed to press in oppressively, as if the building itself conspired with the guards to remind them of their captivity.

At last they were shown into a long, draughty chamber that served as the quarters of the British officers. Here, despite the bleakness, there was a flicker of warmth. A few candles guttered in bottles. A small fir branch, filched from somewhere, stood crookedly in a jug of water and was adorned with scraps of coloured paper, a parody of a Christmas tree. On a trestle table stood a makeshift pudding, the aroma of raisins and suet faint but real. Cigarette smoke curled upwards, and a low murmur of conversation filled the air.

The newcomers were greeted not by silence but by the rise of men from benches and bunks, their faces pale in the candlelight, their eyes alive with curiosity. One man came forward first—slim, brown-haired, with a neat moustache and a manner of brisk authority.

314

'Lieutenant Pat Reid,' he said, extending a hand with firm cordiality. 'Escape officer for this merry band. Welcome to Colditz.' The three airmen introduced themselves in turn to Reid. Names spoken, handshakes exchanged. Seeing their miserable faces, Reid said, 'Well come and join us. Cheer up. You've arrived at the best club in Germany. The membership's exclusive, and the entertainment—well, it's of our own devising. It's called escape. There's a few other RAF boys here.'

'Oh?' said one of the men.

'Yes. Over there by staring out of the window is Charles Sinclair. He arrived last month.'

The new man stared at Charles for a few moments. Then he shook his head and looked gravely at Reid.

'I went to school with Charles Sinclair. We trained together to be airmen.' The next words chilled Reid.

'That is *not* Charles Sinclair.'

The End

315

A Note to My Readers – what happens next is up to you

If you've enjoyed this story, and want to hear more about Carol, Chops, the children and what happens at Colditz, I'd be deeply grateful if you could take a few moments to leave a review on Amazon. Reviews are the lifeblood of any independent author—they help new readers discover the book and keep the words flowing.

Your thoughts, no matter how brief, make a tremendous difference. Thank you for joining me on this journey, and for supporting independent writing.

Author's Notes

Colditz Castle during the Second World War

Colditz Castle, perched above the River Mulde in Saxony, Germany, became infamous as a prisoner-of-war camp for Allied officers during the Second World War. Known officially as Oflag IV-C, it was considered escape-proof due to its sheer cliffs, heavy fortifications and the formidable guards of the Wehrmacht. Despite this, Colditz became legendary for the ingenuity of its inmates, who dug tunnels, built gliders, and devised elaborate disguises in their attempts to escape. The story of Colditz remains one of daring, defiance, and resilience under captivity.

The Bombing of Exeter

Exeter was one of several English cities targeted in the so-called "Baedeker Raids" of 1942, when the Luftwaffe bombed towns chosen for their cultural and historic significance rather than strategic importance. Exeter's beautiful cathedral city centre suffered heavy damage during a series of night raids, with many civilians killed or injured. Fires lit up the skies, and entire streets were reduced to rubble. Yet the spirit of the city endured, with its people determined to rebuild and carry on despite the destruction.

Kim Philby

Harold "Kim" Philby was a high-ranking member of Britain's Secret Intelligence Service (MI6), but also one of the most notorious double agents in history. Recruited by the Soviet Union while at Cambridge, Philby rose through the ranks of British intelligence while secretly betraying its secrets to Moscow. His charm, intelligence and ability to deflect suspicion allowed him to operate undetected for decades. Philby's eventual defection to the USSR in 1963 shocked Britain and confirmed the scale of the Cambridge spy ring's treachery.

Lord Haw-Haw and His Helpers

"Lord Haw-Haw" was the mocking nickname given to William Joyce, an Englishman who broadcast Nazi propaganda to Britain from Germany during the war. His broadcasts, with their sneering tone and doom-laden predictions, were meant to demoralise the British public. Instead, many tuned in for amusement, parodying his accent and rhetoric. Joyce was supported by a small team of German and British sympathisers, who helped write and record the material. After the war, Joyce was captured, tried for treason, and executed in 1946. His voice remains one of the most infamous symbols of wartime propaganda.

Printed in Dunstable, United Kingdom

66902043R00190